THE GODS OF TIME

K.E. DAVENPORT

For Cary
May our descendants know you well.

&

In Memory of Uncle George

"Baa…" "Baaaa…" "Black sheep…"

A cool breeze swept in across the lush, green knoll, gently rocking the tiny, wicker cradle woven from leafy vines and straw. The sounds of cannon fire blasted across the gray sky, but the beaming, little face with big, brown eyes smiled and cooed at the three, fluffy-white sheep heads that were staring down at him, singing their happy tune.

"Have you any wool?"

Kabaam! All three sheep jumped in fright at the sound of a cannonball pummeling the stone wall that was just on the other side of the hill. The baby wasn't bothered by the sound, however, and giggled playfully at the sheep's reaction.

The sheep on the right shook his head disapprovingly and glared at the sheep on the left. "I'm telling you, Wensley, it's not safe to keep the lad here while there's fighting nearby! We need to usher him away to a different part of the realm. Her excellency won't be happy when she finds out we've been standing here chirping about, just waiting to get blown to pieces. From the sounds of it, the Drezel elves have the knights on their heels. If they kill all the humans before they reach us, then there'll be no one left to defend the child."

"Stop all that nonsense, Herdwick!" snapped the sheep who stood between the other two. "You know the plan! If the knights are defeated, then and only then do we follow her excellency's orders and take the child away through the portal. Not a different part of the realm! So stop flapping your jaw about and giving Wensley a hard time."

Herdwick replied, "Well *ooh-eee*, Balwynn. That's some big talk for such a poofy-headed sheep! I don't remember anyone consulting you on the matter, though. How about you let Wensley answer for himself then?"

Wensley, the sheep on the left, nodded and spoke, "You know what will happen if we don't do what she's told us to do, Herdwick."

Herdwick frowned and scoffed. "Well, she can't bloody well turn us into sheep again, can she?"

Wensley frowned too. "No, of course not. But remember what happened to the Doomplar elves when they wouldn't stop warring with each other?"

Herdwick replied, "Oh, sure. She put them in a cryo-time-out, but that was nearly ten millennia ago. I think she's softened a great deal since then."

Balwynn interrupted, "Softened how? She's out there zapping the Drezels with lightning bolts, isn't she? It's not exactly like she's all sugarpills and crystalbows, now, is it?"

"No, no. She's only out there fighting because she has to. Theo took it too far with the Drezels. If she hadn't done something to intervene it would've gotten much worse. She does care for her subjects, you know?"

"Well, if she cares so much, then why did she wait so long to do something about it? And why hasn't she let the Doomplars out of cryostasis?" asked Wensley.

Balwynn laughed cynically. "I can tell you why!" he

exclaimed. "She's forgotten they're even there! That shows you how much she cares for her subjects."

Wensley ignored Balwynn and asked Herdwick gently, "Herdwick, if you're so fond of the empress, then why do you keep suggesting that we disobey her?"

Herdwick sighed and looked sweetly at the little boy in the wicker cradle.

Balwynn laughed again. "Oh, I see. It's not her excellency who's gone soft, is it? It's this old bloke! What could you possibly be thinking of in that thick, sheep skull of yours? You know we can't keep the lad. He belongs to the empress' sister."

Herdwick snapped at Balwynn, "I know that! But that's the reason I don't want him being taken through the portal! He deserves a better life than all that!"

Wensley replied, "But Herdwick, don't you see? That's why the empress came up with this plan. She's trying to make sure he has a better life. If the Drezels win, Theo will surely order them to kill the boy, and then he'll have no life at all."

Suddenly, a loud **boom** echoed from the other side of the knoll, and a plume of thick, black smoke rose above the grassy hill.

"The dark spirit!" Balwynn shrieked.

But Wensley shook his head. "No. That's not Theo. Not yet anyway."

Balwynn sighed, and his voice quivered. "Well, okay. Good. But I think it's time, brothers. Let's get the babe through the portal before it's too late."

Herdwick protested. "No! Those aren't the empress' orders either! We're not supposed to take him unless the knights are defeated. And they can't be defeated yet because we wouldn't be able to still hear them fighting if they were all dead!"

The little boy with light brown hair and rosy cheeks began to sniffle and whine. Immediately, Wensley and Herdwick stood over the child, shushing him quietly while trying to soothe him with soft murmurings.

Balwynn, however, did nothing to help and instead proclaimed loudly, "*See!* This is what I mean. We have to get him out of here now, or we're all done for! They'll surely hear him if he fusses any louder!"

Herdwick refused to give in, though. "No, brother! At this juncture, you're afraid of Theo and the Drezels, but what about the empress? Moments ago, you were insisting that we follow her orders, but you must realize that these are not her orders. You know she'll have our guts for garters if we take him through the portal without good reason."

Kaboom! A spray of dirt flew through the already smoke-filled air, covering the sheep in a damp layer of peat. They each tried to shake it from their curly locks, but it clung to their thick wool and darkened it. The sounds of screaming and shouting from both the men and the Drezels shot into the air like auditory missiles no more than thirty yards away.

Balwynn seemed to lose his mind over the sounds. "See! See! We're practically under attack! The knights are outnumbered! Why else would they have fallen back so far? Any second, they'll all be dead and us next! We have to head through the portal *now!*"

Wensley looked nervously at Herdwick. "What do you say, brother? Do we stay and move the lad, or heed the empress' orders a bit early in the name of ensuring the boy's safety?"

Before Herdwick could answer, a second wave of dirt soared through the air and collapsed over them, finishing the job of soiling their white wool. Balwynn bleated loudly and took a flying, skipping leap at the basket as Herdwick and Wensley watched in horror. "Stop! Noooo!" they yelled at their brother, but it was too late. Large rings of flashing green light stretched out in every direction as a blue fireball encompassed the sheep and the little boy in the basket. Seconds later, all four of them vanished from the side of the lush, green knoll.

For a moment, the noises from the other side of the hill quieted, as if they'd been interrupted by the disappearance of the babe and his sheep guardians. However, the quiet lasted only a short spell before the agonizing cacophony of war replaced it once more.

Less than a minute later, Theia appeared on the hill's ridgeline in the form of a tall woman wearing a flowing, silk gown with knotted shoulders. Her light red hair whipped around in the wind with a frantic energy that seemed to match the expression on her face. She was trailed by a man who was outfitted in a suit of armor and who gripped a long, shiny sword in his left hand. The couple's eyes searched the hillside beneath them, glancing over the spot where the sheep had been attending to the child.

"Herdwick? Wensley?...Balwynn?" called the knight, but Theia grabbed his unarmed hand in hers and squeezed it tight. "They're gone, Logan!" she shouted. "They followed Serena's orders too soon! I knew this was a bad idea! What will we do?"

Logan continued to search the empty hillside for the missing boy and his wooly caretakers, but as the reality of the situation crept in, he locked eyes with Theia and said in a grave tone, "We have to keep fighting. The Drezels have the upper hand, but we can still win this. And when we do, we'll get Serena to bring Heely back."

Theia looked as though she were in a great deal of distress. She shook her head. "No! You don't understand! She *can't* bring him back! That was the whole point of using the type of spell she did. The portal the sheep took him through is untraceable. And without any way to track where he's gone, it could take a million years to find him!"

Logan suddenly looked like he was going to be sick. "But she's a god! She can undo the spell!"

Tears slid down Theia's pale cheeks. "No, Logan. Serena created the spell so that there was no way for Theo to get to Heely if the Drezels won. No god nor mortal can find him now."

Logan fell to the ground on his knees, relinquishing his sword as he did. "Oh, my darling! I don't have a million years to search for our son, though I'd search a billion if I could."

Theia knelt beside Sir Logan and wrapped her arms around his neck. "I know you would, and I swear we'll think of something. I won't let anything happen to you before we see our son again!"

Suddenly a woman with black, wavy hair that hung down her back like winding serpents appeared from the other side of the hill where the battle was taking place. Her eyes were dark green and sparkled like two pools of emerald water beneath the light of a full moon.

She spoke to Logan and Theia who sat together in shock and sadness. "What's going on here? There's no time to rest! You two are needed in the battle! The Drezels have succeeded at offing another dozen knights with that horrible skin-melting contraption of theirs! If you don't find a way to outmatch their weapons soon, you'll have to surrender to Theo!" she shouted at them in a tone of disapproval.

Theia looked up at the dark-haired woman and snapped, "Go easy on us, Serena. Your sheep took Heely. They transported him through the portal alone, even though it wasn't necessary."

"What!?" Serena shouted. "Those blasted, wool-brained creatures! I'll have each of their heads for this! Oh, my darling sister, I'm so sorry! But alas, listen to the violence that's approaching. We must get back to the fighting before it's too late. I swear when this is all over, I'll make it right. I promise!"

The couple looked at each other mournfully and nodded, knowing they had little choice. To find Heely, they would have to defeat the dark god first. It was the only way they would be free to search for their son.

Logan grabbed ahold of his sword with new resolve and rose to his feet, extending his hand to Theia. The three began to head back over the peak, returning to the fight below. But before Serena had disappeared across the hilltop's threshold, she turned her gaze to the exact spot where the sheep and child had vanished.

A devious smile spread across her crimson lips, and she whispered to herself, "Oh yes, my naughty sheep. Take the time gods' son as far, far away as you can. For when his scion returns, all our troubles will come to an end."

Serena turned once more in the direction of the battle and let loose a bone-chilling scream that reverberated far and wide. Then she charged back down the hill and into the thick of war once more.

CHAPTER 1

ON THE WAY TO REBEL TOWN

Max had been riding alongside Dale for the better part of a full day and was mentally exhausted. When they'd left New Waldoff to lead the band of scouts towards the rebels' mountain town, Max suggested that they spend their time quietly strategizing on how to approach the new city in the stealthiest way possible. But Dale dismissed Max's idea immediately.

"Stealthy? What for? Who cares if they know we're coming or not? These fools have no idea we're scouting them out so we can attack them later on. For all they know, we're coming to make peace. Wish them well. Even bring them a house-warming basket for crying out loud. Believe me, it won't be a problem."

Max's true agenda had been to avoid conversation with Dale as much as possible, but he soon learned that Dale was more interested in yammering on to himself than making true conversation.

"That old bitty is in way over her head. You know, she was going to put me on the council? I guess I dodged a bullet there."

Max asked, "How so? I thought you—"

Dale didn't let Max finish his question, though, before he started explaining. "She had that murderous gleam in her eye when we left. I know it well, and judging by that look, I doubt she's going to let any of the council live. Betsy has never known when to go easy.

"When we were tots, we used to play this game called 'fire in the hole.' It's where we'd take turns dropping homemade smoke bombs down prairie dog holes. Whoever got the prairie dogs to leave their burrows first won. But Betsy hated losing. So whenever she did, she started dropping real bombs down the prairie dog holes until we couldn't play the game again for a long time. It's just the same as now."

"How is that just the same as now?" Max asked, feeling disgusted.

Dale snickered like he thought Max was being dumb. "Because that little witch still can't stand to lose. She'll cut off her nose to spite her face if it means she gets to cut off everyone else's noses and their tongues, lips, and ears too. In this case, she's going to kill a bunch of council members who she could've played nice with and recruited to her side. But that's not her style. The council would only serve as a reminder to her that, for a while, they were more powerful than she was."

It was Max's turn to snicker. "Except not really," he said.

"Hmm?" Dale questioned distractedly, but he was already knee deep in another thought and quickly moved on without giving Max a chance to clarify. "You know, Dan and Betsy always thought they were better than me. They thought I was weak compared to them. They never appreciated the power I have over a crowd. Had no respect for my charm and charisma. Getting people to support me by tricking them into believing I'm one of them—just an average loser like all the rest. Well, that's some powerful magic!

"But those two always wanted to strong arm everything. They pushed their way through every obstacle, even when it made more sense to go around the obstacle, or sweet talk the obstacle instead. If I'd been in charge of Waldoff—I mean fully in charge—I bet none of this other stuff would've happened. I'd probably still be leading the city, in fact. I mean all those dumb blokes really loved it when I was in charge. By now, there'd be a dozen gold statues in my likeness all over the city. Two dozen even! Maybe three! Who knows?"

Max was trying his best to tune Dale out but failing miserably. "In this idyllic city of yours, are all these statue-loving citizens still hooked on the mind-altering poison you tricked them into drinking?"

Dale shrugged. "No. The poison was all Dan's idea. Just another part of his strong-arming. I was sensational at working the crowds even before all that. I mean, you probably don't remember, but I was the one who talked all those men into going after the wolves. And that was long before they drank Dan's poison."

"But that was Dan's idea too, wasn't it? Isn't he the one who gave the orders to go after the wolves?"

Dale shrugged again. "I don't know. It's been a long time. It's all kind of a blur now."

Max knew this was Dale's way of putting the topic to bed rather than having to admit that he wasn't quite as powerful as he liked to imagine.

But then Dale said slyly, "You know, I bet *you* probably don't remember going around with my sister back then? Right? I mean it's been so long now."

Max's heart jumped at the mention of Dale's sister. Not only did he remember his relationship with Helen, but it was all Max had thought of for the last month, especially during his time in prison when the only thing he could do was think. Max was surprised that Dale remembered their relationship, though. After all, Dale was highly self-involved and therefore didn't notice much beyond his own set of circumstances. Plus, when Max and Helen had been together, very few people had known about their relationship, and hardly anyone who *had* known remembered it now. And for good reason.

"No, you're wrong," Max said with a hint of sadness. "I do remember my time with Helen."

But something else suddenly occurred to Dale. "Say, what did you mean before? You know, when you made that comment about the council members not being as powerful as Betsy? What was that all about?"

"Well, they weren't," said Max, though he was still thinking about Helen.

Dale argued, "Yes, they were. If Goodman and the council were the ones making important decisions about the city, and Betsy was just Goodman's silly, old secretary—conniving, sure, but without any real power—then what in the world are you talking about?"

Max had to keep from smiling as he realized that Dale was clueless about Betsy.

"You don't know, do you? All those years of the two of you and Dan skulking around together like the little team of hell bandits you were, and she never told you?"

Dale looked annoyed and began to pout. He slowed his horse, letting the other members of their group ride ahead without him. Max slowed too, sensing what Dale was about to ask him, and happy to get to be the one to poke a hole in his riding companion's overinflated ego.

Dale shifted his weight atop his horse to look at Max. "Told me what?"

Max let out a laugh as he began to explain, "Your old friend, the she-devil, is an actual she-devil. She's the dark god's daughter. The spawn of evil."

Dale's face didn't react much to the news, although from

his eyes Max could tell he was trying to understand what Max was telling him.

"The dark god's daughter? You mean…"

But Dale trailed off, and Max didn't know whether he had figured it out or gotten lost in his own self-absorbed reasoning.

Max prompted, "The dark god. The chill in the shadows. The evil lurking behind all the dark deeds you and your psychopathic brother and Betsy got up to."

A wave of understanding flashed across Dale's face. "The dark angel. The one Dan spoke to all those years? That was Betsy's father?"

Max nodded.

"Well, why in the hell did no one tell me!?"

Max shook his head and continued to ride along the same path they'd been following towards the mountains.

"Honestly, I doubt Dan knew either. But as far as Betsy goes, I couldn't say."

Dale hurried his horse to catch up to Max, his flabby skin jiggled as the horse trotted.

"That makes no sense! If Dan didn't even know who was feeding him all his dark plans, then how did some no-brained jackass like you figure it out?"

"Your mom."

Dale flinched. "Is that supposed to be some kind of joke?"

"No. It's not a joke." Max shook his head. "Your mother was the one who told me."

Dale's voice was becoming increasingly high-pitched as he processed the information Max was divulging. In a tone that was on the verge of being shrill, he demanded, "Oh for bloody pickle's sake. How in the hell did *she* know?"

Max had to be careful how he proceeded. It was one thing to let Dale in on the secret of Betsy's family lineage, but he was fairly certain that Dale had no idea about his own lineage either. And Max worried that if he let Dale know that his mother was a goddess, it might give him grandiose ideas—which wouldn't be good for anyone.

"I can't say for sure, but I think one of the wolves told her. Maybe Axel."

Max didn't know if this was the right way to handle the situation, but he figured it was the most likely excuse to work. Dale had spent years convincing himself and others that the wolves were the cause of all sorts of problems, and therefore, he was primed to accept them as the culprit in any scenario.

Dale didn't respond, and for the first time since they'd left the city, the two rode in silence. Max was grateful for the break, and soon his mind drifted back in time to memories of Helen.

He was walking down the streets at the center of Waldoff, on his way home from one of the regular meetings he and his friends attended at Bob and Maude's. It was mere months before the wolf massacre would begin, and he and the others were well aware that the temperature in the city was reaching a boiling point.

Max turned the corner at the city's townhall and entered the large, municipal park with its many plaster statues and monuments, which had been erected to give the park's barren landscape a bit more gravitas. From behind a mediocre replica statue of a naked biblical character, a sweet voice called to him, "Hello there, sailor."

Max looked up at the towering statue of David and smiled. "Well, hello there, David. Your voice is much softer and more lovely than I would've imagined, judging by the rest of you."

Helen appeared from behind the back of the statue with a playful, hurt expression.

"Oh, Helen, it's only you," Max teased.

"Only me? You really know how to twist the knife. I would've thought you'd be happier to see me after all those kisses you planted on me in the alleyway yesterday."

Max looked around nervously to see if anyone else was

near. When he was sure they were alone, he scolded, "I told you we can't keep doing this. You're too young for me. Your parents would kill me if they ever found out we were involved, and honestly, I wouldn't blame them."

Helen smiled and walked closer to Max. "But isn't that part of the fun, Maxie?"

Max looked frustrated. "No, Helen. The idea of your father pummeling me to death isn't fun for me. And just so you know, calling me 'sailor' only serves as a reminder of my old life before the Moon. You know, part of the thirty years I was alive before you were even born."

Helen took another couple of steps closer so that her body was pressed against his. "That doesn't matter to me still," she said. "Who cares about age when we live in a world where most people will never grow a day older?"

Max protested. "But, Helen, you do grow older."

Helen frowned. "Is that what this is about? You don't want to be stuck with me in forty years when I look like I'm twice your age?"

Max tried to fight back the laughter, but he couldn't help it. "No. This isn't about you looking too old for me. This is about the fact that I'm actually more than twice *your* age, which means I've had more than twice as much life experience as you. And as someone with a lot of life experience, I'm telling you this isn't right."

Helen, who was nearly as tall as her would-be paramour, stared deeply into his eyes and suddenly, Max couldn't think of what to say next. He gazed at her dreamily, trying to fight the temptation to lean in and kiss her beautiful, red lips.

Before arriving on the Moon, Max had only ever had one girlfriend—Louisa May, his green-eyed, knobby-kneed, childhood sweetheart. And life on the Moon hadn't exactly presented him with an array of options in the romance department, which meant that Max had lived alone for over a decade. Helen's smooth, tan skin and dark brown eyes beckoned to him. His whole body yearned for her. And though he'd never admit, she was right about one thing. Knowing that their love was forbidden only made it that much harder to resist, though still he tried to put her off.

"Helen, I can't. I've known you since you were a baby, and Bob and Mau—"

But before Max could finish his sentence, his attention moved to the sound of two people approaching the park from the direction of townhall. Max looked over his shoulder and began to take a step back, but Helen grabbed him by the wrist and pulled him down behind the statue's pedestal that she'd been hiding behind earlier.

Max looked at her, his eyes the size of saucers. Helen pressed her finger to her lips just inches from his own, making sure he knew they had to stay quiet. As the other two parkgoers reached the tall, naked statue, they stopped in front of it. Max held his breath, convinced they were about to be discovered. But soon he realized that the couple were only pausing to continue their contentious discussion.

A gruff voice said, "We all know what the plans are for the wolves, so I don't get why Dan's got us sitting around on our hands, waiting. We should be moving forward before those maggots get wind of our operation. Instead, we're playing looky-loo with each other out there in the desert with no orders. And it's got me wondering how true Dan's intentions are to kill the beasts. Everyone knows that most of that dang family of his are wolf sympathizers, after all."

The second person, who Max recognized as Betsy, replied, "Your job isn't to think, Rufus. Dan has his reasons."

"Which are?"

Betsy snapped, "Which are none of your damn business."

Rufus' tone changed, and Max could tell he was getting angry. "Now listen here, you stupid—"

But Betsy stopped him. "Watch yourself. I'm not one of those silly floosies you like to hang around with. There's a reason Dan made me his second in command—a reason I'd be happy to demonstrate if you ever talk to me like that again."

Rufus took a moment, presumably to rethink what he was going to say. "Look, it ain't just me. I gotta whole mess of revved up fighters chomping at the bit, asking me each day when they're gonna get their chance to rain down hell on those sick, four-legged bastards. You gotta give me something more I can pass along if you don't want them going rogue and starting this fight without Dan's permission."

Betsy laughed. "*Them* going rogue might be the last thing that *they* ever get to do. Dan isn't likely to tolerate a group of mutineers with the collective brainpower and patience of a four-year-old. But I suppose, in the interest of less clean-up work for me, you can tell them that Dan's busy focusing his attention on a project that will improve their lives for the better. It's an endeavor even more riveting and complex than wolf genocide if you can imagine that. However, Dan wants to know the outcome of his experiments before he gets involved in the daily tactical maneuvers of beast extermination."

Rufus grumbled. "Well, that ain't a great reason, but I guess it'll have to do. For now."

The two continued to talk but began to walk again and were soon out of earshot.

Max and Helen remained hidden behind the pedestal for a little longer, staring at each other in disbelief. Helen spoke first. "Oh my god! I knew things were bad between my brothers and the wolves, but I had no idea that they were *this* bad. We have to do something to stop them! We have to tell the others!"

Max nodded but didn't respond. He looked deep in thought.

"What is it, Max?"

Max shook his head slightly. "I'm just thinking about what Betsy said."

"I know. That's what I'm saying. We have to go tell my parents and the rest of the group. More importantly though, we have to tell the wolves."

Max shook his head again. "No. Well, I mean yes, of course we need to do that. But it's that other part that Betsy was talking about—the part about Dan working on something to improve lives. What could Dan possibly be doing that's so important he would risk alienating his most loyal followers?"

Helen looked like she was beginning to understand. "So then, you think Dan's new project might be something even more over the top than killing all the wolves?"

Max's gaze met Helen's, and he could tell she was scared. "I don't know, Helen. What I do know is that it might present an opportunity for us."

"What do you mean?" Helen asked.

"I mean that if we can figure out what Dan's working on, then maybe we can throw a wrench into his plans and delay the genocide longer. It could buy us time to find a suitable way to counter his plans altogether."

"So are you talking about sabotaging his experiments, then?"

Max shrugged again. "I don't know. Maybe. But first we'll have to find out what he's working on."

Helen's eyes narrowed. "But how do we even know if what Betsy said was true? And how are we supposed to find out? It's not like we can pay Dan a social visit and say, 'So, we hear you're planning to murder all of our wolf friends and their families. Is there anything else you're up to these days? You know, in addition to wolf extinction?'"

Max replied, "No, you're right. That's probably not the best way to get what we want. But I think maybe you've forgotten what I do for a living."

Helen shook her head. "Of course I know what you do. You make deliveries to and from the market."

Max nodded. "Yes, and you know who I make these deliveries for the most, right?"

Helen shook her head.

"Betsy," answered Max. "I pick up vines from the greenhouse and bring them to the market. For the most part, all the other growers deliver their own plants and produce, but not her."

Helen looked surprised. "You mean you travel back and forth to the Darkside? That seems dangerous, Max. You know, Dan has been spending most of his time over there lately. He's even been getting those jerks he calls followers to build him some type of compound near Black Ice Glacier."

"I know. We've talked about it at your parents' meetings. I don't imagine that there's any danger in me traveling to the greenhouse, though. If anything, I'm helping Dan's cause by keeping Betsy happy. And that could work in our favor."

"In our favor how?"

"Well, maybe if I butter up Betsy, I can get her to tell me what Dan's working on. I doubt she knows anything about me except that I deliver her plants to the market, which means she won't suspect why I'm asking questions. Hopefully, she'll just assume I'm interested in joining their side."

Helen moved her finger back and forth over one of the buttons that held Max's shirt together. "You know, Max, I think you're very brave. Ruth teases you about being young and naïve, but from what I can tell, you're just as brave as any of the knights in the stories Ruth told me while I was growing up."

Helen stared passionately into Max's eyes, and his face flushed.

"That's very kind, Helen, but I don't think—"

But before Max could finish his sentence, Helen lunged

towards him from her crouched position behind the pedestal, pressing her lips against his. Initially surprised, Max started to resist, but Helen leaned into him harder, and pretty soon he couldn't remember why he'd been resisting in the first place. He gently placed one hand on the back of Helen's head and the other around her waist, pulling her even closer to him.

Max's pulse quickened as he lost himself to this memory from long ago, and he let out a blissful sigh. He could remember the way Helen's hair felt wrapped around his fingers, and the electricity that coursed through him whenever they kissed. He hadn't noticed Dale for a while, but if he had, he would've seen that Dale had gone from looking annoyed to downright incensed.

Already on the verge of a tantrum, Dale took Max's sigh as a jab about his prior lack of knowledge regarding Betsy's father. And this perceived disrespect sent him over the edge.

"You're a real no-good bastard! You know that, Max? Something about all of this doesn't smell right! If you and my mom are such good chums, then how about we go pay her a visit when we reach the city? I bet she'd be interested to know who you work for now. Don't you?

"Or is all of this some sort of ruse? I mean, how come Maude's telling you secrets, anyway? From what I remember, the two of you didn't end up on such great terms. I can't imagine either of my parents confiding in you after what you did. From what I recall, they hated your guts once they realized you'd been taking advantage of their *precious* daughter."

Suddenly, Max understood how Dale knew about his relationship with Helen. Dale had still been living with his parents when everything blew up—when Maude and Bob found out about Max and Helen's love affair. Max hadn't realized that Dale had been there that day, listening to the explosive argument that nearly turned into a brawl.

Max wasn't exactly sure what to say, so he told the truth as plainly as he could, "Maude forgave me."

Dale looked peeved. "She forgave you, but you still went to work for Betsy?"

Max shrugged. "I said she forgave me; I didn't say I forgave her."

This made Dale smile. "I see. So, you're working for Betsy to get back at my parents?"

"Something like that," Max replied.

"Hmm, well since we've come all this way, why don't we pay a visit to old Maude while we're here? I could use a pick me up. And what better than the look on my mom's face when she realizes she's been betrayed?"

"No. Betsy ordered us to confirm the rebels' whereabouts, not to cause trouble. If you go up there, you'll start a war."

Dale tsked. "Surely, I'm allowed to check in on my own mother. I don't see why *my* presence would be a problem. It's not like I'm the one who slept with her favorite child."

"That's enough, Dale!"

Dale laughed and then he yelled to the group of scouts who were riding thirty paces ahead. "There's been a change of plans, fellows. I've decided we're going to do more than just confirm the location of the rebel town. We're going to go for a visit. A couple of you will climb the rest of the way on foot while we stay here. I want you to go up there and let those rascals know the honor I'm bestowing on them with my visit. It's not every day that a powerful, former mayor visits a ragtag bunch of losers in their ramshackle village. Oh, and make sure the dopes know I want to see Maude when I get there. Understand?"

Two young men volunteered for the job and quickly dismounted their horses. Then, as they ran off from the rest of the group, up the steep mountain incline, Max grabbed ahold of Dale's arm.

"This is stupid, Dale. Those people up there aren't going to welcome us. Especially not you! So why in god's name would you warn them we're coming? It will only give them time to prepare the spit they're going to roast us on!"

Dale shoved Max's hand away. "Relax. This will be fun. People love sappy nonsense, and what could be sappier than a reunion between a mother and son? You'll see. I'll have those rebel scumbags eating from my hand in no time."

Max shook his head and slumped in his saddle as they began to wait. He knew Dale was going to be sorely disappointed over how his plan turned out. So, to pass the time, Max began to consider all the ways he could avoid talking to Dale on what would surely be a long ride back to New Waldoff. Assuming they made it out of the rebel town alive.

CHAPTER 2

INTERDIMENSIONAL FALLOUT

"What do you mean you have a daughter?"

Mina sat in front of Fred atop a black steed, her shapely torso eclipsing only half of Fred's. Mina's messy hair flowed gently over her shoulders and swayed to the beat of the horse's hooves galloping across the parched terrain. She held what was left of her disappearing arm tightly against her chest. Fred's touch had erased her entire hand and wrist and half of her forearm.

While leaving Earth, Fred had grabbed ahold of her as she began to fall from the glass bridge. And though this noble act had saved her life, she knew it might cost her the entirety of her arm. Mina had mostly managed to ignore the pain in her vanishing arm during her encounter with the misshapen worlds that she'd journeyed through during her return to the Moon. However, now that she'd had some time to relax, the severity of her injury had become much more tangible. It felt like waves of heat spreading upwards towards her elbow in the form of intense, searing pain, alerting her to the fact that her arm's disappearing act was far from over.

Mina tried to refocus her attention on Fred. She'd been

ready to tell him everything she'd experienced on her way back to the Moon, but he'd insisted that they begin their journey to the new city—a large valley in the mountains where many Moon Travelers had fled after living under an intolerable, authoritarian government in New Waldoff.

Mina had been gathering her thoughts as they rode in silence until Fred, who could no longer take the suspense, blurted out his question about her daughter.

Not exactly sure how to explain, Mina decided she might as well dive in. "While I was trying to find my way back to the Moon, I traveled through different places and times. It felt surreal; the places looked surreal. Some of them were stretched out and others were sort of pushed down. It was like viewing the world through a series of curved lenses.

"All of the people and settings were familiar, though. In one reality, I saw my parents, grandfather, and myself sitting in our living room playing a game. But I was older than I should've been—older than when my grandfather died and my mom and dad left me. In a couple of the realities, I was with my professor, Dodgson, the same professor whose class you interrupted.

"In these realities, we were in a relationship, and I guess we eventually got married. About ten years into the future, I watched the two of us get into a car accident. We died, but before all of that, we had a daughter. Her name is Mattie. She's beautiful, Fred. She has dark brown hair, and brown eyes, and she's so full of life and energy.

"She told me she knew I'd come back. Apparently, the older version of me—her mother—told Mattie that if anything ever happened to her, she would find a way back to Mattie through the quantum world."

Mina paused for a few seconds. Her voice had begun to sound sad, but when she spoke again, she sounded hopeful. "It hurt me to leave her. Mattie told me all about her life and how hard it's been for her since her parents died. I promised her I would try to find a way back to her, and I plan to keep that promise. You and Bob have to help me find a way to bring her here."

Fred's heart sank. He was certain that what Mina was describing wasn't real. At least not in the way she imagined it to be. But he had no way to prove it because he wasn't allowed to tell her what he knew. The oracle had ordered him to keep the secrets she'd shared with him private as part of the mission she'd trained him for. Still, Fred didn't want to lie to Mina. The connection they shared was real. Everything he'd learned about in the tunnels had proven it, and he didn't want to risk hurting her by making it seem like she couldn't trust him.

"Mina, I know that what you saw felt real, but don't you see how it can't be? You basically said so yourself. In one of the visions you experienced, your parents and grandfather existed with you in a place and time where they shouldn't have been. If that wasn't real, then why would any of it be real?"

Mina wasn't willing to accept Fred's logic, though. "They weren't visions, Fred. I could touch and feel things while I was moving through the different scenes."

"I understand, Mina. When I was inside the ice tunnels and had to travel through the dark passageways, the oracle showed me visions that felt extremely lifelike. Often, I was able to use all of my senses in those visions, too."

Mina sounded annoyed. "But you were being shown the past most of the time, right? You can call that a vision if you want, but the past is real, Fred. And you and I even shared one of those visions multiple times—the one where you were standing in the middle of the giant wheel and your jaw was frozen shut. Are you telling me that wasn't real either? Even though we both experienced it?"

Fred was frustrated. He wanted to steer away from the

topic. "Look," he said, "all I know is that you're supposed to be here now."

Instantly, he realized he'd made a mistake. Without meaning to, he'd revealed too much.

"What do you mean I'm 'supposed' to be here?" Mina asked. "According to who?"

Fred tried to cover his tracks. "According to me, and also to Bob and Maude. It's like I told you on the train. When Maude died last night, so did Theia—the Moon's goddess. But your real mom is a goddess too, which means you can help rebalance the power shift that happened when Maude died. Without you here, the dark god, Theia's brother, would become much more powerful."

Mina could tell Fred was nervous, and she wondered what he might be hiding.

"But you said on the train that it was my real mother who was responsible for all the horrible nightmares I had, and for kidnapping Bonkers from his deathbed." Mina's voice nearly faltered as she mentioned her beloved basset hound, but she shoved her emotions back down and continued.

"If it's true that she did all those despicable things to guide me towards returning to the Moon, then she must want me here too, right? I mean that's what you told me the oracle said. So then, which is it and why?"

Fred wasn't sure what to say. Parts of what Mina was saying were true, but she still wasn't able to see the larger picture. And Fred hated all the lying he was being forced to do to keep her from figuring it out. "I guess it's both, Mina. But I don't think you should focus on that now. You're here because of the lengths that Maude, Bob, and I went to in order to find you and bring you back."

Mina didn't respond for a while. She could tell that Fred was trying to handle her, and she didn't care for it. She wished they were standing face-to-face so she could look him in the eye and see every facial twitch. She didn't know exactly what more she could glean from watching him, but she thought it would at least help her to know which parts of their conversation were making him uncomfortable.

She turned her thoughts to her daughter again. The girl's soulful, brown eyes had reminded her of her own. "I've been waiting for you." These words—the first ones that the girl had spoken to Mina—nearly stopped her heart. She didn't know what to make of the girl or her strange, knowing expression, and she worried that after everything she'd been through up until that point, she might be facing her tormentor. She'd wondered if it was her mother finally revealing herself to her in the form of a young girl who looked as though she could've been Mina's sister. However, it had turned out, of course, that the truth was even more surprising.

Mattie told Mina how her own mother had been a brilliant quantum physicist who believed that the quantum world was responsible for many odd occurrences in the universe, including the existence of an afterlife. She also alluded to how this other, older version of Mina had sensed the fragility of her own existence in the alternate dimension of space and time she'd occupied counter to Mina's own. Mina knew this had to be true, because why else would she have foretold of her own return if she died one day?

Mattie explained how whenever she awoke in the middle of the night, and called for her mother, her mother would come to her and whisper reassuring words in her ear. "I will be here for you always, my darling. Even if one day you think I've left for good, I promise I'll return to you. You'll never get rid of me, my sweet baby. I will watch over you forever."

Mattie's first words to Mina, *I've been waiting for you,* hadn't been the foreboding words of Mina's absent mother who'd come to life as the spirit of a young girl, but those of a young girl relieved to find that her absent mother's premonition was coming true. Mina wondered, however, if this alternate version of herself had really known she'd return to Mattie in some other form. And if so, how that could possibly be.

The truth was that it seemed far-fetched, and Fred's argument that none of what she'd experienced had been real felt like a fair assessment in many ways. Yet Mina couldn't shake the emotions that her future daughter had drummed up. Mina knew that Mattie had to be real. She wasn't just part of some dream she'd watched inside her own head. She was a flesh and blood child who'd suffered from agonizing grief since losing her parents.

Mattie told Mina that she'd spent most of her days in Mina's old room, asleep in bed, wishing the days away and living only for the nights. For when the world was still and quiet, and there was no one around to ask her about her feelings, Mattie came to life again, finding peace in her dark solitude. She said that during the long nights, she would stare up at the Moon for hours, recalling the stories her mother had once told her of the people who lived there.

Then after recounting this to Mina, Mattie asked her, "Are these stories really true? Mommy said they were, but Daddy insisted they were fairytales."

Mina smiled at this. She could see how Mattie's father might misinterpret her stories about the Moon as fairytales, and she wondered if the older version of herself had spent much time trying to convince Dodgson of the truth behind them.

Before she left, Mina tried to answer as many of Mattie's questions as she could. She knew it was going to be hard to leave her, even though it was obvious that she wasn't the Mina that Mattie had been hoping for. She wasn't her real mother. They shared none of the same memories or experiences. The only overlaps they had were the memories Mattie's mother had shared with her daughter about her past—Mina's past.

Mattie begged Mina to tell her all the same stories her mother had once told her, asking detailed questions along the way, as though she were trying her best to commit it all to memory. Then when Mina told Mattie it was time for her to leave, Mattie asked her if she would be able to return again someday. This broke Mina's heart. She knew that Mattie missed her own mother terribly, and she wished she could've lied to comfort her. But she knew it was important to be truthful so that she didn't end up adding to Mattie's grief.

"To be honest, I don't know if I'll be able to return or not. I'm not entirely sure how I wound up here to begin with. My friends, the ones your mother told you about, they found me on Earth and asked me to return to the Moon. That's what I was trying to do before I arrived in your room. I don't have the wings to fly, like last time. This time I'm having to move through different dimensions to find my way back. I don't know if that makes any sense to you or not. It barely makes any sense to me."

Mattie smiled as a spark of excitement flashed across her eyes. "But I know! You've been using the quantum world to move through different dimensions. My mom was trying to prove that was possible before…well, before the accident. Days before it happened, she told me she had run an experiment that proved different particles could interact with new dimensions by moving through the quantum world in a certain way. You're somehow doing that on your own!"

Mina was shocked. As Mattie spoke, she suddenly felt the answer to one of her longest-held questions snap into place. During her college studies, she'd often wondered if the quantum world had been responsible for her journey to the Moon. And now she knew that some version of her future-self had proven that it was possible. Mina was fascinated, but a little shaken too.

Listening to Mattie felt as if she were receiving a message

sent to her by her alternate self from beyond the grave—from the quantum realm—pushing Mina towards Mattie so that she might help her daughter escape from Earth just like Mina had been trying to do.

As Mina thought about this, she looked down at her arm. This was when she first noticed that the pain had intensified to a level she could no longer ignore.

She said, "I'm impressed, Mattie. Your mom must have considered you a close confidant to share that with you. Look, I want to be as upfront as possible with you too. I don't know what the future holds for me, but I promise I'll do everything I can to return, to find you again."

Mattie put on a brave face, but Mina could see the tears welling up in her eyes. She wanted to reach out and touch her, but she worried it wasn't safe. So instead, she forced herself to think about the difficult times she'd spent by herself after her grandfather had died and her pretend parents had abandoned her for wherever they'd actually gone. She thought about what she would have liked to have heard during all the years she'd spent alone without any adult guidance.

She leaned down so that her face and Mattie's were close together.

"I'm proud of you. I know we only just met, but you remind me a lot of myself at your age. I'm certain your parents would be proud of you too, knowing that you've kept hope alive, even after everything you've been through. I'll try to find a way back, but in the meantime, I want you to be careful."

Mattie nodded but asked, "Careful of what?"

Mina wasn't sure how much to tell her. She didn't want to scare Mattie before leaving, but the whole time they'd been talking, Mina had been wondering how safe her future daughter was in the care of her supposed grandparents—the same two people who'd abandoned her when she wasn't much older than Mattie.

"Just trust your gut, Mattie. If something doesn't feel right, don't ignore it. Look out for yourself the best you can."

Mattie nodded again. "Okay, I will."

After replaying this last conversation in her head, Mina felt determined again and spoke to Fred as their horse began to climb the long, winding path towards the mountain valley where the new city was being built.

"I have to bring her here, Fred. I can't leave her alone with those people who aren't even her real grandparents. My grandfather, or really my father, said my fake parents were put there to guard us. But I don't know who put them there. It could have been someone dangerous for all I know. Like an enemy of my mother's.

"You say I'm supposed to be here, and maybe that's true, but what if the people who were guarding me are angry now that I'm gone? What if they take it out on Mattie?"

The anxiety Fred had felt tapping at his nerve endings was quickly turning into a vicious attack of unease. "Mina, I know what you just went through was difficult, but give yourself some time to process it before jumping to conclusions. I think as the memories and adrenaline fade, you'll begin to realize that none of it was real," he said in a desperate tone.

Mina was glad now that Fred couldn't see her face because it made it easier for her to lie. "Fine. I'll put it out of my mind," she said.

Of course, it wasn't something she really intended to stop thinking of, but for the time being, she decided to give up on trying to persuade Fred.

Fred knew it wasn't like Mina to give in so easily, and he wondered if she was only telling him what he wanted to hear. However, he didn't have time to think it over, because right at that moment, they came upon a group of travelers. Their horse had just completed a long turn along the curved trail they were following, about a quarter of a mile below the valley, when they spotted the group in a wide-open, rocky area at the foot of another uphill climb. There were two figures with their backs to them, sitting on large horses, along with several other men and horses who were standing around looking bored.

Fred pulled the reigns to stop their horse. Nervous about who these travelers might be, he didn't want to make their presence known just yet. Mina looked back at Fred to question what was going on, but she could tell by the intense look on his face that he was trying to determine what to do. She twisted forward again, and right then, one of the travelers on horseback turned to them as though he'd sensed Mina's presence. Mina gasped in horror.

"Oh my god." she whispered. "It's Dan."

"No," Fred said reassuring her. "Dan is dead. That man there is Dale."

Mina wasn't exactly relieved though, considering the last time she'd seen Dale, he'd ordered his guards to kidnap and imprison her.

"What should we do?" she asked.

She could feel a knot growing inside of her stomach over the anticipation of having to face this man she loathed and feared. For a brief second, Dale stared directly at Mina's face, and she thought she detected a hint of recognition flash across his eyes.

The moment was quickly interrupted, however, when the man sitting next to Dale yelled, "Quiet, everyone! Do you hear that sound?"

Mina and Fred and the group of travelers fell quiet, and suddenly, Mina did hear something. It sounded like the quick succession of pounding against the ground mixed with high-pitched screaming. A few seconds later, two young men came crashing down the steep path that wound up the mountain. They were yelling over each other, and from their panicky, disheveled expressions, Mina could tell they'd been through something terrifying.

One of the men implored, "Go! Go! There are people back there with a big ass flashlight that shoots laser beams! And they're coming this way!"

Mina heard Fred snort behind her and knew he was trying to suppress laughter. And though she didn't understand what was going on, she wasn't too concerned for her safety because she sensed that whoever had this oversized flashlight, they were probably on the rebels' side.

The men jumped back on their horses and began riding away without so much as a consideration for the baffled looks on the faces of their comrades. The men who'd been standing around looked at Dale and the rider next to him as though eagerly waiting for instructions.

Dale said, "Yes, fine. Get back on your horses. We got what we came for, I suppose."

Then before anyone had a chance to speak, Dale turned his horse back towards the trail that led down the mountain. Mina held her breath as Dale went by. He stared at her with his twisted smile and right as he moved past, his gaze shifted towards her disappearing arm.

The man who'd been sitting on his horse next to Dale passed by them a few seconds later but avoided eye contact. Then finally, the remainder of the men who'd climbed back on their horses followed the rest of their group down the mountain.

Once they were gone, Mina asked, "What in the world do you think that was about?"

"I don't know," Fred replied, "but I bet we're about to find out." And he gave their horse a swift kick forward as they began their final ascent towards the rebel city.

CHAPTER 3

BETSY'S REVENGE

Betsy's heels tapped loudly on the cobblestone pathway as she took her daily waddle to work. It was early still, and there was no one else stirring on the winding streets of New Waldoff as Betsy click-clacked her way to City Hall. Her long black dress with its pinned, high collar dragged along the street due to Betsy's shrinking stature. Betsy was aware that the hem was coming undone and fraying along the seam, but she didn't care. She'd been much too busy the last several years to concern herself with something as trivial as having her dresses mended.

"Clink."

A black crystal dropped against a stone near Betsy's feet. She ignored it and kept walking; she had business to attend to.

"Clink, clink."

Two more dark stones manifested out of thin air and fell onto her pathway, but still Betsy continued on her way, seemingly unaware of the spontaneous gemstone show happening right in front of her.

"Clink, clink, clink, clink, clink, clink."

Several more glistening, opaque gems tumbled towards

Betsy's stubby feet. This time she kicked them away with the toe of her shoe, sending them flying down the path and out of her way.

She hissed under her breath, "Knock it off! I've got better things to do than take another scolding from you. Stop checking up on me! Surely, you can find something better to do!"

Betsy's outburst seemed to do the trick. The crystals stopped appearing out of nowhere, and Betsy was able to continue her journey in peace. Several minutes later, Betsy arrived in her office, the same large room she'd used to conduct business when Goodman was in charge. The only difference was that in the days since she'd taken over, the room had been overtaken by vines. So much so that it was beginning to resemble an overgrown jungle.

Betsy moved across the room towards her desk and found a mammoth-sized, black crystal seated in her chair as though it had been waiting for her to arrive so they could start their meeting. She glared at the stone. "You've got to be kidding me!"

In a fit of rage, Betsy shuffled around her desk, wrapped her stunted, sausage-fingered hands around the crystal, and with a loud grunt, she heaved the burdensome stone into a corner across the room.

"Damn it, Father! I said I don't have time for this today!"

But as Betsy's fingers touched the black rock, the lights in her office dimmed. The crystal began to shimmer as bolts of electricity wrapped around it like large electric talons gripping it tightly within their clutches. By the time the heavy stone crashed to the floor, a dark vapor was expelling from its center, and a booming voice filled Betsy's office.

"I'm sorry I've become such an inconvenience, Daughter. It really pains me that these frequent tongue lashings are causing a wrinkle in your day or that your punishment is starting to feel like punishment, you dim-witted, little bat.

"How do you think I feel after being weakened by your impertinent disregard of my very specific orders—trapped without minions or a clear path forward after your massive screw up!?"

Betsy sat down at her desk while her father's loud voice harassed her from inside the fuming mist. Then when he was through, she calmly replied, "Just as I've told you every single day, Father, I'm handling it. I'm going to win power for you by destroying the rebels and finding the half-breed who stole your energy. I have it on good authority that she'll soon be returning to the Moon if she isn't back already."

"Yes, or so you say. But all I see when I watch you from this giant cold ice cube I'm forced to suffer atop of, is a greedy, little witch who likes to pretend that killing a bunch of nobodies is going to magically restore me to my former glory."

Betsy slapped her hand down on the desk. "They aren't nobodies! They were Goodman's council, and I'm killing them off to show this city who's boss now! How do you expect me to command fear and respect with this twerpy, little body you gave me if you don't let me demonstrate my skills for evil and torture, first?"

Theo pushed back. "Oh, no! You're not going to blame me for that puny meat sack of yours! That grotesque thing is your mother's fault. I told you she was a forest elf, didn't I?"

Betsy rolled her eyes. "Yes, you've mentioned it a few hundred times."

"Yes, well, Gryobe was the one who talked me into using one of those puny, little creatures to sire an heir. You see, I absolutely despise elves. Every single one of them is a horrid assault to the eyes, but the forest elves are by far the ugliest of them all. They're grossly squatty and partially amphibious. Yet they're the only elves that are changelings. I thought that would be useful. But instead, you inherited all the elves' hideous features and none of their powers.

"That's the reason you're the way you are. I'd hoped you'd eventually develop some useful powers and become an important tool to wield against my enemies. But instead, I had to turn to Dan, who was more devious and cleverer than you. You're an abomination, Betsy. Just like Gryobe. But at least Gryobe had the ability to teleport and turn invisible.

"You've failed miserably at every turn. Even when I assigned you simple tasks, like guarding Goodman or gathering intelligence on Theia, you let me down."

Betsy's face didn't react to her father's harsh words. She simply replied, "Well, this abomination has work to do. So if you're finished—"

But Theo wouldn't be dismissed. "You don't get it, you fungi-brained toadstool! You aren't doing the right work! My sister, Serena, could demolish your whole army with one blast of her siren's cry. You have to find out what she's after. Negotiate for what you want. I guarantee you she's the one responsible for that half-breed, and she isn't going to let you take her without something in return. Besides, you'll need Serena's help to capture the girl. She almost killed me, which means you wouldn't stand a chance against her."

Betsy asked, "But I thought that hadn't happened yet."

Theo groaned. "It has happened! I told you! It's why I've been so weak these last nine years. But the half-breed doesn't know that it's happened yet, and if you can get to her before she completes the time-loop, then there's a chance I can reverse the damage she's done. So, stop playing with your food, and get to work! Real work! NOW!"

Suddenly, the lights in Betsy's office brightened, and the vapor cloud in the corner vanished along with the black gemstone. Betsy scowled. She'd felt bad that her father was in an even weaker state than before he took over control of Goodman, but she was tired of taking all the blame. Plus, if she were being honest, she was glad to be in charge. She felt like she'd earned it after playing second-fiddle to Dan and Gryobe for so long and then eventually Goodman. Always her father's loyal subject, but never his number one henchman.

There was a knock on the door. Betsy knew it was her personal guards showing up for work.

"Come in!" she ordered.

Two large men entered the room, both of whom had spent time torturing Bob when he was imprisoned in the basement of city hall. They were both tall, but one had a round belly while the other was more slender. "Betsy, ma'am, are you ready for us to bring in the last two prisoners?"

Betsy glanced towards the vine-covered windows at the far side of the room and answered, "Yes, I suppose. I might as well get this over with. No point in sparing them. I would never know whether I truly had their loyalty, now that all the rest of the council is dead. They'd pledge it to me even if they didn't mean it just so I'd let them live."

The two men looked at each other as if wondering what they should say.

But Betsy waved her hand at them to dismiss their stupid expressions. "Yes, fine. Go get the prisoners. It's time to be done with this."

As she waited, Betsy thought about what her father had said. "If Mina was so powerful, then why had she needed Helen's assistance to fight Dan?" she wondered. Betsy knew she needed some answers, but she didn't like the idea of confronting Serena herself. In all her years, Betsy had only ever come face-to-face with Serena once, and it hadn't gone well.

She decided she might try a different tactic, one in which she could avoid interacting with Serena again. However, she knew she'd have to wait until Max and Dale's team of scouts returned before putting her plan into action.

Moments later, four guards entered Betsy's office, dragging two prisoners by the arms. The prisoners were an emaciated man and woman who were gagged and bound by their wrists and ankles.

Such a shame, Betsy thought. These two seemed to be some of the more obedient detainees, judging by their scrawny appearance. It was obvious they'd been eating the poisoned fruit she'd been sending them, a trick she'd borrowed from Dan's playbook. Still, one could never be sure why they'd gone along with eating fruit they knew was poisoned. And Betsy was well aware that it was probably to get on her good side.

The guards dropped the prisoners face down on the ground, and Betsy's potbelly guard asked, "Do you want us to bring in the knife or the drill kit this time?"

Betsy shook her head. "Neither today, Lester. I have something else in mind."

The slimmer of the first two guards asked, "Do you still want us to lay out the tarp then?"

Betsy seemed to think about it for a second but then shook her head. "No, leave it all to me this time." She looked at the guards. "These are definitely the last two, right?"

The guards nodded.

"Good," said Betsy. "Then I'll finish them off with a grand finale. You four, go spread the word that the council has been permanently disbanded. And make sure to leave in all the gory details!"

"Yes, ma'am!" The four guards saluted Betsy and left the room, shutting the door behind them.

Once the guards were gone, Betsy could hear the prisoners whimpering, but it didn't bother her. She was focused on preparing herself to do something that she hadn't done in ages, something she'd once loved doing yet had been powerless to do for a very long time. For years, even the thought of trying to perform the ritual she was about to undertake had made her horribly sick, even though the notion of carving a man's beating heart from his chest wouldn't have fazed her a bit. However, thinking about doing this thing she so desperately wanted to do but couldn't had caused her terrible emotional pain and disgust.

But now her powers were back. Just as promised. And she knew what she had to do. She'd grown tired of her father treating her like she was worthless, so she'd decided it was finally time to show him what she was really capable of.

She walked over to the vines which hung across the windows and blocked most of the natural light from entering the room. Then with each hand, she grabbed ahold of two of the thickest vines, took a deep breath, opened her mouth wide and began to hiss like a demented cat.

The lights in Betsy's office flickered as the vines along the ceiling began to slither like snakes, creating a strobe effect as they passed over the lights.

Betsy continued to hiss and spit, and pretty soon her dark, beady eyes had widened and transformed so that they had narrow, golden slits running vertically down the center of them.

"I hope you're watching!" she yelled into the air above her.

The vines from the ceiling dropped down and started to wrap themselves around her body. As they engulfed her, a faint melody began to play. It sounded like children singing a simple, eerie tune. Soon, Betsy's entire body was covered in the swarming vines all the way up to her neck. And this is when the real transformation began to happen.

Betsy's warty head started to grow like a balloon filling with air. Her dark, beady eyes protruded from their sockets, and her mouth widened, forming a bulge at the front of her lips so that they pointed outward. As her skin stretched it took on a greenish luminescence, making it seem sickly like an illuminated corpse.

Once the vines had finished tightening around Betsy, and her head had become even larger than her bulbous torso, Betsy leaned forward over the female prisoner and opened her mouth, creating a gaping void. She lowered the large opening over the woman and began to consume her whole. Her groans and grunts mixed with the woman's shrieks of terror. Then when Betsy was through devouring the woman, she leaned over the man and repeated the process, continuing to groan and grunt even more loudly, as though the act of ingesting her victims was causing her a great amount of dietary distress.

Betsy stood up straight once she was through gobbling the prisoners and pulled her giant head back above her shoulders. The vines sinched around Betsy's torso even tighter than before until her eyes looked like they were going to explode out of her rubbery head. Suddenly, the sound of bones grinding together erupted from Betsy's large mouth in a series of odd and odorous belches. And shortly after the belches stopped, Betsy's body began to heave underneath the tight bondage until, finally, a gargantuan wave of blood, flesh, and bile spewed from Betsy's mouth. The foul concoction covered the ceiling and floor and coated all the vines within teen feet.

The possessed creepers loosened their death grip and unwound from Betsy's body, and the soft, eerie tune faded away. Slowly, Betsy's head reshaped itself so that it was the same normal-sized, warty head as before. She looked around to examine the outcome of the murderous ceremony she'd performed. Blood-soaked vines drooped from the ceiling, and the carpet and walls were slathered in dark red ooze. Betsy's stomach lurched as she expelled one last, rumbling burp. She smiled at her work and licked several droplets of blood from her lips. Then she said, "Well, Father, I guess I'm not so powerless after all."

CHAPTER 4

THE REBELS' STATE

Fred and Mina arrived near the top of the rebels' sloped valley, lined with dull metal homes and buildings, to find a large group circled around Bob and John, talking loudly about what they'd just been through.

"They know where we are! Mark my words! Goodman sent his goons to scare us this time, but he'll be sending his army next!" shouted a gray-haired man who was waving his wooden walking stick in the air.

"That's right!" several of the people around him yelled in agreement.

Then a petite woman who stood beside two young boys shouted, "We'll need at least three hundred of those laser weapons to defend ourselves!"

She pointed at the proton beam that was resting on the ground between Bob and John, the same one Bob and Fred had used to find Mina.

A pale man with light blonde hair replied, "But there's not enough time to make that many weapons! Goodman's army will probably be here in a couple days. A week tops!"

Right then, Bob caught sight of Fred and Mina

approaching the crowd on horseback. He looked relieved. "Look! Fred's returned!" he announced to the group in a desperate attempt to distract them from their collective worrying.

Most of the crowd looked over at Fred and Mina who were climbing down from the horse.

"Who in the hell is she?" a young woman wearing a striped dress asked, referring to Mina.

Bob replied. "This is Mina, everyone, the girl who saved us from Dan. You might remember that she used to have wings."

The woman in the striped dress scoffed. "Her lack of wings ain't the weird part about her! Look, at her! She's all grown up, and part of her arm's missing. How'd that happen?"

Mina explained, "I traveled back to Earth. That's where I've been the last nine years."

Mina glanced down to see how bad her arm looked. There was nothing left below her mid-forearm now. "And as for my arm," she continued, "it's the result of an injury I sustained while leaving Earth the second time. I think I might be in need of some medical assistance." She looked at Bob expectantly.

Bob seemed to be thinking about something else at first, but Mina's gaze pulled him back to the present. "Oh, of course, Mina. Evelyn?" he called, looking around the crowd until his eyes landed on a tall woman who'd been standing a few rows back in the circle of people.

The tall woman with short, dark hair moved past the others and joined Bob in the center of the crowd next to John. Bob asked, "Will you take a look at Mina's arm? You can use Maude's...I mean my—"

Bob's face fell as he tried to find the right words. But Evelyn spoke for him. "I'll take Mina to my house for some privacy. It doesn't have a roof yet, but that's okay, since it doesn't have working lights either."

Evelyn smiled brightly and walked through the crowd

towards Mina and Fred. John took a couple steps closer to Bob and rested his hand on Bob's back.

"Why don't you get some shut eye," he suggested. "You've been through an awful lot. I think it would do you good to quiet your mind for a while. And lord knows this group isn't going to help you do that. I'll talk to them, and we'll work out a plan. Right, folks?"

Most of the crowd nodded at John and Bob, and Bob replied, "Okay, but if anything strange happens while I'm gone—"

John interrupted him. "Oh brother. Don't make me promise that. It seems that there's nothing but strange things happening these days. But you go lie down. We'll let you know when you're needed again."

Bob nodded, and left the others behind, beginning to make his way down the valley road towards the town that his friends and fellow rebels had been diligently working on for several months. Before he was out of earshot, however, he heard a woman say to John, "Wait! If Mina made it back to Earth, then does that mean we can all go back to Earth?"

Bob smiled. He knew what John's response would be, but he also knew that the crowd was too worked up to accept any reasonable answer. They'd gone into survival mode when Betsy's men had suddenly showed up unannounced, and their adrenaline was still pumping. This meant they were on high alert and likely to overreact due to their amplified emotions. Bob knew John had an uphill battle ahead of him if he was going to try to talk sense into the crowd, and he felt a little guilty leaving his friend behind to deal with the mess. But he also knew he'd done his fair share of mess clean-up over the years and was happy to let someone else take care of it for a while.

When Bob caught up to Mina, Fred, and Evelyn, they'd just arrived in front of Evelyn's small house. Evelyn laughed when she noticed Bob and asked, "How'd you duck the crowd?"

He shook his head. "I didn't. John sent me off to get some rest, but I wanted to check on Mina before I decided whether or not to take him up on it."

He turned to Mina. "How you doing, kid? You sure had this guy on pins and needles," he said, gesturing to Fred. "But to be honest, I was nervous, too. We're both very happy you made it. What was it like traveling here this time? And how's the arm? Has it gotten any worse since you arrived? Has it stopped disappearing yet?"

Evelyn looked at Bob with a concerned expression, but she didn't say anything.

Mina replied, "Well, traveling back was definitely unusual. I suspect I might have traveled back and forth through time; I met a daughter I don't have or that I haven't had yet, at least. But Fred says that would be impossible and that none of it was real."

"Time travel!" Bob said in a bewildered tone. "Well, no. Fred's right. I don't think that would be possible. We were tracking you the whole time. If you'd traveled through time, we wouldn't have been able to do that. At least not theoretically."

Evelyn said to Bob, "Time travel and disappearing arms? And here I thought that the weirdest part of my day was going to be when I watched you and John chase those two bozos out of town with your giant laser gun!"

Fred laughed. "Yeah, we saw Dale's men running for their lives on our way up here. Or at least, I assume they were Dale's men. He was waiting on them with several other men a thousand feet down the mountain. Why do you suppose they were here?"

"They said they were announcing Dale's imminent arrival," replied Bob. "But John and I didn't want to take any chances. The last time I saw Dale was when you were escorting me away from my former prison cell.

"When those guys strolled in demanding to talk to Maude, pretty much everyone ran for safety; they assumed Goodman's army was coming for us. John and I were at the site of the proton beam when we heard the others fleeing. John thought we should join them, but I assured him we were safe."

"The men told us that Dale wanted to have a word with Maude," Bob continued. "I told them that wasn't possible, but they wouldn't take 'no' for an answer. So, I grabbed the proton beam, pointed it at them, and told them they had sixty seconds to tell me who'd sent them and why. One of the dopes tried to call my bluff. He said there were no more skilled inventors now that 'Bob the traitor' was locked away in prison. Of course, that made John laugh pretty hard.

"I told the punk that he was probably right but that it just so happened the weapon I was holding was one of 'Traitor Bob's' designs. I then informed him that he had about thirty seconds left to explain himself, and I fired up the beam so it was shining towards them.

"The other kid began squealing like a crazed pig, babbling on about how they got here. I didn't catch everything, but I know I heard him say that Dale told them to find his mom and let her know he wanted to speak with her. He also said that Betsy's in charge of New Waldoff now, which can't be good. Goodman was a snake in the grass for sure, but if Goodman was a snake, then Betsy is the demon empress of all snakes."

Mina asked, "Betsy from the greenhouse Betsy? The crazy woman who lured me into her trap so she could hand me over to Dan? *That* Betsy is in charge of the city?"

Bob nodded. "That's the one. But there's something else you should know about Betsy, Mina. She's the only other human besides my children who didn't travel here from Earth. She showed up on our doorstep when she and the twins were infants. Nobody knew where she came from, and it remains a mystery to this day. It used to frighten me to think about. She's always been one of the biggest parts of our lives that didn't make sense. 'Course that was before I learned that Maude was…" But Bob suddenly remembered that Evelyn was standing there with them and stopped talking.

He looked at Evelyn and smiled, then glanced at Mina's arm and said, "What am I doing? Evelyn, you were going to take a look at Mina's arm, and here I am blabbering on. Fred and I will take a walk for a minute so you can focus on Mina."

Evelyn looked at Bob suspiciously, but she said nothing as Bob placed his hand on Fred's back and they walked away.

She turned her attention to Mina. "Is it okay if I touch your arm?" she asked.

Mina nodded. "I should warn you, though. Even the part that's gone still hurts. A *lot*. It feels like it's clamped inside a vise."

"Hmm. That does seem abnormal, but then again, a disappearing arm is abnormal in and of itself."

"Yes, I suppose so. Were you a doctor back on Earth?" Mina asked.

Evelyn laughed. "Yes, but I actually still consider myself a doctor. I'm a surgeon, in fact. I've never treated a case like yours before, though. I've reattached lots of fingers and toes, and I even managed to save an eye once. But I've never seen an arm slowly vanish. May I ask how this happened?"

Mina replied, "I'm not sure if you'll believe it."

"Try me."

"Well, Bob designed the machine you saw before—the one that shoots lasers. He created it to virtually send Fred and himself back to Earth via a proton beam. Their goal was to search for me, but before they tried it out, Maude died unexpectedly. Fred was going to postpone the whole mission at that point, but Bob insisted they go ahead. Instead of going with

Fred though as planned, Bob had to operate the machine in Maude's absence while Fred was projected to Earth by himself.

"After a long search, they located me, and Fred convinced me to come back to the Moon. But then when I was climbing the glass bridge towards the sky, I got woozy and almost fell hundreds of feet into the ocean. If Fred hadn't grabbed me, I would've died. Unfortunately, my disappearing arm is the result of him touching me in his projected state."

Evelyn had been moving her fingers all around the vanishing arm as Mina spoke—the part of the arm that was left, as well as the area where there should've been a forearm and hand.

"What would make you think I'd doubt all that?" Evelyn asked, giving Mina a playful smile while continuing to examine her arm. She clasped her hands tightly around the bottom of Mina's visible arm and then continued to move her hands along the empty air where the arm should've been, narrowing her grip as she went.

"Can you feel my hands here, Mina?"

Mina shook her head. "No, there's a lot of pain and pressure where the arm should be, but I don't feel any sensation from the outside."

"Hmm. Well, I've made a diagnosis, but I'm not sure you're going to like it."

Mina nodded nervously, waiting to hear what Evelyn would say.

"There's no medicine or surgery in any world I've ever lived in that will bring your arm back from wherever it's disappeared to. And I'm sorry to say if the vanishing is continuing to spread, then I believe it would be best to treat your case like an infection. That means amputating part of what's left of your arm in order to keep the rest of it from disappearing."

Mina scowled. "But hang on a second. What if the vanishing has already stopped? Or what if it's only temporary?

I mean, you said you've never seen a case like this before. Maybe once the disappearing stops, it will reverse course and reappear."

Evelyn replied, "I know this isn't what you wanted to hear, Mina, but you need to try to think logically about this. You're right that this case is new to me, but I think it's highly unlikely your arm is going to reappear. And you need to consider how much of your arm you're willing to sacrifice while waiting around, hoping it will get better on its own.

"If we act soon, I believe we can stop the vanishing before it reaches your elbow. That would give you a chance to be fitted for a prosthetic more easily, assuming Bob is up to the challenge of making you one."

Mina thought about what Evelyn had said and then asked, "How soon do you think I'll need to decide?"

"It's hard to say for certain." Evelyn looked at the sky as if trying to decide what time it might be. Then she looked back at Mina's arm. She touched the part that was left below Mina's elbow again and said, "Probably no later than tonight. I suggest you take it easy the rest of the day. Talk to Fred and Bob about your options and see what they have to say. Then if you decide to move forward, I can perform the surgery first thing in the morning."

"Morning?" Mina asked.

Evelyn nodded. "Yes. Despite being on the Dayside we get short nights here because of the mountains. It never gets totally dark, but dusk will settle over the valley for about six hours."

"I see," said Mina. "And the pain?" Mina asked timidly.

"What do you mean?"

"I mean would I be able to feel everything, or do you have some kind of medicine that can numb the pain?"

"Oh no, Mina. You'd be asleep for the surgery. But yes, I do have some medicine that would numb the pain after the surgery. In fact, come inside. I'll give you a jar of it to start using now. It's a pain relief lotion that you can apply to your skin. I don't think it will help with the phantom pain you seem to be experiencing, but it should at least give you some relief from the pain you feel in the remainder of your arm."

Mina nodded as Evelyn walked past her through the front door of her metal home, waving for her to follow.

"YOU OKAY?" Fred asked Bob as the two walked further down the valley's main path, away from Evelyn's house.

"Sure," said Bob. "Why do you ask?"

"Because you almost let it slip that your recently deceased wife was a goddess. I think John might be right, Bob. It would be good for you to get some rest. You, Maude, and I worked nonstop on the proton beam before Maude died. And then you still kept going, even after losing her. I thank you from the bottom of my heart for helping me race to bring Mina back, but you need to take some time for yourself now."

"Too tired, Fred. Gotta keep going," Bob replied curtly.

Fred stopped and looked at Bob. "Do you even hear yourself? You can't keep going without taking a break. You might think you're invincible, but there will be consequences if you don't let yourself rest a little."

Bob kept walking, forcing Fred to continue walking, too. "I'm an eighty-something-year-old in the body of someone a quarter my age. I'm probably the healthiest eighty-year-old that's ever lived, and I don't need to be lectured by you. You focus on Mina; I'll focus on me."

Fred pushed back. "I don't need to focus on Mina right now. That's what Evelyn's doing. Look Bob, if you won't lie down, can we at least find a place to sit for a moment? Maybe you're not tired, but I am."

Bob looked at Fred suspiciously, as though he thought he might be trying to trick him. But after a few seconds he gave in and pointed to a spot along the path with several large boulders. They made their way over to them, and Fred sat while Bob leaned against the largest rock.

There was silence between the two men for a while, but then Bob said, "All these people came here because I told them we could live a nicer life away from the insanity of New Waldoff. God, it seems like a decade ago I made up my mind we'd be better off if we left.

"I knew that Goodman had it out for me from the very beginning. I thought if Maude and I abandoned the city and brought the like-minded folks with us, then that would put an end to Goodman's obsession with us. I was offering him a win by removing all the people he viewed as a stain on his city. I didn't realize that what he was really after was Maude. How could I have? Neither of us even knew who she was then."

"But you think Goodman suspected it?"

Bob shrugged. "I don't know. Clearly Betsy did, though. I guess it could've been her all along, controlling Goodman, making him into the antithesis of everything I had known him to be. Goodman was a good and loyal soldier, whereas that goblin-woman has always given me an uneasy feeling. To be fair though, I've never been able to figure out why exactly."

Fred hesitated before he spoke his next sentence. He knew that Maude had purposely refrained from telling her husband everything about the world they lived in before she died. On their way to pick up Dale from the Sheep Spa, Maude had told Fred that she didn't want to frighten Bob by divulging everything she'd remembered about their world. And Fred understood her reasoning. After all, there was little about the mortals' lives that was real, and Maude hadn't wanted to ruin the rest of Bob's life by burdening him with the truth.

But even so, Fred had been given orders about what to share, and he knew there was too much at stake to disobey them. "Bob, there's something you need to know about Betsy."

Bob looked at Fred wearily. "Oh yeah? What's that?"

Fred sighed. "When you went to visit Dale at the Sheep Spa, he told you that he'd often overheard Dan speaking to someone who wasn't there. He also told you that Betsy heard Goodman talking to someone invisible too, right?"

Bob stood up straight. "How did you know about that? Did Maude tell you?"

"No, Bob. I'm getting to that part. Just stay with me. Dan and Goodman were talking to the same spirit, only it wasn't exactly a spirit. It was a god, like Maude. But this god is extremely power hungry. His name is Theo, and he lives on top of Black Ice Glacier.

"Few mortals know of his existence because they can't see him. The Moon Walkers were the only mortals who could see the gods, but Serena, the goddess who kept me imprisoned in the ice tunnels, didn't like that."

"Wait, you were imprisoned by a goddess? So, that means that there was another goddess on the Moon besides Maude? Why didn't you tell me?" Bob said angrily.

"Because Maude didn't want you to know. Serena is the reason Maude is no longer here. She's extremely powerful, more powerful than any of the other gods. She has the ability to create and destroy. And not just destroy through scheming like how the dark god used Dan, but destroy with a flick of her wrist.

"Ragher has known about Serena and Theo for a long time. And Neriti knew of them, too. For years, she and Ragher tried to thwart Theo on their own, especially once they realized that Theo had control over Dan."

"But how did this dark god have control over my son? You said that mortals—" Bob stopped. His face suddenly showed signs of clarity. "Dan could talk to the god because he wasn't fully mortal. Dan was half a god because he was Maude's son."

Fred nodded. "Yes, but there's more to it. Your children are not the only demi-gods you've known. The reason Betsy has always given you that uneasy feeling you mentioned is because she's a demi-god too. She's Theo's daughter."

A dark shadow fell over Bob as he processed the information Fred had thrown at him so quickly. Then finally, he said, "Well that explains a lot about Betsy. Of course the little she-demon is the spawn of evil. Her father is a god who wants to either rule the world or destroy it, and her mother is what? A gremlin?"

Fred snickered. "You aren't that far off to tell you the truth. Her mother was an elf and one of the weirdest-looking kinds to be sure."

Bob was incredulous. "An elf? There are elves on the Moon, too? God! Where? And how do you know all of this, Fred? Is it because that other evil god, Serena, told you? The one who stole Maude from me?"

"I know it's a lot to take in, Bob. Maude was trying to protect you by not telling you all of this, but Serena insisted you know the truth. You need to know in order to face what's to come. And yes, there are elves. They work for Serena, but she keeps them hidden from the rest of the mortals because they haven't always gotten along so well with others. They appear to mortals but only when she lets them, usually when she wants them to deliver a message for her.

"And Serena isn't evil. Or at least, if she was telling me the truth, then I don't believe that to be the case. Plus, she told me how to rescue Mina. It's where my plan came from."

"But why did she take Maude away when she was happy here? You really believe she'd do that if she had good intentions?"

"I sympathize, Bob. I do," Fred responded. "But I guess there isn't much else I can say, except that Serena has a plan. Not all of it will be easy. In fact, some of it will be downright miserable I suspect."

Bob looked struck by Fred's words. "That sounds like something Maude told me right before she died. She said that some of my life would be sad and lonely but some of it would be beautiful and amazing too." Bob spoke as though thinking out loud. "She also said there were other gods, but I just assumed they were in faraway worlds or other dimensions."

"Some of them are," explained Fred. "But they are lesser gods, not nearly as powerful as Theia and Theo, and especially not as powerful as Serena."

It was quiet again for a moment until Bob said, "You know, Fred. I think I will have that lie down after all. This was a lot to take in. Possibly too much for one day."

Fred smiled. "I understand. We'll need to discuss what to do about protecting the new city from Betsy when you're feeling up to it, but that can wait. By the way, did the rebels think of a name for the city like you told them to?"

"Yeah, they want to call it Rebelton. I guess 'Revolutionary-opolis' and 'Insurgent-ville' didn't have the same ring."

Fred chuckled. "No, I guess not."

Bob spoke again, "If you don't mind, would you check on John after you find out how Mina's doing? He might need some help if that crowd hasn't broken up yet."

"Of course," said Fred. "But one more thing. I have to know—how did you make the proton beam shoot lasers at those two guys?"

Bob shrugged. "I didn't have to do much, really. The proton device was able to shoot lasers all along. The real trick was to keep it from doing that. I had to build a safety feature when designing the device so that it *wouldn't* shoot laser beams whenever the proton ray was activated. It would have been catastrophic if the lasers had gone off while you were being projected. Likely, you would've been obliterated. I guess your ice tunnel goddess didn't warn you about that part when she gave you the idea for the machine, huh?"

Fred looked perturbed. "No, she didn't. But that would've been nice to know before you used it on me."

Bob spoke in an even tone. "Fred, you already knew your atoms were being caught up in a proton beam and shot across the Moon to rescue the girl you fancy. I can't imagine that the fear of death by laser beam would've stopped you. Can you?"

Fred shook his head. "No, I guess not."

"Anyway, all I had to do was take the safety off in order to shoot lasers at those doofus' feet. You should've seen them run. I bet they'll think twice before trespassing on our turf again, and hopefully they spread the word to their friends too."

"Yes, hopefully so," said Fred who seemed deep in thought. "I'm going to go check on the others now. Try and get some rest, Bob."

Bob nodded in agreement and Fred began the walk up Rebelton's main road. As he went, he thought about what he'd revealed to Bob and Mina. What he'd been ordered to reveal. But even more than that, he thought about what he couldn't tell them—the secrets he'd been sworn to keep. The ones that he knew would change their lives forever.

CHAPTER 5

THE GREENHOUSE FIASCO

In The Days Before the Wolf Massacres

S*woosh!* The sliding door to the greenhouse flew open, and a gust of warm air hit Max in the face. He entered the two-story glass building and paused, giving his eyes a moment to adjust to the fluorescent lighting. Off to the right, at the front of the building, a group of medium-sized vines sat in their pots, waiting for Max to transfer them to Waldoff Market.

Max wasn't in a hurry, however. He was hoping to run into Betsy. Normally, she was right there at the front of the greenhouse, either spraying the vines, repotting them, or enriching their soil with a neon pink formula. Max always assumed her presence was by design—to make sure that he didn't do anything to harm her precious plants as he hauled them off.

"Maybe this is a good sign," he thought. "If she trusts me enough to handle the vines, maybe she'll be willing to talk to me about what Dan's been up to."

Ignoring the batch of vines that had been set aside for him, Max began to wander through the dense tunnels and canopies of creepers. When he found Betsy, she was at the far end of the greenhouse sitting on an overturned pot with her back towards him. Busy at work, she was leaned forward ripping out colorful plants from a series of small pots perched on a table in front of her and discarding their soil in a pile near her feet.

Max heard Betsy breathing laboriously and grunting as she performed the chore, and from the reflection in the windows, he saw that the bottom of Betsy's long, black dress was folded up over her knees to prevent it from getting dirty. Beads of sweat dripped down the back of Betsy's neck, and frizzy strands of hair that had come loose from her tight bun pointed out in all directions. The task was clearly taking a toll on her, and Max felt strange about standing there watching her, as though he'd interrupted something private. He began to turn, but Betsy spoke to him.

"What's the matter, Max? You've never witnessed some good old-fashioned weed pulling before?"

Max was surprised. He hadn't realized that Betsy knew his name. He looked back at her and saw that she was standing up. Her hands were covered in dirt, her face was flushed, and her high collar had been unbuttoned to let her skin breathe.

"No, sorry," he apologized. "I was just wandering around the place admiring your plants. I had some extra time to kill today and thought I'd check out the rest of the greenhouse since I'd never explored it before."

"Aha, so this doesn't have anything to do with what you overheard me and Rufus talking about the other day when you and your girlfriend were hiding behind that naked statue?"

Max didn't know what to say. His entire plan was hinged on the assumption that he and Helen had gone undetected when they overheard Betsy and Rufus talking.

Panic took hold as he tried to sort out how to pivot his plan.

He knew he needed to say something fast, though. Betsy was staring at him with a brutal expression, waiting for him to reply. He decided to stall. "If you knew we were there, why'd you stop?" he asked.

Betsy smiled devilishly as she brushed the dirt from her hands, buttoned her collar, and fastened her ivory neck broach back into place. "What a clever boy you are, Max."

Max snickered at the idea of Betsy talking to him like she was his elder. "You know, Betsy, I remember when you were a baby. I was in my twenties then."

"I'm sure you were, but this is how I speak to everyone. Don't get your big boy knickers in a twist."

Just then, Max heard someone calling from the front of the greenhouse.

"Hey Bets, you back there? Or did you finally decide to hang yourself with one of these ugly, green ropes?"

Betsy ran her hands over her head, trying to smooth down the frizzy, loose hairs that were sticking out. "It's Dan. I wasn't expecting him here now. He's supposed to be supervising the construction on his new place."

Max thought he detected a hint of girlish excitement from Betsy.

"Coming!" she called to Dan.

She motioned for Max to follow her. And he did, even though he felt a huge pit in his stomach, knowing he was going to have to face Dan. Despite being Bob and Maude's son, people spoke of Dan like he was a real-life monster. Or at least that was true within Max's social group—a group that existed for the sole purpose of discussing how to deal with the twins and their followers. Of course Max knew that Dan wasn't a real monster, but he felt like he was taking a risk being in close quarters with him. It was like being in close quarters with a well-fed lion. As long as the lion stayed full, everything *might* turn out okay.

Max noticed when he and Betsy emerged from the dense throng of vines that Dan didn't seem interested to see him. Betsy put herself in front of Dan with her back to Max. "I didn't think you were going to make it today. You said you were busy."

Dan took a puff on his cigar and blew the smoke towards them. "Yeah, well, I got different orders after you left. The big guy says this is important, so here I am."

"The big guy?" thought Max. "What big guy?"

Betsy looked over her shoulder and squinted at Max, as though gauging his reaction to Dan's comment.

"You told him what we want yet?" Dan asked.

Betsy turned herself so she was standing between Max and Dan who were facing each other. She looked annoyed. "No, Dan, but clearly you didn't listen to one iota of my plan. We were supposed to find out why this dope was spying on Rufus and me before all of that."

Dan rolled his eyes. "Fine. Then ask him. Or, geez. I'll just do it. Why were you spying on Bets and Rufus?"

Max replied, "I wasn't spying on anyone."

He knew he had to be careful about what he said. Betsy obviously knew or suspected that he and Helen were an item, but he didn't want Dan to know if there was any way to keep him from finding out.

"I ducked behind the statue because I wanted privacy. I didn't know Betsy and Rufus were going to stop and talk there."

Dan looked at Betsy. "Sounds like he's lying to me. Clearly, he's working for someone." Then to Max, he said, "Who you working for? My brainless parents and their secret team of dolts?"

Max held his breath. He hadn't realized that Dan was aware of their secret group.

Dan laughed. "Look at that, Bets. He didn't think we knew.

You're not a very good spy, you know? Your loser face gives away too much. So, why were you spying? You and those other losers trying to get information to save your pathetic puppy dog friends?"

"I'm not a spy. Like I said, Betsy was the one who stopped to talk. I'd have to be a psychic spy to have known that was going to happen."

"So, you're admitting you're a psychic spy, then?"

Max groaned. He was frustrated but also nervous about where Dan's interrogation was headed. "Oh my god! I'm not a spy."

Dan asked, "Then why were you and my sister hiding behind that statue? You got a thing for my sister? Cause I bet that's something my parents would be interested to know—that their psychic spy is also a fox in their henhouse."

Max's mind raced. He knew he had to come clean without making his relationship with Helen seem too important.

He replied, "I'm not a fox or a spy! I was just walking through the park when your sister ambushed me. I guess she has a crush on me. When we heard Betsy and Rufus coming, she pulled me behind the statue. I didn't even know it was Betsy and Rufus until they were close enough to hear."

"What do you think, Betsy?" asked Dan. "He lying?"

Betsy nodded. "Definitely. He's definitely a spy. He wouldn't have come all the way to the back of the greenhouse to talk to me, otherwise. It's the whole reason he's been delivering my plants to the market all these months. He's been hoping to gain my trust, so he can get information from us."

Max's nerves were starting to get the better of him. It was obvious Dan had come into this meeting with his mind already made up. And Max wasn't sure what to do to convince him that he wasn't who Dan thought he was.

"That's not true," said Max. "I'm just a delivery guy. It's the only job I've ever had on the Moon. Look, I heard what

Betsy and Rufus were talking about—the wolves and some other project you're working on. But everyone already assumed you guys are going after the wolves. If it was supposed to be a secret, then it's the worst kept secret on the Moon."

"Ah, so then," said Dan, "it's the project you're wanting to know about." Dan pulled out a tiny brown jar with a black lid from inside his pocket, holding it next to his face between his thumb and pointer finger.

"This is what you're after," he said giving the jar a little shake. "It's something I've been working on for a long time. Since your girlfriend was a baby, in fact."

"She's not my girlfriend," replied Max hoping he was about to find out what was in the jar.

"Tsk. Tsk. How do you think dear old Maude and Bob would feel about you frisking up their daughter on the sly without even having the courtesy to call her your girlfriend? You might not guess it by their moonbeam-hippie, peace, and love vibe, but those two have pretty old-fashioned notions about these kinds of things. Especially, when it comes to that wolf-loving sister of mine. I doubt they'd be thrilled to find out that one of their trusted companions is getting *his* peace and love vibes all over their pride and joy."

Max wanted to punch Dan in his big, round face, but he knew very well that he needed to keep his cool. It was obvious Dan was pushing his buttons to see what nerves he could strike.

"No, Dan," he said calmly. "Helen isn't my girlfriend because she's too young for me. She has some silly, school-girl fantasy about me built up in her head, but I've told her it could never work. Many times. There's nothing more to it."

Dan mocked Max by making an over-the-top pouty face, the result of which left him looking like a sad clown. "Nothing more? Are you sure, Maxie?"

Max didn't like Dan using Helen's nickname for him. It felt

like a veiled threat, but without knowing whether it was one, Max didn't dare react.

Instead, he asked, "Hasn't it occurred to you that maybe I just want to be a part of whatever's in that jar? I know you have me pegged as one of Bob and Maude's cronies, but that's not who I am. I have no feelings for the wolves one way or the other, and I'm tired of all the talk with no action from Bob and Maude's side. It's a bunch of drivel. They obviously don't have the guts to do anything, or they would've done it by now."

Betsy quipped, "So you're a man of action then, Max? Well, why didn't you say so? If you're looking to prove yourself to us, you can start by bringing that doe-eyed sweetheart of yours over to the Darkside. We'd love to have a word with her."

Betsy raised her eyebrow at Dan and smiled wickedly, but Dan didn't seem to notice.

"Okay, here's what's going to happen," said Dan cutting to the chase. "I don't really give a flip if you and my sister are shacking up, but I'm certain you'd be in hot water with my parents if they found out. So, to keep that from happening, you're going to lure my sister to Black Ice Fort. After that, the three of will chat about what comes next.

"If you come on board, I'll keep your dirty secret hidden. But if you fail to show up within two weeks' time, I'll not only reveal your relationship to my parents, but I'll also make sure my followers know that you and my sister are trying to infiltrate their operation in order to protect the wolves. And I'm sure you can imagine how Rufus and his crew of idiots would treat spies. Can't you, Maxie?"

Max nodded. He understood now that they'd been set up. "Yeah, I can imagine. But what do you want with us? You need to give me an idea, at least. It's going to be hard to get Helen to agree to meet you on your turf without being able to explain why it's necessary."

Dan looked annoyed. He took another puff on his cigar.

"Remember the good 'ole days, Bets, when all you needed was a solid threat to get people to do what you asked? Whatever happened to that?"

Betsy waved her hand back and forth, trying to fan away Dan's exhaled smoke. "We were children then, Dan. And the people we were threatening were also children. At least in the sense that they never grew up. Adults are harder to persuade. They have too many thoughts. It gets them all confused about what their priorities should be."

Dan rolled his eyes. "Dang it, Betsy. It was a rhetorical question. I'd tell you to keep your mouth shut and look pretty, but one of those ships sunk in the harbor before it ever had the chance to sail."

Betsy lashed out. "You've lived on the Moon your entire life, Dan! Stop making nautical metaphors like you're some god-damned sea captain! You sound like a dumbass!"

Dan took Max firmly by the arm and pulled him away from Betsy, towards the sliding door. The door whooshed open, but Dan stopped short in front of the open doorway.

"Just ignore that old witch," said Dan. "She gets hysterical sometimes. It's why I had to hide her way out here in the middle of nowhere. Her face couldn't launch a rubber band, let alone a thousand ships. But her horticulture comes in handy every once in a while, which is why I keep her around."

"Damn it! I can hear you, Dan! You egotistical, fat-faced buffoon!"

Dan went on. "Listen, Max. I don't give a rat's ass about the wolves, but I know your girlfriend—"

Max gave Dan a look like he was going to protest, so Dan said, "Fine, not your girlfriend. I know my *sister* would like nothing more than to save those beasts from the likes of Rufus and his gang of thugs. So, here's what I propose. If you can get her to come meet with me before the two weeks are up, I'll get Rufus and the others involved in another project for a while, something to do with building dungeons in my fort or what not. That would at least postpone the wolf massacre and buy my sister and her cohorts some time to think of ways to stop my followers."

"But why would you do that when you've spent years turning everyone against the wolves?"

Dan replied, "Because I need my sister for the special project I'm working on. It's a formula that acts like a truth serum, and I want to test it on Helen."

Max didn't like the sound of this. "A truth serum? What for? Why don't you test it out on Rufus or one of those other numbskulls?"

Dan smiled. "Because I think my sister is harboring a secret that she might not even be aware of. And if I'm right, this serum will reveal the truth."

Max's anxiety had begun to spike again. He knew what Dan was describing could be dangerous for Helen and that was assuming Dan was even telling the truth about his intentions.

Dan sensed Max's reluctance. "I don't want to hear a 'yes' or 'no' out of you. This isn't your decision to make. Take my offer back to your woman and let her decide. Got it?"

"On one condition," Max replied. "I want to know what secret you think Helen is hiding."

"Nope. No conditions. Either my sister is willing to risk her own safety to help those mangy beasts, or she isn't. That's the deal. Take it or leave it." And with this Dan pointed Max towards the exit.

Max looked back over at Betsy who was staring at him intently. She didn't say a word, though, so he walked through the open door. He felt the cool air from the outside hit him in the face like the icy fist of reality clobbering him across the chin.

He thought about turning around again and telling Dan and Betsy to go to hell. It was obvious that they'd had an ulterior motive all along—setting him up to hear Betsy and Rufus talking in the park as a way to lure him in and make him an offer.

But Max knew Dan wasn't someone to be trifled with. The best thing he could do now was get as far away as he could from the Darkside's deranged madman and his pint-sized colluder. Max hopped back on his horse and began riding back across the Darkside.

He realized he was pulling an empty wagon, but there was no way he was turning around to pick up the vines he'd left behind. It was going to take a whole day to get home, which should've been enough time to decide what to do next if he'd been dealing with an ordinary problem. But Max already knew that this was no ordinary problem. He'd walked headfirst into a complicated dilemma, and as he rode away, he thought about how even if he'd had all the time in the world, he still might not know how to solve it.

Back in the greenhouse, Betsy asked Dan, "You think he'll tell her?"

"Yeah, he'll tell her. He'd be a coward not to, and I don't think he's a coward. Not too clever, but not a coward either."

"You think he believed that part about you thinking he was a spy? He got all squirmy then, just the way you like."

"I don't know. It doesn't matter, though. It got him scared enough to bend the way I want him to. He needs to believe that he and my sister will be in danger if he doesn't give me what I want."

"True, but there's no guarantee they'll go to the glacier, even if he does believe you. And honestly, Dan, I still don't think it's likely that your sister is Theia."

Dan snarled. "Shut it, Betsy. It doesn't matter what you think. If the dark spirit senses my sister is Theia, then who are you to say otherwise? Anyway, one way or another, we're gonna find out. Everything depends on this. I won't be fully in control until we know what's happened to Theia."

"You mean *he* won't be fully in control. Right, Dan?"

Dan shrugged. "Sure. Fine. It's all the same, though. When *he* takes power, I get to be in charge. After all, nobody except his stupid minion can see him. Kind of hard to be a ruler when you're invisible to the ones you're ruling over."

Betsy smiled. "Hmm, I suppose you're right."

But Betsy knew that Dan wasn't right at all. In fact, he was completely wrong because unbeknownst to him, *she* could see and hear the dark spirit. And not only that, but unlike the flimsy tricks Dan was beginning to learn from her father, Betsy had real powers. Dark powers.

But Betsy knew she had to keep this part of herself hidden for the time being. Even from Dan, the only person she'd ever cared for. Because soon when the time was right, Betsy planned to show everyone what she could really do. And then she'd be the one to rule over them all.

CHAPTER 6

IN THE MOMENT

When Mina and Fred rejoined the dwindling group of rebels who were circled around John, the large Irishman seemed as though he'd reached his wit's end. "Fine! Yes! We'll pluck all the feathers from every last bird on the Moon and build a bunch of wingsuits to fly every last one of ye devils back to Earth. Would that make you happy?" he shouted at the crowd.

Fred laughed, but Mina nudged him. She hadn't officially met John yet, but she remembered what it was like to deal with an unruly group of Moon Travelers. She stepped into the middle of the circle with John to address everyone. "I know all of you are longing to go home and see loved ones again, but it's not as easy as I've made it seem. You see, I thought I was going to die when I reentered Earth's atmosphere. And honestly, I nearly did. I was on fire at one point and realized I was going to burn alive. Plus, what John here doesn't realize is that the wings Bob created were made from synthetic feathers that no longer exist. That means it's impossible to send people back to Earth the same way that I went."

A young woman in the crowd yelled, "So why did *you* get to

use the feathers? We should've taken a vote on who got to go back!"

Mina felt discouraged. She'd wanted to help John talk sense into the group, but instead her explanation had created a whole new problem for them to deal with.

John snorted before answering the woman. "Well, first of all, *she* got to use them because *she* saved all you rascals! Or have you already forgotten about that? We'd all be toast— wiped out by a cloud of toxic gas fumes—if Mina hadn't come here to save us."

Mina smiled at John and said, "Thanks."

"No problem. I'm John, by the way. I didn't have a chance to meet you last time because I was working as a 'go between' for Bob and Maude, carrying supplies back and forth between the market and our secret base on the Darkside. However, I did see you from afar one time."

"Great," said a man in the crowd. "We're all delighted that you two have met. Now can you please tell us what we're supposed to do about Goodman's army? One laser isn't going to do diddly squat to stop them. They have a whole lot more weapons than our one, and I know that for a fact because I was working in a factory for the last five years helping to build them. We need to do something!"

Everyone in the crowd began talking frantically to each other upon hearing this news. The young woman who'd addressed the crowd before shouted, "We're doomed! If we can't go back to Earth, then I vote we abandon Rebelton while we still can! Find another place to live! Somewhere more secluded where Goodman's army can't find us!"

John sighed. "We've been through this, Barbara. It's why more than half the original group has already gone home and left the rest of us here twiddling our thumbs.

"There's nowhere else to go that would be easy to defend. Not with a group this large. Why can't you all just let it go for one night? Let Bob have a chance to rest up. He's been through the ringer and needs a moment to breathe, but once he's better I'm sure he'll think of a wonderful way we can defend ourselves against those bastards in the old city."

Fred stepped into the circle. "I think what John's trying to say is that it's going to take more than one meeting to come up with a plan. He's heard your concerns and he'll take them to heart. How about we plan to hold another meeting tomorrow afternoon? That will give us all some time to process today's event and come up with some better solutions."

John whispered to Fred, "Are you daft? There's no appeasing these folks. They aren't going to leave us alone *that* easily, and now you've done offered them another go around tomorrow."

Fred rested his hand on John's shoulder to reassure him. "Does that sound fair to everyone?" he asked.

Several of the people in the crowd groaned, but most of them nodded or gave a vocal affirmation. Then they began dispersing.

"Well, I'll be," said John. "I didn't think that would work. Good on you, Fred. However, there's no way I'm going to be at tomorrow's meeting if that's fine and dandy with everyone. These people nearly drove me insane with all their circular reasoning and repetitive questions. I thought when we left New Waldoff we were bringing the best of the Moon Travelers with us, but now I'm not so sure."

Fred chuckled at this. "Don't be so hard on them. They've been through a lot, just like the rest of us. Most of them have families with young kids, right? I can't imagine what their daily reality must look like, caring for children who they know will never grow up."

"Yes, I suppose it must be a blessing and a curse," John agreed. "The parents get to enjoy them at their most precious stage forever, but they also never get to see them grow up and fulfill their potential."

"Yeah, except what potential?" Mina asked. "It's not like they'd ever get to live a normal adult life even if they did grow up. Not on the Moon, anyway."

"Fair point," noted John. Then he asked, "Do either of you know whether our friend, Bob, has actually taken my advice and gone to rest?"

Fred shrugged. "I wouldn't bet on it. He seems to be under the impression that he won't have to deal with Maude's death if he just keeps going. He reminds me of one of those bouncing wind-up toys headed for the edge of the table."

"That's what I was afraid of," said John.

"Do you think Evelyn has something that she can give Bob to help him sleep?" Mina asked. "Like a sedative? I saw all the pill boxes and medicine jars in her living room after she examined me. I think most pharmacies back on Earth have smaller drug stocks than Evelyn's house."

"Oh, yes," replied John. "Evelyn spends all her time coming up with new medicines whenever she isn't seeing patients. Just like Bob and his gadgets or me and my ales."

"Oh, you're a brewer?" asked Mina.

"Yes, practically all my life. It was the family trade back home."

Fred interjected, "I'm sure Evelyn must have something to help Bob sleep if she's a prolific pill producer. The question is will he take it?"

A devious expression appeared across John's face. "Well, he can't object to what he doesn't know about, can he?"

Fred was surprised. "But how are you going to get him to take medicine unknowingly? It's not like you can slip it into his drink; there's nothing to drink here."

John winked at Mina as though she were in on his secret and replied, "Let me worry about that. In the meantime,

Mina's going to need a place to rest tonight. Why don't the two of you find Bob and inquire about where Mina should stay now that she's here. Get him to take you to Maude's house if you can. He hasn't spent much time there yet since he began working on that proton machine of yours the moment he arrived. That is to say, he might need to be coaxed into going there, especially if he's put off by the idea of facing Maude's death."

Fred asked, "Did Bob tell everyone how Maude died?"

John nodded. "Yes, and what a truly awful tale that was. Falling off the side of the mountain during that freak storm. I suppose she must have fallen under some sort of spell for such a thing to happen. That or she got swept off her feet."

Then looking around to make sure no one was listening, John whispered, "I'll tell you two and no one else that I was quite surprised by the tragic news. I'd had it in my head for a while that Maude might be part fairy or witch, possibly invincible. I wouldn't have thought she'd meet such a careless end. If anything, I'd have thought she would've just up and disappeared into the darkness one night, never to be seen again."

"A fairy?" Fred laughed a bit nervously. "You certainly have an imagination, don't you?"

John ignored Fred, and said, "I've been hesitant to ask, but I guess I'll go ahead and get it out. Were you able to find Maude's body when you went looking for her? And how did the two of you end up crossing paths?"

Fred and Mina looked at each other, not entirely sure what to say. Finally, Mina spoke. "It was luck. When I arrived, I walked towards the old city at first, but of course I didn't find anyone, so I began to wander. That's when I ran into Fred. He was on his way to search for Maude's remains."

Fred added, "I didn't find Maude's body, but I'll search again soon. I also need to pay a visit to the wolves, but now that Mina's back, I guess I'll put it off a little longer."

"The wolves?" asked John. "What for?"

Fred was ready with his answer this time. "I want to form an alliance with them on behalf of Rebelton. We're both vulnerable to whatever New Waldoff has planned. It would be good if we could agree to help each other out."

Mina said, "I think that's a great idea, Fred. But you don't have to wait on account of me. I'll go with you. I'd love to see Axel again."

Fred looked at Mina for a second as though trying to think of how to respond. "That's not a good idea, Mina. No matter what you decide to do about your arm, you're going to need some time to adjust to the new normal. Hopefully, Bob can fit you with a prosthetic quickly, but it might be months before you get the hang of using it."

Mina laughed. "That's silly, Fred. I don't need a new arm to visit the wolves."

Fred replied a bit testily, "Yes, you do. It's dangerous out there."

Mina sounded irritated, too, now. "It's not any more dangerous than it was when the Moon was being controlled by an evil madman who wanted to gas the whole place. And even if it were, I don't see how having less of an arm makes any difference."

Fred's face suddenly flushed, and he looked away. "I don't want to fight, Mina. Let's just go find Bob and ask where you're staying tonight."

As a previous pub owner, John was well versed in the wide spectrum of human embarrassment, which meant he understood where Fred was coming from. "I think, dear Mina, what the lad here is having trouble saying is that his feelings for you are what's different now. It seems to me he's trying to keep you safe."

Mina bit her lip, and her cheeks turned rosy. She looked at Fred who was too embarrassed to look back at her. So she walked to his side and took his hand in hers. Fred looked down at their entwined fingers and then back up at Mina's face. He smiled shyly but with a hint of relief. "I didn't know if you…" He stopped. Then he said, "You backed away before."

Mina shook her head. "I know, but let's not talk about that now. We'll go look for Bob while John drums up whatever weird potion he's planning to slip him."

Then to John, she said, "Just please don't do anything to Bob that can't be undone. Okay?"

John nodded. "Oh, I've never been in the business of poisoning my patrons, but there's many a man who could attest to the fact that I'm able to serve a drink that would knock even the largest of arses into next week. Pardon my foul language, love."

"It's fine," Mina replied, "but could you serve Bob a milder drink? Maybe knock his bottom into tomorrow instead of next week? That is unless you want to handle that restless crowd by yourself again tomorrow."

John laughed. "No. That I don't. You two go on. I'll see you at Bob's in a short while."

Mina and Fred walked back down the slope towards the rows of metal homes, still holding hands. Mina had applied the numbing lotion that Evelyn had given her, which meant the pain in her arm had subsided, and she was able to concentrate on her emotions again.

Mina could feel electricity running between their fingers, and she thought back to the train ride they'd taken together. She had yearned for him to touch her, but of course when he finally had, it had been too soon. And now she was left with little more than half her arm.

During the horse ride to Rebelton she had enjoyed the feeling of Fred's strong arms around her, but she'd been fully aware that this embrace had only occurred out of necessity. This time was different, though. It was a declaration of their mutual feelings, and it brought back all the longing Mina had felt for Fred while they were riding the train together back to her hometown.

"I've decided to let Evelyn amputate," Mina announced suddenly. "There's no point in waiting until I've lost my whole arm. I might as well let her try to fix me now."

"Oh," said Fred.

"Oh? That's all you're going to say?" Mina questioned.

Fred stopped and looked at her. "No, it's just that I wasn't expecting that. I'm still shocked that your arm could even get this bad. I don't know what to think about it, except that it's upsetting, of course. And confusing, too."

"Confusing how?" Mina asked.

Fred paused before answering. "I guess it's just confusing how the proton beam even worked. For instance, how was I able to touch you if I was only being projected? Right?"

Mina narrowed her eyes at Fred. "Aren't you the one who helped Bob come up with the idea for the beam? Why are you doubting the science behind it now when it's already worked? Or is there something else?"

Fred looked worried. "Like what?"

"Well," Mina began. "I've been wondering how you helped Bob come up with the idea for the proton beam ever since you told me about it on the train. I mean, it's not exactly like you have a background in science or engineering."

"I told you. The oracle gave me the idea. She said it was important to rescue you in order to keep the Moon balanced after Maude died."

"There's something you're not telling me," Mina said, pulling her hand away. "Your story doesn't exactly add up. You told me on the train that my mother is the one who wanted me to return to the Moon. But then you also said that it was this oracle who wanted me to come back so I could help restore the balance. Then on the ride here you said both of these things are true, even though they feel like conflicting stories. So why aren't you telling me everything, Fred?"

Fred sighed deeply He knew he was going to have to divulge more, but luckily there was more he was allowed to tell her. "The oracle isn't the oracle, Mina. She's a goddess just like Theia. Her name is Serena, and she's the one who wanted you back on the Moon. In fact, she's the reason that either of us are here to begin with."

Mina was surprised that Fred was being honest with her all of a sudden. "What does that mean?" she asked.

Fred shook his head. "All I can tell you is that Serena controls pretty much everything on the Moon. She doesn't like attention, though. She prefers to stay hidden from mortals and semi-mortals, except for the elves."

"Elves?" Mina asked. "Like in my dream."

"You've dreamt about elves?" Fred asked sounding surprised.

Mina nodded. "When Dan abducted me after I passed out in the greenhouse, I had a couple of intensely strange dreams. One of them was about elves."

"I see," said Fred.

"So then if Serena was truly the one responsible for my return, what about my—" Mina stopped as a thought suddenly popped into her head.

"Serena is my mother. Isn't she?"

Fred nodded. "Yes, Mina. Serena is your mother."

"But how can that be? My mother's name is Cate. At least that's what my father told me. Plus, how could Serena be my mother if she lives on the Moon?"

"Serena's full name is Serena Hecate, or Serena Cate for short, or just plain Serena. The reason she's your mother despite living on the Moon is a pretty simple question to answer. For example, how are *you* here?"

Mina grew excited. "I get it, Fred! That means she can

travel to different dimensions. Just like I did! Don't you see what this proves?"

Fred looked at Mina quizzically. "No."

"It proves that Mattie *is* real. If I'm able to travel through dimensions like my mother, then obviously, I found Mattie in a different dimension while escaping Earth."

Fred shook his head. "No. Please don't start this again, Mina."

Mina looked annoyed. "Why, Fred? Unless maybe there's something else you know that I don't."

Fred looked at the ground in frustration and then back at Mina. "No, Mina. There's nothing else," he said sounding resigned.

Mina begged, "Well, then stop doubting me! I know what I experienced was real. It was just as real as you and I standing here together right now."

All of a sudden, Fred took a step towards Mina, grabbed her around the waist and kissed her full on the lips. Mina began to pull away, stunned by Fred's forwardness, but then stopped herself. Resting her good arm on Fred's shoulder, she grabbed on to the back of his neck, pulling him into her as they continued to kiss.

Fred moved his kisses to the side of Mina's neck, scooping her hair back with his hand. Mina was breathing hard. She felt dizzy and raw with passion. Every part of her wanted to give herself over to Fred.

As if he could sense Mina's feelings, Fred whispered to her as his lips grazed her ear, "I've loved you for longer than you could possibly know. I loved you on the day you made me hum that horrible tune for hours on end while we waited for Axel to rescue us. I didn't know it then, but I did. And I promise you, Mina, until the second I cease to exist, I'll never stop loving you."

Fred's pulse beat fast. He wanted so badly to tell Mina

everything he knew, not just what he was allowed to. But Serena had made it abundantly clear that there would be grave consequences if he told Mina the truth. So he held it back, even though it was painful to do so.

Mina pulled away and placed her hand on Fred's chest. "I love you too, Fred. I don't understand why exactly, but my feelings for you have always been incredibly strong. Even before we met. That's why I knew I had to rescue you from Dan. It's obvious we have some kind of deep connection. That day years ago in the small tunnel when we were humming together in harmony, I think I saw your past life—the one you lived before you arrived on the Moon. You were younger, playing ball with your friends outside. I didn't tell you before because I knew you wouldn't be able to remember, and I didn't want to hurt you."

Fred forced himself to smile, even though it was killing him to ignore Mina's acknowledgment of their powers. "Thank you," was all he said, and he raised her hand to his lips and kissed it tenderly.

A voice they recognized called to Mina from nearby. "Oh my goodness! Mademoiselle! It is true that you have returned!"

Mina and Fred looked over their shoulders at the same time to find the little French chef bustling towards them with a bouquet of flowers in hand. Fred looked around and realized that there were quite a few people walking up and down the street and that he and Mina had somehow tuned everyone out while engulfed in their moment of passion.

"Jacques! It's wonderful to see you," Mina greeted the chef, leaning down to give him a hug. "How have you been?"

Jacques' rosy cheeks darkened to an even deeper shade of red at Mina's warm embrace. "Oh, you know. Things have been better. I still do not have the gourmet kitchen I desire, but it is at least bigger than the horrible ass stall…oh, no, no. I mean, donkey stall I was forced to work out of in New Waldoff. You have heard of this awful place? No?"

Mina nodded. "Yes, Fred told me about New Waldoff. It sounds like the Moon Travelers went through a terrible time the last few years. I'm just glad some of you were able to escape."

"Yes, well thank you. But Fred does not really know about such things. He never lived in New Waldoff. Surely, you'd like to hear the stories from someone who can give you a first-hand account of the terror we lived through while you were away?

"Oh, I know! I will have a dinner party for you soon. I will invite Bob and John and you and Fred. Mind you, there is not a lot of food here to make a sumptuous meal. And the others, they always say to me, 'Non, Jacques. You cannot leave the valley to get good ingredients to cook your food, or you will be killed.' And I say back to them that life without good food is no life I want to live. But then they threaten to lock me up. Anyway, I work with what I am able to. Will you come to my dinner party?"

Mina smiled. She knew the chef's invitation was heartfelt. "Of course, Jacques. I wouldn't miss it for the world."

As she spoke, Jacques' eyes drifted to Mina's disappearing arm. "La vache! What has happened to your arm? Please tell me this did not occur on account of the space suit I made for you."

Mina had to suppress a laugh, thinking of the lumpy cheese suit that Jacques had made for her. Of course, she'd almost turned into human fondue while wearing it, but she didn't blame the chef for that.

"No, Jacques. This is a recent injury. It happened on my way back to the Moon. Your space suit worked well. I would have burned up in Earth's atmosphere if it weren't for the suit."

Jacques beamed with pride. "Well, of course. As you know, my cheeses have always been the finest. I am just happy they could help you with your space travels too.

"Now, if you will excuse me s'il vous plait. I have to get home quickly. The building crew I work with is going to help me install my cabinets this afternoon. It will be good to no longer have to stack my things on the floor. However, it will also be a sad occasion for it is our first time together without our Maude. I fear we will all have a big hole in our hearts, which is why I have been out picking these little cactus flowers," he said tearfully holding out his hand to show them the violet-colored flowers he was clutching. "I hope they will make people feel better."

"That's lovely," said Mina. "I'm sure that your friends will enjoy the flowers, Jacques."

"Yes, well, I'd better go. I will see you soon. Until we meet again!" And the little chef strolled away, down the main road.

Fred laughed. "He's certainly fond of you. I'm not sure he even noticed I was here."

Mina looked at him with concern. "Are you jealous?"

"No, nothing like that." Fred laughed again. "To be honest, I have a hard time remembering there are other people around when I'm with you, too. Like a few minutes ago when we kissed, everything around us kind of melted away."

Mina smiled. "I know what you mean."

The lovebirds stared dreamily at each other for a few more seconds. Then Mina said, "Well, I guess we should go find Bob like we told John we would. If he's not resting, I'd like to find out where I'm staying."

"Good idea," said Fred as they began to walk. "I'd offer you my place, but at the moment, all I have is a tiny tent. Hopefully, Bob can find nicer living arrangements for someone of your caliber."

"My caliber, huh?" Mina said as her wheels spun. "I want to ask you something, Fred."

"Okay," Fred replied drawing in a deep breath.

"If my mother, Serena, was here on the Moon all along, then why hasn't she ever tried to meet me?"

Fred reached out and took Mina's hand in his own. "I can't answer that," he said.

"You can't or you won't?" she asked staring at him from the side, studying his reaction.

Fred hesitated. Without looking at her directly, he said, "I can't."

He knew this was only a small lie because he actually couldn't tell Mina, as per Serena's orders. But Fred hated not being honest with Mina, and worst of all he feared that someday it might ruin everything between them.

Mina was disappointed. She knew that Fred wasn't telling her everything still, but she sensed there was a reason, so she didn't press him further.

Fred looked at Mina after the quiet became too much to bear. She looked disappointed, which awakened Fred's anxiety.

"Look, Mina," he said. "Let's just live in the moment as much as we can for now. I don't know if you can feel it yet, but there's a storm coming. And once it reaches us, I suspect more will be revealed than any of us ever wanted to know."

Mina didn't like the sound of Fred's cryptic warning, but she squeezed his hand anyway and said, "Okay, Fred. We can live in the moment. For now."

CHAPTER 7

CATCHING DALE UP

"Umm, love what you've done with the place, Bets," Dale announced as he waltzed into Betsy's office, eyeing the mess of tangled vines that were drenched in sticky, clotted blood.

Betsy looked up from her desk where she was huddled over an army map featuring the Moon's Darkside, a map that Bob had commissioned when he and his soldiers were toiling away in the dark, waiting to fight Dan.

"Why are you here, Dale?" she asked coldly. "Your debriefing isn't scheduled until tomorrow."

Dale ignored Betsy's rude greeting and walked to her desk where he stood staring. "You've got a little something…" He trailed off but used his hand to make a circular motion around his face in an attempt to alert Betsy to the blood that was splattered over hers.

Betsy took a handkerchief from her pocket and wiped it on her cheeks and forehead; however, this only served to smear the blood across her skin so that it now looked like carelessly applied war paint.

"Yep. You got it," Dale lied giving Betsy a thumbs up.

"Fine. But I have a lot of work to do, so if you have something to say, make it quick."

Glancing over at the blood-soaked vines again, Dale suddenly wasn't sure if he wanted to ask his question. Carefully, he said, "Max revealed something about you when we were journeying to the rebel's city, but I'm not sure whether to believe it."

"He told you I'm the dark god's daughter?"

Dale nodded, relieved that Betsy had said it for him.

She looked over at the bloodbath from earlier and then back at Dale. "Yes, that's right. I was born a demi-god. I'm half time god, like my father and half forest elf on my mother's side."

Dale looked a bit sulky all of a sudden, although it was unclear whether this was because Betsy was only now telling him the truth, or because he was jealous.

"I don't get it," he said annoyed. "What's a time god? A god that keeps time? And what the hell is a forest elf? I thought elves weren't even a real thing!"

"Calm down, Dale. Nothing's different than it was before you found out. Time gods are gods who have the power to move through time. The extremely powerful ones can sometimes even change the outcomes of events. They have other divine powers, too. My father, Theo, is able to get inside the heads of some creatures and coerce them into doing what he wants. He isn't able to do it with everyone, though.

"And yes, elves have lived on the Moon longer than any of the other mortal creatures, but they were banished a long time ago. They mostly live underground now on the south side of the Moon."

"Okay. Okay, okay," said Dale, trying his best to frantically process what he could and file away the rest for later. "But why didn't you tell me before? We could've used your father all those years we were pushing people to join our side. Right? If he can control people, then he could've forced them to obey us."

"No, Dale. That's not what I said. That's not how his powers work. Regular people can't even see him. Dan only heard him, remember? And I'm pretty sure that was only possible because of who your mother was. To control Goodman, Theo had to hide inside of a crystal for years. Goodman wouldn't have been able to hear Father, otherwise.

"Besides, my father isn't interested in being some ridiculous attraction that humans can use for political gain. There are rules in this realm that were created by a god who has even more power than my father. And Theo isn't able to break these rules, although he's tried."

"Okay, but why did you say who my mother *was*, Bets?"

Betsy sighed. "Maude's dead, Dale. That powerful god I just mentioned, her name is Serena. She killed your mother a few days ago."

Dale was shocked. "What do you mean she killed her? Why would she do that!?"

"Now, don't go getting sentimental about Maude. I know you don't really mean it. Serena killed her because your mother was a time god too. She was Theia, Dale. But as far as I can tell, Maude didn't know it until the very end. Or at least she never acted like she did."

Dale looked angry. "That doesn't make any sense, Bets. How could Maude be a time god? She's a Moon Traveler, just like most of the humans. If she was a goddess, then how can we be sure that all the humans aren't gods?"

Betsy rolled her eyes. "Look, Dale. I don't have time to try and convince you why all the humans aren't gods. I'm sure if you spent ten seconds thinking about it, you'd be able to deduce that one on your own. But as far as Maude is concerned, I think Serena transformed Theia into human form and erased all of her memories as punishment."

"But why?"

Betsy sighed. She hadn't planned to have a heart-to-heart with Dale, and she was starting to resent Max for telling Dale about her father in the first place. Nevertheless, she needed Dale to do something for her, so she continued to answer his questions.

"A long time ago, when Theia and my father were living as gods in the Moon Realm, with only the wolves and bryobane to lord over, Theia reached out to Father by sending some messengers to speak to him. According to Theo, these messengers were the parents of the most powerful wolf—Neriti.

"At the time, Father didn't know of Neriti because she was still young. Neriti's mother explained that she had been talking to Theia through the crystals in Crystal Crater for many years, but that Theia had ordered her to keep it a secret until that day. Supposedly, Theia ordered Neriti's mother to go to my father and give him a special crystal that would allow Theia to speak to him, too. Of course, Father killed both wolves as soon as they explained who they were and what they wanted, but Theia presented herself to Father anyway and told him a story from long ago."

Betsy reached out her blood-stained hands to Dale, but he visibly recoiled.

"Take my hands Dale. I have the power to show you what happened since my father once showed it to me. It's the watered-down version of time travel I possess as the daughter of a time god. You may possess the same power, although I suspect your powers have more to do with your silver tongue."

Dale didn't like the idea of holding Betsy's hands, even when they were clean. But he was curious to see what would happen, so he did as he was told.

Suddenly, Betsy's office blurred out of sight, and Dale found himself standing on top of a thick sheet of ice lit by dozens of glowing red, dark crystals. Two wolves lay dead a few feet away with their throats slashed. Out of the corner of Dale's eye, he saw a black haze swirling around. He turned his head towards the haze and realized that he was standing right next to Theo. He jumped, startled by the dark god's appearance. Theo was in the shape of a terrifying beast made of black smoke. He seemed to be partly human, but he also had horns pointing out of his head and giant fangs. "Holy crap, Bets!" Dale cried, and for a split second, he thought he saw Theo flinch towards him ever so slightly.

"Keep it down!" he heard Betsy scold him, though he couldn't tell where her voice was coming from.

Dale could hear another voice. It spoke in a strange tone and sounded like nothing he'd ever heard before. As he began to listen, he noticed there was a small crystal laying in front of Theo's smoky feet. It glowed like the other crystals, but its light was golden white and far more powerful.

"I have memories of a time before the crystal worlds came into existence," said the voice. "You and I lived on Earth as gods, but we took the form of humans. We weren't alone, either. We traveled with the other time gods, chasing our sister, Serena Hecate, across time as she reincarnated herself into different bodies.

"We tried to save her from herself—to bring her back here to the one true realm. But she rejected us, and eventually, she tried to destroy us. She killed our two weaker siblings and blew up the Earth realm in the process. Only you and I survived.

"When Serena realized that she'd lost everything important to her, she acted remorseful, at first. She found us and took care of us, but as we grew stronger, she decided we still posed a threat to her. To neutralize us, she stole our memories."

Theo scoffed. "That's quite the story, sister. But how do you expect me to believe it when you *do* seem to have these memories that you claim were stolen from you?"

The voice from the crystal spoke again, "Serena has stolen

our memories many, many times over our long existence. And there have been other times she has restored them, as well. Once, after the Earth realm was destroyed, Serena stole our memories and trapped us together inside a crystal world filled with elves. You and I were the gods that ruled over all the elves, and we were very much in love with each other.

"Of course, we didn't know we were siblings during this time because we didn't know who we were or where we came from. We had a child—a little boy named Heely. But right after I gave birth to him, fighting broke out between the different elf species.

"I begged you not to get involved with the fighting; I knew that any meddling would only make it worse. You promised me that you'd stay neutral, but I soon found out you'd betrayed me, and not only that but you had chosen to side with the elves who were the most belligerent, the Drezels.

"The Drezels had decided to use the elves' infighting to make a power grab. They turned the stronger elves against the weaker ones. By doing so, they were able to get the stronger elves to do their dirty work—wiping out entire villages of weaker elves. But once the stronger elves were finished exterminating most of the weaker ones, they were betrayed. Immediately, the Drezels killed off half the population of stronger elves, which was an easy task considering how worn down these elves had become during the fighting they'd done on behalf of the Drezels. And thus, the Drezels managed to seize power over all the remaining elves.

"When I realized what you were up to, helping the Drezels with their despicable plan, I took our newborn son and fled. I visited the elven villages that were suffering the most from the civil war and did what I could to help them.

"What I found in these villages was heartbreaking. Most of the elves there had been displaced—their homes destroyed due to the fighting. The villages had become safe havens for refugees, a place the elves could heal after losing their families, their friends, and their livelihood. I cast a protection spell over these villages to keep the Drezels from finding them.

"I spent several weeks taking care of the sick and wounded, going around with Heely strapped to my back. A month had passed when a group of more than a hundred knights appeared, miraculously, right outside the village I was staying in. They were confused and disoriented. They'd been on a quest, journeying through desert lands when suddenly they found themselves in a lush green world, unlike anything they'd ever known. At the time, I believed they'd been banished from their own realm by an angry god, but I'm certain now that Serena placed them in our crystal world to usher in the events that followed.

"Upon hearing of the elves' plight, the knights decided to make it their mission to defeat you and the Drezels. I told them I would help by using my powers as a time goddess, but I warned them that our chance for victory was slim. I didn't want to scare the knights; however, I knew the Drezels to be ruthless. If you could only remember how cold their eyes were, how grotesquely conniving their tight-lipped, little smiles were. Even with our army of knights, I knew we would be heavily outnumbered. Your army included not only hundreds of Drezels, but also what was left of the strongest elves.

"Soon after we began preparing to fight your side, Sir Logan, the leader of the knights, revealed he was in love with me. He asked me to marry him and said he wanted to adopt our son, Heely, as his own. He promised that once the war was over, he would take us to the most beautiful place in the realm to start our new lives together.

"I accepted his offer, even though I didn't share his feelings of romance. I think mostly I agreed to marry him to get back at you for your betrayal. Plus, I knew Sir Logan to be a good and simple man, and he was the kind of father I wanted for our son. A father who'd put their child first.

"Then, as luck would have it—or so I thought—a week before we were set to carry out our first attack on the Drezel armies, our sister Serena Hecate showed up with her talking sheep. She introduced herself as my long-lost sister and told a story of how a jealous god had placed her under a sleeping spell for many years. She said that when she woke up, she knew she had to come find us right away because the same god who'd put her in a coma had also placed a memory spell on you and me.

"I had no reason to doubt her, even though I was mortified to learn that you and I were siblings. Serena seemed so sweet, and when she heard of all that had transpired, she offered to sneak across enemy lines to spy on your army. After she returned from this covert mission, she told us that you had learned of my plan to marry Sir Logan and had gone into a mad rage. She said you'd ordered your army to find me and our baby and to kill us on sight.

"Logan was outraged when he heard the news, but I was terrified. I wanted to take Heely and hide. Serena insisted, though, that this would be the worst possible move I could make. She said that it was safer if we stayed with the knights, and that she would stay and fight too. She also showed great concern for our son, offering to have her three 'guard sheep' watch over him whenever we were in battle.

"When I told Serena I didn't feel comfortable letting the sheep watch Heely on their own, she told me she would make sure our son was safe by casting a protective spell over him. However, for the spell to work, Serena first needed the consent of the parents. Since Logan had already adopted our son, he was able to give his permission as one of Heely's parents. But we didn't go through with it right away because I was beginning to have a bad feeling about the plan.

"The spell worked by allowing the sheep to take our son through a portal along an untraceable path through time and space. The problem was that because it was untraceable, no god or mortal would ever be able to find Heely once he was taken.

"Logan and I talked about alternative plans, including hiding Heely with the elves who'd stayed neutral during the fight. But we were too scared that your minions would find Heely while we weren't there to protect him. Eventually, we approached Serena again, willing to give our consent but with one condition. The sheep were only to take our son through the portal if both Logan and I were deceased or if Heely was in imminent danger.

"Serena happily agreed to these terms and cast the spell right in front of us. For a while, everything was fine. The battles were bloody and went on for days before one or both sides would retreat, but Heely was always safe nearby. And we could check on him whenever we liked.

"Our side held out much longer than I thought possible. The knights had constructed all kinds of war instruments— ones that launched fire and brimstone at your army. But it wasn't enough. We made major gains in the beginning of the war, but eventually the Drezels created their own weapons, and we lost too many men and elves to be able to continue fighting much longer.

"We knew the last battle was near. All the knights were prepared to die for the cause, even when it became apparent that the cause was all but lost. I wasn't prepared to die, however. All I cared about was protecting my family and most of all our son. Plus, during the months Logan and I spent fighting together, I witnessed what a heroic warrior he was and grew to love him.

"The thought that you, Theo, might once again keep me from living happily was too much to bear. I begged Serena to recast her spell so that when our situation became dire, Logan and I could leave the fight and travel through the portal with our son. Serena insisted that it wouldn't come to that, though. She still thought she could save our army with her powers. But nothing I'd seen during the fighting made me believe that was true. She could zap the enemy with electricity and stun them with her loud cries, but her powers didn't always work. And when they did, they only worked for a short while.

"I asked her what harm it would do to recast the spell, but she pointed out that it would never work because Logan would never leave the battlefield. I conceded and told her then to recast the spell so that I could go through the portal with Heely. Serena hesitated for so long that I didn't think she would agree. I'd already grown suspicious of her motives, and I wondered why she wouldn't change the spell if she was really on my side. But finally, she granted my request with the caveat that the sheep would still take Heely through the portal so long as he were in imminent danger. I agreed but decided that I would stay close to wherever Heely was so he'd never be in imminent danger. When I told Logan of my plan, he decided to stay close, too.

"The final battle came, and it was horrible. We were so far outnumbered that it took less than thirty minutes for the Drezel army to kill half our soldiers. Logan and I fought the soldiers who made it past the first few lines of warriors on our side. Serena, on the other hand, was all over the place. She came near to us at one point while dueling with one of the largest elves I'd ever seen. Yet she was smiling the whole time, as though she were only toying with the creature. She shouted to us that things were starting to look up, but Logan and I had no idea what she was talking about. It was obvious to us that we were going to lose the war that day.

"Soon after her comment, our situation became even more bleak. There were cannons firing on us from close range, and clouds of dirt and smoke had filled the air, making it nearly impossible to see more than a foot in front of our faces. I yelled to Logan through all the muck, even though I didn't know if he was still alive. I told him I was going to Heely, and a second later I felt his hand on my arm. He pulled me close and told me he loved me, ready to say goodbye, but before he could, a blinding flash of light came from the other side of the hill we were fighting on.

"In my heart, I already knew what had happened. Logan and I took off up the hill, yelling for Serena's sheep. When we got to the top, we looked around for any sign of them or Heely, but they were gone.

"I began to weep while Logan tried to find hope in the situation. A minute later, Serena joined us at the top of the hill, pleading with us to come back to the fight. I explained what had happened, but she already knew, even though she pretended not to. She beckoned us to come with her to the other side of the hill—to continue fighting your army so that we would still have a chance to save Heely afterwards.

"We had no choice. There was nothing we could do at that moment except fight. So, we did. But right after we started back over the hill towards the battle, the strangest thing happened. Serena came storming over the hill, screaming a banshee's cry unlike anything I'd ever heard before. And I watched as lightning bolts and fire fell from the sky towards the soldiers on your side, wiping out nearly everyone in one fell swoop.

"When it was done, Serena laughed with glee while our last few soldiers finished killing the last few of yours. At first, I was in shock, but then I lost myself in a mad rage. I screamed at our sister for not having used her powers earlier and demanded she explain herself.

"That's when you showed up. You came racing across the battlefield in your human form, but at a speed that far surpassed that of any human. Then before I could stop you, you killed the rest of the knights, including my sweet Logan. Next you turned your anger towards me. You yelled at me to hand over our son and insisted that all the bloodshed was my fault. You said you never would've allowed the Drezels to attack us if I hadn't stolen our son.

"I held my ground, staring you down, ready for you to strike me dead. But Serena intervened before it came to that. She told you of the bargain we'd made and how she had tricked me into going along with her scheme. She even explained that this wasn't the first time she had played with us, alluding to the long history we all shared.

"I fell to my knees and began to sob for our lost Heely and for my Logan and for these horrible lives we were being forced to live. I realized then that Serena was a terrible trickster, an evil god of deceit. I begged her to let me go to Heely, but she refused. Then, with the most devious look I've ever seen, she told us that she had her own plan for our son.

"I continued pleading with her to let him go and begged her to tell us what she was going to do, but she said that Heely was no longer our concern. At this point, you lost your temper and ran towards Serena, ready to strike her down. I tried to stand in your way screaming for you to stop. I knew we needed her alive to have any hope of finding our child. But as you flew through the air, you pushed me to the ground, grabbed Logan's sword, and thrust it into Serena's stomach.

"I watched in horror as Serena smiled. Dark blood poured from her wound, and her breath turned to frost. I was sure you'd killed her, but then something astonishing happened. Serena grabbed hold of the sword's hilt and pulled the blade from her stomach. I saw your face as it happened. You were still angry but shocked too. Before either of us could react, Serena said, 'Very good, Theo. This was exactly what I needed to know.'

"Then she snapped her fingers and erased our minds. But she didn't just erase our minds, she started everything over from the point when the knights first appeared. She even returned Heely, only I didn't know he'd ever been missing. She reanimated all the elves and all the humans, and we went about fighting the battles again, just like none of it had ever happened before.

"This time, however, Serena threw the battle to your side after Heely disappeared, and your army quickly killed the rest of the knights, including Logan. I realized that I'd been completely betrayed by Serena. Believing her to be a spy that you'd sent to kidnap Heely, it was I who took Logan's sword and ran it through Serena's chest in this alternate timeline.

"Serena smiled at me with a look of relief and pulled the sword from her heart. She said, 'Thank you, dear Theia. You've done well.' Then she snapped her fingers again and sent me to a different crystal world without my memories for who knows how long.

"The next thing I knew I was on the Moon again with you, and we were the rulers of the Moon Walkers. But of course Serena had bound you to Black Ice Glacier and me to Crystal Crater.

"Look, brother. I know we've had our differences as we've vied for power over the Moon, but can't you see that this is just Serena's way of controlling us?

"I started to remember everything when Serena stepped in to help reset the Moon Walkers—after you corrupted so many of them. I hated the deal we'd all made to change the Moon Walkers into the bryobane and wolves. It felt wrong to steal their memories and force them to be something they weren't. I think that's because part of me instinctively knew that Serena had done the same to us.

"I stopped using my powers for a while as a way to reflect on this horrible deed and taught the wolves their own magic to avoid having to use any of mine. I think it's possible my memories came back because I refrained from magic. Steadily over time, all the scenes I've shared with you today trickled back to me.

"I thought about confronting Serena to tell her what I knew, but I feared she'd punish me by wiping my slate clean again. So instead, I've kept quiet all these years, waiting to see how much I'd remember while devising a plan. The best strategy I've ever come up with is for us to join forces and work together.

"Theo, we have to destroy Serena and this place. All these millennia, we've been living in hell when we could be back in paradise. I remember what it was like. We all lived here together once—you, me, our siblings, and Serena. We were happy then. We called our home Ortus, and it was blissful.

"It wasn't until Serena created Earth that everything fell apart. And the only way to start over is to kill Serena so that she has no more power over us or our world. Only then can we rebuild it from scratch and make it good again."

Theo growled disdainfully, and Dale's heart skipped a beat. He'd been so captivated by the story that he'd lost himself in it for a while and was only now remembering that he was inside of a completely different time and place.

He whispered to Betsy, "So this talking rock is what convinced your father to destroy the Moon?"

But Betsy shushed him.

Theia continued trying to persuade Theo. "I wish you could remember what Ortus looked like before Serena ruined it. We could do whatever we wanted. We had everything we wanted. There was an endless variety of beautiful music to listen and dance to. It poured from the heavens or out of the flowers and trees or from practically anywhere in nature we chose to hear it. We could eat or not eat everything or nothing. We lived in a paradise just for us gods, and it was perfect.

"Serena stole that from us, Theo, and if we don't work together, we may spend the rest of eternity just as we are now —Serena's puppets. I do realize it won't be easy, though. Serena is incredibly strong, and she keeps robbing us of our memories.

"When I tried to kill her, she sent me to a tiny crystal world, abandoning me there without my memories. And without my memories I couldn't use my time-leaping powers to go back and remember what I'd been forced to forget. I'm sure she's done the same to you. She clearly has some twisted thirst for torture. So, what do you say, Theo? Will you help me take her down once and for all?"

Theo snickered. "How do I know your story is real? I take it you want me to stop using my powers in order to bring back my own memories. But surely, you'd agree that this reeks of a setup. I think what's happening here is that you've come to realize I'm going to find a way to eat your wolves and ingest their energy so that I can free myself from this damned glacier and rule the Moon realm on my own. You're only trying to get in my way with these ridiculous lies!"

The voice in the stone sighed. "I'm not lying, brother. And I'm not asking you to stop using your powers. However, if Serena begins to suspect that I've remembered everything and finds out that I've told you the truth, she'll come for us both. You need to have a way to remember all of this, just in case. If you'd like, you can capture the memory of this encounter inside this dark crystal that I'm speaking to you from now. I am offering it as a gift for you to use however you wish, even though I know you might use it against me one day."

Theo seemed intrigued by the offer. He picked up the crystal and studied it for a moment. Then, he asked, "Assuming your story wasn't all lies, what have you done for yourself in case our sister tries to steal your memories?"

The crystal inside Theo's smoky palm answered, "I've

traveled back through time to create records of everything that happened. I had to take precautions, of course, so I entrusted the stories to the Moon Walkers I knew best. I told a select few of them everything that I knew I'd want to remember and asked them to create a system for keeping the memories safe. They produced a coded language to record what I'd told them and then hid the records.

"Then I moved forward through time to when the Moon Walkers were changed into the wolves. I told the elder wolves that they, too, were responsible for guarding these records. However, I never told them what the records contained, so now I'm the only one who knows how important these documents are—except for you.

"I'm telling you this so that you'll see you can trust me. If we don't work together to take Serena down, I fear we'll be doomed to repeat our own tragic history over and over until kingdom come."

Theo laughed defiantly. "Well, I don't believe you, Sister. But I'm taking this crystal, nevertheless," he said as he closed his fist over the stone.

The light from the crystal continued to shine between Theo's clenched fingers. Theia said, "I beg you to reconsider. We may not have another chance to escape our fate."

Annoyed that he hadn't gotten rid of his sister so easily, Theo replied, "I'll think about what you've said. My minion will inform you if I change my mind."

Suddenly, Dale was transported away from Black Ice Glacier back into Betsy's blood-soaked office.

"Holy crap, Bets! That's quite the story that rock told your father. Was that really my mother inside of there?" Dale asked as he tried to ignore the whopping case of vertigo he was experiencing from the time travel.

Betsy shook her head. "I can't say for sure."

Dale looked confused. "But that's who she claimed to be, right?"

"Yes, that's right. But Father told me he didn't believe it was Theia speaking to him that day. He did end up storing the memory of the conversation in the stone in case Serena ever showed up to steal his memories. But she never did.

"The thing is, Father said that Theia was protective of her wolves. It didn't make sense that she'd send two of them to their deaths. There should've been no doubt in her mind that he'd kill them because she knew he had long sought revenge for what she did to the bryobane. It just didn't add up."

"I see," said Dale. "But don't you think there must have been some truth to it all? I mean Theia did end up in human form as Maude later on. Maybe Serena found out Theia had gotten her memories back and then punished her just like Theia said would happen."

Betsy leaned even further back in her chair so that she was practically horizontal. "I don't have all the answers, but here's what I do know. Father believed the talking stone was a hoax— a red herring to throw him off his quest for control of the Moon realm.

"He said that centuries earlier, Theia asked Serena if she would help her prevent Father from killing her Moon Walker subjects and stealing their energy. Serena agreed to help but told Theia that the only way to stop Theo was to divide the Moon Walkers into two separate groups and transform them into different non-shifting forms. She said doing so would allow her to cast a spell that would block Theo from killing Theia's new subjects if he tried to steal their energy and break free from Black Ice Glacier to take control of the Moon.

"Serena went ahead and transferred all the Moon Walkers' energy to the wolves and then placed a spell on them so that this energy could no longer be stolen from them. From then on, the energy was only transferrable if the wolves granted it to someone. In return, Serena demanded that Theia take a less active role in the lives of her subjects. She also forbade Theia and Theo from talking about her with mortal creatures.

"According to Father, Serena expressed a desire to be left alone and live a quiet existence in her ice tunnels. She used this opportunity to put a spell on her domain to keep it hidden from all mortals. There was a caveat, though. Serena exempted the Moon Walkers from her spell. She had to because of the last demand she made of Theia—to be given one of Theia's Moon Walkers before the rest were changed."

Dale asked, "What did Serena want a Moon Walker for?"

"Beats me," said Betsy. "Maybe to keep her company, although I doubt it. Father thinks Serena wanted a Moon Walker so she could train it to be her personal spy. That's why the moment Theo detected Ragher's presence on the Darkside, he sent Gryobe to keep tabs on Ragher."

"Gryobe?! You mean that insane looking dog my brother kept around his fortress?"

Betsy snickered. "That wasn't a dog, Dale. Gryobe was my father's treasured minion. He created him by harnessing the energy of a million crystals and casting a dark spell on the bodies of a wolf and bryobane."

"Huh," said Dale, scratching his chin. "Seems like it would've been easier just to buy a dog if he wanted one so badly."

Betsy shook her head. "No, Dale, you're missing the point. Theo didn't want a pet dog. Gryobe had powers. He was able to teleport and become invisible, making him the perfect spy.

"Anyway, when Gryobe reported back to my father, he informed him that Ragher's energy was surrounded by a powerful protection charm, which meant Theo couldn't steal Ragher's energy either. Father suspected that this meant Ragher was part of Serena's big plan for the Moon. By then, he'd come to the conclusion that whoever it was speaking to him from the stone that day, they were telling the truth about Serena.

"So, Father made a plan to pull Ragher to his side. He knew he couldn't eat him, but he thought if he could get Ragher to work for him, then he'd at least be able to create problems for Screna. Unfortunately, getting Ragher to switch sides was harder to do than Father thought.

"Father sent Gryobe to follow Ragher's every move, but Ragher wanted nothing to do with Gryobe. In fact, he avoided him at all costs. Gryobe spent years wasting time, chasing after that stupid creature with nothing to show for it. It wasn't until Gryobe had followed Ragher for a couple of decades that Gryobe finally gained something useful from his assignment— he overheard Neriti and Ragher talking about how Theia was missing.

"Father knew this had the potential to change everything, but he needed to know where she was, first. He worried the news of her disappearance might be a trick designed to get him to leave the glacier so that he would lose his powers and become weak and vulnerable."

Dale frowned. "Why would he lose his powers?"

Betsy sat up again. "Millenia ago, when Serena brought Father and Theia back to the Moon's surface, she erased their memories and told them that each of them had been granted part of the Moon. Theo was given Black Ice Glacier, Theia got Crystal Crater, and Serena had her underground ice tunnel fortress. However, Father always felt as though he'd drawn the short straw, since all he had was a large, cold glacier that never saw the sun. He wanted a different part of the Moon, but Serena made it clear that if any of them tried to leave their domains, they would forfeit their powers for a length of time. She explained that each of them was bound to the same rules, but if one of them ever managed to leave their territory, for whatever reason, then the other two gods could also leave their domains without giving up their powers.

"Theo tried several times to leave Black Ice Glacier when he suspected the other two gods might no longer be in their territories. But he was wrong each time, and it greatly diminished his energy. And once this happened, it took many years for him to regain the full extent of his powers. So, when Gryobe overheard Ragher and Neriti talking about Theia being gone, Theo knew he had to be careful how he proceeded. Before he did anything, he needed to know that what Gryobe had overheard was true.

"He devised a plan to have Dan annihilate the entire realm, hoping it might draw Theia out of hiding. At the time, he suspected your sister, Helen, was Theia, reborn into human form. But that turned out to be false; Helen was just a pawn.

"After Dan lost the battle to your sister, Father became very weak. His energy was so greatly diminished that he thought he might die. He knew more than ever that he needed to find Theia and steal her energy while she was in a weakened, mortal state.

"He took the crystal that had supposedly come from Theia and used it to control Goodman. The crystal brought out the very worst in Goodman, effectively making him a paranoid dictator. At Father's request, I stepped in to help Goodman build a city that could keep surveillance on everyone in it. I also created a secret network of agents who reported directly to me. Their purpose was to let me know if they ever saw or heard about any supernatural occurrences within the city walls.

"I was confident it would be easy to find Theia this way, but all I ever found out is that there are a lot of drunks in this city who claim to have magical powers, and citizens who like to spend their time accusing each other of witchcraft. I knew I was going to have to approach the problem in a new way, so I set off the explosions around the city.

"I'd long suspected that your parents might have something to do with Theia, but Father didn't believe me. He'd been so close to Dan all those years that Father was certain he'd have known if Dan's parents were hiding Theia. Plus, he'd already suspected Helen of being Theia, and that hadn't panned out, so he went in a different direction with his suspicions. He decided if Theia were in hiding as a human, she was probably living an incognito existence.

"I didn't buy that, though, and I wanted to test my theory about your parents. That's why I visited you at the Sheep Spa and told you to pass along the information to Bob regarding Goodman's plan to kill your parents. When I was positive your parents had taken the bait and were planning to flee the city, I blew up several of the cyakine gas lines and waited to see what would happen next.

"I ordered the guards at both city exits to keep a lookout for Bob and Maude. If they survived the blasts, I was going to have them arrested and charged with high crimes so I could interrogate them. But when your mother managed to get away and your father proved useless, I again had to rethink my plan.

"Fortunately, after Max spilled the beans about Maude, I knew we were back on track to restoring my father's powers. I went to tell Father the good news, but in my haste to move things along, I released Father from the crystal too soon. I thought it would be best for him to take possession of Goodman and go after Maude immediately. But it turns out that Maude was already dead, presumably banished to a crystal world inside Crystal Crater. And because I forced Father to manifest on the Dayside—away from Black Ice Glacier —Father is now even weaker than before."

"Geez, Bets! It doesn't exactly sound like you have everything under control here. What are you planning to do next? Blow up the rest of the city and then stab your father in the eye?"

Betsy snapped, "I didn't tell you all this so you could pass judgement, Dale. Besides, I'd be less quick to throw stones if I were you. You've never been anything more than a thorn in the side of all those who knew you. But lucky for you, I'm going to give you a chance to change all that. I'm sending you on another fact-finding mission, and an important one at that.

"We've got to find out what Serena knows. Regardless of who was talking to my father through the crystal, it's painfully obvious that Serena holds most of the power on the Moon. We need to know what her plans are and if she's willing to make a deal that'll give us Mina."

Dale looked surprised. "Mina? You mean, that annoying girl from Earth? I just saw her near the rebel town. She's older now, and she looks different without any wings and a partially missing arm. But I'm sure it was her."

"Hmm," Betsy moaned. "That's good information. But we need to know why she's here and what Serena plans to do with her."

"Well, I don't mind helping you Betsy, but I just got back from the mountains. I'm going to need a few days of recuperation before I can go back out again."

Betsy narrowed her eyes. "Are you thick, Dale? Mina is back, Theia is dead, and there's a memory erasing goddess who may or may not be coming for us next. And you think it's naptime? Pull it together! I'm only sending you on this errand because I need you to prove to me that you can handle tough work.

"Your brother wasn't as smart as my father gave him credit for, but the one thing that attracted me to Dan was that he put in the work it took to carry out his schemes. Now, do you want to do something useful for once in your impotent life, or don't you?"

Dale looked hurt. "Fine, Bets. But you know, you really are a nasty witch. What do you want me to do?"

"Good. You'll start by going to the Sheep Spa, and—"

Dale interrupted, "The Sheep Spa!? No way! I spent nine years rotting my brains out in that rancid-smelling factory. There's no way I'm going back there!"

Betsy smiled wickedly. "Oh, yes you will, Dale. And this time you're going to burn it to the ground."

CHAPTER 8

THE NEW NIGHTMARE

When Fred and Mina found Bob, he was standing outside Maude's little, metal home. As they approached Mina wondered how long he'd been standing there, staring at the front door.

"Hiya, Bob," Fred greeted him. "We hoped we would find you here. Mind if we come in for a visit?"

Bob looked over his shoulder at the couple and gave them a half nod, like he was lost in a daze. Mina tried a different approach. She walked to Bob's side and wrapped her good arm around his as though he were about to escort her somewhere.

"You're missing her, aren't you?" she asked. "Every day I came home from school after my father died, I dreaded going in. The empty rooms and deafening quiet were horrible reminders that he was really gone."

Fred sidled up to Mina and whispered, "How's this supposed to help?"

Mina glared at Fred, but before Fred could get defensive, Bob said, "I guess I better go ahead and face the music. Standing here missing Maude isn't going to solve anything. I'm fortunate to have a home to go to after everything that's happened."

Bob took a step forward but stumbled. Mina sturdied him though, and Fred stepped to Bob's other side in case he needed help.

"I'm fine," Bob reassured them, but as he took a few more steps, Mina could tell that he wasn't. It seemed that in the short time since they'd been apart, Bob had begun to show signs of his age, no longer steady on his feet.

He wobbled up to the front door with Mina and Fred on both sides of him ready to intervene. "I said I'm fine. I just need to lay down."

Mina opened the door to the house. "Yes, Bob. But Fred and I want to make sure you make it to your bed first."

Bob snickered. "You sound like her, you know? She always made silly comments like that whenever I was tipsy or being pigheaded."

"I take that as a compliment. Maude was a great lady," said Mina as she and Fred followed Bob through the front door into what had formerly been Maude's small living room.

"Looks just like the first house we lived in together," said Bob sadly. "I guess she drew up the same plans while I was away. Funny how when you're young and in love, a cozy home seems just perfect. Then you get older, and you start to think you need more space for whatever reason—a growing family, more workspace, better social status, *whatever*.

"But you know, I think this would have suited me fine at any stage of our lives. All I ever wanted was to be with her doing what we did best, helping others solve problems and working together on our inventions. We really had a nice life, and this house would have been…"

Bob had walked to the center of the room. And as he spoke this last sentence, he collapsed into a metal chair, leaving his unfinished words hanging in the air.

Just then, there was a knock on the front door, and a second later, John entered the living room, holding a pint of ale. Mina and Fred greeted him, but Bob didn't look up from where he sat.

"Well now, Bob. I had a feeling you might not go down so easy, which is why I've come to offer you a pint. It's some of the last few drops of ale I've been saving. The boys and I only managed to bring one keg when we left New Waldoff. So, enjoy it now. Because until we run some proper water lines into the valley, there won't be any more brew."

John winked at Fred and Mina as he held the pint out to Bob. But Bob remained despondent.

"Oh, come on, man. Don't let it go to waste. I recognize well that look across your face, and if there was ever a gent in the whole world needing a pint, it's you at this very moment."

Bob still didn't respond, but before John could try to twist his arm again, there was another knock at the door. It was Evelyn. She poked her head in and looked around the crowded living room. "Sorry to bother you all, but I came by to see if Bob had taken the sleeping pills yet."

John whipped around still holding the ale, splashing his arm as he turned. "Evelyn, dear. I was just trying to convince our good friend, Bob, to drink this ale to help his troubles."

Evelyn looked at the ale and then back at John with a concerned expression. "John, did you crush up the medicine I gave you and mix it into that beer?"

John looked flummoxed, like he wasn't sure what to say. But Mina answered for him. "Yes, Evelyn. That was John's plan all along. He told us he was going to make a concoction to put Bob to sleep."

John griped, "Well, I didn't know everyone was going to make such a fuss about it! It isn't like I'm trying to kill the man, you know? We can all see that he needs his sleep! And this spiked ale is the only way he's going to stop thinking about his dear, departed wife, and get a moment's rest!"

Evelyn replied, "Relax, John. Nobody here is against you, but you should've been honest with me about your plan. I've never tested those drugs with alcohol before, which means I can't guarantee it's a safe combination."

Suddenly, Bob reached out his hand, grabbed the drink from John, and began chugging.

Evelyn moved towards the group that was surrounding Bob.

"Stop him!" she ordered as she reached out to pull the cup away. However, John and Fred got their hands on it first and between the two of them, they managed to wrestle the cup out of Bob's hand, spilling what was left of the drink onto Bob's lap and chest.

Mina tried to suppress a laugh. She understood that Bob had grabbed the pint in a desperate attempt to deal with his pain, and she felt horrible for him. But she also couldn't help thinking he looked funny grabbing the cup and drinking so impetuously. It reminded her of how an upset toddler would behave at bedtime.

"I guess it's too late to find out where I'm staying," said Mina trying to lighten the mood.

"You didn't have to do that, mate," John spoke to Bob. "If I'd known it might cause you trouble, I never would've mixed those drugs with the ale."

Bob shrugged. "It's okay. You were right. I can't stop thinking about Maude. And I need to. At least for a while, so I can get some sleep. I don't feel like myself anymore. I don't know if sleep will help that, but I do know I'd rather conk out than keep feeling this pain."

Evelyn moved toward Bob and leaned down to give him a hug. Then she said, "Help me move him to the bedroom, gentlemen. He needs to lie down quickly."

Fred and John took ahold of Bob from each side and helped him walk to the bedroom that had been built for him to share with Maude. Bob's vision had started to blur, but he saw the soft, thin mattress stuffed tightly with wool and the suitcases that Maude had packed for them before she left New Waldoff.

He felt Fred and John ease him onto his back. His head was swimming, but he could feel his waking mind falling away as he lost himself to the darkness that was creeping in. Before he drifted off, he said, "Tell Fred to set up a tent for Mina in the living room. It will give her primacy and a place to sleep for now."

"Primacy?" Mina asked from the doorway.

Evelyn put her hand on Mina's shoulder and led her back into the living room. "He meant privacy, I'm sure. Are you okay sleeping here tonight or even until we can build you your own house, maybe?"

Before Mina could answer, Fred walked back into the room and said to her, "I could stay here too if you want some company. I'll help you keep an eye on Bob to make sure he doesn't have a bad reaction to the medicine and alcohol."

Evelyn smiled knowingly at the young couple. "That's fine, but keep in mind that I'll be coming and going throughout the night to check on Bob's vitals."

John walked back into the living room with a hangdog expression.

Evelyn asked, "Everything okay, John?"

"I didn't mean to put Bob in any danger with that drink. You all know that. Don't you?"

"Of course," said Mina. "You were just trying to help him. We all were."

Evelyn agreed. "Yes, we know you would never hurt anyone, John. But promise me you'll consult with me before slipping anyone a mickey next time. Okay?"

John nodded, and he and Evelyn began to head towards

the front door. Evelyn turned back, "So you two are officially planning to stay here tonight then?"

Fred looked at Mina questioningly, and Mina answered, "Sure. It will be like all the times I built forts out of couch cushions to sleep inside of."

"Was this recently?" Fred asked.

Mina laughed. "No. It was when I was a kid and my grandfather, I mean my father, would let me stay up late watching movies with him."

John chuckled. "A grown-up sleepover in Bob's living room, huh? Well, I hope you two actually plan on sleeping. I'm sure you could both use the rest after the day you've had."

"You have no idea," Fred replied.

Evelyn grabbed ahold of John's arm and began to guide him out the door. Then, before she closed it behind them, she said, "Just remember, I'll be back in an hour or so to check on Bob."

Fred saluted Evelyn jokingly, and Mina nodded as Evelyn walked out the door.

"Why do I suddenly feel like Evelyn is our mom?" Fred asked.

Mina smiled. "I was thinking that same thing."

LATER THAT EVENING, Mina and Fred lay on their sides facing each other inside a two-person tent they'd set up in the middle of Bob's living room. Mina rested her head on her hand, and Fred ran his fingers lightly through her hair as they talked.

"Did you remember anything about your past, Fred? When you were in the ice tunnels?" Mina asked through a muffled yawn.

"Not exactly." Fred frowned. "Serena showed me bits and pieces of scenes that I should have remembered, but I didn't. The memories actually spooked Ragher. He didn't understand how I was able to view memories from my life on Earth."

"Why not?"

"I guess Serena told him that the labyrinth only contained memories from the Moon."

"But that's not true?" Mina asked.

Fred waited a beat, then said, "Guess not."

Mina closed her eyes. She was nervous about falling asleep, perhaps because the only time she'd ever slept on the Moon, it hadn't felt like she was asleep at all. The dream about the woman in the yellow dress had haunted her for years. She'd thought of this nightmare and the dream about the elves often, only she had a hard time thinking of them as dreams and not memories.

When Mina returned to Earth, this feeling lingered; it began to feel like every dream she had was more than a dream. The vividness and intensity of her dreams strengthened so much, in fact, that Mina had to remind herself often that she'd been asleep once she awoke.

As she allowed herself to surrender to the dreamworld that awaited her, she whispered to Fred. "I wonder if it's time for you to take me to my mother."

Seconds later, Mina was asleep. This felt like a blessing to Fred, because the one thing that Serena had emphasized the most, before setting him free, was that under no circumstance was he to bring Mina to the ice tunnels.

His stomach had stayed twisted in knots the entire day, as he thought about how he was going to continue following Serena's orders without alienating the woman he loved. He let out a deep sigh and laid his head down to watch Mina sleep. He fell into a daydream where he imagined taking Mina to a faraway corner of the Moon realm, to a place outside Serena's reach—though he knew no such place existed. There they would live happily together, loving each other and possibly even starting a family of their own.

It was a sweet dream, but it broke Fred's heart a little. He knew that none of his fantasies of their future might ever come to fruition. He and Mina and all the rest of them had betrayed Serena, and it didn't matter that he was the only one who remembered what had happened. Serena remembered, too, and Fred suspected that no matter how carefully he followed her orders, she would still find a way to make them pay.

Mina awoke to the sound of metal gears clicking. Exhausted, she tried to pretend that the noise wasn't there, but the sound only grew louder the more she tried to ignore it. She opened her eyes while instinctively reaching for a pillow to cover her head. But to her dismay, she found that she was back inside her bedroom in the tiny cottage by the sea.

"What the...?" she blurted out as she jolted into an upright position. Her eyes darted frantically around the room as though trying to make sense of what they were seeing. Mina flew out of her bed and ran to the window. It was bright outside, brighter than she ever remembered seeing the little clearing before. Unnaturally bright.

"Think, Mina, think," she told herself. But her mind felt clouded. She remembered being back on the Moon, high up in the mountain valley with Fred and her friends. "Did I fall asleep? Is this just a dream?"

She walked around her room to test her theory. Her mirrored vanity was right where it should have been with her hairbrush and tiny porcelain jewelry box on top. She picked up the brush to examine it. Silver hairs were wrapped around the cylinder-shaped handle and woven through its bristles like fine silk thread spun around a loom.

"That doesn't seem right." Mina looked in the mirror and stepped back in horror at the sight of her reflection. Instead of her own smooth skin and dark hair projecting back at her from the glass, there was a woman she'd never seen before staring back at her. The woman had long white hair and prune-textured skin. Mina looked down at her own youthful hands and realized she had two of them again.

She stepped closer to the mirror and leaned in. The gnarly looking woman leaned closer too, perfectly in-sync with Mina's movements as though she were her reflection. Mina positioned her head so it was inches from the glass, staring into the woman's eyes to see if she recognized them as her own. They were dark, just like hers, but something about them looked different. They seemed colder.

Just as Mina began to take a step back, the woman in the mirror lunged at her from the other side of the reflection, causing Mina to fall backwards in fright. The glass shattered and burst into hundreds of tiny pieces, leaving only the mirror's empty frame behind. A horrible cackling laugh bounced off the walls of the bedroom, and the sound sent shivers down Mina's spine.

Suddenly, Mina understood that this room wasn't her bedroom. It had been made to look like it—but by who, she didn't know. The thought terrified her. She raced to the bedroom door and turned the crystal doorknob in her hand. She yanked open the door, and was met with a swarm of screaming, brown bats that flew past her into the bedroom. They screeched and clawed at her flesh, ripping at her hair and whipping her in the face with their wings.

Mina screamed for help, though she knew there was nobody to save her. Not knowing what else to do, she retreated from the door where the steady stream of bats continued to invade her room. She fought her way through the terrible creatures, making her way to the window where she planned to escape. After a few steps she realized there was something gritty covering the floor. It felt like sand. She kept walking, but when she reached the window, she found what was causing the grit. Several of the flying bats had caught fire and were disintegrating into ash right in front of her eyes.

Mina shoved her hands against the bottom window sash, pushed it upwards, and flung herself out of the cottage just as two fiery bats collided above her head. The window fell shut again with a loud crash, startling Mina who was face down in the grass with her eyes closed.

"This has to be a nightmare," she told herself. "You're on the Moon with Fred and Bob. You just have to wake up, Mina. Wake up, damn it!"

She hoped that when she opened her eyes, she'd be back inside the tent in Bob's small living room. But before she raised her head, she heard the loud clicking sound that had first alerted her to this new reality. She pushed herself off the ground and stood up. During the seconds she'd been lying face down, it had turned to nighttime. In front of her in the grassy field was a sight she recognized. There was a huge metal wheel, level to the ground, that sat in the clearing.

Mina's heart was pounding. Something about the loud, ticking wheel made her feel like she was being tested. She looked behind her. The bats were still flying around her room in a cyclone of flesh, fire, and ashes. She turned her gaze back to the wheel and held her breath as she spotted Fred standing in the center of the giant cog.

"Not again," Mina thought. She walked along the outside perimeter of the slowly rotating disc, digging her heels into the damp grass with every step. She remembered this recurring nightmare well and how it always ended with a tidal wave crashing over her and pulling her away, like the hand of the sea plucking her from the face of the Earth.

As she aligned herself with Fred's frontside, she was surprised that Fred didn't seem concerned at all about his predicament. He stood quietly in the center of the wheel, staring back at her calmly. The block of ice covered more of his face than it had in any of her previous nightmares. Fred's skin tone was palish blue, but only the area around his eyes and forehead were visible.

"Are you okay?" Mina called to him.

Fred didn't respond except to pull his hand towards himself in a waving motion, beckoning her to walk across the wheel to join him. Mina looked over her shoulder, expecting to see the giant wave coming for her. But there were only trees and darkness and a stillness that felt eerie.

"I can't, Fred," she told him, glancing down at the turning wheel. Long planks of metal ran from where Fred stood at the center of the wheel to the outer ring. However, there were wide gaps of space between the narrow planks, and it looked like a long fall into a dark hole if Mina were unable to keep her balance.

Fred beckoned to her again, but Mina was too scared to step out onto any of the rotating walkways which led to him. The sound from the clicking gears became louder, and Mina took a step back, nervous about what would happen next. The ground shook, and suddenly a solid wheel appeared underneath the top one, filling in the wide gaps. Mina relaxed a little, even though the clicking gears were now accompanied by a nauseating scraping that sounded like sharpened fork prongs being dragged across metal.

She looked at Fred. He motioned for her to come to him. Holding her breath, she walked out onto one of the moving planks, worried the solid wheel beneath her might not stay in place for long. Then she took quick steps across the walkway, and in no time, she was at the center with Fred. She threw her arms around him, relieved to have made it. She looked at his face and reached for the ice, but Fred grabbed her hands gently.

"But Fred, you're going to freeze to death! I mean, how can you even breathe like that?" she asked as she examined his face where a thin piece of ice seemed to be forming over his nostrils.

Fred shook his head again, sending up a cloud of frost around them from the tiny water crystals that had formed on the block of ice.

"Why did you want me to come to you if you don't need my help?" Mina asked.

But Fred ignored her. He moved to the side of the round platform where they stood, bent down, and pulled open a manhole cover that he'd been standing on top of. Fred pointed at Mina and then pointed down into the dark hole he'd opened.

"You want me to go in there?" she asked.

Fred nodded.

"No way! It's pitch black down there, and you can't even tell me where it goes!"

Fred became agitated. He pointed at Mina emphatically and then pointed again to the hole.

"No, Fred!" said Mina firmly. "You go!"

Fred shook his head and moved towards her, but Mina yelled at him, "I said no!"

Fred was finished arguing, though. He wrapped his arms around her and began to force her towards the hole. Mina screamed and kicked, trying to push Fred away from her. But he was much stronger than she was, and seconds later he had dropped her into the hole feet first.

Mina replayed the moment from years earlier when Dan had pushed her into a dark hole. Unlike that time, however,

Mina didn't fall. In fact, it felt like she'd gone nowhere at all. Instead, she was standing straight up, staring down a long tunnel made of ice. She took a few steps, but instantly the scene changed, and she was standing along a wooded trail. Rain was pouring down, and the air had a damp chill, which caused her to shiver.

She began running to get warm. Lightning struck, and the forest lit up around her. A second later, the ground shook as a loud clap of thunder rumbled across the sky. Then before the rolling thunder ceased, the scene began to glitch. The walls of the ice tunnel quickly came into view and then vanished. Reappeared and then vanished again. Sometimes the ice tunnel took the place of the forest, and other times it merged with it.

"It's not real," Mina said aloud. "So where am I?"

Suddenly, the forest scene took over once more, and Mina was flung down the trail by an invisible force. The cold rain pelted her exposed skin as she flew with her arms pushed out to her sides and her legs and torso in a stiff, upright position. The rain came down at a faster rate as time sped up, and lightning illuminated the forest's canopy, as if there was a wild party happening in the upper reaches of the forest.

Mina tried to scream but couldn't. She thought back to the insane ride the wings had taken her on when she first traveled to the Moon. Just like then, she had no idea where she was headed or whether she might be in mortal peril. She noticed signs hammered into the trees as she zoomed along the trail. They looked like the same ones that had forewarned of the last time she would ever see her beloved father and basset hound.

The moment had occurred soon after she first spotted the signs. She arrived home to discover Bonkers was missing. When she went searching for him, she found her father and lost pup in the ocean. They'd been formed by the sea's very mist and were standing atop the rolling water, staring back at her.

Mina knew she was being ushered through the memory of this day, but she didn't understand why. Just as this thought occurred to her, the scene changed. Her cold, damp skin was instantly dry, but she felt a weight on her back that she hadn't felt in some time. Dozens of people surrounded her, staring at her in amazement, including two familiar faces. It was the market's welcoming committee, Larry and Carla. The couple talked and fidgeted at twice that of any normal speed. Mina couldn't hear what they were saying, but it didn't matter because she'd already lived through this moment when she first arrived at Waldoff Market.

The scenery rearranged again, leaping to when Mina had fled the men in blue suits. The pace was even faster now than anything Mina had experienced before, and her body was beginning to feel the strain of all the quick motions. It was as though she were trapped inside a heavy robotic suit that she had no control over.

She was hit from behind, and her body lurched forward. She looked over her shoulder, but there was no one there. Seconds later, she was diving onto the ground between two market stalls, attempting to hide from the men in blue. She knew what came next—the poem and note she would find attached to her wing. It was a mystery she'd never solved, although she'd wondered about it several times over the years. Mina figured it had been someone connected to Ruth that pinned the little slip of paper to her wing. After all, a short time later Ruth had given her a similar note that'd tipped Mina off to Dan's existence.

The scene was moving so fast that Mina wasn't able to read the note this time, but she remembered what was written on it. It was a poem referencing *Jack & the Beanstalk*. And on the reverse side there was a message that read "You're in danger! Be like Jack!"

The message had prompted Mina to stop moments later in

front of a vine-covered stall where she was eventually kidnapped by a vine and launched over the top of the market. The whole thing had been quite unusual, and yet it was how Mina finally found Maude, her mysterious marketplace contact.

Suddenly, an idea came to Mina, and without thinking she asked aloud, "It was you all along. Wasn't it, Mother?"

The marketplace dimmed from view, leaving Mina back inside a long ice tunnel that sloped downwards into darkness. A stream of cold air blasted towards her.

"Why are you here?" boomed a deep voice.

"I don't know! Aren't you the one who brought me here?" Mina yelled back, shaking from the cold.

Sinister laughter echoed through the tunnel, and Mina's eardrums screamed in pain.

"I think you do know. You're lazy like the others. You don't try to remember. I was soft before when I allowed you to run and hide, but those days are over. No more childish games. It's time to begin."

"Begin what?" Mina demanded. She had tried her best to hold back her fear and confusion, but tears were trickling down her face now. The tears warmed her cheeks, but she hated how they gave away her emotions.

The loud voice didn't reply. The walls in the tunnel sprang to life in a display of thousands of sounds and scenes moving at warp speed. Millions of colorful flashes and sparks flowed across the walls, leaping out at Mina and assaulting her senses. It was horrific. She could feel herself pulling in every tiny nuance of every scene, like she was a microscopic sponge absorbing an ocean's worth of water all at once.

"Stop it! I can't take it!" she screamed, falling to her knees. She tried to cover her ears but realized that she no longer had any arms or even a body. She had transformed into the air around her. Mina felt sick, and though she no longer had a physical head, the place where her head should've been felt like it would explode.

Mina diverted her vision from the tunnel walls and stared straight into the darkness at the bottom of the slope. She wanted to run to it and face her monster, but before she had the chance to try, she was pulled once again by an unforeseen force, down the long corridor towards the darkness. She let out a warrior's cry, ready to take on whatever beast lay hidden behind the dark veil. But just as she reached the bottom of the icy incline, Mina awoke. She heard herself scream as she came to, although the sound was muffled by sleep.

"Wake up, Mina. Wake up," she heard Fred saying to her.

Mina opened her eyes but immediately burst into tears of pain. She pulled herself into a fetal position, grabbing onto both sides of her head with her hand and the stump on her forearm.

"Mina, what's wrong?" Fred asked. He sat up and rested his hand on her back.

"Help!" she cried. "My head! Help me! Please help me!"

Fred stared at Mina, not knowing what to do. Then all of a sudden, the tent flap was pulled back, and Evelyn appeared on the other side, peering in with great concern.

"What's going on?" she asked.

Mina had begun to whimper and shake, still holding onto her head.

"I don't know," Fred replied. "She was having a nightmare. Then she woke up and started screaming. I think it's her head. It seems to be hurting really bad."

"It's beginning!" Mina yelled at them. "She said it was time!"

Fred and Evelyn looked at Mina and asked in unison, "Who?"

Mina shrieked, "The Moon witch! My mother! Help me, Evelyn! Please!"

Fred felt his heart skip a beat at the mention of Serena. He understood now what was happening. He motioned to Evelyn to move out of the way so they could talk outside of the tent.

Once they were standing in Bob's living room he asked, "Do you have anything you can give Mina for the pain?"

Evelyn stared at the tent where Mina continued to wail and sob. "For a headache? Yes. But I'm pretty certain that whatever's happening to her goes well beyond a headache, Fred. I'm not even sure she's fully lucid right now. That talk about her mother being a Moon witch? Has she ever said anything like that before?"

Fred shook his head. "No, Evelyn. But look, she told me this kind of thing happens a lot," he lied. "It could just be worse this time. Could you give her an extra dose of the headache medicine? Maybe it will help take away some of the pain."

Evelyn looked suspicious. "Yeah, I can grab the medicine, but if Mina suffers from frequent migraines, I'll need to evaluate her once she's feeling better."

He nodded. "Sure, that's fine. But hurry back, okay?" Fred looked at the tent. "She's really suffering," he said tensely.

Evelyn left, but Fred didn't return to Mina right away. Her cries of agony were ripping him apart inside, and he clenched his fists in anger. Serena had told him what would happen to Mina, but she hadn't mentioned it would be painful. Not like this.

Fred felt helpless, and he began to question whether he'd done the right thing by bringing Mina back to the Moon. Serena had promised him that Mina wouldn't be physically harmed if he went along with her plan. But if the torment Mina was experiencing didn't seem like harm to Serena, then Fred wasn't sure it was right for him to trust anything she'd ever told him.

He remembered that Serena had insisted his loyalty to her

would be tested on his journey, but the excruciating pain Mina was being forced to endure felt like more than a test. It felt like a betrayal. And with those feelings sitting heavy in his chest, the tale that Serena had woven for him began to come unraveled.

CHAPTER 9

FIRE AT THE FACTORY

Dale arrived at the abandoned Sheep Spa the afternoon following his visit to Betsy's office. After Dale left her office, Betsy sent one of her henchmen to the old factory with a message for the guards who'd been watching Dale's empty jail cell for a couple of weeks.

The message was short. It explained that the men had been reassigned to the Moon's south pole and that they were to keep watch over the wolves who lived there until further notice. It also stated what would happen to them if they disobeyed Betsy's orders and returned to New Waldoff without permission. This part involved their bowels being chopped up and served in some sort of delightful delicacy that would be offered at all the finest eateries in New Waldoff—a threat made to prevent the news of the unauthorized prisoner transfer from ever leaking out.

"You've got to prove to Serena that you're tough," Betsy had told Dale before he left. "In fact, I'd like to see that side of you too. Setting the factory on fire will make a statement. Most normies don't have it in them to kill someone, especially not their own father. It will draw the attention of Serena's spies.

When they approach you, I want you to go along with whatever they say. Understand?"

Dale agreed to do everything Betsy told him to, but he still wasn't sure whether he'd be able to go through with it. He stood and stared at the outside of the ghoulish-looking, metal factory that had been his prison for so long. He pictured his father sitting alone inside the same jail cell that he too had occupied, wondering why the guards had left and if they were coming back.

Dale hated himself for thinking of his father at all. He knew it was a sign of his weakness. Weakness he'd spent his whole life trying to exorcise.

"What would Dan say if he could see your silly ass cowering in front of a big, dumb building like it's some kind of monster?"

He imagined his brother's voice. "Dale, you're a pathetic loser. Go set fire to that building so you can get a meeting with the lady god. Not our mother, the other one. Hopefully, she's attractive. Tell her you want an important position with power. Not that you deserve it, you coward."

Dale responded to his brother's imaginary voice, "I may be a loser and a coward, but you're extremely dead, Dan. Maybe if you'd been more cautious like your pathetic brother, you wouldn't be so dead. Also, I think the sinister lady god is our aunt. Not that you'd care, you sicko."

Dale knew he was just stalling, but it didn't matter. A tiny part of him considered going inside to say a final farewell to his old man, but he couldn't bring himself to do it. The thought of getting near his old cell again made his body break out in a cold sweat.

He walked around the outside of the building until he found what he was looking for. Up at the top of one of the boarded-up windows there was a tiny hole that Dale knew had been connected to an air filtration system from when the factory was used as a slaughterhouse. While the Sheep Spa was being transitioned into Dale's prison, the filtration system had been removed, but the vents were left inside the walls. In the first few weeks that Dale was locked up, he realized the vent at the top of his cell worked like a two-way amplifier between the outside walls of the Sheep Spa and his prison chamber.

He'd first noticed it when the guards were taking a smoke break at this particular corner of the building. Of course Dale hadn't dared to test whether the vent worked both ways. He knew that if it did and the guards heard him, they'd most likely find a way to seal the vent shut. It wasn't until a few weeks later when the three-headed sheep were talking to each other as they passed by the outside vent that Dale decided to try it out.

"Hey, sheep brains! Can you hear me out there?"

The sheep stopped talking, and Dale wasn't sure what had happened. But then he heard one of the sheep say, "Did you hear that?"

Another sheep spoke, "Why yes, but where in god's name did it come from?"

The third sheep explained, "I think there's a miniature person talking to us from that very tiny hole up there near the roof."

Dale was relieved at first, though the conversation that followed wasn't what he'd hoped for. It turned out, the sheep had a difficult time processing the concept of vents and amplification, and Dale spent more than an hour that day arguing with them about how he was a full-sized person who lived inside the factory and not a miniature person who lived inside the hole in the wall.

For years after this encounter, Dale tried to convince the sheep to go find Betsy, or as he described her in simple terms for the benefit of the sheep, "the lumpy lady in the black frock."

On multiple occasions, the sheep had reassured Dale that

they were off to go find 'the lumpy lady,' but each time when they returned to the vent, weeks later, they had little to no recollection of any of the conversations they'd previously had with Dale.

Eventually, Dale gave up, but in an effort to relieve some of his boredom, he adopted the hobby of screwing with the sheep, telling them all sorts of ridiculous stories to either frighten or annoy them. Dale's favorite was the one where he was King of the Moon. In this story, Dale claimed that he was the deceased ruler of the Moon realm. He stated that his evil godparents had put a spell on him so that his spirit would stay trapped inside the factory's walls forever.

Dale told the sheep that the one benevolent thing his godparents had done when casting their spell was to allow him to come to life again whenever the blue and green planet was at its highest point in the sky above the Moon. He declared that once he was brought to life again, he would be able to feast on the flesh and bones of the animals who surrounded the factory.

Dale repeated this story nearly every day for months. Then after he was through, he would ask the sheep if the blue and green planet was at its peak. But every time he asked, the sheep swore that the planet was low in the sky or not in the sky at all.

"Are you sure?" Dale would ask. "I'm feeling mighty hungry today. How about you send one of your animal friends into the factory for a chat?"

Other times, Dale would shout, "Oh boy! I think I can feel my hands coming to life again! Soon the rest of me will follow, and I'll eat like a king once more!" At this point, Dale would begin banging on the walls below the vent to scare the sheep into thinking he was coming for them.

Sometimes, on lazier days, Dale would only moan and howl whenever he heard the sheep passing nearby. And if he felt up to it, he would mention a few words about how desperate he was to devour the tender meats of all the scrumptious barnyard animals.

Later on, when Dale grew tired of messing with the sheep, he began to tell all the animals that he heard passing by to eat the 'delicious' hay from the forbidden haystack at the far side of the Sheep Spa. He knew that there was rotten hay that had been moved to a fenced off section on the far side of the factory because he'd overheard the sheep talking about how it had gone bad after being treated with the wrong pesticide.

The animals believed Dale's story because they wanted to. He had made the hay sound too appealing for them not to want to at least try it. He told them that it was magic dried grass that would take away all their aches and pains and keep them from ever getting sick again. And then once the animals were good and sick from sour hay stomach, he sold them on drinking the non-potable water to cure their terrible indigestion.

Dale had a decent enough time pulling off this silly scheme, and he eventually used it to get the council's attention so that Bob was forced to pay him a visit. This made Dale happy for three reasons. One, it meant he was upsetting Bob's day-to-day life. Two, he got to pass along the information that Betsy had told him to in exchange for freedom and a spot on the council. And three, it gave him a way to break up the monotony of his day.

"Bob?" called Dale, though not too loudly since he wasn't sure whether he was making the right decision by trying to contact his father. "It's me, Dale, your last remaining offspring."

There was no reply, and Dale wondered if the vent might have been sealed up after he left the Sheep Spa. It was easy to imagine his father alerting the guards to the vent that wasn't meant to be there. He always was a do-gooder, even when it didn't do him any good to be that way. "Especially then," thought Dale.

In that moment, Dale decided to go ahead and say what he wanted to say without thinking about whether Bob could hear him or not. "Look, Bob, I know we don't get along, but I'd still like you to know that this isn't personal. I have an important job to do, maybe the most important one I'll ever do. This place isn't being run by who we thought. It turns out, Theia was Mom all along. Can you believe that? And she has a couple of siblings. One of them is an okay guy, but he's kind of frightening at first sight. The other one is a complete nut job from what I can tell, and I guess she's the one who's actually in charge of everything.

"Anyway, the only way I can find out what she wants is to burn this place to the ground. So, I'm going to do it. I just want to say that I'm sorry for the inconvenience it might cause you. Hopefully, you can see why I've gotta go ahead with the plan, though. We all know I've spent my life acting as someone else's stooge, but this is how I'm finally going to break out of that mold and make my own mark. It's probably too much to ask, but maybe you could finally be a little bit proud of me."

There was still no answer, so Dale decided he'd take this as a sign that his father had accepted his fate and planned to die stoically instead of begging for his life. Dale knew, of course, that there was an even better chance that his father hadn't heard a word of his speech, but he chose to ignore that possibility because it wasn't what he wanted to believe.

Dale returned to the horse he'd ridden to the Sheep Spa and opened the satchel that hung from its saddle. He took out several gray paper packets and a jade lighter. Then he gathered up kindling from some nearby scraggily bushes and began to scatter the sticks and twigs in six different spots around the factory's perimeter. Each time he laid the kindling down, he lit one of the packets on fire and dropped it on top of the pile.

Alas, by the time Dale had set the last gray packet on fire, the front of the Sheep Spa was completely engulfed in flames. He stood thirty feet back from the building next to where his horse was tied up and watched as the prison was swallowed by the fire, pondering what it would be like to be an orphan now.

Soon however, his thoughts were interrupted by a voice next to his ear. "Such a shame. A mad ghost-king lived inside of that factory once. Do you remember?"

Dale jumped out of his skin as he turned to face the three-headed sheep. He hadn't been expecting to see any animals at the factory; he'd assumed Betsy's men had hauled them all off to New Waldoff already.

"What in the mother of tin can rat bands are you doing here?" Dale shouted at them.

The second sheep ignored Dale's reaction and replied to the first sheep, "Oh yes. If I recall correctly, his fairy godmother trapped him inside for being naughty. Then, she took away all his toys and made him eat and drink hay soufflé and poisoned water until he became a good little king again."

The third sheep stared into the flames and said, "All hail, the mad ghost-king! May his lust for flesh be put to rest, and may he never come back to haunt us!"

"I don't understand," said Dale. "Why didn't the three…or one…or however many of you there are go with the men who took the animals away?"

The first sheep replied, "Go with the men? To our deaths? No thank you. I'd rather stay here and make smores with you."

The second sheep corrected him. "No, no. This man isn't here to make smores like the lawyer doctor detective used to. Can't you see? That fire is much too big to make smores with. If you got close enough to roast a marshmallow, you'd end up on fire too."

The third sheep protested, "Well, if you had a big enough stick and marshmallow, you could make a really big smore.

However, I never cared much for smores. The marshmallows get stuck in my teeth and the chocolate and crackers taste like hay."

The first sheep scoffed. "They were hay. The doctor lawyer detective wrapped the marshmallows up in hay. Only the little ones got to eat the chocolate and crackers."

The second sheep recounted, "Oh, yes. That's right. Those little boys used to wipe their hands on our backside when they were finished eating. I haven't seen those pip squeaks in a while. What do you think ever happened to them?"

The third sheep added, "Oh, yes. There was melted chocolate, cracker bits, and sticky marshmallow covering our wool when they were through. Then that one goofy horse would follow us around for weeks, biting all the spots where those little brats had wiped their grimy paws on us. To answer your question though, brother, one of those brats is dead, and the other is right here. See!"

The first two sheep looked at Dale aghast. "Oh dear, oh dear. Why does he look like that? Did he eat too many smores?" asked the first.

"He's old now and his hair looks like straw. I feel repulsed and famished," stated the second.

"Yes, well embrace that feeling, brothers, because this is who the empress has sent us to fetch."

"Wait, what?" Dale asked as the roof collapsed into the burning factory.

The sheep and Dale took a couple of steps back. "You're saying Serena sent you? You three are her henchmen? Geez, maybe Bets got this all wrong. I mean, if you three are Serena's henchmen, that doesn't exactly say much for her."

The first sheep looked puzzled. "Who said a lot about her?"

The second sheep snickered. "You're one to judge! You don't even have henchmen."

"I'm not a god!" Dale fired back.

The third sheep said, "No, certainly not. You don't have the countenance or the demeanor to be a god. If we're making comparisons, then you're more like a worn-out shoe or a sad puppet that no one likes to play with. But you'll have to excuse my brothers. Their memories aren't as sharp as mine. Serena zapped their brains too many times. She realized a long time ago that she doesn't need all three of us to know everything. So, to keep things simple, she fries their memories whenever they find out things that she doesn't want them to know. She does it to me, too, sometimes. But less often, since one of us needs to be able to carry out her orders without forgetting what they are. Or at least I think so."

"So, she ordered you to come find me?" asked Dale.

"Is that right?" asked the first sheep. "I thought we were supposed to be picking up one of the demi-gods. This man looks like an old clown, and not even one of those evil-looking, funny ones. Oh, look! The campfire is almost finished eating the Spa," said the first sheep.

"We better move out of the way. I think the walls are about to come down," said the second sheep.

"Yes, well it was time to move anyway. Ready, brothers? Let's go!"

Suddenly, giant rings of electric blue light shot out around Dale and the three-headed sheep. Dale ducked, sensing something scary was about to happen. Then he glanced back at the burning Sheep Spa one last time before they disappeared.

CHAPTER 10

THE VOICE INSIDE

In The Days Before the Wolf Massacres

From a very young age, Helen knew she wasn't like the other humans on the Moon. For one, her mom and dad were the first and most well-known of all the Moon Travelers. This meant that she'd never known a time when her parents weren't being stopped in public or visited in their home by people who had some sort of problem they needed solving—whether it be related to relationship or mechanical mishaps.

Helen sensed early on that people were magnetically drawn to Maude and Bob, but she was told it was because her parents had helped the other travelers make it across the neon bridge. However, Helen secretly learned that this wasn't the true reason people gravitated to them.

Another difference Helen was aware of was that she and her brothers grew older, unlike all the other Moon Travelers. Her parents told her this happened because humans were supposed to grow older. They said that when the Moon Travelers crossed over the neon bridge, their internal clocks transformed so that their bodies no longer showed the effects of time. But again, Helen was aware there was more to it than what her parents knew.

Helen also wasn't like the others in that she had an unparalleled kinship to the wolves. The only other human who had become close with the wolves was Ruth, but Ruth's relationship with them wasn't the same as Helen's. Ruth had been good to the wolves, acting as a human ambassador to the packs, whereas Helen had been accepted by the wolves as one of their own from the time she was an infant.

Helen was told that her kinship to the wolves was due to the fact that they'd saved her from a terrible illness when she was small. She was told that this had created an unbreakable bond between them. Yet again, Helen knew this wasn't the whole story.

The final and most important way in which Helen understood she was different from all the others was that her first memories were not of her parents, or of her brothers, or even of the lunar wolves. Helen's first memories were of a voice that whispered to her from inside her own head. It was a sweet voice that told her how special she was, how smart she was, and how brave she would one day become. But unlike all the other ways that Helen knew she was different, no one ever attempted to explain the voice to her, because no one else in the entire world knew about the voice that told Helen of the Moon's secrets.

MAX RACED through the streets of Waldoff on his way to Bob and Maude's. He'd decided on his long ride back to the

Dayside that he needed to come clean with his old friends and was prepared to tell them all about his relationship with Helen and what had happened at the greenhouse. It was the only way he knew of to protect Helen. He just hoped that Maude and Bob would go easy on him when they found out how much he cared for their daughter.

Max was a few blocks away from their house, passing by John's pub, when he nearly plowed into Helen as she exited the building. Her long dark hair was pulled back in a ponytail, and she was wearing a flowing, yellow sundress that complimented her dark tan skin. Max's heart skipped a beat. In all his angst, he'd forgotten he was supposed to bump into Helen "casually" at John's after the greenhouse so they could discuss what'd happened.

"Max!" she exclaimed. "Where are you running off to in such a hurry?"

Max held his breath, scolding himself for not remembering to take a different route to Bob and Maude's. "I can't talk now, Helen. I'm on my way to see your parents."

Helen kept her cool, but he could tell by her eyes she was concerned.

"Oh, I see," she said. "Well, I'm headed that way now. I'll join you." Helen looped her arm through his and pulled him forward as the two began to walk side by side.

"What happened at the greenhouse?" she asked in a hushed tone. "You were supposed to meet me at John's. Remember?"

Max surveyed the street as they walked, nervous he might find prying stares everywhere he looked. "I know, but I changed my mind. And you shouldn't be holding my arm like this. It will draw people's attention. They'll wonder what I'm doing walking around like this with a twenty-year-old who's not my daughter."

Helen pulled her arm away but said, "For the last time, we look the same age, Max."

Max stopped and turned towards her. "But we're not the same age, Helen. And *you* might not think that's a big deal, but everyone else here does. They know who you are, who your parents are. And people will talk, especially in this climate. It won't matter soon though, I suppose. I've decided to tell your parents everything. They need to know so they can protect you."

Max started to walk again, but Helen grabbed his arm and pulled him back around to face her. "No, Max. You don't get to decide this. They're *my* parents."

Max looked at Helen's hand on his arm and then glanced around at the other street-goers. They were starting to draw attention. "We can't do this here. Come on," he said as he pulled his arm away, motioning for her to follow him down the block to a narrow side street that was practically devoid of other pedestrians.

Max stayed silent until they were far enough away from other people so as not to be overheard. "Look, I'm sorry, Helen. But I should never have allowed us to get involved like this. Maybe it's true what everyone says—that nobody ages physically or emotionally once they get here—but that doesn't make our relationship okay. And now Dan and Betsy know about us. We were set up to overhear Betsy and Rufus that day. They wanted us to confront them because they want you to come to the Darkside. I'm supposed to deliver you to your brother."

Helen looked shocked. "What? Why?""

Max groaned. "Dan's developed a truth serum that he wants to use on you. He thinks you have a secret locked away in your head that not even you know about. He's hoping he can find out what it is."

Helen laughed in disbelief. "That's ludicrous! What secret?"

"I don't know. Dan wouldn't tell me, but he wants us to meet him at Black Ice Glacier where he's building his fort."

"Well, that's silly. I just won't go. It's not a problem, Max."

Max argued, "It is a problem, Helen. He says he'll tell your parents about us if we don't show up there in the next two weeks. But it won't be a problem soon because I've decided to save him the trouble by telling them myself."

"No, Max. I won't allow it," Helen said with a sudden seriousness that made her sound more like a seasoned general than a young woman.

"Yes, Helen. I have to, and honestly, I want to. I need to come clean."

Helen felt a flood of hurt rising up inside of her, but she did her best not to show it. Instead, she listened to the voice that she knew so well as it gave her instructions on how to react.

He's weaker than you, Helen. If you really love this man, then you'll have to remain calm. Show him you can be mature about the situation.

Helen did as the voice said and asked in a matter-of-fact tone, "Is that all Dan threatened to do? To turn us in to my parents? That seems pretty tame for him."

"No," said Max, "at first he threatened to tell his followers we were spies." Max was relieved he didn't have to lie about this part. Omitting the truth was always easier than lying, and this was exactly how Max planned to handle the situation regarding the carrot Dan was trying to lure Helen with.

Max had already decided on the way home that he wasn't going to tell Helen of Dan's offer to temporarily spare the wolves in exchange for her presence on the Darkside. He feared what she would do if she learned that surrendering herself to Dan could keep the wolves safe, even temporarily.

He's hiding something, Helen. You need to find out what it is.

Helen said to Max, "I should've gone with you. I would've told my brother what he could do with his threat."

Max shook his head. "Don't talk like that, Helen. He's much more dangerous than you give him credit for. He and Betsy mean business. Dan made it clear his followers are planning to go after the wolves soon. We need to tell your parents everything. Also, you need to stay as far away from the wolves as possible. Everyone already knows how close you are to them. I get that Dan's your brother, but if his band of hoodlums decided to come after you, I'm certain he wouldn't lift a finger to protect you unless he thought he had something to gain from it. Now that you know he wants something from you, keep that knowledge in your back pocket and use it as a bargaining tool if, god forbid, you ever need it."

Helen felt a massive swell of anger and heartache. It was as if she'd just learned that the wolves had been defeated before the attacks even began. She wanted to run to Neriti and Axel and let them know what was coming, but the voice inside of her told her to do otherwise.

It's going to be okay, Helen. We knew this day would come, and Max is right. For you to complete your mission, you will need to stay out of the way for a while. Tell Max that you want him to go to your parents too. But instead of telling them the truth, tell Max to ask them for their permission to be your bodyguard. This is a gift I am giving you. It will buy you more time to spend with your beloved.

Helen and Max turned down a secluded alleyway a block from her parents' house, one they'd become familiar with during their secret affair. Helen stopped in front of a large brick wall and leaned against it. She grabbed ahold of Max's hands and pulled them to her waist. Tears formed in her eyes, but she wiped them away with the back of her hand and said, "I understand the need for honesty, Max, and I've listened to every word you've said. You clearly have feelings for me, or you wouldn't be trying so hard to protect me. But what do you *want?*"

Max shook his head. "I don't know what you mean, Helen. I mean, I want you to be safe, and—"

Helen cut him off. "So, keep me safe," she said softly, pulling his body against hers. Whispering in his ear, she said, "While the wolves are busy fighting, I'll need someone to watch out for me. You could be my bodyguard if we don't tell my parents about us just yet."

As she spoke to Max, Helen positioned her leg so that it was pressing against Max's inner thigh.

He tried to guard himself against the spell she was putting him under, but he felt hypnotized. For years, he'd convinced himself it was fine that he was all alone on the Moon, telling himself that he was strong enough to live for ages without any romantic prospects. Yet whenever he felt the fire between him and Helen ignite, all those notions of eternal celibacy flew out the window. Their chemistry was unlike anything he'd ever known. More than just magnetic, it was like every single atom in his body wanted to attach itself to her.

He took one of his hands from Helen's waist and wrapped his fingers around the back of her neck, pulling her into him with a firm but gentle tug. Then he leaned in and kissed her while running his hands through her hair and up and down the back of her silky, yellow sundress.

Part of his brain was telling him what a fool he was being, but he didn't care. He wanted her so badly that nothing else mattered in that moment. She could've asked him to do anything for her—even drink Dan's truth serum which he assumed was poison—and he would've gladly done it.

As the heat between them continued to build, it was Helen who finally pushed away. She clutched his hands in hers, and they both caught their breath.

"Does this mean you agree with me, Maxie? You'll ask my parents if you can be my bodyguard?" she asked sweetly.

Max looked like a lovesick puppy with Helen's lipstick stains covering the bottom half of his face. He nodded helplessly, even though his gut was telling him he was making a mistake.

"Oh, that's wonderful! Thank you, Max! Now, we better go tell my parents what you found out. But they're not at the house right now—they're working out of the barn today."

Fifteen minutes later, after spending most of the walk composing themselves, Max and Helen made their way up the small hill to her parents' work barn on the outskirts of the city. The large door at the front was wide open, and as they approached, they saw Bob and a young-looking Maude hovering over a long table. On one end, there were giant beakers filled with colorful liquids, and on the other sat long, curved metal scraps and several toolboxes.

Maude was the first to notice Helen and Max entering the barn, and she nudged Bob to look up. "Hi, Helen. Hi, Max. What are you two up to?" she asked.

Max resisted the urge to look at Helen for support. He'd tried to prepare himself for what he would say when he and Helen went to see his old friends, but once they were there, it all became a little too real. Max felt the bottom drop out from underneath him as self-consciousness reared its ugly head. He worried that anything he did or said might give away his feelings, even the slightest smile or bat of an eye.

Before he was able to find any words, Helen spoke for them. "I ran into Max on the street looking for you. He said he just got back from picking up Betsy's vines at the greenhouse and overheard Dan and Betsy talking about how your lunatic son is planning to go after the wolves soon. There could be an attack any day now."

Max looked at Helen from the corner of his eye and

nodded, still trying to find the courage to speak to Maude and Bob.

Maude seemed a bit suspicious. "Is that right, Max?" she asked.

Max nodded again and said, "Yes. It's true. But apparently, Dan is working on something else too. Possibly a truth serum. I heard Betsy say that it will make everyone's lives better. Whatever that means."

Bob frowned. "That's not good. Maude and I have long suspected that Dan's been making his own formulas, anticipating the day he might come up with something sinister yet hoping it would never come to that."

"What are we going to do about the wolves, though?" Helen asked. "I need to go tell them what's about to happen. Axel hasn't been around lately. I know he and Neriti have been busy preparing the others, but I'm worried they don't realize that Dan's followers are ready to pounce."

Maude shook her head and said, "Absolutely not. No way, Helen. If what Max overheard is true, then you have to stay close. Nobody else has been as close to the wolves as you, and everyone in this town knows it. If you go heading off to them now, Dan's disciples might think to target you also."

"That's exactly what I told her," Max interjected. "No offense, but I don't think your son has ever cared for anyone else's best interest. I expect there'll be some serious bloodshed between the wolves and those who go after them, and I don't think it's a good idea for Helen to be anywhere near that. If these ruffians get it in their heads to go after the humans who they suspect are supporting the wolves, I don't think Dan will do anything to stop it."

"I agree," said Bob. "Helen, it would be best if you stayed close to your mother and me during the next several weeks. We could use your help here working on the new inventions and formulas we've been tinkering with. What do you say to helping us out?"

Helen looked around at these three much older adults who looked like her contemporaries. Each was staring at her with a look of worry and hope, and it made her furious.

"What I *think* is that I don't want to be cooped up with you guys here for weeks or even months! And also, I expected a lot more out of you! What was the point of all those top-secret meetings with your friends if you were never planning to do anything to protect the wolves? You all remember that they were the ones who saved my life, right? And now you're just fine hanging them out to dry? Without even a warning about the evil that's headed their way?"

"Don't be ridiculous," said Maude. "Of course we'll warn the wolves. We just don't want you to be the one to do it. I'll send a silver bird to Neriti and Axel right away. I'm sure they'll alert the other wolves as soon as they get it."

Helen shot back, "It's not that simple, Mom. The other wolves are spread out over great distances. It could take days, even a week, to alert them all. This isn't right! I thought there would be a plan!"

Helen began to weep, which made Max even more uncomfortable since his instinct was to take her in his arms and console her. Luckily, Bob was already rushing to his daughter's aide. He put his arms around her, and Helen buried her face in her father's shoulder as she continued to cry.

In the meantime, Max made his way over to Maude to have a private word. "Look, Maude. I can't blame Helen for not wanting to be cooped up all day while the fighting is going on. I don't mind watching her, though, for however long the fighting takes. She can accompany me as I make my daily deliveries. It will give her some exercise, which might help her expel the dark thoughts she's bound to have on account of what her friends are about to go through. I'm not planning to do any deliveries outside the city anyway, since I doubt it will be safe for a while."

Maude raised an eyebrow. "You really wouldn't mind? You know that's a lot of responsibility to take on, Max. Bob and I would need to know that you'd be willing to put yourself in harm's way if it came to that."

Max felt a little funny about responding to Maude's question, but he told himself it was okay. After all, he had known Helen her entire life.

"Definitely I would," he said. "I'd do anything to help you guys out, and Helen too. It can't be easy for her, knowing that her brothers are responsible for all the malice towards her friends."

She sighed. "Yes, I'm sure that's true. Honestly, it's not easy for any of us. I wish there was more we could do besides talk. But as you know, we'd be risking the entire town's safety if we tried to go against Dan and all the people who seem hell bent on taking down the wolves. I just hope to god the wolves can protect themselves against what's to come."

"Me too," agreed Max. "Because to be honest, from what I've gathered about your son, if the wolves fall, I think we might be next."

Maude bit her lip. "Yes, well, let's hope it doesn't come to that. Now, if you'll excuse me, I need to send that message to Axel and Neriti."

Maude walked towards the back of the large barn while Max went to check on Helen, who was using her father's handkerchief to wipe her eyes.

"I'd be happy to walk you home if you feel like getting some rest," Max told her.

Helen looked at him and nodded. "Yes, thank you. I'd like that."

Bob smiled with a look of relief. "That's thoughtful of you, Max. I appreciate it."

Max smiled back, though a bit sheepishly. "It's not a problem. I talked to Maude, and we agreed that if Helen doesn't want to spend all day with you here, then she can accompany me on my daily deliveries."

Bob asked his daughter, "What do you say, darling? Does that sound like something you'd like to do?"

Helen looked at Max. "Yeah, I guess so. It's probably better than being stuck here or in the house all day."

Max knew Helen was only acting aloof to throw her father off the scent of their secret love affair, but her words still stung a little.

"Great then. It's settled. Let us know if you ever need a day off, Max. She's a handful sometimes, you know. I think it must be that wolf side of her that makes her so wild," said Bob teasing.

Max started to feel extremely awkward again, and so he only nodded in reply. He knew Helen must have sensed his unease, because she quickly said her goodbyes to her parents, and they left.

On their way back to her house, Helen was quiet, lost inside a cloud of emotions. Finally, after a long silence, Max asked, "Is everything okay? I mean, despite, you know, that nothing is?"

Helen responded, "I guess I just never really thought about what it would actually feel like when we arrived at this point in time. Neriti knew this day would come; she tried to prepare me for it my entire childhood. But I was so focused on how it would happen and what it would mean that I didn't think about how it would make me feel."

Helen paused for a moment, then continued, "Can I tell you a secret, Max?"

"Of course," he answered. "You can tell me anything."

The voice spoke to Helen before she could go on, though.

Don't do it, Helen. Men don't always handle it well when they find out the woman they care for is some kind of 'chosen one.'

But Helen ignored the voice's warning. "I want to run away from here and fight with the wolves, only I know I'm not supposed to. Neriti told me about a prophecy she received before I was born. It stated that one day I will have a major role to play in keeping my brothers from taking control of the Moon. The wolves have been training me for this my entire life. They said that I would sense when the time is right, but it's hard to know what that means. I thought that the time might be now, but I've been led to believe otherwise."

Helen was keenly aware that she had to be a bit vague with her explanation because she couldn't let Max know about the voice. She knew it was too dangerous. The voice had warned her that her entire family would perish if she ever told a soul. And when Helen once dared to question this, she'd spent months afterwards having terrifying nightmares about her family's demise, which she understood was no coincidence.

Well, I guess we'll see where this goes. Hopefully, he won't want to know who made you believe otherwise.

"What does that mean that you've been led to believe otherwise?" Max asked.

I thought so.

Helen bit her lip, a habit she'd inherited from her mother. Stumbling over her explanation, she said, "I just mean that if it were my time to protect the Moon from my brothers, then wouldn't Dale be more involved in all of this, too? Yet lately, whenever he's not at one of his rallies, he's holed up in his room, sulking. I think maybe he and Dan got into a fight. My parents think he's depressed. All he does anymore is sleep."

"I see," said Max, although his thoughts had begun to stray from their conversation. He wasn't sure what to make of Neriti's prophecy. He'd never given the wolves' belief in the Great Energy much credence. However, it did seem strange that Helen had revealed this secret about a prophecy from long ago on the very same day that he'd withheld information from her that might give her the opportunity to save the lunar wolves from her maniacal brother. Max didn't know if he truly believed it was all connected, but it did make him feel more anxious about keeping the secret.

Helen noticed that Max had gotten quiet.

I told you. Men want to be the savior or the villain in their story. Clearly, he's taking this hard. Either that or he knows more than he's telling you.

Helen talked back to the voice in her head by thinking, "You don't know that. That's the way Father looks when he's thinking about food. Maybe Max is just deciding what he wants for dinner."

When they arrived at Helen's house, Max walked her to the front door. "Okay. I'll see you tomorrow," he said.

Helen looked disappointed. "Don't you want to come in for a little while? Dale is normally at one of his rallies during this time of day. We could discuss what I was telling you before. I'm sure you have some questions."

Max shook his head. "No, Helen. I get it. You've always had a special connection to the wolves. I'm guessing this is one of the reasons why. But I need to go to John's now for a meal. It's been a long couple of days, and I'd like to get a bite to eat before I turn in for the night."

"I could come with you," Helen suggested.

"No, that's okay. I need some time to think."

And this was true. Max did need some time to think about everything he had learned. But in addition, a twinge of guilt was beginning to fester inside of him—guilt for not telling Helen about Dan's offer. Max still wasn't going to tell Helen the truth, but he no longer felt justified about this decision.

See, my dear. He's avoiding you now.

But Max alleviated some of Helen's fears by reaching out

and squeezing her hand gently. "I'll come over around eight tomorrow to pick you up. I've got to warn you, though. Hauling other people's junk around may seem glamourous from the outside, but it's not exactly all it's cracked up to be."

Helen laughed. "That's okay. As long as I'm with you, I'm sure it will be ten barrels of monkcys."

Max smiled at Helen's attempt at an old expression. Then, he let go, leaving her standing outside her parents' home, watching him as he walked away.

CHAPTER 11

DALE & EMPRESS SERENA

"Oof!" Dale hit the ground with a sickening thud. He was disoriented from the teleporting journey the sheep had taken him on, but immediately, he noticed that the light around him looked odd. It had a bright, sterile glow, the kind that felt unnatural and slightly ominous.

Dale rolled over from his stomach onto his back. Slowly, he sat up. The sheep were standing next to him, but there was something strange about them. "Why do you three look different?" Dale asked rubbing the growing knot on his forehead where his skull collided with the ground.

"What do you mean different? Different how?" asked the first sheep.

"Don't be stupid," the second one said to Dale. "We're no different and neither are you. You're still fat and ugly, and we're still sheep."

The third sheep attempted to explain to the others, "Brothers, he's referring to the fact that we've come apart. Separate bodies, you see?"

The first sheep looked down at himself. "Looks the same to me."

The second sheep copied the first by glancing down at himself also. "Oh yes, I remember. We used to be attached. Seems like ages ago now."

"It was thirty seconds ago," said the third in disbelief. "But okay, fine. I'm glad we've all moved on. It is much nicer not to have to share a digestive tract anymore. I don't know what you two were eating besides hay, but it caused a ton of bloat."

"Dirt and twigs," confessed the first sheep.

"I sucked on a few house mice from time to time. Much sweeter than a bitter dormouse. Plus, I enjoy the way their tiny paws tickle the inside of my mouth."

"We're sheep! We don't eat mice!" exclaimed the third.

The first sheep said, "If I recall, we were humans once."

"I don't *eat* mice," the second sheep said to the third. "I just suck on them occasionally. Wait, we were humans? I don't remember that."

The third sheep confirmed, "Yes, we were humans thousands of years ago, but we've been sheep much longer. But just so you know, humans don't eat..." The third sheep paused, then looked at Dale and asked, "You're a human-like creature. Humans don't eat mice, right?"

Dale shook his head. He hadn't been listening to most of the sheep's conversation because he was trying to wrap his head around where they were. "No," he muttered in response. "At least not the sane ones. What is this place?"

The sheep started walking towards a white dome with a dark doorway in its center. It stood like a giant eyeball rising out of the vast stretch of land that was bathed in the ominous light. Dale felt the eye watching him, and this made him shiver slightly.

"Am I supposed to follow you?" he asked the sheep as they continued to walk away from him.

"Follow us if you dare." The first sheep giggled.

The second one looked over his shoulder at Dale. "This

way to the empress. Not like you have a choice. There's nowhere else to go."

The third sheep countered, "Well, actually he does have a choice. The entry to the labyrinth isn't enclosed. That's the Darkside right out there. He could make a break for it if he wanted to. Not like any of our stubby legs are going to catch him, even if he is round in the middle. But I imagine the empress would just make us go after him again if he did."

Dale rolled his eyes and started following the sheep. "Well, when you put it that way. You know, you three bozos talk too much. You remind me of all the women I know. Next time, you should just say 'yes' or 'no.'"

"Yes," said the first sheep.

"No," said the second.

"Dear heavens," said the third. "This meathead is calling *us* long-winded? Brothers, we should reassess how we converse if this walking stream of consciousness thinks *we're* too chatty. Do you think only one of us should speak from now on? You know, sum things up on behalf of the rest of us? Keep it short? I've often heard that brevity is the spice of life."

"That's absurd. We don't talk too much. Well, you do maybe," said the first sheep.

"Not going to happen. We all get a turn. Always have, always will," added the second.

"Yeah, I didn't think so, but it was worth a shot," said the third.

They reached the entrance to the labyrinth, and Dale peered into the dark, rectangular gap in the dome.

"Hmm. That's funny," the first sheep commented. "There's normally a light on in the tunnel. Do you think the empress has gone to sleep?"

"I can't remember the last time I slept," said the second.

"Do I think the immortal, disembodied goddess that lives down this hole went to sleep? No, I do not. It's more likely we each have permanent brain damage and have misremembered that there was ever a light in the tunnel at all."

"Well, I'm not going down there," said Dale.

The first sheep said, "No one's making you, you know? But could you do us a favor and look down the tunnel to see if there's a light on at the bottom? None of our necks are long enough."

Dale moved into the doorway and leaned his head inside to try and get a better view of the bottom. "Nope. It's pitch black —" But before he finished his sentence, the first sheep charged Dale from behind, headbutted him in the back, and sent Dale headfirst down the steep incline. Dale shouted a series of swear words as the second sheep laughed mockingly.

"What an idiot! Hard to believe he's a demi-god."

The third sheep replied, "Well, he was never as clever or diabolical as his brother, but that made him more trusting. Probably not a trait we should beat out of him. Hmm, brothers?"

The other two sheep shrugged indifferently. Then they each took a turn jumping into the dark ice tunnel and riding it down on their bellies with their legs splayed out in front of them. The third sheep followed, landing at the bottom of the steep incline on top of the others.

There was light in the small room at the bottom of the slide. A tall sheet of ice scraped quickly along the frozen ground behind them, blocking the pathway out. All three sheep stood up and shook themselves off. The first one let out a grumpy bleat. "Baaaa! I hate how cold it is. It doesn't matter if my coat is thick; I always feel as if I need five more layers to keep warm! Why does she keep it so frigid?"

The second sheep answered, "Too warm and the tunnels would melt! You see that they're made of ice, don't you?"

The third sheep spoke to Dale, who was once again face down on the ground, "Sorry for the dirty trick my brother played on you, but we have to follow orders. The empress is expecting you. Come this way and mind the twirling ice walls. They move pretty fast, but if you walk in a straight line and keep up, they won't bother you."

"Twirling ice walls? What the blazes?" said Dale as he brought himself up to a standing position. But pretty soon he had his answer as the walls around them began to break apart into separate sheets of ice. They moved swiftly to and from like they were following coordinated dance steps.

Dale jumped out of the way fast to avoid being run over by a gargantuan piece of icy wall.

"Holy hell! These things have a mind of their own!" he exclaimed, reaching out to push against one of the thick sheets that was headed right for him.

The first sheep laughed and said, "You'll be flattened if you do that. Flat as a pancake! The empress will be forced to work her magic to keep you alive. Then you'll be a puddle of goo and flesh, but a talking one, I suppose."

Upon hearing this, Dale changed his mind and moved behind the third sheep, following the small herd down the long, cold corridor that was taking shape around them.

"Oh come, come. I don't think that's what would happen. The ice would just push him forward, maybe sweep him off his feet a bit, but nothing as dramatic as a flattened torso."

The third sheep continued ignoring his brothers and spoke directly to Dale. "It shouldn't be long now. The empress knows we're here, and soon—"

Just then, one of the walls in the newly formed ice tunnel collapsed.

"Aww, yes! See there you go!" exclaimed the sheep. "Like, I said, she knows you're here, so here you go. Right this way into the void, and Bob's your uncle!"

Dale looked at the third sheep confused. "My father, you mean."

"Your what?" asked the first sheep.

"You say your father's mean?" asked the second.

"No time for this nonsense," stated the third. "We already know the lawyer doctor detective is your father, but that's not what I meant. And you're wasting the empress' time, which is hardly the right way to start off with her."

Dale stared into the nothingness in front of him. He had never liked the dark. It was one of the reasons he hadn't gone with Dan to the Darkside sooner; the thought of being blind to his surroundings scared him silly. "What's in there?" he asked the sheep.

"A surprise. Just lean in closer, and you'll see," said the first sheep.

"I'm not falling for that again," Dale said firmly.

"Go and see for yourself," answered the second. "We can't very well tell you what you'll find because it's different for everyone."

Dale didn't like the sound of that, and he began to move away from the giant hole.

The third sheep shook his head. "Wrong way, sir. No use fighting it. The choice you think you have is an illusion. You're going in there whether you like it or not."

Dale panicked. He turned away from the sheep and quickly shuffled down the long, icy tunnel. He knew there was a dead end ahead of him, but he hoped he might be able to push the ice barrier out of his way once he got there.

Before he made it halfway, he heard a loud whirring noise like an old-timey machine coming to life. Then in a flash, hundreds of moving pictures appeared on both sides of him, covering the walls. Dale was fascinated. He looked around and noticed that there were several scenes from his life playing out nearby—including a few from when he was the mayor of Waldoff Market. There were also a lot of scenes of three little wolf pups.

Dale spun around, not focusing on any one scene, when out of nowhere a cacophony of sound erupted from the walls. Dale covered his ears, but the volume from all the scenes playing at once was deafening. He ran down the tunnel again, not knowing how else to escape the noise. A moment later, the ice walls broke apart, but this time, instead of forming a new tunnel, the walls created a tiny room around Dale that was growing smaller by the second. Dale thought for sure he'd be crushed, but just as the walls transformed into a coffin-sized space around him, a sliver of a void opened up inside one of the tall ice sheets, and with a little, effort Dale squeezed himself through.

Just like he'd feared, he found himself in the darkness, in a space devoid of all light and sound. Dale took a few steps and stretched his arms out to see if he felt a wall or any kind of structure. His hope was that he could position his back against something so that at the very least, nothing would be able to sneak up behind him in the dark. But there were no walls or structures. In fact, Dale felt a bit like he was floating whenever he walked, and he wondered if there was a solid surface beneath him even.

"Hello?" he spoke to the void nervously.

There was no answer. So Dale, who wasn't much on patience, spoke again. "The sheep told me I'm here to meet with the empress. Is she in here?"

Still, there was no answer, and Dale started to feel frustrated. "You know, I'm a very important person on the Moon. A demi-god, in fact. I was once the mayor of a huge marketplace full of people. I have charm, and I understand the humans very, very well. I could be useful to you. After all, I've heard you're pretty powerful too. If we team up, there's no telling what we could do."

This time, a booming voice cut through the void. "Demigod. Demi-human. Wolf. You think I brought you here to team up with you? You think you could be of service to me now? It may surprise you to learn that you've already been of service to me in many forms. But it is time for you to retire, Dale. You're of no further use to me on the Moon. I've summoned you here to make other arrangements."

"What kind of arrangements?" asked Dale. When he'd imagined meeting Serena, he'd imagined a beautiful, young woman—similar to the way his mother had looked when he was younger, but maybe taller. But this goddess was clearly much more powerful than his mother, and from the sound of it, she thought Dale was disposable. He hated to admit it, but he was beginning to sense he was in over his head.

Before Serena could respond, Dale added, "You know, I'd be happy to work for you. Those sheep you have don't really know what they're doing. Two of them get mixed up a lot, and the third is a know-it-all jibber-jabberer. Let me take their place. I take orders pretty well, and I can keep things simple. I did whatever my brother told me to do for years, and now I've got Betsy telling me—"

Dale stopped before he finished, wondering if he should've mentioned Betsy.

"What's the matter, Dale? Witch got your tongue?"

"No, it's just—"

But Serena interrupted him before he could tell her a lie, "You don't need to worry. You haven't revealed anything I didn't already know. Betsy is one of the many reasons I had the sheep bring you here."

Dale was surprised. "Why?" he asked.

"I'm going to tell you a secret, but it's one that you must never repeat. Do you promise?"

Dale nodded his head to the void. "Sure. I promise," he said, hoping this meant he'd be around long enough to tell a secret—any secret.

"Good. Do you know that during all the millennia I've

lived here in my ice labyrinth, not one curious soul has ever asked me why I choose to live inside a system of revolving ice sheets, hidden away from prying eyes."

"Well, I'm guessing you don't get a lot of visitors besides the sheep. Could be the reason, you know."

Serena laughed. "Oh, no. On the contrary. I have lots of visitors. The elves have always come and gone as they pleased, granted they enter a different way than you did."

"So, it's true? There really are elves on the Moon."

This made Serena laugh even harder. "Oh yes. Many, many elves."

"Well, I'll bite. Why have you chosen to live inside a bunch of cold tunnels for so long?"

"Alas, Dale, it's not 'a bunch of cold tunnels.' You see, this is my time calculator."

"Time calculator? You mean, like a clock or calendar?"

"No," said Serena, sounding more serious now. "The time calculator isn't for measuring time; it's a machine that measures events. Or more precisely, the outcomes of events."

Dale was confused. "How do you measure the outcomes of events?" he asked.

"By building a massive calculator underground that can store and analyze every single moment that's ever happened, even ones long forgotten."

"But why would you need something like that? You're a god, right?" Dale asked as he tried to wrap his head around Serena's bizarre revelation.

"I'm a god to you. But really, I am all. I create all and destroy all. The irony of this is that even though I could once create anything and everything, I cannot see into the future to know what the outcome of my creations will be. Over time, this has caused a lot of trouble. Your mother and the god that your brother served were part of this trouble. So, I created a solution to my problem by building this machine."

Dale still wasn't sure he understood. "But where's the machine?"

"You were inside of it before; the ice tunnels are part of it. The memories you saw on the walls were your own. The machine detected your presence and displayed different scenes from your life. You recognized some of them, no doubt. Like the time from your very naughty stint as Mayor when you were in charge of all those poor people you and your brother poisoned."

With no attempt at sounding remorseful, Dale said, "Sure. I saw some of those scenes. Wish there'd been more from when I was younger. I was quite the handsome devil."

"Right," said Serena ignoring Dale's egotism. "The wheels under the surface of the Moon are also part of the machine. I developed them to be perfectly balanced. They run on the harmony between the day and night. The heat of the day warms the giant wheels until they reach the level of heat where they desire to be cooled. And the cool of the night chills the wheels until they reach a level of cold where they desire heat once again. Thus, the wheels are always turning, never satisfied with staying still."

"You're saying these giant wheels of yours have feelings?" Dale asked skeptically.

Serena snickered. "I've told you I have the power to create and destroy everything, and this is what you choose to question me over? You embarrass yourself, Dale."

Dale felt a twinge of anger, but he knew he had to be careful not to show it. "But if we're surrounded by the machine like you say, then where are we now? Where is this void?"

"Well, that is a good question, indeed, Dale, but not one I'm willing to answer. Suffice to say, we are nowhere at all and everywhere all at once."

"You're right. That answered nothing."

"Well, it wasn't supposed to. Anyway, I think it's time we discuss my plan for you."

Dale began to panic again, worried what Serena's plan for him might entail. He decided to stall. "You know, Betsy thinks you have some big plans that involve Mina. It's why she sent me here. To find out what it is."

"Yes, Dale. I do have plans for Mina. Plans that involve destroying everything."

"That's pretty bad," quipped Dale.

"Yes, I suppose so. But do you know why I've told you this, Dale?"

"Because you like me?"

Serena replied, "No, not at all. In your current form, you are completely detestable. However, I feel I've put you through enough. But I can't have you running back to Betsy's side. The time calculator has made that abundantly clear. You would ruin my best laid plans. So, I must do something else with you."

Dale gulped. "Does that mean you're going to kill me? Because my offer to work for you still stands. Hell, I'll even be your fourth sheep if it means I get to live. Just let us all have our separate bodies. I have no interest in being any part of a four-headed, wooly freak."

"I'm sorry, but I can't have you working for me. That would—"

Dale didn't let Serena finish. He bent down on his knees and began to plead to the darkness for his life. "Okay, okay. You can make me the fourth head. I don't care. Please, Ice Queen. I mean, Empress. Or Serena. Whatever you prefer to be called, please just let me live!"

It was clear by Serena's voice that she was finding it hard not to laugh.

"I was going to say that allowing you to work for me would require you to stay on the Moon's surface, and I can't have that. It's become obvious to me that you will ruin everything if you stay. However, I never thought of running the scenario where you become the fourth sheep head—the muted one, of course. You'd have to be mute for safety reasons. I can't have you telling my secret to everyone, lest they figure out my plan."

"You mean I'd have to go around attached to those buffoons without any way to tell them to shut up even? Well, then you better make me deaf, too, or I swear I'll find a way to saw their heads right off."

"I see," said Serena. "You know, I was going to offer you an entire kingdom of your own to rule over, but I do sort of prefer your way better. It's definitely more of a punishment than a chance at redemption, but certainly you know what's best for you."

Dale began to grovel again, "No, no. Please! I had no idea. Please let me take it back. Really, I'd prefer to rule my own kingdom than live the rest of my life as a dumb sheep."

"Hmm. Well, you have lived most of your life as a sheep already. And even part of your last one. In that one, too, you spent all your time following your brother around, though it was hardly a blip of a life."

"What do you mean my last life? You mean when I followed Dan around as a kid?"

Serena explained, "No, Dale. Didn't you wonder why I addressed you as 'wolf' before? You and Dan and Helen used to be wolf triplets long ago. You were Neriti's grandchildren."

Dale was horrified. "Wolves!? No way! I'm the son of a human and a god, not some mangy beasts!"

"Oh yes. You are all of those things you just said, but you were once the son of wolves, also. You see, Dale, energy never dies here. It can only transform. It is part of the problem I've faced while trying to make things the way I know they should be. But that's all set to change soon."

Dale asked in a pouty voice, "If it's all set to change, then how do I know this deal you're offering is on the up and up? Offering me a kingdom right before you destroy the entire world sounds like a pretty raw deal if you ask me."

"You can take it or leave it. But I should warn you that if you don't take it, you will be disposed of."

"You just told me that you can't kill me! Energy doesn't die! Remember?"

"True, but I can put you into a cryo-chamber and freeze you for the rest of eternity, which would basically be death for you."

"Fine then," said Dale. "I guess I'll be king for a day. Who are my subjects going to be?"

Serena responded, "Oh, you'll have many. I'm sending you into a crystal world. It's one of the thousands of leftover fragments of Earth from when the Earth existed long ago. You'll exist in a quantum world there, but you'll never know the difference. In fact, that world will likely seem even more real than the Moon."

"But how will people know I'm their king?"

"Your subjects won't have any memory from before. I'll make sure of it. You'll find it rewarding at first, Dale, but if you choose to be a lazy king—that is if you don't work hard to make your kingdom prosperous and good—it will one day feel like a punishment to be king. The choice will be entirely yours."

Dale asked, "Can I return to the Moon if I don't like it?"

Serena replied in an amused tone, "Yes, of course. Just click your heels together and wish to come home."

"Really?"

"No, Dale. I wouldn't be very good at exiling if I let you come back the instant you got into trouble or grew bored."

"But what if my subjects try to kill me? Then can I come back?"

"Look at that. You've become more self-aware during your

time in prison. Yes, there's always the chance that will happen if you don't change your ways. However, the answer is still no. Also, I should mention that your subjects will be elves."

"No! That's not fair! You made it seem like they'd be humans!" Dale whined.

"No, I didn't. That was an assumption on your part. However, it won't bother you as much once I restore your memories from before. Just like every creature I've ever made, you have lived many different lives in many forms.

"All the humans were once elves, even the ones who lived on Earth long ago. Some of those humans became elves again —or Moon Walkers, wolves, bryobane, or even other humans. The calculator has helped me decide how to distribute energy throughout this realm and beyond. It's all part of the grand experiment I've been conducting."

"But elves? Really?" Dale moaned.

Serena laughed. "Yes, elves. And you will be their wolf king."

"Wait what!?"

But before Dale could complain again, several beams of white light shot through the darkness and right into Dale's pupils. For a split second, both his eyes shone bright white and then the light faded.

"Oh my god," said Dale seriously. "I've been so blind. I remember now. Mama and papa and my siblings…and…and that monster! It led us into the darkness with its little ball of light and murdered us!

"Yes, Dale. That's right. It was Gryobe acting on Theo's orders. It terrorized Ragher and Neriti for many decades; your deaths were part of its terror campaign. You will remember much more now that I've unblocked your memories. Hopefully, these memories will serve you well as king. Farewell, Dale."

A ball of strobing green light sped towards Dale. It expanded as it moved closer, transforming into rings of electricity. The rings encompassed Dale, flashing faster and faster. He screamed in terror, but then suddenly his body disappeared from the void, leaving only a small, shining crystal hovering in his place.

Serena called, "Wensley! Balwynn! Herdwick!"

The three sheep burst into the void with a loud *pop!*

"Baa! Fiddle sticks! That hurts!" said the first sheep.

"Baa! Can't you let us walk in through the ice hole like all the others?" asked the second.

The third sheep corrected the second, "But that's not how most of the others enter, is it? She zaps all the elves into the void too."

Serena ignored the sheep. "The deed is done. You three will deliver this crystal to Theo's daughter, Betsy, just like I promised," she ordered.

The crystal that had taken Dale's place began to hover in front of the three sheep, shining brightly. "That little demi-demon is expecting it, so don't mess this up! Return to me as soon as you're finished. Everything is beginning to fall into place. It's time to prepare for our special guest."

CHAPTER 12

A BIG REVEAL

In the days of the wolf massacres

A few weeks had passed since Max's encounter with Betsy and Dan at the greenhouse, and during that time Waldoff had changed from a bustling town to a city on the edge. Not only were there fewer people in the streets during the day, but during the designated evening hours of the never-ending daytime, the city turned into a ghost town.

Dan's followers were mostly gone, off to prepare for their hunt. But this hadn't brought much comfort to the citizens who were against what Dan and his followers stood for. These Waldoffians worried about what would come after the ruffians had their fill of the wolves.

A deep sense of dread hung over the city like a dark cloud. The winds of change blew through the streets, whipping up anger and fear. There was fear over what was about to happen to the wolves but even more so over what would become of the city once the atrocities had been committed.

Unfortunately, the people who disagreed with what Dan's followers were planning to do also disagreed with each other about what should be done. And because these citizens were never able to reach a consensus, those who pushed the others to remain neutral were the ones who got their way.

Yet in the midst of all the city's friction, Max and Helen had entered into a full-blown love affair. It would've made little sense to anyone on the outside who knew Helen and her connection to the wolves, but Helen had found a way to distract herself from her devastation by making love to Max every chance she got.

Spending each moment of the day together delivering items across town with Max had given Helen exactly what she'd hoped for—plenty of opportunities to sneak away together without drawing suspicion. At first, Helen and Max would slip down alleys, like they'd done many times before, to engage in hot and heavy kissing sessions, but as these sessions grew steamier, Helen suggested they move them to Max's apartment.

Max was reluctant at first. He already felt like he was crossing a line by allowing their relationship to continue, and he knew that moving things to his place would be going a mile over that line. There was no turning back after that. However, after he and Helen were nearly caught several times by shop owners taking out their trash, Max decided he either had to give in to Helen or stop their affair for good. So, Max gave in.

As the city drew into itself more each day, the demand for deliveries dried up to the point where Max and Helen were able to spend half of each morning and afternoon tucked away between the sheets. When they were tired, they held one another close and caressed. And when they were energized, they were like wild animals, giving into their raw hunger for each other.

Weeks passed with Helen and Max soaking in every

moment they spent in their lover's cocoon. Although the thought of the trouble brewing outside was never far from their minds, the horror of what was happening didn't dampen their love making. If anything, it made the fire between them even stronger. Not because of any macabre fantasy about what the wolves were going through. But because the terror served as a reminder of how fleeting life could sometimes be, even in a place where most people never grew any older. The sense that the moments they spent together were only temporary made their longing for each other grow, as they tried desperately to hold on tight to what they had for as long as they could.

Then, one afternoon while they were lying naked in Max's bed with Helen running her fingers over the muscular curves of his chest, Max got up the courage to say something that had been weighing on his mind. "Why did you pick me, Helen? I mean, I know you couldn't pick someone your own age since dating a child is even more scandalous than what we have going on. But why me? Why not one of the other guys trapped in a twenty-something year old body?"

Helen pulled away from Max's side, holding the sheet tightly to her chest as though to hide herself. Her face flushed, and she bit her lip, a sign that Max had come to recognize as a nervous tell.

"Wait, what's wrong? Am I not the first guy you chose? Do you have other secret boyfriends around town?"

Helen laughed. "No, Max. It's just that I'm not sure you're going to like my answer. I already know how weird our age difference is for you, and this might make it even weirder."

Max rolled over and rested his hand on Helen's stomach. "I'm sure nothing you could say would make this weirder. Unless you tell me that you're really a robot in a human costume."

Helen waited a second and then asked, "What if I told you that I've been in love with you since I was seven?"

Max flinched. "Okay, you were right. That does make it weirder."

Helen smiled, even though she knew Max was struggling with what she'd just said.

"Well, maybe not in *love*, but I definitely had a schoolgirl crush on you growing up. Do you remember that time when Ruth asked you to help her deliver the wool mats and pup toys to the wolves, and the two of you set up a workshop in my parents living room for a couple of weeks?"

Max laughed as he thought about this time. "Oh, yeah. I remember Ruth told me it would only take a day or so to prepare the deliveries, but when I got there to help, there were items spread out everywhere. She never mentioned that people had been dropping supplies off at your parents' for weeks and that nobody had boxed anything up yet. As I recall, you were a great helper. How old were you then, ten or eleven?"

Helen bit her lip again and said, "No, I was seven. It was then that I first realized I cared for you deeply. You were silly and kind. You took care of Ruth like a loving son. She struggled constantly to recall where she'd put certain items while you were packing, but you never got frustrated or lost your temper. You helped her find whatever she misplaced no matter how long it took.

"You made up games, too, while we worked, challenging us to see who could organize the supplies into piles fastest. And whenever I lost, you'd tickle me endlessly. You also showed me how to do magic tricks, and at lunchtime you would make the three of us grilled cheeses. It was the most fun I'd ever had, and I remember thinking that when I grew up, I wanted to spend every day like that with you, having fun and getting lost in our own silliness."

"Oh, Helen," said Max. He was flattered, but he also knew that some of these feelings Helen cherished were due to their unfortunate circumstances. He thought that if she'd had the chance to grow up like a normal girl on Earth instead of the Moon, then she wouldn't have had to cling to a bland memory of them working on Ruth's deliveries to satisfy her need for young romantic notions. She would have had real romantic stories, involving suitors more appropriate for her than him.

Max rolled onto his back and stared up at the cracked stucco ceiling in his apartment. "I wish I had known. I would've told you to forget about me. That you could do a lot better with—"

"With what, Max? With someone else? Really? Like *who*?"

Max shrugged as if he realized he were already defeated. "Like anyone, I guess."

Helen chose to ignore him because she knew that he didn't really mean it. "You know you wore your hair differently back then. Remember? You had brown, shaggy curls that hung down over your forehead."

Max ran his hand through his short hair. "Yeah, I remember."

Helen inched towards him, draping her arm over his chest. "The curls made you look boyish, even more handsome if such a thing's possible," she said teasingly.

Max sighed longingly and rolled towards her. "I could grow it out again, I suppose," he said in a heavy whisper as he began kissing her neck up and down.

Suddenly, there was a loud banging at the front of Max's apartment. "Oh crap!" Helen exclaimed in a hushed, frightened voice. Helen and Max tore out of bed, grabbing their clothes quickly and throwing them on.

Tangled up in his white shirt that was still halfway inside-out, Max said firmly, "You wait here while I find out what's going on."

He tore his shirt off again, fixed it and pulled it back on. As he left the small bedroom, he glanced at Helen; she looked terrified. "It's going to be okay," he said reassuringly.

The loud banging continued as he made his way across the living room, and once he was a few feet from the door, he heard John's voice call to him on the other side. "Max! Come on! You better open up quick if you're in there! It's an emergency!"

For a second, the thought of getting caught with Helen vanished from his mind, and he threw open the door, worried what the emergency might be. John stood in the doorframe with red cheeks, huffing and puffing as if he'd just run ten miles to get there.

"What's going on?" demanded Max.

John pushed past him into the living room, and shut the door behind himself, yanking the doorknob out of Max's hand as he did. John started to move towards Max's bedroom, but Max leapt in front of him and shoved John backwards with all his might, which was necessary, since the pub owner was a half foot taller than Max and had a much larger build.

"Stop, John! You can't just barge in here saying it's an emergency and then not tell me what this is all about."

John pointed towards Max's bedroom, "I'm doing you a favor, Max. You're lucky it's me here and not Bob, since I'm certain what I would find if I shoved you aside and marched into your bedroom."

"I don't know what you're talking about," Max fired back, although nothing about his tone sounded innocent.

"Oh, yes you do, lad. You've got Helen back there. The two of you aren't as clever as you think. The shop owners who come around my pub have been talking about seeing you two necking in all the back alleys for weeks now. Lucky for you, none of them would dare tell Bob and Maude what they've seen because none of them wants to be the poor sap to deliver *that* news."

Helen walked into the living room, looking well-groomed

instead of disheveled the way she'd looked seconds earlier. "Hello, John."

John nodded at Helen. "Hello there, Helen. I'm glad to see you fully clothed; you need to hurry and get home now."

Helen protested. "Why, John? We've done nothing wrong. I don't see why I should be forced to tell my parents anything when I'm a grown—" she stopped, however, as the voice inside of her interrupted the argument she was making. *Your parents already know something's amiss, Helen. Dan sent them a silver bird this morning.*

"Oh my god, they already suspect us," she said aloud so John and Max could hear her.

Max looked at John. "Is that right, John? Maude and Bob know about us? You told them that you suspected our affair?"

John looked at Max angrily. "No, you dumb-dumb. I already told you that nobody in their right mind would want to pass along that message. But Helen's brother, the Darkside madman, sent a silver bird to her parents, and now Bob has every single person out scouring the streets for you two. I think Dan's message has him worried that Helen's been kidnapped."

John said to Helen, "You'll at least have your parents' relief working in your favor when they see that you're safe. How safe you'll be after that initial relief wears off, I surely can't say."

It's time to face the music, Helen. You knew this relationship would be fleeting. I've prepared you for more important things than laying around all day hiding from the world with this doof.

Helen replied to the voice, "I want you to respect Max. He's not a doof; he's a sweet man. Plus, you never told me I'd have to give up the relationship *this* quickly. And honestly, I don't plan to. I'll make my parents see things from my perspective. And if I can't, then who cares? They can kick me out if they want. I'm old enough to live on my own."

The voice didn't say anything back, which surprised Helen since it never let her have the last word during a disagreement.

To Max and John, she said, "Okay, it's time to face the music. Max and I will just come clean and ask my parents to accept us."

John laughed, "Are you sure you want to do that, Max? You know that Bob and Maude aren't likely to accept their precious daughter going around with an old man like this."

Max took Helen's hand in his own and said, "I know, John, and honestly, I don't blame them. It took me a long time to accept the feelings that Helen and I share for each other. But I do now, and I won't give up on us so easily."

"I love you, Max!" said Helen, throwing her arms around him and kissing his cheek.

Max embraced Helen. "I love you too," he said. "I think John is right, though. Your parents aren't going to take this well. I think it would be best if we keep our cool when we talk to them."

Helen nodded. "Of course, Maxie. We'll be as cool as cucumbers," she said in an over excited tone.

Max glanced at John. He knew Helen still seemed very young at times, which bothered him for reasons he couldn't entirely pinpoint. After all, there were lots of people he knew who didn't always act their age. Even people much older than Helen. In this particular instance, however, he wished he could get Helen to act like the most mature version of herself without upsetting her, mainly because it would help their case in the court of social opinion.

"Okay. You two best be heading off to Maude and Bob's now. I wish you well," said John, although Max thought he detected a hint of judgement in John's tone.

Max, John, and Helen exited the apartment as John prepped them for what to expect once they were outside. "I wasn't joking when I said that the whole town is out there searching for your whereabouts. That's only to be saying that if I were you, I'd refrain from making this your relationship debut. You're not likely to get the kind of attention you're hoping for."

John opened the large door that led out of the multi-story apartment complex and held it for the couple. Right away, Max and Helen understood what John had meant. Groups of people were standing in front of the building as if waiting on a famous celebrity to walk outside. When they spotted the couple, several of the groups started to cheer, and someone yelled, "Hallelujah! They're safe! John found them!"

Helen and Max smiled at the crowd self-consciously, and Helen gave a little wave, not entirely sure how to respond to this unusual gathering of people that was entirely focused on them. Luckily, John had a great deal of experience managing people and spoke for them, "No need to worry any longer, folks. These two were just taking a break from their delivery duties."

"But it's been hours since they went missing," said a larger woman who was standing near John.

"Yes, well they didn't have much work today. Anyway, you can all go back to whatever you were doing before," urged John.

Helen and Max began their walk to Helen's home, but much to their dismay, a man at the front of the crowd shouted to the others, "Come on! Our work's not done yet! We've got to get them to Bob and Maude safely, just like Bob told us to do!"

Max tried to dissuade the man. "No, no. That's okay. We can manage on our own."

But nobody seemed interested in what Helen and Max thought, and so the couple was followed street after street by a crowd that continued to grow. It seemed that everyone was eager to be part of the team that delivered the two missing persons to Bob and Maude. Helen suspected that this was because the search for the missing couple had come as a welcome distraction for most of the town.

When they arrived at Helen's, Maude rushed out the door and threw her arms around her daughter, shaking and crying. "Oh, thank heavens! I was so scared! Where were you two?"

Just then, Bob emerged from the front of the crowd. "Let's go inside, Maude. This is family business," he said seriously. "Thank you to everyone for helping us locate these two. Maude and I appreciate you. We'll let everyone know if we hear any news regarding the wolves, and we ask that you do the same."

There were loud murmurings from the people who filled the street, and it was clear to Helen from what she overheard, that the search party felt dissatisfied being disbanded so unceremoniously. Nevertheless, people began to turn around and leave, as Maude, Bob, Max, and Helen disappeared into the house and closed the door behind them.

As soon as they were inside, Helen tried to speak first, "Mom, Dad, we didn't mean to—"

"I'm going to stop you right there, Helen," said Bob. "I spoke with John on the way back here. You know he did you two a real favor today. Nobody even thought to go to Max's apartment until an hour ago. It never occurred to anyone that you'd be holed up in some kind of sick lover's den together! John was the one who guessed it, and lucky for you he insisted he go alone because if I'd been there, I don't know what I would have done! Max, you have some nerve! How could you possibly justify taking advantage of someone so much younger than yourself?! And our precious daughter who we trusted you to protect! Was that why you offered? So that you could fulfill some perverted fantasy?"

Before Max or Helen could say anything, Maude, who was looking visibly shocked by the revelation, asked, "Helen, is all of this true? Have you and Max been...been together? Like *that?*"

Helen began to talk fast and loudly, "It's not what you're

making it out to be. I'm just as responsible for this relationship as Max, if not more so! And Max didn't come up with the plan to watch out for me; I did. He wanted to come clean to you about our relationship after he got back from the greenhouse."

Maude scoffed. "Just how long has this been going on between you two?"

Max felt like he needed to say something instead of standing there looking cowardly, so he replied, "It's been a few months. And I just want to say that I'm so sorry I didn't tell you when it all first started. I knew it was going to upset you, but I want you to know that I really love Helen. I promise this isn't some disturbed fantasy. I actually have real feelings for her."

Bob lashed out, "She's basically a child!"

"No, I'm not Dad! I know we've all tiptoed around this conversation for years, but what did you think was going to happen? That I was going to spend my entire life never falling in love? With anyone? Is that really what you want for me? To never fall in love?"

"Not with *Max!*"

Helen rolled her eyes. "Then who? There's nobody my age on the Moon! And the ones who are closest to my age have the bodies and minds of children still! You guys never wanted to talk about this because you knew there was no perfect solution. But if you're honest with yourselves, you'll realize that the only real solution was for me to follow my heart."

Bob and Maude looked at each other. Helen's words were hard to argue with, even though neither of them liked the idea of their daughter being with a man more than twice her age.

Finally, Bob shook his head and said, "This is ridiculous. Maude and I have always treated you like a close friend, Max. You've been part of our inner circle since the beginning. Allowing yourself to get carried away with our daughter was just plain wrong! End of story! There's no way I can ever look past all this deceit and betrayal. The two of you won't see each other! Ever again! I don't care if you have to go live alone on the Darkside, Max!"

Helen intervened on behalf of her paramour. "Daddy, if he goes, then so do I. You don't want to acknowledge it, but I'm an adult now. Yes, I've continued to live here, but that's only because I enjoy being close to you both. But I am perfectly capable of living on my own, and if you try to force Max out of my life, then I'll defy you."

Bob looked angrier than any of them had ever seen him. His typical calm had vanished, and he looked like he might explode with rage. Maude put a hand on his arm, sensing her husband was about to blow his top.

She spoke gently to Helen, "Darling, I know you want this for yourself, but I think we need to let everyone cool down before we discuss this further. Nobody in this room is being very reasonable at the moment."

Bob had begun to take deep, shallow breaths through his nose, causing his nostrils to flare. Concerned over the dark direction the conversation was headed, Max said, "Maude's right. The four of us need to take a step back and think this through. There's got to be a way we can work all this out like adults."

Suddenly, Bob lunged at Max, grabbing his shirt in both fists and forcing him backwards against the wall of the front entryway. "Stop talking! You're not part of this family! You don't get to have a say in how we handle our business!"

Helen screamed and ran towards her father, reaching for one of his arms to try to pull him off of Max. "Stop it! You're hurting him!"

Max's eyes had grown large with fright. He didn't dare say a word, too afraid that it would cause Bob to tear him apart.

Maude moved to Bob's other side and said, "Let him go, honey. You know you'll regret it if you do something rash."

Bob didn't let go, though. Not until he looked at Helen who'd started to cry as she continued trying to pry his arm away from Max. "Please, Daddy," she pleaded with him.

Something about his daughter's terrified expression snapped him back to his senses. He let go and backed away from Max, rubbing his sore hands. "You're right, Maude. I'm sorry. I didn't mean to lose control."

Helen hugged Max who looked like he was in a state of shock. "It's going to be okay, Maxie. Let's get out of here. We can come back when my father's ready to be rational."

Bob didn't react to Helen's remarks. He was too busy hanging his head in defeat. Maude spoke, though. "Helen, do you know the reason we were so worried about you today?"

Helen nodded. "John said you received a silver bird from Dan. He said you thought I'd been kidnapped."

"Yes. That was part of it." Maude pulled a flat piece of silver from her dress pocket. "Read it for yourself," she said handing it to Helen.

Helen took the silver note from her mother and read it aloud.

To Whom It May Concern:

A promise broken is a debt owed. My dear sister and her delivery boy didn't show up to Black Ice Glacier as we agreed upon. I guess that wolf-associating shrew isn't quite as fond of the beasts as we all thought. Oh well. I was probably going to let Rufus' men kill them eventually. Helen didn't make it here in time, so we'll never know, will we? It's time to pay up. No more delays.

-Dan

Instead of turning to Maude, Helen looked at Max and

asked, "What does Dan mean I'm not as fond of the wolves as everyone thought? Why would he say that?"

Max, who was still shaken from his encounter with Bob, wanted to run out the door. He knew that there was no good way to answer Helen's question. The truth would make her angry, but playing dumb could put her in danger if she decided to go searching for answers on her own.

Yet not wanting to put Helen's safety at risk was the whole reason Max had withheld the truth in the first place. So, he confessed. "When I was at the greenhouse last time, Dan asked me to bring you to Black Ice Glacier, just like I told you. What I didn't tell you was the deal he was offering. He said if we met him there within two weeks' time, he'd give his followers a new project to work on—to distract them from going after the wolves for a while."

Maude put her hand over her heart. "Oh, Max," she said.

Helen, on the other hand, flew into a blind rage. "Oh my god! How could you, Max!?," she screamed at him. "You had no right! No right to make that decision for me!"

She slapped Max across the face. "I could've saved them! We could've found a way to stop those scumbags from going after my friends!"

Helen started to beat her fists against Max's chest, which got Bob's attention, breaking him from his spell. He grabbed Helen around the waist and pulled her away from Max.

"Let go of me!" Helen screamed. "This man is responsible now for every single one of the wolves' deaths! Just as much as Dan is! Just as much as his followers are! Let me go, Dad!"

"No, Helen. You have every right to be mad. He should've told you, but he was trying to protect you, just like your mom and I have been trying to do."

"I don't need protection from any of you! The wolves are the ones who need protection! From *us!*"

Bob acknowledged Max for the first time since attacking him. "I think you better go now," he said.

Max looked at Bob and then back at Helen who was struggling to free herself from her father so she could go after him again. He wanted to say something to make it all better, but he knew there was nothing left to say. He nodded his head and walked to the door. As he began to leave, he heard Helen yell after him, "I will never forgive you for this, Max! Never!"

Max felt his heart being ripped in half as he walked down the path to the road. He gasped for breath, feeling like he was suddenly drowning. Luckily, the crowd that had followed them to the house was gone. He had never enjoyed being the center of attention, and he especially didn't want to be in the spotlight right then. His relationship with Helen had been the best thing to happen to him since he'd first arrived on the Moon decades earlier, and he didn't want it tainted by others' judgements.

As he walked home, he wondered how he could possibly fix what he'd done, or if it was even worth trying. He loved Helen, but he had never felt like he was good enough for her, not just because of their age difference, but because she was so full of life and passion, unlike himself. He might not have aged since arriving on the Moon, but something inside of him felt much older, as though his internal clock had never truly stopped ticking.

Max decided to get some rest, hoping it might help him to think of a solution, one that would keep Helen from hating him the rest of her life. He knew she might be better off without him, but even if they were no longer together, he didn't want her to despise him for what he'd done.

When Max arrived on his floor, he walked down the hallway to his apartment. Along the way, he noticed something shiny hovering in front of his door. It was a small, silver orb with thin, metal wings on both sides—a silver bird right outside of his apartment.

Max felt sick. Nobody ever sent him silver birds. Mostly, they were used by people who didn't mind sharing their business all over town. The only people he knew who used the silver birds for important business were Bob, Maude, and Dan.

He reached out and plucked the mindless bird out of the air, quickly tapping it twice on top to stop its wings from flapping. Exhaling a deep breath, Max felt his torso deflate. The sensation reminded him of how far he'd fallen since that morning. He unlocked his door, still clutching the little silver bird in his hand. He knew whatever message was inside would be private, possibly even dangerous, for he already sensed who had sent it. However, what Max didn't know, what he couldn't have known, was that the contents of this little bird's stomach would change the course of his life forever.

CHAPTER 13

LIVING WITH THE MEMORIES

Two months had come and gone since Mina's dream, and barely a moment had passed when she wasn't in pain. The nightmare she'd had inside the tent her first night back had somehow triggered one long excruciating headache, fueled by a constant flood of memories that bombarded her senses every single moment of the day.

None of the stories that played out in her mind's eye belonged to her, and once they flashed across her vision, they nestled into her brain for good, taking up space inside of her that she didn't even know existed. Mina attributed the agonizing pain to the new memories that kept coming to her for reasons unknown. It was as if her brain was having to recalibrate itself over and over again in order to store all the new information that was being forced on her, like a cosmic flow of information pouring from a faucet into an ever-expanding balloon.

Evelyn spent days with Mina inside the tent in Bob's living room, doing what she could to help her with the pain and keeping an eye on her arm. After Mina's pain began, her arm quit vanishing, which Evelyn took as a small win, since it would've been risky to place Mina under anesthesia in her fraught condition.

Fred slept next to Mina at night, holding her hand and readministering the pain medicine Evelyn had given him to use on Mina. Evelyn had tinkered with her extensive collection of medicines until exhausting every option she could think of to produce a painkiller that was strong enough to ease Mina's suffering. Fortunately, some of the pills Evelyn came up with during these trials seemed to take the edge off a little, and when Mina took them with a sleep aid, they relaxed her to the point where she could almost get an entire night's worth of sleep.

The sleep was hardly restful, though. Mina slept, but she was constantly moving, physically interacting with the scenes that were being fed to her subconscious. Mina spoke in different voices too—some deep, others childish. Fred often closed his eyes and pressed his forehead against her cheek while she slept, imagining what she was seeing and wishing he could take away her pain.

During the days, while Evelyn stayed with Mina, Fred helped the other Rebeltonians build their new city. He felt guilty for leaving Mina, but John made it clear to him that it would be heavily frowned upon if an able-bodied, young man, such as himself, didn't pitch in with the construction work that the whole town was busy doing. And honestly, Fred felt relieved to have some time away. There was nothing he could do for Mina, and truth be told, he felt responsible for the misery she was going through. After all, he had known that Serena was planning to stuff Mina's head full of memories that didn't belong to her. He just hadn't realized what a horrible ordeal it would be for her.

One evening, after weeks had gone by living this new life, Fred returned to Bob's just as Evelyn was walking out the door. She smiled at him brightly, which Fred was surprised to see, since normally, Evelyn appeared tense after spending the day with Mina—the same appearance Fred tended to have in the mornings.

"Our patient had a good day today," Evelyn said to him. "I've been worried that she might be building up a tolerance to the pain medicine, but hopefully, it won't matter now. Her migraine seems much improved."

Fred knew that what Mina had been experiencing was much worse than a migraine, but he and Mina continued to describe it as such, because they didn't think it wise to tell anyone what was really going on. To be fair, Mina didn't even know the full extent of what was happening to her, but she understood that it had to do with her mother filling her head with memories. Evelyn and Bob, on the other hand, believed the memories were mere hallucinations brought on by the headache.

"That's great! When was the last time she took her medicine?"

Evelyn replied, "That's the best part. She hasn't taken any medicine since last night. She refused when I offered it to her this morning, and she hasn't asked for any since. She says it still hurts some, but I think the worst might be over. One thing I'm concerned about, though, is that she seems just as distracted as she did when she was hurting. I'm nervous she may have had some neural damage as a result of whatever was causing the pain. I wish to the heavens that I had the same equipment up here that I had on Earth. If I could just get Bob to focus his engineering skills on building some machines that have already been invented instead of spending all his time on new ones."

Fred laughed. "I'm not sure that Bob's capable of such a mundane project. Speaking of that, have you heard the rumor going around that some of the Rebeltonians want to halt construction of the city so that everyone can begin working on building weapons instead?"

Evelyn nodded. "Yeah, I did hear that, but it's not just a rumor. Bob told me last night that some of the townsfolk petitioned John to hold a meeting later this week about doing just that."

"Wow. What did John say?"

"Well, as the town commissioner, he has to agree to their request. They got over a hundred people to sign their petition. My guess is that they're planning to call for a vote at the meeting."

Fred said, "I'm sure you're right. Honestly, I'm surprised it took them this long to organize themselves after those men from New Waldoff showed up the way they did. People still talk all the time about how harrowing that day was. Anyway, I better go in and check on Mina. Thanks for taking care of her again today."

"Of course," replied Evelyn. "Let me know if there are any changes to her condition. Otherwise, I'll probably go back to building houses tomorrow while I still can. Hopefully, the town will come to some reasonable consensus regarding the petition. As a doctor, I'm not keen on the idea of building weapons."

"That's a good point," he said. "You should bring it up during the meeting. I bet there are others who are morally opposed to building weapons too."

"Oh, believe me, I will. See you later, Fred."

Fred walked into Bob's house and made his way into the tent where Mina was sitting.

"Hey there," he spoke softly to her. "Evelyn told me you're feeling a little better. That's wonderful. Have the memories stopped?"

Mina looked at Fred with a weary expression. "No," she said and paused. A few seconds passed, and Fred wondered if Mina planned to tell him anything else, or if something was wrong,

But then she continued, "I don't know how to explain it. I

guess there's been a shift. My head still hurts, but it's more of a dull ache than the stabbing pain from before. I can still feel, hear, and see all of the thoughts my mother is sending me; it just doesn't feel nauseating anymore."

Fred gazed at the side of Mina's face. She was staring at the tent wall right in front of her, but it looked like she was watching a movie, or that her mind was lost in space.

"Are you able to see what's actually around you, also?"

He reached out and stroked the back of her head with his fingers. "Do you feel me here with you?"

Mina nodded but kept staring off into some other world. "I do. You'll have to give me some time to get used to all of this. It's hard to ignore the memories. They seem just as real as anything that's occurring in our own reality, but they're even more demanding of my attention. I'll work on it, though. I promise, Fred."

Mina looked at Fred for a split second and gave him a smile. Then she looked away again, allowing herself to be pulled back into the everchanging creases of time where she watched millions of memories play out over thousands of years.

Fred was disheartened. When Evelyn told him that Mina was doing better, he'd hoped it meant she was finished absorbing the vast amount of memories Serena intended to transfer to her. For a moment Fred thought about Ragher and all the obstacles he'd gone through when building his life with Neriti. Fred knew that these were obstacles Serena had put into place to keep Ragher and Neriti from straying off the path she wanted them on—the path that kept her plan in motion.

When Fred learned what Serena had put Ragher through, he knew that the same fate might befall him one day. Yet even so, if Serena had been telling him the truth about what Mina was destined to do, then Fred knew he had to follow her orders. It would be far too dangerous not to.

Fred knelt beside Mina for ten minutes, watching her. He was so close he could've easily wrapped his arms around her and held her, but he knew that even though she was there, her mind wasn't fully present. And he didn't think it was right to bother her with his need for affection while she was burdened with the nonstop memories playing out in her head.

Still, it felt like torture to watch her close-up. For years he had dreamt of what it would be like when they were together again. And now here they were. But in reality, Mina was a hundred miles and a million hours away from him. Frustrated with the situation, Fred lay down in the spot he'd slept in every night since Mina arrived. He didn't bother to see if his movements had drawn Mina's attention. He was certain they hadn't.

Fred slipped into an aware dream state, a state in which his mind was relaxed enough to escape his control, yet he could still feel the pull of the waking world he'd left behind. He was watching a group of people he'd never seen before, sitting around a table in an old-timey saloon. The people were playing a card game, and one of them seemed interested in a man who was sitting at the bar with his back to them.

Suddenly, Fred was yanked out of his pseudo-dream when he heard Mina yell, "No! Stop! Get off him!"

Fred sat up, startled, and Mina flinched.

"You scared me," he said in a tone that sounded slightly scolding.

"I know," said Mina. "I didn't mean to. I'm working on it. Really, Fred. It's just these memories that have been coming to me this afternoon are so familiar. I guess they aren't the best ones to practice detaching myself from."

"Yeah, I guess not," he replied. But Mina had already been dragged back into her own waking dreams. Fred left the tent feeling annoyed, although he was mad at himself for it. He plopped himself into one of the living room chairs right as Bob walked through the front door.

"Hi there!" he greeted Fred cheerfully. "I saw Evelyn a little while ago. She said Mina is doing better today."

Fred looked at the tent and said, "It depends on your definition of better, I guess. But yes, her headache seems to be almost gone."

Bob smiled knowingly. "The hallucinations are still keeping her distracted, huh?"

Fred nodded. "Yeah. It's been tough for her. It's like she's living somewhere else, even though she's right here."

Bob sat down in the chair opposite Fred. "It's been tough for you too, I imagine. It's hard to love someone who isn't there. I'm learning more about that every day."

Fred turned his head and looked at Bob. "Sorry, Bob. I know you've been missing Maude," he said, feeling embarrassed.

Bob laughed. "You're right. I have been missing her, but I wasn't trying to guilt you with my sadness. I'm just saying I can relate to what you're going through. One of the differences between us is that Maude and I had a lot of years to enjoy our relationship, while I'm guessing you and Mina haven't even begun to enjoy certain parts of yours yet."

Fred looked away from Bob as he felt his face begin to flush.

"Yeah, that's what I thought," said Bob as though he were responding to an admission of guilt.

"Well, there will be time for you two. Mina just needs to get straightened out first. Evelyn and I have been spending a lot of time lately talking about what we might be able to do to replace Mina's arm, and I think we've got a good plan in place. We've even built a prototype together. Evelyn has given me a lot of insight into the anatomy of the arm and the nervous system, and we've come up with a design that we think Mina will be able to control with her brainwaves."

"Wow, Bob. That sounds pretty impressive. But when have

you two had time to spend on that? Evelyn's been here every day while you've been helping with the construction."

Bob gave a little shrug. "Oh, well I've been going over to her place most evenings to give you and Mina some privacy. It's been nice to have somewhere to go with my thoughts. Evelyn was always a good friend of Maude's and mine. She's been our go-to person on all things medical related."

"I see," said Fred. "Evelyn told me there's going to be a meeting in a few days about halting the city's construction so that we can begin making weapons instead. You think if they call for a vote, it will pass?"

"Yeah, probably," said Bob. "It's a terrible idea, though. If Betsy gets wind that we're building weapons over here, it will only escalate whatever craziness she's already planning."

"So, what do we do then?"

"Evelyn and I have been working on that. I think I might have an idea, but I'm not sure yet. Anyway, you don't need to worry about this right now. You've got enough on your plate looking after Mina."

Fred frowned. "I'm not really doing anything. Just waiting for her to come back to me. Again," he said gloomily.

Bob reached over and patted Fred on the shoulder. "Hang in there, buddy. Maybe now that her headache is subsiding, the visions will fade too."

"Yeah, let's hope," Fred agreed.

A few days passed, and Mina did make some progress refocusing her attention on the here and now rather than the long passed. She and Fred began to have conversations that lasted more than twenty seconds at a time, and when Mina did find herself being drawn back into the memories, she was able to fight it. Sometimes.

And as Mina became more present in reality, Fred became comfortable expressing his feelings towards her again. On the fourth night, after Mina's pain had dulled to a mild headache,

Fred even tried to kiss Mina as they snuggled next to each other before they fell asleep.

Instead of kissing him back, however, Mina blew a raspberry right into Fred's mouth and then began to laugh. Fred pulled away and then sat up, feeling a white-hot rage begin to flood his chest.

Sensing his anger, Mina sat up too and quickly began to apologize. "I'm so sorry, Fred. I didn't mean to do that. I was already allowing the memories to take over again, and right now I'm experiencing four…no wait, seven…nope, now nine at once. But when you kissed me, I was having a memory of being in a horse stable on Earth, examining horses, and I was right at the back end of a rather large horse with my nose near its rear. Hopefully, you can understand why the kiss was a bit off-putting before I realized what was going on."

Fred's heart rate had slowed enough that he didn't feel angry anymore, but he was still hurt. "Mina, I know you have the weight of the world—well, really multiverses—upon you right now. But I've been having trouble not feeling close to you these last two months. I guess I'm worried that, considering how new everything was between us when this all first started, maybe things have changed between us. Maybe your feelings for me went away completely."

Mina grabbed Fred's hands and pulled them to the top of her chest, right above her heart. "No, Fred. My feelings are the same, and I still want us to be together. It's just difficult to focus still. I thought you understood when I told you I was trying to get better, that it was for you. Or for us, really.

"But you're right that things have changed. I don't know how my mind has been processing the amount of information it's been given at such a rapid rate for these last two months, but surprisingly it has. I've started to think that the terrible head pain I was experiencing was my brain learning how to constantly mend itself back together as it got ripped apart and restructured to fit all the data it was receiving.

"It doesn't make sense, but every single day, I feel myself becoming more adept at not only storing all these memories, but also accessing them and processing them. I'm starting to get good at synthesizing and analyzing everything that's been given to me in the form of billions of memories. It's like my brain has turned into a super processor. It feels exhilarating but also extremely weird, if I may be so gauche with my choice of words."

Fred looked at Mina like she was speaking a foreign language. "I see. Well, you certainly sound like a whole new person."

Mina smiled. "Sorry. I will try not to let all of this go to my head too much. Get it? Go to my head?"

Fred winced at the pun, but this made Mina laugh, which made Fred laugh too.

Mina looked deeply into Fred's big brown eyes. "You know, Fred. I've seen a lot of men these last two months while lying here in the tent, suffering through these visions. But the entire time, I didn't see one man who came anywhere close to being as handsome as you."

Then, in an awkward lunge, Mina threw herself towards Fred and began to kiss him all over his face. After a minute, Fred stopped Mina, by gripping her around the back of her neck with one hand and cupping her ear with the other. He leaned into her, kissing her lips gently at first, then gradually applying more pressure.

Mina leaned her head back when the pressure became too intense, and Fred began to kiss her neck. Suddenly, Fred lost himself in the moment, moving his hands quickly all over Mina's body, like a hungry animal.

Mina pulled away. "This doesn't feel right, Fred. We don't

have any real privacy here, you know? Isn't Bob in his bedroom?" she asked breathlessly.

Fred stopped moving his hands but held Mina close. "I don't think so. I think he's at Evelyn's. They've been spending a lot of time together working on your new arm."

Mina bit her lip. "Really? You think so? Even this late?" she asked, and Fred could tell that she was stalling.

"I can go check if you'd like," Fred offered.

Mina nodded nervously, and Fred turned around and crawled out of the tent. Mina heard him walk around the outside towards Bob's bedroom.

"Bob? Are you in there?" he called, making a show out of checking for Bob.

Mina lay down in her nook and waited for him to return. Fred crawled back in a few seconds later and said, "Nope. He's definitely gone. We're all alone."

Mina yawned. "That's good, but I think I'd like to wait until we get our own place, Fred. The idea of being interrupted our first time by Bob or Evelyn or maybe even John or Jacques is too mortifying to put into words."

Fred looked hurt again, but he said, "Yeah, I understand. But that's really all this is, right Mina? There's nothing else going on?"

"No, Fred. There's nothing else going on. I swear. Try to get some sleep. Tomorrow we can ask Bob about accelerating the timeline to get our own place."

Fred lay down next to Mina, feeling discouraged. "Sure, we can talk to him. But nothing's going to change. Not after the meeting they're about to have tomorrow night. I'm pretty sure that more than half the city has decided they want to build weapons instead of houses."

"Oh," said Mina.

She and Fred stared up at the tent's angled ceiling, neither saying a word for a long while. Fred was tense. He knew he seemed insecure, but he couldn't help it. He wanted desperately to be with Mina, but he sensed more than ever that Mina realized he was keeping something from her. And even if she didn't realize it, he felt riddled with guilt over what Mina had been forced to go through since he'd brought her back to the Moon.

"Actually, Fred. I'm not being entirely honest with you. There is something else going on."

Fred felt a lump rising in his throat. "What is it?" he asked, waiting for the other shoe to drop.

"Well, ever since we started kissing, I can't get this image of a giant robot out of my head. But it's not just the vision that's alarming. There's something else about it that I can't quite put my finger on, and it's been bothering me this whole time."

Fred blew out a deep sigh of relief. Though Mina's confession was odd, he was happy she wasn't telling him that she'd received a memory from his time in the ice tunnels with Serena —a memory that could implicate his complicity regarding Serena's plans.

"A giant robot? Well, that's a relief I guess."

"How so?" asked Mina.

"No. I just meant that I was worried it was about me. Why do you think this memory is bothering you so much?"

"That's just it, Fred. I don't think it's a memory. It feels like something else. Like something bad is coming our way."

Fred tried to reassure her, "You've been through a lot recently, and you're doing a great job at getting back to normal. This vision could just be a byproduct of how hard you've been working to refocus your attention on the present. I mean, unless you think you're seeing a memory of a futuristic movie, or something like that?"

"No. It's not a memory of a movie," she sighed.

"Hey, come here." Fred reached over and pulled Mina against him to comfort her. "I'm really glad to have you back.

These last couple of months have been tough. I worried I'd sort of lost you. It was horrible watching you go through that. I wanted to kill Serena!"

Mina hesitated, then asked, "Fred, you didn't know that was going to happen to me, did you? Beforehand?"

Fred paused, and after a loaded silence, Mina looked around at his guilt-stricken face. She sat up. "How could you? You knew my mother was going to torture me like that and you didn't even try to warn me?!"

Fred knew he wasn't supposed to be broaching this conversation with Mina, but he couldn't keep lying to her. "I'm sorry. I had no idea that it was going to be like what you experienced. I didn't know about the pain. I'm not supposed to talk to you about any of this, though. It could mess everything up, and if Serena finds out, she might try to pull us apart."

"Pull us apart? Like how? Imprison you in the ice labyrinth again?"

Fred shook his head. "I can't say, Mina. Please just know that I would never do anything to hurt you. I meant what I told you when you first arrived. I love you. More than you could possibly know," he said in a deep, sad voice.

Fred tried to hold her hand, but she pulled it away. "No, Fred. I need to think about this first. I spent a lot of time while I was in pain, trying to accept what my mother was doing to me. It took time, but I finally came to the conclusion that she was hurting me for a good reason. Clearly, if you allowed it to happen, I must've been right. But it still doesn't excuse the fact that you've been lying to me. How am I supposed to trust you when I know you're hiding things from me?"

"You think I want to hide all of this from you? Carrying around Serena's secrets has been the biggest burden I've ever faced. But you have to understand, she made it very clear before I left the tunnels that it's the only way we can be together. Keeping her secrets is the price I pay to be with you.

And I'll happily do it for the rest of my life if it means we'll always be together."

Mina patted the top of Fred's hand. "Okay, Fred. I think I understand. Get some rest. I don't know if it's a coincidence or not, but I'm starting to get pulled back into the memory world. I think I'll try to sleep to avoid having to deal with these new sets of images. We can talk some more in the morning."

She lay down again and closed her eyes. Fred rolled on his back and looked at the tent's ceiling. He thought to himself—for he didn't dare whisper it aloud—"Dear god, Serena. You better not forsake us after all of this."

CHAPTER 14

THE TRAP

In the days of the wolf massacres

After Max walked out the door, Helen fell to the floor and sobbed. "I loved him, Mama," she cried. "How could he do this? I thought he was a good man."

Maude bent down and wrapped her arms around Helen's shoulders. "I know you did, baby. And I think Max *is* a good man, although I'm currently finding it difficult not to seriously question his decision-making skills."

"But if he knew me at all, he would've known that I don't need him to protect me. He would've let me save the wolves. Instead, he put his own feelings before the safety of an entire species. You can't convince me that a good man is capable of doing something like that."

Bob, who stood behind his daughter and wife, said, "I am madder than hell at Max, Helen. But I think he did what was right. There are two things that everyone on the Moon knows for certain—that you have a soft spot for the wolves, and that your brother, Dan, isn't someone you can trust. Max was smart enough not to put you in an impossible situation. He knew what you'd do, and he knew how dangerous that might be. Chances are you would've been walking into a trap. Max was trying to prevent that."

Helen shook her head, although she didn't look up to meet her father's eyes. "I'm not dumb, you know. I could've found out what Dan wanted from me first without being lured into a trap."

Helen felt her mother turn her head to look at her father, which made her angry. She knew what it meant when her parents exchanged silent glances. They thought she was being unreasonable, but they didn't want to say it in front of her. She pulled away from her mother's embrace and stood up.

"I'm so sick of you two treating me like a child still. *This* is why I couldn't tell you about Max. I knew you would make it out to be some big scandal, but why should it have been? Yes, he's older than me, but it's not like we all have so many options here. You two forget how lucky you were to find each other and fall in love on the Moon. Most people who came here alone are still alone. And then there's us four freaks who actually age— your three kids and Betsy. I don't know what you were expecting me to do. Live my life alone? Marry one of my brothers? Or maybe Betsy?"

Bob scolded, "Don't be absurd, Helen."

"Then what, Dad?! You both spend all your time solving everyone else's problems in this stupid place, except for your own children's. It's like you discredit us because you think it's easier being normal, or because we never knew what it was like to live somewhere else. But what you don't seem to understand is that just because we never lived somewhere else doesn't make this life any easier."

Maude spoke softly, "We know this life isn't easy for you, Helen. And don't think for a second that your father and I haven't spent countless hours and days talking about what to do to make things better for you and your brothers. The problem is that there aren't any simple solutions. I think you might have found that if circumstances were different, your father and I would have eventually accepted your relationship with Max. It would've taken some time to adjust to, but we want to be open-minded, honey."

"Right, Mom. Daddy really seemed open-minded when he was choking Max against the wall earlier."

"That's not fair, Helen," said Bob.

Helen shot back, "You know what's not fair? The fact that you assume I'm no match for my brothers. You have always acted as if they're so much smarter than me. It made sense when I was younger, but now that I'm an adult, it's insulting. Have you ever stopped to consider that maybe the reason Dan and Dale act the way they do is because of you? You two have always put us into these tidy, little boxes. Dan's the evil child, Dale's his trusty sidekick, and I'm the perfect but naïve child."

Maude looked hurt. "I don't think you mean that, Helen. Certainly, you don't think your father or I would ever purposely pigeonhole our children, especially not in such terrible roles. We've never wanted anything but the best for you all."

Bob added, "You're hurting, sweetheart. It's been a long day. Go get some rest, and we'll talk about this later."

But Helen was too mad to take her leave. Years of frustration had suddenly risen to the surface, and she no longer cared about hurting her parents, not when she felt like they were the cause of all her suffering in that moment.

"Don't tell me what to do! You no longer get to control me. If I let you continue to have a say over my life, I'll probably end up just as crazy and vindictive as the twins! If you only knew what I go through!"

Again, Maude and Bob looked at each other, nervously this time.

Helen screamed in frustration. She couldn't take it anymore. She stormed upstairs to her room. The voice had been whispering to her the whole time she'd been talking to her parents, but she'd chosen to ignore it, too lost in her own emotions to deal with the pesky prompts and asides from the parasitic specter she unwillingly harbored inside of her. Yet as the fire within her began to dwindle, the voice became clear to her again.

You know you prove nothing to them by acting out like that.

Helen replied heatedly, "Did you know about Max? Did you know he'd betrayed me?"

The voice asked her, *If I'd told you what he was hiding, would you have believed me? You needed to find out for yourself. He was right to keep it from you, though. Just like your parents said, he would've been putting you in a terrible position if he'd told you about Dan's bargain. It's not time for you to face your brothers yet. Too soon, and it will all be for naught.*

Helen fumed. "Yes, you keep telling me that, and yet you give me no indication as to what timeline I'm dealing with here or how in the hell you actually know any of this! Come to think of it, maybe you're just a figment of my overactive imagination, or a sign that there's something wrong inside my head. Just like there is with my insane brothers!" she yelled out loud.

Watch it, Helen. I've been kind to you because I know how much you've had to endure. Unlike your parents though, I have limits to how much of your childishness I'm willing to put up with.

"Go ahead and do your worst!" Helen spoke to the spirit inside her head again. "Give me nightmares for a year! I don't care anymore!"

Just then, Helen saw a shadow out of the corner of her eye. Startled, she jumped as she turned her head to find Dale standing a couple of feet back, lurking in her cracked doorway. "What are you doing?" she asked in an accusing tone.

Dale, who had a devious, boyish look to him opened Helen's door and walked in.

He snorted. "I heard that fight you were having with our good old 'rents, and I came to check on you. But then I thought I heard you talking to one of them still."

Helen shook her head. "No, I was just blowing off some more steam."

Dale raised his eyebrows. "Oh, I see. Well, sorry for your troubles. I know what those two are like. I just never thought I'd see the day when the three of you were fighting like that. Guess all it took was adding a little sexual seasoning into the mix, huh?"

Helen gave Dale a look of disgust. "Gross, Dale."

Dale put his hands up as if to show her that he hadn't meant anything by his remark. "Forget what I said. I was just trying to tell you I know what it's like to be on the receiving end of Maude and Bob's 'holier than thou' act."

Helen scoffed. "Mom and Dad are upset with you and Dan because you've been leading your followers towards violence for years now, filling their heads with garbage about the wolves and about our parents and our parents' friends. I don't think our situations are exactly equal, Dale."

Dale shrugged. "Fine, whatever you say. I just came in here to lend you some support, but clearly you don't need it. Guess if you're not in the mood to gossip about Mom and Dad, then you probably don't feel like hearing what Betsy has planned for that special friend of yours either."

Helen's breath caught in her throat. "What are you talking about?" she demanded.

Dale had started to walk out of the room but turned around again to face her. "Oh, nothing," he said coyly. "You probably wouldn't care anyway. After all, I'm pretty sure I heard you tell that silly man that you'd never forgive him. 'Never!'" said Dale mockingly as he raised the back of his hand to his forehead and lifted the other one up to cover his mouth. "I doubt what Bets has in store for Max would even matter to you at this point."

Helen grabbed a wool-stuffed pillow off her bed and threw it at him. "Stop it, Dale. Either tell me what's going on or get out of my room."

Dale stood in the doorway for a second as though contemplating what other torments he could inflict on his sister, but then eventually he said, "Betsy decided that if Dan couldn't entice you to come to him, then she might as well have some fun with Max. He's probably already on his way to the greenhouse now. She sent him a silver bird after Dan sent the one to Mom and Dad."

Helen stared at Dale trying to determine whether he was lying. However, her brothers had always been difficult to read due to the permanent detached stare they'd both mastered in infancy. "Why would Betsy decide to take Max if Dan really wanted me? That doesn't make sense."

Dale threw his hands in the air. "Beats me. But if you don't believe me, then go check for yourself. That drip of a guy you suddenly hate so much is almost definitely headed to the greenhouse on some stupid noble quest. I guess that's some people's idea of romance. To me, it just seems dopey."

"God, Dale. It's hard to imagine why you and Dan have never had any relationships," Helen said sarcastically.

Dale laughed. "Who says we haven't had any relationships?"

Helen looked at Dale curiously for a second but decided not to pry. She knew she had to get to Max's apartment fast, to convince him not to go to the greenhouse. "Okay. I guess I'll go check, but if Mom and Dad ask where I've gone, just tell them that I needed to get some air and that they don't need to send the entire town after me this time."

Dale shrugged. "Sure, although I doubt they'd listen to me."

Dale left her room, and a few minutes later, Helen snuck out by climbing from her bedroom window into the back alley behind her house. She'd done the same thing countless times before whenever she'd gone to visit Max or gone to see the wolves when she wasn't supposed to. Before she left, she changed into a dark dress and wrapped a brown scarf around her hair, hoping not to draw any attention from the people on the street who might want to stop her to discuss what had happened earlier in the day.

Keeping her head down and walking fast, Helen made it to Max's apartment in what she suspected was record time. She knocked on the door, but after a few seconds with no response, she took out the key Max had given her and opened the door. Just as she feared, Max wasn't home. She walked around the apartment, looking for any sign that he was just out making deliveries or at John's having a bite to eat.

When she reached the bedroom, though, she found an open silver bird lying on top of the bedsheets that were still strewn about from their lovemaking earlier in the day. Helen leaned over and picked up the little piece of metal next to the bird, reading the note that had been carefully etched into it.

A little birdy told me that you've been naughty, Max. We know you didn't tell Helen about the deal. If you still want to protect her, then meet me at the greenhouse right away. It might be too late to fix things between you and your lover, but you can still save her from the horrible fate that will befall her if you don't do what we say this time. Get here fast, and we'll leave her alone. For good.

-Betsy & Dan

Helen read the note a few times over. Something seemed strange. Dale had told her that Betsy sent the note, but it was written as if both Betsy and Dan had sent it. It didn't sound like something Dan would write, though. Plus, Helen was pretty sure that Dan would never have allowed his name to be put second to anyone else's, which made her think that Dan might not be behind the note at all. "Is Betsy laying a trap for Max?" Helen asked herself.

The voice suddenly appeared in her thoughts. *What are you going to do, Helen?*

"I have to go after him, of course…right? What Max did was wrong and extremely upsetting, but he wouldn't even be in this predicament if it weren't for me. I have to save him."

Are you sure that's a good idea?

Helen laughed and said aloud, "I mean, I'm sure you'll tell me if it is. I assume you want to have some big say in all this."

No, I think you should do what you feel is right. I trust your judgement.

For the second time that day, Helen was surprised by the voice's reaction, but she tried not to show it because she didn't want to give it any reason to doubt her. "Okay," said Helen. "I'm doing this, then. I'm going to the Darkside to save Max."

CHAPTER 15

THE GREENHOUSE FACE-OFF

Max arrived at the greenhouse on horseback twelve hours after leaving Waldoff. He'd almost turned around several times due to his growing anxiety over what he was about to endure, but he kept pushing forward. He knew he wouldn't be able to live with himself if anything bad happened to Helen. He had to face Betsy and Dan and do whatever they demanded to keep them from going after the woman he loved.

The sliding door at the front of the large glass building swooshed open, releasing a warm blast of air that hit Max in the face. Upon entering, he noticed a quiet melody. It sounded like children humming a cheerful tune. Carefully, he took a few steps into the tangled throng of vines that hung from the partitions along the ceiling and wound their way around each other, forming woven archways and tunnels.

Max knew he should probably alert Betsy and Dan to his presence, but he was too keenly aware of his role as the fly that was kamikazeing its way straight into Dan and Betsy's web. So instead, he savored his last few moments of freedom before giving himself over to whatever depravity his soon-to-be captors had in store.

However, when he reached the clearing at the back of the greenhouse, there was no one waiting there like he'd expected. There was, on the other hand, an unusually long table that occupied a large section of the otherwise open space. At the far end of the table was a place setting for one with a tan mat made of cloth and a fork, knife, napkin, and plate all arranged right where they should be. A candelabra had been positioned behind the place setting, and in each of its three arms, a yellow candle sat aglow in a dark turquoise flame.

The scene made Max even more apprehensive. He sensed he was being watched—that someone was hidden in the thicket of vines waiting to see how he was going to react to this table set for one. His heart started to beat loudly inside his chest.

"Betsy? Dan?" he called, hoping that by identifying his potential stalkers, he might lure them out of hiding.

There was no response, except Max was fairly certain that the sound of humming had grown louder all of a sudden. He began to panic. His hands and feet grew sweaty, and his knees grew weak. He moved along the length of the table towards the place setting where he grabbed the candelabra in one hand and the knife in the other, holding onto them tightly in case he needed to use them as weapons.

A burst of laughter erupted from nearby. Max recognized it as Betsy's laugh. He turned in the direction he'd heard it coming from, but before he was positioned properly, there was another burst of laughter, only this time it sounded like a hundred shrill laughs echoing off of every surface inside the greenhouse. Max raised his hands to cover his ears without thinking and nearly cut himself on one side and burned himself on the other.

"Dang it!" he exclaimed, furious with his own carelessness. Yet the mishap steeled him for a moment. "What's the meaning of all this?! You and Dan wanted to see me, so come on out here and see me already!" he yelled towards the general vicinity of where he'd first heard Betsy laugh.

The volume of the humming increased steadily, and Max suspected that something terrible was about to happen. Still clinging to the knife and candelabra, he ran in the direction he'd originally come from. But before he could make an escape, two thorny vines slithered their way around his ankles and wrapped themselves tightly around his legs, piercing Max's flesh with their spikes.

He screamed bloody murder as the vines raised him off the ground upside down and dangled him above the long table. The candles fell from the candelabra, extinguishing as they bounced off the tablecloth below him. Max didn't let that stop him from using the candelabra as a weapon. He beat it like a three-pronged club against one of the vines that had entangled him, while stabbing at the other with his dinner knife. His defensive moves only seemed to agitate the vines, though, and they pulled even more tightly around his legs, causing Max so much agony that he let go of his weapons.

Max continued to scream, but a few seconds later a hole appeared in the dense mess of vines and Betsy emerged into the open space where the table had been set. Max stared upside down in horror, not entirely sure that the creature he was looking at was indeed the Darkside witch. Her torso was covered in vines that had tightened around her, which seemed to be the reason that her head was several times larger than normal. Her skin glowed a ghastly green, her lips pointed out, and her dark eyes looked like they might burst out of her skull at any moment.

Through clenched teeth, he whispered, "My god, Betsy. Is that you?"

A hoarse voice rattled from Betsy's wide mouth, "Yesss,

Max. So nice of you to come to my little party. You must be exhausted from your long journey. Please have a rest."

Suddenly, Max dropped to the table on his back, though the vines remained wrapped around his legs. His head was centered atop the metal dinner plate while the rest of his body pointed down the length of the table. Max screamed in pain again, and Betsy winced at the sound.

"Oh no," she said, pulling a small scalpel from her pocket. "No more of that nonsense from you. Whatever will your dear Helen think when she arrives to find that her knight in shining armor is really a pathetic cry baby?"

Max's eyes widened as he watched Betsy pull out the sharp blade. "What are you going to do?" he asked in a terrified tone.

Betsy didn't respond. Instead, she slid the knife under her glowing green epidermis and sliced a thin piece of skin from her forearm. Max was fascinated by the ease in which Betsy seemed to be mutilating herself. The skin hung by a thread from Betsy's arm for a second as she returned the scalpel to her pocket. Then, she plucked the ten-inch piece of flesh and rolled it between her palms. As she moved her hands back and forth, the skin transformed into a sapling vine.

Once she was finished rolling the baby vine between her hands, she lobbed it at Max. The small vine wiggled as it flew through the air. When it landed on Max's face, it stretched out, wrapping around his mouth and the back of his head until he was firmly gagged. Max tried to yank the growing vine away from his mouth, but it was no use. The harder he fought, the stronger the vine became.

Betsy laughed. "Do you have any idea what trouble you've gotten yourself into, Max? I knew you wouldn't come unless I signed Dan's name to that silver bird message because every single person on the Moon thinks *he's* the scariest threat here. People always think of me as his sidekick, if they even think of me at all. But all that's about to change. Wanna guess why?"

Max tried to reply, but his voice was muffled by the vine that was holding his mouth shut.

Betsy continued, "It's because I have incredible powers, ones that nobody knows about, but soon they will. Making the vines move around and do my bidding is only the tip of the iceberg. But you'll see soon enough. I'm going to show my father, the dark god, that he's entrusted his dirty work to the wrong creatures.

"But I bet, right now, you're wondering what I'm going to do to you, so I'll tell you. First, I'm going to devour your hands. If you're being honest with yourself, I think you'll admit they're not the best hands. Sure, you might miss having them for practical purposes, but that's assuming that you live through this at all.

"Then, once I'm finished eating your hands, I'll wait until Helen arrives to take the next step. You see, Dan and my father are certain that your darling Helen contains a very important secret. They think that my father's sister, Serena—a goddess even more powerful than Theia—forced Theia, to become human, turning her into Helen. But I think that's rubbish, and I plan to prove it by consuming you whole in front of your beloved."

Max was horrified not only by Betsy's demented appearance, but also by how determined she seemed to carry out her threats. He burst into a fit of silenced screaming, struggling against his rope-like constraints. But it was no use. And soon, he stopped fighting because he realized he was using up all his energy with nothing to show for it.

"That's right, Max. Go ahead and surrender. There's little hope for you, after all. The only shot you have is if it turns out Helen really is Theia, and she somehow manages to save you before I finish you off. But like I said before, I don't think your girlfriend is any more a god than you are."

Max tried to yell at Betsy through his gag.

"Can't hear you, Max! Vines got your tongue!" Betsy laughed sinisterly. "Time for some finger food!"

Again, Max struggled against the vines holding him captive, but this time he stayed quiet, trying to channel all the energy he could muster into freeing himself. He felt the warm blood dripping from his leg wounds where the long thorns had punctured his skin. The pain that had been hot and electric at first was fading, and Max felt himself getting woozy.

Betsy glided along the length of the table towards him, opening her mouth wider and wider as she drew closer. Her dark eyes looked primal, staring at his hands like a hawk staring down at a mouse in a field. Betsy slowed her pace when she reached Max, and he sensed from this slight hesitation that she was about to lunge at him, going in for the kill. He held his breath and let his mind go blank, readying for the attack as best he could.

Just as he'd expected, Betsy dove headfirst towards his right hand that was pulling at the vine around his mouth. Max felt her rubbery lips clamp down over his entire fist. The vine over his face loosened and helped Betsy by pushing Max's hand towards her open jaw. Betsy inhaled deeply, but it wasn't a normal breath. A powerful vacuum formed inside of her mouth, one that could rip flesh from bone.

With the vine around his mouth loosened, Max screamed as loudly as he could. The sound seemed to surprise Betsy, who stopped for a second. But in that moment, Max heard someone shouting from close by. "Leave him alone! You can have me, but first, you have to let him go!"

Betsy's head snapped to an upright position, and the vines that held her torso spun her in a half-circle to face Helen. "Well, didn't you get here fast, princess. Heavens to me! I guess it must be true love between you two, after all! That sure makes this easier for me."

"Run, Helen! She's going to eat me in front of you. Run!" Max pleaded as the vine tightened over his mouth again.

Before Helen had time to respond, the vines behind her quickly unwound, grabbing her around the waist and forehead and tilting her backwards so only her heels were on the ground. Helen gasped and began pulling at the vines just as Max had done. Betsy reached into her pocket again, but this time, she pulled out a vial full of clear liquid. She uncorked it and tossed it to the side of Helen. A long vine unfurled from a series of hooks along the ceiling, catching the vial and pouring it straight into Helen's mouth in one smooth motion.

Helen's first reaction was to spit the liquid out. However, the vine was already wrapping tightly around her jaw, preventing her from expelling the mystery concoction.

Betsy's swollen head cocked back as she let out a monstrous laugh. "Welcome to my palace, dear. I do hope you enjoy the show. You'll find there's nothing I can't do here, for between these glass walls, I'm all powerful!

"Those folks on the Dayside called me crazy for building my greenhouse in the dark, but what they don't know is that every day I spend over here, my powers grow stronger. My father, the dark god, has been so busy with his puppets Dan and Gryobe that he hasn't bothered to keep a close watch on me. And since he's been distracted, I've been honing my skills and am ready to take my place now as his most trusted advisor. But first, I need to prove that his little fantasy about you and Theia being one in the same is false."

Helen, who appeared to go into a trance while Betsy was talking, suddenly furrowed her brow as if the mention of Theia had struck a chord.

Betsy smiled a wide, deformed grin. "Yes, that's right. My father believes you're Theia in human form. There are three gods on the Moon, and Theo thinks that Serena—the most powerful of them all—punished Theia by erasing her memories and banishing her to live a human existence amongst the other semi-mortal humans.

Helen's eyes glazed over again, which seemed to annoy Betsy. "Hmm. I guess that relaxant worked better than I expected."

The vines around Betsy's waist guided her over to where Helen was leaning back, propped up by the vines who held her in a state of suspended animation. Betsy snapped her fingers in Helen's face in an attempt to pull her out of her stupor. "Helen!" she called to her in a singsong fashion. "I'm going to eat your boyfriend if you don't wake up! Well actually, I'm going to eat him anyway, but it will all be for nothing if you aren't conscious while I'm doing it."

Helen didn't even blink. She looked as if she'd fallen asleep with her eyes open, giving her the spooky appearance of a body whose soul had jumped ship.

"How in the hell am I going to pull this off now?" Betsy asked herself. She turned her giant head to look at Max. "Well, I guess I could wait until your lady friend wakes up, but I'm not much on waiting. I'll just eat you slowly, starting with your legs. That way by the time she comes 'round again, we'll have already made some progress."

The vines turned Betsy's entire body towards Max, squeezing her waist, which enlarged her noggin even more. Max struggled and moaned as Betsy's gargantuan head hovered over his feet like a psychotic, man-eating hot air balloon. She lowered her mouth, and he felt his shoes and socks being ripped off, drawn into the vacuum that Betsy's intestines had created. There was a grinding noise as his footwear disappeared into her bowels, and immediately, Max felt all the skin below his ankles pulling away from his bones and tendons.

He closed his eyes, hoping to escape the excruciating pain, but a bright blue flash illuminated the inside of his eyelids.

Max thought he was hallucinating until it happened again—this time accompanied by a loud rumbling.

The pain in his feet eased, and he opened his eyes to find Betsy standing upright, bathed in a bright blue aura. She turned away from him, and Max lifted his chin to see what was happening. His view, however, was blocked by Betsy's boulder-sized head.

"What the devil!" Betsy exclaimed.

Suddenly, her head began to shrink as the vines loosened around her body, and Max could see what was going on. A beam of light shone from Helen's lifeless eyes, and inside the beam was a woman made of dark blue, reflective crystals, staring at Betsy through black onyx eyes. The woman spoke in a voice that sounded like it didn't belong to their world.

"That's enough, Betsy."

The crystal woman waved her right arm, and the fluorescent lights dimmed. A second later, all the vines began to smoke and sizzle, as they dried up and flaked apart. And pretty soon, all that was left in the big open space were piles of ash and soot spread across the greenhouse floor.

"My babies!" Betsy screamed. "No!"

The woman put her hand up, and Betsy's mouth snapped shut as though on the woman's command.

"The vines are not your children, Betsy. I understand that you've been dealt a rotten existence. My time calculator has a difficult time predicting what your father will do. More so than any other being in all the realms. Your life was therefore unforeseen, which means you've always been a thorn in my side, dark child of Theo.

"You're the anomaly that keeps me on my toes. I should destroy you, but I worry that removing your snakehead would cost me—that a dozen more Betsy-sized anomalies would take your place. So, I've come to offer you a deal instead.

"First off, you can't eat Max. I'm no more in favor of this

mortal man than you are against him. But I have unfinished business with Helen, and if I allow you to kill him, it will only get in the way of my plan.

"You want power, which is something I'm prepared to grant you. I will give you unlimited power. You won't have to be your father's top dog. You'll be even *more* powerful than him —traveling to any end of the Moon realm that you choose, wielding your power freely. But first you have to do all that I ask."

Betsy's eyes had shrunk back to their normal beady size, but they were fully alert. She was obviously intrigued. "You're my father's sister? Serena?"

The woman nodded. "I am the goddess, Serena."

"So, my father got it half right then. Helen has a goddess inside of her; he just guessed the wrong one."

Serena shook her head. "I speak to Helen when I need to, just like your father speaks to Dan. We're not one in the same, though."

Betsy smirked. "Okay, so what do you want me to do?"

Serena answered, "To prove you're worthy of possessing the powers I can bestow on you, you must accomplish several tasks. First and foremost, you must practice patience as it will be many years before these tasks will be carried out. Two children will arrive on the Moon with wings on their backs.

"Once they're here, Helen will bring them to you separately under false pretenses. You will know for certain it's them because they will tell you they're looking for the blueprints to your greenhouse. Whatever you do, do not let Dan kill them. They will be your father's and Dan's undoing. Without these children, you will never have the power you crave."

Betsy scoffed. "Oh, really? How about instead I kill Dan, the winged brats, Helen, and Max? I don't have some fancy time calculator like you, but I bet if I did, it would show me that the path I plan to take to power is much faster than yours. Besides, I trust my father a whole lot more than I trust you."

"Don't test me, Betsy. This deal isn't one to refuse."

"Are you saying I don't have a choice?" Betsy asked.

Serena responded, "I could make your life very difficult."

"Ha! You must not know anything about my life if you think you could make it much worse. Father said you were the most powerful of all the gods. He said you erase memories to punish other gods and mortals. But I think you may have met your match in me.

"You see, I'd be happy to have my memories wiped. You'd be doing me a favor, really. Nothing about my life up until now has been worth remembering."

Serena looked angry. She thrust both arms behind her, and her whole body lit up in pure white light. Waves of golden dust suddenly flew out of Betsy's skin towards Serena.

"What are you doing to me?" Betsy screamed in pain.

Serena continued to focus her energy for several more seconds and then relaxed her body again. "You weren't being cooperative, so I've taken away the powers you possessed."

Betsy shook with rage. "You can't do that!"

Serena laughed a deep, haunting laugh and flew towards Betsy so that she was standing right in her face. "Of course, I can. Didn't your father ever tell you what I am? The reason I am more powerful than all the others? I can create and destroy whatever I'd like."

Max, who'd been released from his botanic bondage as soon as the vines disintegrated, sat up on the table while watching the exchange. He wanted to run to Helen and carry her out of there, but he didn't dare. It was obvious that whatever powers this goddess named Serena had, they might be tied to Helen, since she was being projected from Helen's very eyes. And Max worried that if he moved Helen, it would vanquish Serena and allow Betsy to have at him again.

"So, you're going to destroy me now?" Betsy hissed.

"Not at all. With each task you complete, I'm going to restore some of your power. Then, when you've done all that I've asked, I will give you the greatest power you can imagine. It will come to you in the form of a precious crystal, one that will allow you to do great and horrible things. It'll give you the strength to take your powers to the next level and beyond."

Serena's dark eyes started to glow. "You must never tell your father or anyone that Helen isn't Theia. Keep searching for her if you wish; I can already see that you will. But it won't get you what you truly desire. Help your father and Dan as they ask, but do not allow the winged children to be harmed. One day, after I grant you ultimate power, the girl child will become your enemy. Only then do you have my permission to pursue her."

"Why would I waste my time on a child?" Betsy asked dismissively, still livid over what Serena had done to her.

"She will no longer be a child, and by then you will have a better understanding of who she is."

Betsy said, "Okay, but how do you plan to deal with these two? Your host might be stupefied, but I can feel Max breathing down my neck. If you ask me, it would be best if you gave me back some of my power *now* so that I can eat him. Then he won't be able to go blabbing about all of this to whoever'll listen."

Serena shook her head. "As you said before, my best-known power lies in erasing memories. I've already decided to remove Max and Helen's love affair from all recollection. For as long as neither Max nor Helen remembers their affair, no one else will either."

"Wait! What?" Max asked, jumping off the table to stand before Serena. "No! I beg you, please don't do this! Can't you steal the memory of today instead? I'd be fine parting with it. Really. But I'd be nothing again without my memories of these last few months. I love Helen. There was nothing for me in this world before we fell in love, and it took me so long to accept us. Please don't take her away from me now that I finally do."

"No, Max," replied Serena. "Helen told you she has an important role to play with her brothers, and it's true. The time you two spent together in this life is over. I will not allow her to be distracted by her love for you anymore.

"Besides, one day, you will need to help Betsy move forward with her plan to rule the Moon. That's why it's important that these feelings you have for Helen no longer hang over your heart like a hard stone. You may not understand it now, but hopefully one day you will."

"I don't understand! I'll never understand! Not if you erase my memory of it! Please, goddess! Please don't take this away from me!" Max groveled.

Serena nodded at him solemnly. Then in one swift movement she raised her multifaceted fingers to the side of his head, and Max dropped to the floor, unconscious.

"Leaping cockroaches!" Betsy exclaimed.

"He's fine. Memory theft takes a toll, but it's not lethal. Through him, I have just removed the memories of his and Helen's love affair from everyone but you. I will lead Helen back to the Dayside without her knowing where she's been, but you'll be responsible for getting Max out of here. When he comes to, put him on his horse and take him to the border. By the time he's regained his faculties, he'll be so puzzled over what's happened that he'll think he's suffered Darkside poisoning."

"Balderdash! Like hell I will!"

"Agreed," said Serena. "Like hell you *will*. And make sure you follow my other orders too. I trust that you understand the importance of what I've told you?"

"Not really," replied Betsy. "I mean, you haven't told me why any of this matters to you. Why do you care so much about what happens to these winged children? And why offer me so much power when clearly I'm not even part of your plan?"

"You're part of my plan now, aren't you, Betsy? Just do what I've asked. It's not for you to know why. Then one day, when you've finished all your chores, I'll reward you by sending you a stone that will make all your dreams come true."

"And how long will all this take?"

"It's going to take a while, but it will be worth it in the end," said Serena

"And if I don't play along, you'll what? Pop out of Helen's eyeballs again and scold me? Seems like you've already done your worst by stripping me of my powers."

Serena laughed. "Stripping you of your powers is far from the worst thing I could do to you, and I think you know it. Just go about your business like normal, and don't tell anyone what's happened here today. No one! Got it?"

Serena raised her hands above her head, and suddenly, the layers of ash and soot disappeared, and the greenhouse became a lush jungle once more.

Betsy looked relieved, though she tried not to show it. "Yeah, fine. I got it."

Serena smiled. "That's a good, little elf-demon. Oh, and Betsy? Stop blowing up animals in your spare time. It attracts the wrong attention, and I'm tired of listening to a bunch of pissed-off elves moan about it."

Betsy started to respond, but before she could, the light shining from Helen's eyes faded, along with Serena. Then like a mechanical toy, Helen quit hovering in her leaned back position, stood up, and began to sleepwalk away.

"That last order doesn't count, Serena!" Betsy called after Helen. "I don't care how pissed-off the elves are!" But a minute later, Betsy heard the door at the front of the greenhouse swoosh open and knew Serena was gone.

CHAPTER 16

ASHLEIGH & THE RATS

Ashleigh River Nate had spent most of her adolescent life on the Moon—going on some sixty odd years. Since arriving with her family decades earlier, she'd lived in a constant state of limbo, having already left her childhood behind yet not having reached true adulthood. Like all of the Moon Travelers, Ashleigh River hadn't matured at all since she arrived. However, considering the fact that she was a thirteen-year-old, she believed she was already as smart and mature as she or anyone else could ever be.

She was certain she knew all there was to know, even though she'd received terrible grades during the years that she was still allowed to attend school. And seeing as how smart and mature she was, Ashleigh thought she should be allowed to make all her own decisions, even though whenever she did make her own decisions, they tended to get her into trouble.

For instance, the first couple of decades that Ashleigh River attended mandatory schooling on the Moon, she had been suspended ninety-six times. While most of the adolescents her age tried their best to cope with the rotten set of circumstances life had handed them when they reached the Moon, Ashleigh did her best to rebel.

She cut her hair during class; cut other students' hair during class; tattooed her calf to read 'Death to Ms. Davis' (her seventh grade teacher); blew up the chemistry lab twice; started a fire in biology when she tried to roast a dissected frog over a burner; spoke in burps for an entire day; threw an open container of venomous spiders at a boy who called her cute; and bit off each of her toenails before spitting them one by one at the girl who sat in front of her.

Of course, there were minor offenses that Ashleigh committed routinely in class as well, like drinking and swearing. But these were often overlooked since most of the kids her age swore by the time they'd been on the Moon for ten years, and nearly half of them had drinking problems. There were, however, two incidents that stood out from the rest, the first one being the precursor to her expulsion and the second one being the incident that culminated in said expulsion.

The first incident occurred several years before Dan burned down Waldoff. It was a regular sunny day on the Moon when all the children arrived for their daily lessons at the sprawling school campus. The morning bell rang, signaling the start of the day, but when the first wave of children lined up to enter the school, a flood of rats scurried out of the building towards them.

Right away, the older kids started to scream, "Plague rats! We're all going to die!"

A stampede broke out in the schoolyard as the students and teachers ran for their lives. Unfortunately, many of the youngest children were too scared to move and stood in place sobbing until they were either snatched up by a teacher or knocked to the ground.

Over a hundred injuries occurred that day, and someone had to be held responsible. The head of the school appointed an investigative team to find out how so many rats had invaded the school's main entryway. It didn't take them long to find the culprit, though. Whether by accident or as a calling card, Ashleigh left her monogrammed etching pen near the school's front doors, which she later admitted to using to pick the locks.

During her confession, Ashleigh River told the story of how she spent her entire weekend filling the school with every harmless, non-plague rat she could find around the city. From her tone, it was evident that she felt no remorse, so the head of the school pulled together a committee to review Ashleigh's record and decide on an appropriate method of punishment.

The consensus was that Ashleigh was a troubled child who was better served by being kept in school than by being expelled. And as punishment, they assigned her afterschool chores that would be carried out under the supervision of the school's custodian crew. Ashleigh and her parents were brought in to hear the committee's recommendation. Her parents were told all sorts of disturbing information about Ashleigh's school behavior, much of which they didn't want to know about. But overall, they were satisfied with the committee's decision since they preferred to have Ashleigh out of the house as much as possible. What Ashleigh learned from the meeting, however, was that she would have to try harder next time.

So began another long list of borderline criminality. First, she stuffed a racoon into a younger girl's locker. Suspension. Then she etched swear words into her teacher's desk while everyone was gone to lunch. A Saturday spent learning how to refinish a desk. There were stink bombs, and spitballs, and other forms of chaos. But nothing got Ashleigh River the expulsion she was gunning for until she decided to revamp the only plan that had ever gotten her close to being in *real* trouble.

It was risky for sure. With the arrival of animals on the Moon came the arrival of several forms of pests. Cows brought flies. Cats and dogs brought fleas, ticks, and mites. And the rats brought themselves. But they also brought additional fleas, and some of these fleas were infested with plague. The Moon Travelers found this out the hard way when several of the earliest travelers were bitten.

Luckily, there were enough doctors to quickly identify what had happened and contain the spread. However, the Moon Travelers who'd been bitten were the only ones to ever die from any sort of illness. Therefore, the doctors recommended that everyone in the city work together to eliminate the disease-riddled fleas by exterminating their rat hosts.

Bob and Maude and their friends handled the situation by coordinating an effort to set out poison and traps for the rats. But after a few weeks, a group of travelers got together to oppose the work they'd been carrying out in order to destroy the plague infested rats. At first, Maude, Bob, and the others thought the pushback was a joke. The opposing group of travelers claimed that the work being done was inhumane. Yet not inhumane to the rats; inhumane to them.

They said that the plague rats and their fleas had been sent to the Moon by God so that the travelers could defend themselves against each other. Bob and Maude's group asked the others why they thought it was a good idea to use a deadly bacterium to defend themselves when that same bacterium might kill them and everyone else too. But the group wasn't interested in hearing this kind of logic. They said they knew very well what their god-given rights were and could recognize when those rights were being infringed upon. Then they announced that it wasn't the other group's place to tell them whether they could or couldn't keep their rats.

Bob and Maude didn't relent control completely, though. To ensure everyone's safety, their side created a city ordinance that forced the rat supporters to keep their morbidly frightening "pets" locked away in solid metal cages that only allowed air to flow in and out through a complex series of filters. For years the rats remained stored inside these types of cages in closets, sheds, and attics with very few incidents of escape. Most travelers thought very little about the rats at all until one of these escapes would occur, and then there would be panic for a few days until it became evident that nobody had caught the plague.

Ashleigh River's parents kept their plague rats hidden just like most people, but unlike most people, they kept the keys to the cages hanging on a hook by their front door so that anyone who came inside had access to them. Ashleigh's father regularly reminded his children not to touch the keys or go near the rat cages. Yet on several occasions, while her parents were away, Ashleigh and her older brother, Wayne, and younger sister, Perin, had dared each other to go into the attic so they could sneak a look at the families of plague rats that lived above them inside their secure metal homes.

Ashleigh had never dreamed of actually taking the rats out of their cages. She was old enough to understand the dangers and consequences of handling animals that carried a deadly disease. Nevertheless, after spending decades living through the same mundane routines with no end in sight, Ashleigh was ready to do whatever it took to break free from her purgatory.

So early one morning, long after her parents had drawn the curtains and her family had gone to sleep, Ashleigh got out of bed and dressed herself in her school uniform. Then she snuck out of the room she shared with Perin and quietly tip toed down the hallway until she was underneath the little door to the attic. She climbed the ladder just as she'd imagined doing over and over again for weeks.

She grabbed the smallest of the metal cages and slid it towards herself. To make sure that there were still rats in the cage, she looked through the glass peephole at the top. There were several furry, gray bodies scurrying around, alarmed by the sudden movements of their cage. Ashleigh grabbed hold of the handle on top with one hand, and with the other, she held the bottom as she lowered it down the attic stairs, trying to keep her balance.

When she reached the bottom, her father was waiting for her with a stern look of disapproval. "What in the hell do you think you're doing with those?" he asked in a hushed voice, trying not to wake the rest of the house.

Ashleigh's pulse quickened. She reached into her pocket and pulled out the key to the cage, the one she'd stolen from the key ring by the front door when nobody was paying attention after dinner.

"Back away or I'll open it," she threatened. "I know what I'm doing, Dad. This isn't just some prank I decided to pull on a whim. Go back to bed and tell no one you saw me, or else you'll end up in even more trouble than me."

Ashleigh's father's expression changed from anger to concern. "Don't do this, Ash. If you let those creatures go, it'll kill people. Then those holier-than-thou peacemongers will take our rats away for good."

Ashleigh took a step towards the living room, away from her father. "You don't understand. You have no idea what it's like to live through seventh grade for all of eternity. I HATE it here! And no one cares! All the adults are so grateful they get to live forever. All the babies, like Perin, are thrilled to play forever. But I'm neither of those things, and I never will be! *This* is how I'm going to find my own way, and don't tell me there's other options because that's a lie!"

Before her father could offer a rebuttal, Ashleigh ran from the house. She was fueled by anger and hurt, as well as by hope that she could make her circumstances better. When she reached the schoolyard halfway across town, she stopped to catch her breath. It was still early, so nobody was out walking the streets or in the schoolyard with her yet. She looked to see if she'd been followed, but the path she'd taken was clear.

Ashleigh walked to the front entrance of the school and set the rat cage by her feet. She pulled her engraving pen from her pocket and began to pick the locks, but soon realized they'd been updated and were no longer easy to pick. Ashleigh concentrated on the task for several minutes before she decided it was no use. She knew that people would be up and around the city soon, which meant she needed to get inside quickly so that she had time to get the rats to her classroom and unlock their cage before she made her escape.

It was obvious what she was going to have to do next. She was going to have to find a discreet window at the back of the school and smash it with a rock. Ashleigh picked up the rat cage and began moving to the back of the school when a group of men, that included her father and three law officers, came rushing towards her. One of the officers tackled her to the ground before she could reach for the key in her pocket.

"Dang it, Neil! You could've broken the cage open doing that!" Ashleigh's father yelled, grabbing ahold of the cage and examining it for damage.

Neil pushed himself off the ground while holding Ashleigh tight. "Sorry Arthur," he said addressing Ashleigh's father. "But us officers are trained to use surprise tactics whenever necessary to take down hooligans. If the department issued us proper weapons, I suppose we'd have a better way to handle these types of situations."

The other two officers came to Neil's aid by grabbing Ashleigh's arms and cuffing her.

Ashleigh spit hair out of her mouth and screamed at her father. "I won't go back to that school again. They'll have to expel me this time! I might not have killed anyone, but I could have. I need to be free to live whatever life I choose for myself. I don't belong in this adolescent hell forever!"

Ashleigh's father shook his head. "Honey, you're right. And you aren't going back there ever again. These men are going to be escorting you to jail this morning to face trial for what you attempted to do. You'll be serving prison time over this for certain, but I'm sure you'll get out one day, if they ever deem you fit to live among people again."

Ashleigh looked shocked. "They can't put me in prison! I'm only thirteen!"

Arthur chuckled. "You and I both know you're well past thirteen. But anyway, that's something you should've thought about before you tried to kill the whole city."

"No, Daddy! That's not fair! Everybody knows that no one ages. I'm still thirteen! If I wasn't, then why did I have to go to school all these years!?"

"I'm sorry, hon. But this isn't really about you. It's like I told you before you ran out on me this morning. Those donkey-headed folk who run this city would love to have a reason to exterminate all our plague rats. They tried once before, and we can't give them a reason to try again. You've got to serve some time to show them that there are ways to address the risk associated with our rats."

Ashleigh looked furious. "You're throwing away your own daughter to save your rats!? What a rotten father you are! You sold me out!"

"No, Ash. You've had this coming for a long while. Go ahead and take her away, Neil."

Ashleigh struggled against the guards, but at barely five feet, she wasn't able to give them too much trouble.

That was the last time she saw her father before the trial. And just like her father had promised her, she was made an example of—sentenced to serve twenty years in Waldoff's small prison. However, when Dan and Dale started offering the poisoned water to everyone, they forced all the prisoners to drink it and then let them go so they could rejoin society within the confines of the market.

For years Ashleigh River roamed aimlessly around the

market, mostly in the center where the golden fountains provided the serum for forgetting her problems. Unfortunately, once the market was freed from Dale's tyranny, and the decision was made to build New Waldoff, most of the ex-prisoners were re-arrested and imprisoned in City Hall, the same prison Bob eventually spent time in.

After Ashleigh was re-arrested, she had a slight stroke of luck when she received a visit from the Moon's bat-faced crone, Betsy. Betsy had been studying up on the unfair treatment the prisoners were receiving including their re-arrests, and she'd taken it upon herself to review each case on her own. Or so she said.

"From one old hag to a much older, albeit youthful looking hag, you've got real grit. I wish you'd gotten those rats into your school the day you got arrested. It would have served those lamebrains right for forcing kids to continue their education without any point. None of you are ever going to grow up or put what they teach you to practical use, right?"

Ashleigh shrugged. She didn't trust Betsy. She knew how close Betsy had been to Dan and his twin brother, Dale. And though Ashleigh didn't think anything about Dan and Dale one way or the other, she also knew that Betsy wasn't the type to talk to her unless she wanted something.

"I guess so," said Ashleigh, unwilling to get too friendly.

Betsy continued, "I guess what I'm saying is that if it were up to me, maybe you wouldn't be behind bars at all. There are plenty of people who deserve to be in here more than you."

"Like you?" asked Ashleigh with a smirk.

"Hmm," said Betsy. "I would have thought after all these years locked away in one institution or another, whether it be school or jail, that you might have wanted to live freely for a change."

"Are you saying you can get me out?" Ashleigh asked.

Betsy shrugged. "I'm saying that power tends to be a fickle

thing. One day you might be king of the mountain, and the next you're no more than a beggar."

"So, are you a king or a beggar?"

"I'm neither, dear. But one day I will be bigger than either, much bigger than a beggar like you could imagine."

Ashleigh frowned. "I'm not a beggar."

Betsy nodded. "No, of course not. But you might be wise to play the part for a little while. That is, if you do actually want your freedom."

"What do you want from me?" Ashleigh asked. She didn't have any interest in playing Betsy's game and thought it best to cut to the chase.

"Sometime soon, although I can't say exactly when with any certainty, I'm going to wield a great deal of power on the Moon. Maybe more than anyone has ever wielded. From what I understand, it's going to happen quite suddenly. And since I know how much humans hate change, I'm lining up some early supporters."

Ashleigh looked at Betsy cynically. "And you want me to do what? Be your cheerleader? That's really not my style."

Betsy waved off the idea. "What the hell would I do with a cheerleader? No, from what I understand, your style is cracking heads and lighting fires. Is that right?"

"I guess," said Ashleigh, as though she were bored.

"Well, what I'm asking is for you to harness that energy into creating an army—one that will follow me into battle if need be."

Ashleigh laughed. "I'm no drill sergeant, either. What kind of army do you think would listen to little old me?"

Betsy smiled devilishly. "An army of children and teenagers just like yourself. People who have lived in the bodies of six, eight, twelve, and fifteen-year-olds for twenty, thirty-six, forty-seven, or even fifty plus years. I know there is a large population of disgruntled youth out there like yourself, people who have been overlooked for far too long. I want you to bring them to my side so I can lead them to freedom."

"What kind of freedom are you talking about? Did I miss when all the other kids got locked up too?"

"No," Betsy replied. "I'm talking about the kind of freedom that allows you to live your lives however you want, free from what society and your families expect of you. No more ridiculous rules. You can live how everyone else does—doing what you want, when you want."

"And how are you going to give that to us?" Ashleigh asked suspiciously.

"By blowing up the social norms and everything else, for that matter. This place—New Waldoff—it's fine as far as human cities go, but it's awfully small considering how gigantic the rest of the Moon is. I have plans to take over the whole thing, and you can help me. In return, I will let you live however you want."

Ashleigh asked, "But how am I supposed to trust you, Betsy? As far as I can tell, you've never been loyal to anyone but yourself."

Betsy pointed at her nose. "Yes, you've said it perfectly. And that's why our arrangement works so well. You support me getting what I want, and I support you getting what you want. It's a fair trade. Do we have a deal?"

Ashleigh threw her hands up in the air indifferently. "Sure, Betsy. One magical day when you become the most powerful person on the Moon, I'll lead an army of children to fight for you. Whatever you say."

Betsy knocked twice on one of the iron bars of Ashleigh's cell and said, "Perfect. Enjoy the rest of your incarceration because once it's over, the real work begins."

CHAPTER 17

AXEL'S NEW ROLE

Axel had returned from the south side of the Moon and rejoined the pack of wolves in their ancestral home, determined to stay neutral in whatever wars might occur between the humans and gods. Unfortunately, he quickly found his new, ordinary life of neutrality rather boring.

Axel, after all, was the son of the most revered healer who'd ever lived and the oldest living Moon Walker. Neither mediocrity nor a dull existence were in Axel's nature, and he quickly found himself developing an itch for excitement.

To make matters worse, he hadn't exactly been welcomed back into the fold of the above ground wolf pack. It turned out that the wolves who had chosen to live in the ancient ancestral territory were rather hung up on tradition and order. And the elders seemed somewhat miffed that Axel's presence complicated the strict hierarchy they'd come up with.

When he chose to return to the largest remaining pack, Axel had assumed he'd be assigned a role as a healer or, even more likely, as an elder. He'd never had the opportunity to finish his healer training once the wolf massacres began, but he had been the leader of his small wolf pack during all the years they'd lived in hiding underground.

The elders, however, many of whom were younger than Axel, didn't think he deserved to be given a high-level role within their ranks. So once Axel announced his intention to live with them permanently, the elders met in private for many days to discuss what to do with him. Axel thought it was absurd that it would take so long to find him a role, but he assumed it was because they respected him and wanted to create a special place for him.

When they reached their decision, the elder council invited Axel to meet with them. They told him they'd decided not to grant him a role in their community. They said that they couldn't in good conscious appoint him to a position that he'd done nothing to earn within their pack. Yet they also would not disrespect him by assigning him with a role that he would surely feel was beneath him.

But Axel did feel disrespected. He pushed back swiftly, asking the elders to reconsider giving him some sort of assignment—even if it was in a lesser role such as a healing assistant. He told them that he felt he could finish his training quickly and earn a higher spot among the healers. Again, the elders declined his request, but Axel didn't give up. He began to build a case for himself, sighting his past experience training under the guidance of his mother, the most powerful wolf healer ever. But the lead elder, a silver wolf named Chaxtan, who'd been a puphood acquaintance of Axel's, cut him off before he could finish.

"Our minds are made up, Axel. Hopefully you do not believe we came to our decision lightly, knowing the amount of time we spent mulling over your unique situation."

Axel shook his head. "No, Chax. It's not that I doubt how much effort you've put into deciding my case. I just don't feel that you've considered everything I have to offer. I mean, you say that I have done nothing to earn a spot within the pack, but when I first came here, I retaught the wolves how to speak and how to reclaim their Moon Walker powers by shifting. Does that count for nothing?"

Chaxtan replied, "We are grateful to you for these things, of course. The problem we see is that your story is not straight like a line but broken into pieces that don't always make sense. We know you trained under Neriti, who you now claim to be your mother. But it seems that if Neriti were truly your mother, then other wolves would have known about this long ago. And none of us understand your relationship to Ragher, who we all knew to be Neriti's actual child. It just seems as if you have decided to blur the lines between what is real and what is not."

"Why would I do that? I have no reason to lie about these things."

"That may be. But there are wolves among us that remember the year you went missing after Tahissi took her life. Many believed you were in love with her and that's why you chose to leave your wife and abandon your training. You can see how it is difficult for us to reconcile this information, especially when it wasn't the last time you disappeared."

Axel felt like he'd been punched in the face. Once again, the lies that his parents had told for decades were coming back to haunt him. He explained, "I didn't know Tahissi was my sister then, and I did love her. But that's not why I disappeared. I left because I felt responsible for her death, and I didn't know how to cope with my guilt."

Chaxtan asked, "And the last nine years? You say you were with Ragher and the human, Fred, being held prisoner inside a moving ice labyrinth by some unseen oracle that nobody else on the Moon has ever heard of. Is that correct?"

Axel nodded. "I know how it sounds, but now that you've all reclaimed your Moon Walker powers, there's a chance you could find the ice tunnels too. I could try to lead you there if it would help."

The elders looked at each other intrigued, but Chaxtan quickly struck down the idea. "No, Axel. Even though it is hard to know if what you say is the truth, I cannot allow our wolves to take the risk of also being imprisoned by this evil oracle that you claim exists."

Axel was beginning to wonder if Chaxtan had chosen to be against him no matter what he said or did. "So, you refuse to believe me, and you won't allow me to prove my story or give me the opportunity to take on any role in the pack. Is it actually that you'd prefer to see me leave all together?"

Another elder, a female wolf named Dalia, who was a decade younger than Axel, spoke, "We don't wish to see you leave, but this is how we feel you will fit in best. Our hierarchy is strict and there are many conditions you would have to meet to be matched to any of these roles. We do not see that you can change your ways this late in life, to do well within the hierarchy and keep from causing friction. This is why we made the decision to keep you on the fray.

"You are welcome to stay and prove yourself as a member of our pack. But you will have to make your own way, and truly, Axel, if you are being honest with yourself, I think you know that this is best for you. All those who know you, know that you have the heart of a loner. Though you may crave the comfort of a pack, you do things outside of the norms, like interacting with the humans."

Axel reacted, although he already knew he'd been beat. "Is that what this is really about? The connection I had to Helen? Because when I first came here, I told you of my plan to stay neutral regarding all human business in the future."

"No," said Chaxtan. "You are trying to make this about one thing, but it is about everything we've spoken of today. Dalia is right. You will do your best making your own path whether you end up staying with us and accepting your place among the pack, or not."

Axel gave up trying to change the elders' minds. There was no point in arguing further because he could see their hearts were against him. For days after this exchange, Axel roamed around the ancestral territory as though hoping to find an answer in the dirt, rocks, or wind. Finally, he made the decision to pay a visit to the underground pack. When he'd left them months earlier, he decided he would return on occasion to inform them of what was going on above ground so that they wouldn't stay cut off from the other packs.

Also, Axel had great respect for their leader, Elu. She was strong and wise like her mother, Imgu, and since he had no one else he felt comfortable turning to, Axel hoped she might be willing to counsel him on some important matters, including what he should do with the rest of his life.

So, Axel informed several of the elders that he was leaving to visit the underground wolf pack and that he would return in a few weeks. In the back of his mind, he wasn't sure whether this was true or not. But he thought it didn't matter really, since there was nobody there to miss him if he didn't return.

When he'd made it past the border of the pack's territory, Axel felt a weight lift from his shoulders, which surprised him. He'd believed he made the right decision when he chose to live with the larger pack after returning from the Moon's south side pack, but that was when he still thought he'd be able to assimilate into the pack by taking on an important responsibility. He wondered if Dalia and the others were right. Maybe he did have the heart of a loner.

But if that were true, then it was likely due to the circumstances he was raised under—with no real guardians, and secret parents who were careful to keep a certain amount of distance so as not to reveal their true identities to him. Certainly, that was enough to make any pack animal feel alone.

After all, he'd only ever had himself to look after his best interests.

Axel pushed these thoughts from his mind and took off running. He wasn't as fast as he once was. The years he'd spent cooped up in the ice tunnels had worn away some of his muscle, and now that he was older, he didn't expect that he'd be able to get much of it back. Even so, he still loved the feeling of running free with the cool breeze blowing through his fur.

He went about ten miles without stopping when he spotted what looked like a wide group of little figures dotting the horizon up ahead.

"What in the world?" Axel wondered out loud. He knew it couldn't be the humans because the shadowy outlines weren't large enough to be that of humans. Then, suddenly, it dawned on him what he was looking at.

Oh my god, he thought. Had the oracle sent an entire army of elves after him for disobeying her? He stopped in his tracks, as he decided what to do. He knew it would be wrong to run back to the pack because he'd be leading the elves right to them. On the other hand, he was having a difficult time thinking of this army in serious terms. The encounter he had with the elves on the south side of the Moon had left him with the impression that they were mischievous creatures, possibly even downright naughty, but also goofy, and certainly not dangerous.

After another moment's thought, Axel decided to hold his ground. He knew he might be facing another round of imprisonment by doing so, but he felt it was unlikely that the elves were there to kill him, and he was curious to find out what they wanted. He walked towards them slowly to show them he had no intention of attacking.

As they got closer, Axel saw that there were thousands of the creatures, and although none of them were much taller than the ones he'd met on the south side of the Moon, there were some who were so small that the top of their heads only reached halfway up one of Axel's legs. The creatures looked sad with droopy expressions, and their heads hung down towards their round, unclothed bellies.

"Woot, woot, moon doggy! Woot, woot!" squeaked one of the larger elves who'd pushed himself towards the center of the wide group to come face-to-face with Axel. Axel bowed his head in acknowledgement of the large elf's greeting.

"Did the empress send you all here to turn me into crystal soup?" he asked, referencing the threat the elves on the south side had made.

"Woot. No, the empress ordered us to come to you. Not to make crystal soup, though."

Axel was curious. "Alright, then why did she send you to find me?"

"This is a fine question, moon doggy. The empress has decreed that we are your responsibility now. She has evicted all the elf tribes from our cozy homes. The empress says we are no longer welcome underground and that we are to live above ground with you hen's fork. Woot."

Axel's jaw fell. "You mean hence forth?"

"Oh yes. That too," replied the elf.

"So you're telling me that the crazy lady who lives in the void has so much power over you that she can kick you out of your homes? Why didn't you just stay? What's the worst she could do?"

All the elves who were close enough to hear Axel's question began squeaking to each other in tiny voices.

The large elf sighed dramatically. "Woot. There are so many wicked things her excellency could do, it's not worth speaking them all. My least favorite is the electro-zappies when she sends lightning into our bodies through whichever orifice she deems most worthy."

Axel chuckled in disbelief. "Okay, so maybe the better question is why you didn't leave the empress behind long ago and make your own way on the surface. Why would you put up with such a terrible ruler?"

"Oh no. Empress Serena isn't really terrible. She only punishes us when we disobey. Most of the time we elves are very good. It's the rest of the Moon creatures that have been bad, but the empress plans to fix all that soon. Woot."

Axel asked, "Oh? And just how is she planning to fix it?"

The big elf shrugged and smiled. "Couldn't say, moon doggy. The empress is mighty and brilliant, and I'm just a lowly elf."

"But you said—"

The elf cut him off. "Knowing that plans exist isn't the same as knowing what the plan is. But speaking of plans, where will you have all of us elves live now? And may I live with you?"

Axel felt caught off guard. "I don't care where you all live! I'm not your new master. Live anywhere you'd like. And no, you can't live with me. I'm on my way to visit the underground pack, and I don't even know you!"

"Oh. Well, I am Exigor, a good and kind elf. I would make an excellent living companion. Woot."

Axel had become frustrated with the way the conversation was going. He said, "That's great, Exigor, but you still can't live with me. It's not just because I didn't know your name. I also find the way you speak extremely irritating."

Exigor looked hurt. "How so? I am an excellent orator, which is why I was chosen to speak on behalf of the whole. I feel I've done a decent job of adapting to your own way of speaking. Do you not think so? Woot."

"No, and partly it's because of that blasted word you keep saying. 'Woot.' Is that some kind of nervous tick from all the electro-zappies?"

Exigor shuddered at the thought. "No. This is how we were told you like to be addressed. You are a woot moon puppy, no? You and your kind speak, of course, but you also howl and say, 'woot, woot.' Isn't that correct?"

Axel suddenly understood the misunderstanding, but it didn't relieve his frustration any. "We are wolves, not 'woots' or 'moon puppies.'"

Exigor's gray skin pinkened with embarrassment. "My deepest apologies, moon wolf. I didn't mean to offend. Now, could you please tell us where you would like for the elf tribes to live?"

Axel looked around at all the childlike faces that were staring back at him with big, sad eyes. He knew if he gave in, then he was most likely allowing the empress, or oracle, or Serena the evil Moon witch, to win. She'd clearly sent all the elves to him as either a punishment or as a way of putting pressure on him to unite the wolves against Theo. He couldn't be sure which of these it was, although he knew very well that it could be both. Despite this, though, Axel couldn't disregard all these homeless elves who were looking to him to solve their problem.

"Fine. I'll help you get settled. But the first time any of you tries to convince me to do the empress' bidding, you won't get one more second of help out of me. So spread the word. Also, I don't want to be your leader. You already have packs, or tribes, as you call them. The leader of each tribe can be in charge. I was recently told that I have the heart of a lone wolf, and therefore I have no interest in governing anyone. However, I know some wolves who would be more than happy to help you out if you decide you want to be ruled by wolves."

Exigor squealed excitedly, and all the other nearby elves began to shimmy and shake as they let out their own happy squeals. "Oh, thank you, Axel the moon doggy! We are eternally grateful to you for your kindness!"

Axel groaned softly but nodded. He already felt burdened by his offer to help the elves, but he reminded himself that he was doing the right thing. Besides, he would've been emotionally blind not to feel a sense of comradery with these helpless creatures who, just like him and his family, had been abused by the oracle for so long.

Axel turned and signaled for the elves to follow him. He already knew exactly where he was going to lead this ridiculous exodus of squeaky underground dwellers, and he smiled as he imagined how Chaxtan and the elders would react when Axel presented them with these several thousand gray-skinned, overly enthusiastic humanoids.

Axel snickered at the thought and said to himself as they began their walk, "Maybe this will be worth it after all."

CHAPTER 18

THE PROMISED CRYSTAL

"Baaaa! Where are we now?" cried one of the sheep.

"Well, surprise, surprise! We're in some sort of human dungeon. I *told* you to take a left at the spinning vortex!" the second sheep scolded.

"Never mind that now. We have bigger problems! I'm trapped!" yelled the third sheep.

The first two sheep, who were facing each other, turned to look at the third. He was stuck behind bars in one of the prison cells underneath City Hall. And he wasn't alone.

"Who are you?" asked his cellmate—a young woman wearing a shabby-looking school uniform.

The third sheep was startled. He turned his head to see who was talking.

The first sheep spoke, "We're three sheep. Who are you?"

The second sheep said, "We used to be a three-headed sheep, but that's all behind us now."

"Brothers! We need to stay on task! It's been over a month since we began our journey to deliver the crystal to Betsy," said the third, sticking out his tongue to show them the crystal. "And I've almost choked on this damned thing a million times, which is not a way I care to die. Focus! We're close now. I can feel it. Break me free from this cage so we can go look for her."

The first sheep began the rotation again. "Are you Betsy?" he asked the young woman.

"No," she replied. "I'm Ashleigh. But I know where you can find—"

The second sheep interrupted her. "Why are you in there, anyway? Is this where they keep the poor children?" he asked eyeing Ashleigh's grungy clothes.

The third sheep snapped at the first one, "How could you mistake this girl for Betsy? She doesn't look anything like her. Betsy may be small too, but she's lumpy in the middle with a face like an ogre that ate a dozen frogs."

Ashleigh laughed. "Yeah, that's a good description of her. But what about this crystal you're carrying? What are you delivering it to Betsy for?"

The first sheep answered, "The empress told us to. She's the supreme goddess of the Moon, you know."

The second sheep pondered, "I'm not sure we're allowed to talk about our mission. Serena would certainly silence us for good if she found out we were spilling her magic beans."

The third grunted. "You two blabber mouths have already said too much. Now get me out of here so we can get on with this!"

Ashleigh tried again. "But surely you can tell me what the crystal does. I mean I'm not exactly a threat locked up like this."

The third sheep knew right away they were doomed. He shook his head frantically at the other two sheep, attempting to warn them not to talk.

It didn't work. The first sheep said, "Yes, well quite right I suppose. The crystal gives whoever uses it incredible power. Thought about using it myself, but I'm just a lowly sheep and don't really have any need for power."

The second sheep said, "Huh! I hadn't even thought of using it! I guess after all these years of having my brain zapped, I've lost the will to dream big."

By the time it was the third sheep's turn to speak, Ashleigh's arm was already wrapped around his neck, and she was reaching her entire fist into his mouth.

"Aghhh!" The third sheep tried to scream, but his cry was muffled by Ashleigh's prying fingers.

Ashleigh grabbed ahold of the dark crystal and held it above her head. "Aha! Got it!" she cried victoriously.

The third sheep sputtered, "You don't know what you're doing! The last human to use a crystal wound up possessed with his eyeballs rolling across the floor. Is that what you want to happen?"

But Ashleigh wasn't interested in hearing about the crystal's side effects. She had finally found a way to obtain what she wanted—power to rule over her own life and to get a bit of payback against those who had wronged her. She held the crystal up to her eye and stared into it. An electric current ran across its surface, and Ashleigh smiled gleefully. She could sense the energy from the crystal beginning to course through her, and she suddenly felt very strong. With her free hand, she grabbed hold of one of the iron bars on her cell and bent it to the side, opening a hole in the cell that was just big enough for her to squeeze through.

"Sorry, sheep. Hope that empress goddess of yours doesn't punish you too harshly."

Then holding the crystal out in front of her like a tiny shield, Ashleigh took off down the dank, dark hallway.

The third sheep tried to push himself through the opening Ashleigh had created between the cell bars, but immediately, his head got stuck.

"What do we do now?" asked the first sheep. "Serena will surely zap our hides over this one!"

"Well, if you ask me, we should teach that brat some manners. That dirty child had terrible etiquette. I mean, really! Who told her it was fine to stick her fingers in a stranger's mouth like that?"

"Fudge nuggets!" exclaimed the third, who'd been trying to push himself through the bars. "I can't do anything now. My shoulders are completely wedged. You two will have to go on without me. One of you, catch up to that little lady and follow her. The other one, find Betsy and tell her what's happened. She's likely to be just as upset about the crystal being stolen as we are, which means maybe she'll help us get it back."

"What about you, brother?" asked the first sheep. "Wouldn't you prefer that we zap our way out of here so that you can come too?"

"Ha! He's probably happy to be stuck! Thinks he's on vacation, he does!" said the second.

The third retorted, "If you think it's such a vacation, then I'll help you try it sometime. But right now, there's no time to waste zapping ourselves out of here. We're closer to Betsy than we've been so far, and who knows where we'll end up if we try to apparate again. So, go!"

The two sheep nodded at their brother and took off galloping in the same direction Ashleigh had gone. The third sheep slowly wiggled his way back into the cell and lay down carefully, resting his body on top of the cold, stone tiles. A moment later, he heard a commotion at the front of the prison and knew his brothers had run into some guards.

He didn't worry about it too much, and after a few moments passed and the commotion died down, the third sheep said to himself with a laugh, "Well, maybe it is kind of a vacation."

. . .

THE FIRST AND second sheep scampered through the hallways, following Ashleigh's scent until they reached the prison's exit. Here, it became evident that Ashleigh had met some resistance judging by the large doors at the front of the chamber that had been blasted open and the five guards, who were splayed out on the ground.

"How the bloody hell did you two get in here? I don't recall us having any sheep prisoners!"

The first sheep said in an offended tone, "We're not prisoners! We work for the empress, the ultimate goddess of the Moon!"

"Shut up!" scolded the second. "Remember? We're not supposed to talk about that."

"Oh, right," said the first. "I mean, nothing to see here. We've just come by to inspect your prison. It's lovely. In fact, we'll write that in our report. 'Lovely prison. Wouldn't want to stay, but an excellent place to hang if you're one of the bad apples.' Haha! Get it? Hang? Ha!'"

The second sheep rolled his eyes. "Come on! We have to get out of here."

The two sheep hopped over the guards' bodies that were blocking their way.

"Stop them! Betsy will want to have a word with these two!" shouted the guard who'd spoken before.

But none of the guards moved an inch. It appeared they'd all been stunned.

"Oh, no. Don't trouble yourselves. We can see our way out!" said the first sheep as he and his brother made their way through the splintered doors.

When they arrived in the next hallway, they quickly dashed to the end where they found an elevator waiting on them. "What do we do now?" asked the second sheep.

"It smells like the girl rode in this metal box a moment ago. Get in!"

The sheep jumped into the elevator, and the second sheep smashed his head into the front panel of numerical buttons. Several of the buttons lit up, and the doors to the elevator closed. Slowly, the sheep rode the elevator up, stopping at nearly every floor until they reached an empty lobby where they picked up Ashleigh's scent again. The first sheep looked questioningly at the second.

"You go after the girl," ordered the second. "I'm going to keep riding inside this box for a while. I think I caught the stench of a demi-demon a little while ago. I bet I'll find it again if I keep riding this thing upwards."

The first sheep said, "Now who's taking a vacation from work? Maybe I'd like to be the one to ride inside the fun metal box all day long."

The second sheep looked at his brother and said, "So, you're not too scared to confront the spawn of evil all by yourself? You, who's still afraid of the dark after all these millennia?"

The first sheep scoffed. "I'm not afraid of the dark! I'm just afraid of what might be hiding there! Like Serena…or Betsy. Okay yes, fine. I'll go after the girl. You deal with Betsy."

The first sheep got off the elevator, and the second sheep pushed his head into the upper set of numerical buttons. The doors closed again, and the second sheep rode the elevator up four more floors, stopping at each one until he caught a strong whiff of Betsy. He stepped off the elevator and into a carpeted hallway that had several doors connected to it.

Sticking his nose in the air, he followed Betsy's musky scent all the way down the corridor to the last door at the end of the hall. There he stopped and shuddered. Along with Betsy's woodsy, amphibian odor, he picked up some older smells too. They were the smells he associated with death. Blood and organs and rotting flesh. The second sheep prepared himself. He knew no matter how scary Betsy was, that his punishment for losing the crystal would be worse than anything Betsy was likely to do. He had to confront her.

The door was ajar, and he could hear Betsy moving around the room. Since he couldn't easily tap on the door, he cleared his throat and said, "Knock, knock. Anyone there?"

The swishing sound of Betsy moving stopped, and there was a long pause. The sheep wondered if Betsy was trying to trick him into going away by making him think she wasn't there, but a second later, the door flung open with Betsy standing on the other side.

"Who are you?" she asked.

The sheep pulled his head back as though he didn't know what to say at first. Then he replied, "I'm a sheep. Are you Betsy?"

Suddenly, Betsy seemed to understand what was happening. "She's sent you, hasn't she? It's finally happening. I'd started to think I'd been betrayed, but that crazy goddess actually kept her promise. So where is it?"

"What?" asked the second sheep, choosing to play coy, fearing what Betsy might do when she found out.

"The crystal, you thick-headed creep! Give it to me!" she yelled as she grabbed the sheep around his long neck.

"Ohhh, the crystal. Yes, well there's been a slight hiccup with that. You see, my brothers and I began our journey here many weeks ago, but we had some delays. We didn't know where to find you, so we had to make some educated guesses. Long story short, we really did some traveling. We ended up inside several different holes; trapped in a bordered-up pub; stuck atop a glacier on the Darkside; and then wandering around this rubble-filled city of yours for an entire week trying to make sense of how you humans live. Turns out, some of you live in apartments and the rest of you curled up in nests on top of the rubble. Weird."

"Your educated guess where to find me was inside of

different holes?" Betsy asked condescendingly. "But you do work for Serena, right?"

The second sheep paused as though waiting for someone else to speak, but then he realized he was all alone. "Oh, yes, we work for her. She's the one who sent us to give you the crystal."

"So where is it now?" Betsy asked.

"A rude girl stole it from my brother's mouth. She yanked it right out of there with her grubby paw and then used it to break out of jail and get past the guards. She looked like a misfit, this one. Probably she's planning to sell it at the nearest pawn shop."

Betsy looked baffled. "What do you mean a girl stole it? Who is she?"

"Her name was Assley, I believe. She used to live in the prison downstairs until a few minutes ago. My brother and I followed her scent using the metal box. He went after her, but when I got a whiff of you, I came here to tell you what had happened."

"I see," said Betsy. "The girl's name is Ashleigh, though after today her name won't matter. She'll be toast. Come with me!"

The second sheep nodded. "Ooh! Yes please. I love toast. Can we have it with jam? You know, you're quite the proper host. Much more so than I was expecting, anyway."

Betsy ignored the sheep and moved towards the hallway, calling for her guards. Three large men wearing tight white t-shirts and dark pants came rushing into the hallway from the office next to Betsy's. "One of you, take this sheep into custody. He's going to be my hostage until I get what I was promised. The other two of you, come with me. We have a bratty little turd to finish off."

"Wait, a turd? I thought we were having toast!" said the second sheep, taken aback.

The men looked at each other as though they weren't sure they'd heard Betsy correctly, but when she ordered them to move, they sprang into action. One of the men grabbed the second sheep around the neck and dragged him into the men's office while the other two followed Betsy down the hall, into the elevator, and then out of the building.

When they reached the sidewalk in front of City Hall, they had no problem knowing which way to go. The cobblestones that normally lined the street had been ripped up and flung everywhere. Stones had been shot into nearby buildings, creating gaping holes in the walls. Street lanterns and sidewalk benches were completely destroyed, and several fires had begun burning inside the damaged buildings.

Betsy saw people cowering under benches that had been left intact and peeking around building corners to see if the danger was gone. Growling at the sight of it all, Betsy headed towards the path of destruction. "Who does this diva think she is? I made her a deal! She can't just waltz in and take over my city using my crystal! Oh, I'm certainly going to teach her a thing or two!" Betsy declared loudly, although it was obvious she was talking more to herself than the two guards who were trailing her.

Betsy and her guards wound their way through the streets, passing dozens of horrified-looking people who were standing around as if they didn't know what to do with themselves. Several of them yelled at her as she passed, telling her about their missing children and begging her to bring them back. Betsy waved them off, though. She didn't have time to deal with runaways or kidnappings right then, not that she would've normally cared about such things anyway.

About a mile later, Betsy knew she was getting close when she heard a ruckus up ahead. She turned a corner and found a hundred school-aged children crowded together down one long street. All of them were pointed in the same direction and staring at Ashleigh. But Ashleigh's appearance had changed dramatically. She'd grown roughly ten feet taller and now had dark black eyes and glowing, pasty flesh that was ripping apart in places. Next to Ashleigh, stood a panicky middle-aged man, who kept glancing back and forth between Ashleigh and the crowd.

The teenage monster spoke to the other adolescents in a deep voice. "We are the forgotten citizens! For too long we've been forced to live in the shadow of our elders, doing what was demanded of us instead of what we wanted. Yes, we might be young in mind and body forever, but does that mean we should never be allowed to live a life we desire? Our parents and government have told us that we must always go to school and follow their rules for our own protection, but this is a lie. They don't want to protect us! They want to control us! Today, we rise together against them. With me as this city's new leader, you'll never have to obey these rotten ageists ever again!"

The crowd cheered, and Ashleigh grabbed her father by the neck with her giant hand, causing him to flail and gasp for air. She continued, "Many years ago, I tried to free myself from their shackles, but this man, my so-called father, wouldn't allow it. He was threatened by my desire for freedom and made sure that I was locked away. I offer him up as our first sacrifice. Tonight, we will build a pit outside the city and fill it full of plague rats. Then this man and anyone who tries to stand in our way will be tossed into the pit!"

The kids cheered again, but Betsy had seen enough. She began pushing through the crowd and throwing elbows at the children who were smaller than her. A few seconds later, Ashleigh spotted Betsy and her guards.

"Stop those old people!" she yelled at her followers. "They want to arrest us! They'll be the next ones we toss in the pit!"

The adolescents tried to restrain Betsy and her men. However, Betsy's massive guards easily thwarted their attempts.

Every kid who tried to grab or lunge at them got a giant hand, fist, or knee shoved into one part of their body or another.

When Ashleigh realized that Betsy was getting close, she let go of her father, dropping him to the ground with a loud thud. Then she held the crystal out towards Betsy with the intention of lifting her up, just like she'd lifted all the cobblestones off the street earlier. But Betsy raised her open hand in the air, and the crystal flew out of Ashleigh's hand and into Betsy's.

The second Ashleigh lost control of the crystal, the light shining through her skin faded, and she began to shrink. She screamed and cried for help as the cracks that had formed along parts of her arms, legs, and face began to ooze blood.

"Oh, dear." Betsy laughed. "You certainly overestimated your abilities. I guess I should've mentioned at our last meeting that I'm a demi-god, and demi-gods, just like their god parents, are able to control crystals. I didn't want to bore you with all the details before, but it's too bad I didn't since now you've gone and gotten yourself into quite the blood-soaked pickle."

Ashleigh's body deflated into a pile of skin and bones, lying lifeless on the sidewalk where she'd just stood like a giant only a second before. Betsy took this as her cue to take the spotlight. Clutching the crystal by her side, she walked to Ashleigh's remains and stood on top of her decomposed body.

She addressed the crowd. "As you witnessed here today, bad things happen to those who oppose me. Yet my plan has always been to include your kind. If you follow me, I will give you even more freedom to choose your own fate than this one was promising you." Betsy tapped her toe on top of the cluster of hair that had been Ashleigh's scalp.

"A new existence is dawning for us all! Follow me into battle against our enemies who wish to keep me from conquering the Moon! Fight for me! Die for me! And I will reward you with any existence you like. What do you say?"

The crowd of juveniles took a moment to glance around at

each other somewhat apprehensively, but then eventually, they began to nod and cheer.

Betsy smiled. "Good," she said.

All of a sudden, Betsy's head inflated. Her mouth grew wide, and her eyes bulged out. The ground shook as she reached her arms above her head, and many of the children toppled over. Then two things happened simultaneously. The children began to age rapidly, turning from little kids or young teens into elderly adults. And at the same time, hundreds of vines appeared from out of nowhere, crawling over buildings and wrapping themselves around lampposts and people, as though they were the same.

Betsy laughed as she soaked it all in. But after a few moments, she noticed something out of place. The first sheep emerged from behind a row of trash cans on the other side of the street, knocking a few of them over as he tried to escape the chaos. Betsy looked at her two guards who were staring at her with their mouths agape. She signaled to them to grab the sheep, and they nodded and took off.

The hundred or so people who'd just been through puberty in a matter of seconds were beginning to gather themselves as they eyed the others in the crowd and then stared down at their own bodies to make comparisons.

"Listen up!" ordered Betsy. "This is my first gift to you. Now none of you will ever have to worry again about being mistreated for looking too young."

Someone in the crowd grumbled, "Well, fine! But I didn't want to look like my grandpa either!"

Right then, a vine snatched the man out of the crowd and lowered him into Betsy's mouth where she quickly ground him up and belched out his remains on the sidewalk next to her. The crowd of seniors gasped and screamed in horror, but Betsy continued, "Like I was saying, this was my first gift to you. And soon I will call on you to return the favor so that I know we can trust each other."

Just then, the guards showed up in front of Betsy with the wrangled sheep, who had a thin green vine tied around his neck.

"Oh good," said Betsy as she bent down to pick up what was left of Ashleigh's hair.

Betsy tossed the smoking scalp at the sheep's feet. "Take this to your master and tell her, 'Package received.'

The sheep asked, "Do I have to? I could just give her the message, you know."

Betsy snickered. "No, you'll take it to her like I asked, and tell her that the next time I send her a scalp it will be Mina's."

The sheep nodded, and the guards cut him loose. Reluctantly, the sheep lifted the bloodied hair with his mouth and walked back towards City Hall to collect his brothers and return to what was quickly becoming the safer side of the Moon.

CHAPTER 19

NO HOMES FOR WEAPONS

The construction teams had already completed half the city when the meeting to discuss the weaponization of Rebelton was called. Granted, the homes that had been built lacked some important features such as running water and energy to fuel a modern kitchen. But the houses were designed so that these missing features could easily be installed later on, once it was possible to bring water and energy to the city. Nearly two-thirds of Rebelton's citizens were now living in homes, but all the government buildings and private businesses were still waiting to be built.

Mina and Fred walked hand-in-hand to the meeting as the sun fell below the valley's highest peak, and dusk descended across the mountains. Nobody could have guessed it, but Fred was helping to guide Mina along the path to the outdoor spot where the meeting was to be held. Fred had spent the day with Mina, assessing how easily she was able to keep the nonstop memories at bay.

Mina hadn't left the confines of Bob's living room in two months, and Fred wasn't surprised that once she began opening herself up to the world again, it had reversed some of the progress she'd made. He already suspected it would be harder for her to tune out the memories flooding her brain when there was more than just the tent's sloping wall to focus on.

"It's not harder to tune them out," she'd told him. "It's just that the memories sort of jumble together with whatever's going on in reality. It all gets mixed together. For instance, if I'm listening to you but also walking, then my vision tends to focus on whatever memory is racing through my brain instead of what's right in front of me."

Fred knew this was bad. He begged Mina to stay home instead of going to the meeting, but she insisted that it was no big deal. "Now that I'm up and about, I'd like to test my sea legs," she had told him. "Besides, it doesn't matter if I come across as odd. Everyone knows I've been sick; they'll just assume that I'm still on the mend."

So, they came up with a plan that involved Fred slowly escorting Mina anywhere they went while outside Bob's house. They also agreed that Mina would listen and not speak during the meeting, just in case her reality-based senses went on the fritz from sudden over-stimulation.

"Hey, do you think that if I mention I'm the daughter of a powerful Moon goddess they might build me a house quicker?" Mina joked as they walked together holding hands.

Fred looked to make sure that no one else who was headed to the meeting was close enough to have heard her comment. "I'm not sure it's a great idea to be making jokes like that when you can't even see who's around us."

Mina laughed casually. "Relax, Fred. I'm not completely blind. Plus, like you said, it was just a joke."

"I know but remember what we agreed. You're just going to listen tonight, even if you feel like saying something. Right?"

Mina squeezed his hand. "It's going to be okay. I won't talk, but even if I did and something went wrong, it's not like people are going to automatically assume I'm some sort of demi-goddess weirdo."

Fred pushed back. "That's not what I'm worried about. This meeting was called because of the paranoia that's starting to stink up the air here. You showed up the same day those guys that were with Dale did. I'm worried if you start acting funny, it will only make things worse."

"Make what things worse?" Mina asked.

Fred groaned. "I didn't want to tell you any of this when you were sick, but there have been some rumors. Stupid rumors going around that you were sent here by Goodman."

Mina scoffed. "But Goodman isn't even in power anymore. Betsy's in charge still. Isn't she?"

Fred replied, "Yes, as far as I know, but we haven't bothered to tell anyone yet. Bob thinks it would only serve to stoke people's overactive imaginations. Anyway, that's why it would be better if you just listened tonight. Don't give them anything to use against you."

"Geez," said Mina. "I don't exactly see how people could think I'm a spy when I haven't left Bob's living room in almost ten weeks. If I were a spy, I'd be a pretty lousy one. All I've learned since arriving in Rebelton is that once we have a place of our own, and a normal bed to sleep in, I never want to set foot in a tent ever again. I guess I could take that piece of anti-camping espionage back to Betsy, but she'd probably execute me on the spot for being the most useless spy ever."

"Can you please stop using the word 'spy' over and over again? It's not going to help your case if someone hears you."

Mina laughed. "Yes. But again, I'd have to be the absolute worst spy in the world if I went around outing myself constantly by talking about being a spy." She paused and said, "You know actually, that wouldn't be such a terrible cover, come to think of it."

"Oh my god. Just stop. Please."

Right then, Mina and Fred heard familiar voices approaching from behind.

"Of course it is possible, John! I have always said that people's love of food outweighs their desire for anything else. And it is even true in this desolate purgatory of a world where nobody needs food."

John replied, "You've lost your mind if you think you're going to get anyone to back you, Jacques. These people are scared, and it has been my experience that nobody wants to eat when they're scared."

Jacques snickered. "Well, we shall see."

Jacques suddenly noticed the couple walking a few feet ahead. "Oh, bonsoir, Mina! It is so nice to see you out again finally. We have heard terrible rumors that you were most unwell. Are you feeling better now?"

John and Jacques caught up to Mina and Fred as Fred squeezed Mina's hand, letting her know he was there for her if she became overwhelmed.

"I am feeling better. Merci, Jacques," she responded, keeping her eyes focused forward so that he wouldn't notice that she couldn't see him.

Luckily, John took the attention off of her. "Yes, it's great to see you both out together," he said giving Fred a friendly nod. "Jacques was just telling me that he plans to introduce a separate agenda at tonight's meeting."

"Oui, that's right," Jacques said testily. "The people, they think that they want protection from a city that is too many miles from here to count. But I think what they really want is to get on with their lives. And what better way to do that than to be able to cook again? To enjoy the taste and fragrant aroma of a roasted lamb chop or an asparagus bisque. This is the only thing that makes this world an okay place to live. Building weapons will not fill a man's stomach."

Fred asked, "So what are you proposing then, Chef?"

"I am proposing that we bring in some gas and water lines right away. To make these useless kitchens of ours actually do the work they were intended for. What good is it to have a sink or a stove when there is no water or heat?"

John interjected, "I told the fellow that his idea is ludicrous. There's no way people are going to turn their focus to making their kitchens functional when most of them don't even remember how to make a sandwich, let alone a homecooked meal.

"I see," said Fred. "Well, it's an interesting idea, Jacques, but I'm afraid I agree with John. I don't think you'll get many people to back you. Right now, the masses seem less interested in asparagus spears than they do actual spears."

Jacques stuck his nose in the air with a pouty expression. "And you mademoiselle? Do you think my idea is ludicrous like these two bozos?"

Mina shook her head without looking at Jacques. "Oh, no. You aren't going to drag me into this. I'm just along for the ride. Right, Fred?"

Fred smiled. "That's right. Mina is building up her stamina again after her long illness. She doesn't want to overexert herself, which is why she's only coming along to listen to the ideas tonight."

A few seconds later, they arrived near the top of the sloped valley where a few hundred people had gathered in a circle several rings deep. Mina squeezed Fred's hand nervously, sensing that more people had shown up to the meeting than she'd expected.

Fred said to Jacques and Fred, "We're going to find a place on the outskirts of all of this in case we need to leave early. We'll see you both later."

John nodded. "Of course. It's a large turnout. I guess I better go ahead and get the event started. But first, I'm off to find Bob."

Jacques and John walked towards the right of the crowd, and Fred led Mina off to the left.

"No homes for weapons?" Fred said aloud to himself as he helped them find a place to stand near the back of the gathering.

"What's that?" Mina asked.

"Are you able to see the outlines of the signs people are holding up?" he whispered. "They all say, 'No homes for weapons.'"

John took center stage atop a metal box and began calling the meeting to order.

"That's a stupid slogan," Mina whispered.

Fred explained in a hushed tone, "We're not supposed to be talking now." Then he said, "But I think what they're saying is that they don't want any more homes built until we've built an arsenal."

"Right, but what I'm saying is that those signs make it seem like they're promoting homelessness for guns, bombs, and sling-shots." Mina laughed.

An older woman next to Mina shushed her.

"Slingshots?" Fred asked.

"Sure, why not? They can take down giants, can't they?"

Fred sounded exasperated. "Do you think you could stay quiet if I stayed quiet?"

"You could try," Mina replied with a sly grin.

The two stopped talking and listened to John address the crowd as he summarized each sides' position. Then when he called for representatives from both sides to come up, Mina leaned over and said, "You know, when you were talking to Jacques about his plan, I was having a memory of some-thing that happened the day I went back to Earth. The memory was of Bob and Maude and Jacques. They were all watching me leave, but then Ruth showed up with a man. He looked familiar. I think it's the same person we saw sitting next to Dale when we ran into them on our way up the mountain."

"Oh yeah?" asked Fred sounding only semi-interested.

"Yes. And I've been given several other memories of him from much earlier, too. His name is Max, and he was in a secret relationship with Helen."

Fred looked at Mina as if this had piqued his interest. "You're saying one of the Moon Travelers had a relationship with Maude and Bob's daughter? Wouldn't that mean that he was a whole lot older than her?"

Mina nodded. "Yeah, it's why the relationship had to be secret. But eventually, Bob and Maude found out, which didn't go well. I wonder though why he would be in cahoots with Dale if he and Helen were together. It seems like there's a missing piece to the puzzle. I think I'll ask Bob."

Fred looked at Mina questioningly. "Are you sure that's a good idea? Maybe the reason this Max is working with Dale and Betsy is because of how poorly it went when Bob and Maude found out about his relationship with Helen."

Mina bit her lip. "No, that's not it. I can sense it. There's something else—another memory I haven't been given yet that would explain it. I just have a really strong feeling that I need to know what happened."

"Well, maybe if you wait a few more days, the memory will come to you."

Mina shook her head. "No, Fred. It's hard to explain, but I've started to find logic to the order that the memories are arriving. It's like there's a special code embedded inside each one that signals they're coming in the right order. But there's a gap where this memory should be. It's the only reason I'm even mentioning it to you now."

"I see," said Fred. "Well, I guess I can understand that. Or at least, I know that you understand it. But do you really think it's a good idea to approach Bob about this? It might not be something he wants to talk about, especially not after losing Maude just a few weeks ago."

"I know. But I think it's important that I find out sooner rather than later. I think there's a reason I'm having this revelation now."

"Yeah, okay," Fred said giving in. "But you're going to at least wait until after the meeting, right?"

Mina nodded, and they focused on what was going on in the center of the circle again. A heated argument had broken out between Jacques and the man who was leading the group in favor of weapons.

"This is outrageous!" exclaimed Jacques. "You've offended me! How dare you question my loyalty to our new city! Do you know how terrible my situation was in our last home? I had nowhere to chop, nowhere to baste, nowhere to ferment. And here, I have plenty of places to chop, to baste, to ferment, just like my friend, Maude, promised. But I have no way to cook and nowhere to get water from. It is nearly as bad as the New Waldoff, but I am a believer in this city. It is why I am using my democratic right to protest. You and your friends think you are protesting for something good for our city. You have no idea what kind of box of pandora you could be opening. Instead, you are happy being ignorant cows!"

"Grow up, Chef!" shouted the medium-build weapons supporter with thinning, red hair. "You're the most easily offended person in our entire city. Just because our side doesn't have the passion for food that you do doesn't make us ignorant cows. What's ignorant is the notion that outfitting our kitchens with a few conveniences is more important than protecting ourselves from the likes of Dale the conman and Goodman the autocrat! Nobody here even needs food, and we definitely won't need it if we get our brains blown out!"

Jacques scoffed. "With you, who could tell?"

The man moved towards Jacques like he was about to

punch him, but Bob and John intervened, getting in between the two and pushing them apart again.

"Okay, that's enough debate for tonight," said John. "Now that everyone in Rebelton knows what our choices are, I propose that you go home and debate it with your friends and families. We can reconvene in a couple of days to take a vote."

Bob, who was still holding on to a red-faced Jacques, raised his hand to speak. John smiled at him and said, "Yes, Bob? You have something you'd like to say before we adjourn?"

Bob replied, "Yes, well there is one more proposal that Evelyn and I would like to make. We know that the majority of you want us to stop building the city in order to focus on creating and stockpiling weapons. But there are also many of us who'd like to keep working on our city instead of allowing it to sit unfinished for…well, for who knows how long? Evelyn and I understand both sides of the argument, and we believe there's a compromise to be made."

Jacques fumed, "There are also those of us who don't care about building houses or weapons until we have proper kitchens!"

Bob nodded. "Yes, of course, Chef. But I think we may have to make sure that everyone at least has a roof over their head before we begin focusing on utilities."

Jacques groaned in frustration, but Bob continued. "Evelyn and I have come up with a plan that would keep our city from being attacked or spied on, and it wouldn't require us to halt construction while we spend months or maybe even years building enough weapons to defend ourselves from every sort of attack."

Evelyn joined Bob in the center of the crowd now. She rested her hand on Bob's shoulder and said, "That's right. We've come up with an idea that would actually prevent any would-be intruders from getting within a mile of us."

John, who looked surprised, asked, "So what is this you two have cooked up then?"

Bob grinned and said, "We've created the plans for a mega-robot, one that can be controlled by a remote. It's designed to be indestructible against any weapons that New Waldoff currently has. And as far as its own weapons, it will be armed with lasers and heat-seeking missiles in order to deter anyone from going around it. We'll position it at the base of the mountain where it will make rounds. We've mapped all the possible routes that lead to our valley and have deduced that the mega-robot will only need to guard a span of five miles to ensure that no one gets by."

Fred looked at Mina in shock. "Did Bob just propose building a giant robot? Just like your memory?" he asked whispering.

Mina nodded. "Yeah, he did. But I told you, Fred. I don't think it was a memory."

"That doesn't make sense, though. Serena never mentioned anything about giving you visions of the future. I don't even think that's possible. So how in the world did you know about it beforehand?"

Mina shrugged. "I don't know. You're right. It doesn't make sense."

Fred asked, "Do you think Evelyn might have mentioned something about the robot when she was taking care of you? Think hard, Mina."

"No, Fred. It's not like building a mega robot is something someone just casually hears in a conversation and then immediately forgets. I'd remember if she'd told me. Now, shh. I want to hear what they're saying."

Evelyn was talking. "Right, and we'll have several guards positioned at different stations throughout the day and night to be on the lookout for trespassers."

A woman in the crowd asked, "But how is this a compromise? With a robot the size you're talking about, won't everyone have to stop building houses to help make it?"

Bob reassured the woman, "It will take a lot less time to create one giant weapon than an entire arsenal of smaller ones. Plus, the mega-robot covers all our bases. If we stopped working on the city to create weapons, we can't be certain how long that would take. We don't even know how many weapons we might need. And if New Waldoff really did send troops up here, we'd be in a weak position if they managed to surround us from above."

One of the men holding a 'No Homes for Weapons' sign said, "That's right. That's what happened during the first wolf massacre!"

Bob nodded. "We don't need nearly as many people to help build the mega-robot as we would to build tons of smaller weapons. Evelyn and I have created a project plan that calls for a team of twenty workers. There will be a few times when we'll need some extra help of course, but for the most part, everyone can continue working with their construction teams while the team of twenty builds the robot."

The man who'd argued with Jacques earlier asked, "But we need to defend ourselves starting like yesterday. How long is it going to take to build this guy?"

Evelyn answered, "We predict that if all goes right, we can have the robot up and running in three months."

"Three months?! We could all be dead by then," said the man.

Bob spoke again. "I understand that you're worried, but to be fair, it would take us twice that amount of time to build the number of weapons we'd need to defend ourselves against a direct attack on our city. And that's with everyone building the weapons. In fact, it would take nearly three months just to get everyone trained on how to build them safely."

The man with the thinning, red hair grumbled, "I'm not

sure how you did the math there. Seems like you're erring in your own favor if you ask me."

Evelyn offered, "Not at all, and as a show of good faith, I invite everyone here to meet with Bob and me during the next couple of days. We'll be working out of my house. Come by and let us show you our designs and project plans. We're happy to discuss it as much as you want and answer any further questions you may have."

"Alright, folks," John addressed the crowd again. "There you have it. You have three choices to consider over the next couple of days—no weapons and more new homes, weapons but no new homes, or mega-robot and new homes. We'll—"

But Jacques interrupted John by clearing his throat loudly.

John smirked. "Sorry, Jacques. I meant four options. You could also have no weapons, no new homes, but working kitchens in the homes that've already been built. We'll meet back here in two days to take a vote. Meeting adjourned."

The crowd began to disperse into groups with a lot of the sign holders talking to each other rather seriously in low voices. Mina said to Fred, "Lead me to Bob. I want to speak to him."

"What, now?" Fred asked.

"Yes, now. I want to ask him some questions about the mega-robot."

"Oh," Fred replied sounding relieved. "I thought you were planning to talk to him about Helen's secret relationship."

"No, of course not. Is he talking to anyone?"

Fred began walking Mina around the groups of people who were chatting with each other. "He's talking to Evelyn, of course. Those two have been spending a lot of time together lately."

"What does that mean?" asked Mina.

"Nothing. It's good, honestly. It seems like Evelyn is helping take Bob's mind off of Maude." Fred paused and then said, "Okay, we're almost there. Can you see them?"

Mina nodded. "Barely, but enough, I guess."

Bob and Evelyn stopped talking as Fred and Mina approached them. "So, what do you guys think?" asked Evelyn.

"I think it's a great idea," Fred responded first. "I'm not sure we really need it, but if it gets the weapon-pushers to quiet down, then I'm all for it."

"Good!" said Evelyn. "Because we want you to help us build it. Will you two join our team?"

"Oh wow!" said Fred as he looked at Mina to gauge her reaction. "What do you think? Do you feel well enough to help them build the robot?"

Bob spoke, "Well, we don't know if we have the votes yet, but if we do, we'd love for you to help us. We'll of course need to accelerate the timeline on Mina's prosthetic before undertaking such a large project, though. Do you think you could come by Evelyn's tomorrow, Mina? We need to finalize a few measurements before we draw up the plans to attach it."

"Sure," said Mina. "But can I speak with you alone for a moment, Bob?"

Evelyn and Fred exchanged glances, but Bob said, "Of course, Mina. Let's take a walk."

Mina asked, "Do you mind if I hold onto your arm as we go? I'm still feeling sort of weak."

Bob nodded and stuck out his elbow so Mina could loop her arm through his. "What did you want to tell me?" Bob asked when they'd gotten far enough away from all the people who'd hung around after the meeting.

"I need to ask you to do something, but I can't tell you why I'm asking. I just need you to trust me, okay?"

Bob replied, "Okay, but I'm glad you pulled me away from the others before you said that. Did Fred tell you there's a growing belief that you might be a spy sent by Goodman? Absurd, I know, but paranoia makes people believe strange things."

"Yes, Fred told me, although I don't think I believed it until just now. I thought he was being overprotective. Anyway, I need you to promise me that there will be a kill switch on the robot. Not just a switch to shut it down quickly, but a switch that will fry its insides and make it completely useless. Forever."

Bob took a moment before he replied. "And you can't tell me why?"

Mina shook her head. "No, I can't. To be honest, I don't exactly know myself, but I do know it's important. You wouldn't need to tell anyone about the kill switch except for the people you trust to operate the robot, of course."

"Well, I will say that the thought of a kill switch had crossed my mind, although I would never have made its function quite as extreme as what you're asking for. However, being married to a goddess for fifty some odd years, without either of us having a clue who she was, has made me a great deal more open minded. I'll do it for you, Mina."

"Thank you, Bob. I'm sure it sounds crazy, but I'll sleep a lot easier tonight knowing you'll do it."

"Speaking of sleeping, Evelyn and I have been talking about what to do with you and Fred now that you're feeling better. We've decided to move you into Evelyn's house for the time being and let her go back to sleeping in a tent for a while. Her place is so filled with all of her medicines and chemistry sets that we barely have any room to work as it is. It's going to take a lot of space to begin working on the robot parts—if we get the votes. Some of the build will need to happen outside, but we're going to do all the workshopping at my place."

"That's very generous of Evelyn to give up her house like that, though. Are you sure she's okay with it?"

Bob nodded. "Yes, it was her idea actually. Granted she'll still want to have full access to her house during the day, but we'll leave you two alone at night. It's just temporary until you get your own place. We can't move you up the list obviously since you were the last ones here, but this should work until then."

Mina gave Bob a hug, although she fumbled a little since his body was mixed in with the memories flinging themselves across her mind's eye. "Thank you, Bob. I feel like I owe you a lot. You sent me home, brought me back, and have helped me feel comfortable here. You're a true gentleman. Maude was lucky to have you."

"Thank you, Mina. That's kind of you, but really, I was the lucky one. Anyway, I'll walk you over to Evelyn's place. I suspect she will have already told Fred of the new sleeping accommodations. They're probably already over there now. How much are you able to see, anyway?"

Mina smiled. "So, you can tell, huh?"

"Oh, yes. I mean, I only suspected it before, but when you raised your arm towards my chin for a hug a moment ago, I knew for sure."

Mina brushed it off. "It's just a mild case of blindness left over from the migraine. I can see shapes, and my vision is returning a little more each day."

"Well, okay. But I think you need to talk to Evelyn if your vision isn't back to normal in the next couple of days. Deal?"

Mina nodded. "Can I ask you something else?"

Bob laughed. "Well, I assume it's too early in the relationship for you to be asking me to install a kill switch in Fred. So, go ahead."

"Years ago, when Helen was still pretty young, she had a relationship with a man that was a friend of yours and Maude's. What happened?"

Bob stopped in his tracks. "Max!" he exclaimed as if the words Mina had spoken had suddenly brought back a long-forgotten memory. "Oh my god. I can't remember the last time I thought about that. I guess I must have shoved it out of my head right after it all happened. I can't believe I hadn't thought about that since that day. Heck, we worked together for years after that, and I never even gave it any more consideration. That doesn't seem like me."

"Hmm," pondered Mina. "I suspect it might not have been your fault that you forgot."

"What do you mean?" Bob asked.

"I mean there's clearly more going on in this world than any of us knows, and I want to get some answers," explained Mina.

"You think this has something to do with that other goddess Serena? The one who kept Fred, Axel, and Ragher prisoner in the ice tunnels? Fred seems convinced that she isn't bad, but I think he might have Stockholm syndrome. How could he not be angry that she stole nine years of his life, for crying out loud?"

"Yes, I think this does have something to do with Serena, but I'm not comfortable saying any more about it right now. I don't think Fred has Stockholm syndrome, though. I think he's just been tasked with keeping secrets that he'd rather not keep."

"I see," said Bob. "I suppose I shouldn't ask any more about it then, since you probably wouldn't tell me anyway."

Mina smiled. "I don't know that much to begin with, but hopefully, I will soon."

They arrived at Evelyn's a few minutes later to find Fred there by himself. Fred took Mina by the arm and helped her into Evelyn's living room. "I've already thanked Evelyn several times over, but I want to thank you too, Bob, for giving us a place to stay these past few weeks. It was kind of you to share your home with us."

Bob waved him off. "I don't know how kind it was with you two having to sleep on the floor, but it was my pleasure to have you."

Mina took hold of Bob's hand. "We appreciated it, Bob. I

know it must have been tough having a patient as a guest. Please thank Evelyn for me, too, when you see her later, and tell her that I love her new roof."

Bob bid Mina and Fred goodnight and then showed himself out. That evening, Mina went right to sleep, exhausted from her first night out since the memories began and happy to be sleeping in a normal bed again. Before she conked out, she reached over and draped her arm across Fred's muscular chest. Through a yawn, she said, "I love you, Freddie."

"Freddie?" he asked. "Hey, Mina. Before you fall asleep, will you tell me what you said to Bob?"

But Mina was already out like a light.

A few hours later, once the city had gone to sleep, Mina sat up straight in Evelyn's bed and stared into the darkness. She realized right away she could see again, although the light was so low there wasn't much she could see besides the long shadows across the bedroom floor.

"Fred! Wake up!" she yelled, pushing against his shoulder frantically.

"What is it?" he asked sleepily.

"The city. I think it's under attack," Mina said in a loud whisper.

Fred sat up next to her. "Mina, I don't hear anything. I think if the whole city were being attacked, we'd hear—"

Suddenly, there was a blinding flash of light and a loud explosion from just outside Evelyn's house.

Mina and Fred jumped out of bed and went running to the living room as more explosions rang out across the city, rattling the very foundation of the house. Mina moved towards the window, but Fred pulled her back. "No! We can't. Whoever's doing this might see us and try to break in. We have to stay hidden!"

But Mina shook her head. "We have to find out what's

going on out there! If their plan is to blow up the houses, then we're sitting ducks in here."

Without waiting for Fred to respond, Mina flung the front door open and stepped out into a wild scene. There were people wearing black clothing and hoods running through the streets and throwing grenades into windows while hundreds of Rebeltonians fled their homes in nothing more than their night clothes. Some of them were holding their children in their arms as they ran.

Mina could feel the adrenaline coursing through her. She sped towards a man dressed in all black, who was about to throw a grenade. She pushed him to the ground from behind. Fred called to her from somewhere that sounded lightyears away as Mina watched the grenade tumble from the man's hand. Right away, she realized what she'd done. By shoving the man to the ground, she'd interrupted his throw which meant the grenade had only gone half the distance between the man and the house he was targeting.

Mina panicked. She turned to run, but it was too late. The explosion went off with a loud bang and a bright flash. As she was launched through the air, she heard someone screaming, but she couldn't tell who it was. For a second, she thought of the man she'd pushed to the ground, but the thought didn't last long. Because once the second was up, her thoughts went quiet as the darkness sunk its fangs into her.

CHAPTER 20

THE FORGOTTEN

A very long time ago

"Hello, young man," came a woman's sultry voice.

It was getting late, and Heely had been gathering sticks in the forest so he could build a fire at his campsite. Startled by the woman's presence, he dropped the firewood and turned to see who was behind him.

A tall lady with ebony hair and porcelain skin stood before him. She wore an ivory silk slip underneath a dark velvet robe that was tied together loosely by a silk sash. Her eyes and skin glistened in the fading light, and for a moment Heely thought the woman might be glowing.

Mesmerized by the sight of her, he stood and stared, forgetting to speak. He couldn't recall having ever seen a woman, or any other human during his twenty-five years of life. It was the reason he'd decided many years earlier that nobody else like him existed—that he was an anomaly. Heely shared his planet of lush forests, grassy plains, and sparkling blue seas with other creatures, but not one of them looked anything like him.

In his early youth, Heely had been raised on-and-off by a trio of talking sheep, but no matter how many times he'd asked the loquacious animals where he came from, he was given no reply. Or at least not one that made any sense.

"Hello there, ma'am."

"Ma'am?" asked the woman feigning a pout. "You would address me as your elder when I look as youthful as you? Maybe even more so?"

Heely shook his head. "No, I'm sorry. You're right. You do look very young, but to be honest, there's an aura about you that seems as old as the sky itself."

The woman took a step closer, smiling so sweetly that she looked practically fiendish. "That is kind of you to say. I wouldn't have expected you to be such a smooth talker when you've had no one to talk to for so long."

Heely held his ground, although he felt intimidated by the woman's approach. "Do you know me?" he asked bluntly. "For you speak as if you do. Are we related somehow?"

The woman laughed, and her bosom heaved, accentuated by her tight robe and slip. "Do we seem related? The way you're staring at me suggests you believe otherwise."

Heely blushed and said, "It's just I've never seen a woman before. In fact, I've searched this whole world and never come across another soul. Where did you come from?"

"Would you believe me if I told you that I came from your dreams?"

Heely thought about this for a moment and said, "Yes, I believe so. You do seem familiar now that you mention it. But how?"

The woman wrapped her arms around Heely's shoulders and drew herself into him. "My name is Serena Hecate, but you can call me Cate," she said. Her mouth was so close to his that he could feel her breath tickling his lips like a warm kiss. "I've been watching you for a while now, and I think we could have fun. Would you like that, Heely?" she asked.

Heely nodded his head. He was so overcome by the new feelings he was having that he wasn't capable of thinking clearly anymore. He leaned into Cate and kissed her with a longing he'd never known. The two of them fell to the ground, rolling on top of one another over the leaves, moaning and panting wildly.

But quickly, the scene changed, revealing another place and time. Heely was older, somewhere in his early thirties. His face was covered in black and gray stubble and his hair had begun to turn white along the sides. He stood in front of a cottage staring at the large trees that formed a border to the clearing he was standing in.

He spoke to the air, "Are you there, Cate? I'm ready."

Suddenly Serena appeared in front of him, wearing a long white gown that billowed in the salty sea breeze. She smiled lovingly. "Are you sure, darling? You've considered every angle of my proposal carefully?"

Heely nodded. "Yes. We can bring a child into this world as long as you promise that he'll never be alone. I don't want him to suffer the way you made me suffer."

Serena reached out and stroked the side of Heely's face with her long fingers. "No. I know that was a mistake now. I tried to protect you by keeping you from others, but I realize it was at too great a cost. Our child will want for nothing. As soon as they are born, I will fill this world with people and cities and incredible stories. That is what you want, yes?"

Heely nodded. "Yes, Cate. And you will live here with us like you said you would? At least for a while?"

Serena nodded. "Yes, I'll stay close until our child turns five. But you remember the deal, don't you? Once I leave, your memory of me as I am now will be erased and so will the child's.

For our son or daughter to fulfill their potential, they must not know who I am, which means you must not remember either."

Heely sighed. "Yes, I understand, although I wish it weren't so. What will our child think of having a father who can't remember anything about their mother?"

Serena Cate took Heely's hand. "You don't need to worry about that, my sweet Heely. I have a plan that will prevent our child from ever thinking less of you."

Heely asked, "Do you think you could at least let me keep a few of my memories? Or maybe give me some fake ones with you mixed into them. I don't need to remember you're a god after all, just that you were the woman I loved."

Serena wrapped her arms around him. "Yes, Heely. Because I love you so, I will grant you that, although it won't be much. But don't be sad. Once our child is born, they will bring you so much joy, you won't pine for me the way you do now. And when I'm truly gone, you won't pine for me at all."

Heely shook his head. "That's not possible, Cate. I believe that a piece of me will always pine for you. Despite everything you've done, I believe our love story to be greater than any other love story in any of the other worlds that exist out there."

Serena pulled Heely into her and kissed him tenderly. "I do love you," she said, "which makes it so much harder to fulfill my plans. But Heely, I *will* one day move on. There's a clock inside of me that I cannot ignore, a constant ticking of gears. It drives me mad most of the time, though when I'm with you I feel a little less so."

"Then, maybe once you spend some time with me and our child, the ticking will go away, and you'll be able to find peace again."

Serena shook her head. "No. You must understand; that will never happen. The possibilities that were once present in my life, in this existence, are no longer attainable. Something was taken from me long ago that I can never get back. The only hope I have is to keep moving forward. I have spent longer than you can imagine planning all the steps that must be taken to get to where I need to be, and nothing that anyone does will ever stop that from happening."

Heely looked disappointed, but he said, "Alright, Cate. I understand."

Serena knew he still had hope that things would change, but she couldn't risk talking him out of the decision he'd made to have a child with her. She took his hands and placed them on her hips. "Are you ready then?"

Heely held Serena in his arms and kissed her. Then he swept her up before laying her down in the grass outside the cottage. Serena began to shine brightly from inside. He looked at her quizzically, but she nodded at him. And so, he began to make love to her.

A second later, the sky above them lit up in a cosmic spiral of orange, gold, pink, and purple, like a spinning sunset. From inside the heavenly spiral, a glowing pebble of bright light emerged and floated towards the trees. Like a playful fairy, it bobbed up and down through the air, bouncing off several of the large evergreens until it implanted itself deep inside the middle of a solid pine, halfway up. The enormous tree lit up in blinding white light. Then as it dimmed, it began to glow a fiery red as though it might burst into flame. But soon, the tree returned to normal, except for a small mound that had developed over the spot where the tiny orb had entered through the bark.

Time jumped forward again to a stormy night outside the cottage. The same tree that had accepted the little light was now dying, rotting from the inside out as a huge radiating embryo clung to its decomposing wood. Heely stared at the tree from the backdoor with a worried expression. The light inside the plasma-filled sac was pulsating. Something he'd never seen it do before.

Serena Cate moaned in pain from inside the little cottage. Heely passed through the kitchen to the living room where Serena sat in an armchair wrapped in blankets in front of a flickering fire. Heely stood by her side and held her hand, not quite sure what else to do.

"It's time," she said, pressing her hand to the wool blanket that was pulled tightly over her stomach. "I can feel it. Grab the ax and go! *Now*, Heely!" Serena ordered as she began to moan again.

"Are you sure, Cate? There's lightning close by, and the rain is coming down in buckets."

Serena shot him a dirty look that made it clear she thought he was being a coward. "I don't care if there's a tornado riding atop a tsunami out there. It's time, Heely. Get the ax," she said grinding her teeth.

Heely let go of her hand and walked to the closet where he put on a warm jacket and grabbed a shiny ax with a long wooden handle. "This won't hurt you, will it?" he asked standing in the entryway to the living room, ax in hand.

"No!" she shouted as she cried out in agony. "The only thing hurting me is watching you act like a fool when you should be out there getting on with it!"

Heely nodded and said, "Yes, Cate."

Then, like a man on a mission, he left the cozy cottage behind and walked headlong into the clearing as he made his way towards the tall trees that guarded the border between the land and the sea. When he reached the dying tree, he paused to gaze up at the large embryo clinging to the diseased-looking conifer. The light from the thick pod was pulsing faster than before.

Heely felt uneasy about what he was about to do. Stalling for another second, he carefully ran the tip of his finger along the ax's narrow edge, making sure it was still sharp from the last time he'd used it. He winced. The glistening blade sliced his finger and several drops of blood collected on its tip. Heely lifted his finger to his mouth and sucked the blood away.

"Alright, child. Your mother says it's time for you to come into this world. So be it!"

Heely pulled back his ax and swung it with all his might into the side of the decaying tree. The world around him lit up in a flash of brilliant blue light as though the electrical storm was responding to his newfound determination.

He pulled back the ax a second time and swung it again into the same notch he'd carved out on the first strike. Again and again, he sliced into the trunk as tiny bits of dying wood sprayed from the tree with each blow of the ax.

Minutes later, there was a loud crack, and Serena Cate screamed like a banshee, a frightening sound that echoed throughout the clearing. The tree fell, and Heely jumped out of the way to give it room. A loud thud shook the ground as the tree made contact, and Heely hurried to the spot where the embryo now lay looking less plump with barely any light left inside of it.

Kneeling down, he grabbed the gelatinous blob. Then he stood up and threw it over his shoulder like he was hauling a sack of potatoes. He moved swiftly across the clearing with both hands holding the pod firmly so that his long strides didn't jostle the delicate package. When he reached the cottage, Serena was cursing his name. Her forehead and the sides of her face were glistening with sweat, and dark strands of her hair clung to each.

"You wretched mook! You took forever! Bring me the capsule!"

Heely obliged, laying the squishy sac at Serena's feet. "I know you're in pain, Cate. What can I do? I long to make this easier on you."

"What can you do!?" she yelled. "You can go back in time and prevent your treacherous parents from messing up all of existence! This job of bringing about life was much simpler before they forced my hand. Because of them, I had to destroy the Earth and all of my most beautiful creations. It was an unimaginable feat that permanently degraded my energy. Before that, I would've been able to create a million divine children with just a snap of my fingers!"

Serena groaned loudly and dropped her head back, still holding onto the blankets that were pulled tightly around her.

After the groaning subsided, she continued, "So, you think you can do that, Heely? You think you can fix all of creation? I mean, I, as a supreme goddess, have been trying to fix it for the last several thousand years, but I'm sure that *you*, as a non-supreme god, could just breeze right in and fix it all in a jiff. Right?" Serena doubled over in pain.

Despite the dressing down, Heely stayed by Serena's side. When she was able to sit up again, she looked at him with remorse and said, "I'm sorry I lashed out. I just want this part to be over. Go into the kitchen, darling. You won't want to see the rest of this."

"I'm fine, Cate. There's nothing about bringing our child into the world that could disgust me. I want to stay with you."

But Serena shook her head defiantly. "No, this part must remain private. This life we're about to meet is powerful. It has been here before many times. More than anyone, save for me. It needs to be eased into the world gently, or it might not survive the process. It is jarring to put so much energy into a confused and helpless vessel. It's like trying to trap a powerful storm inside a tiny jar."

Heely didn't quite understand what Serena meant by this, but he knew it was important to her that he go. So he leaned over, kissed her cheek, and said, "Okay. I'll be close by in case you need me."

Then he left her side and walked to the kitchen. He sat at the little table and drummed his knuckles lightly against the uneven wood, in rhythm to his own heartbeat. A minute later, the living room went eerily quiet, and Heely worried that something had gone wrong. Yet before he could call to Serena to find out if she was okay, a loud commotion rang out like the sound of a melon being ripped apart. First, there was sloshing, then tearing, then the sound of water splashing against the wood floor.

Heely rapped his knuckles faster against the tabletop, nervously waiting on news from the living room. From what he'd heard so far, he felt certain that Serena Cate had opened the pod, but there was no indication that a baby was inside— no cooing, no crying, not even a gurgle. He stopped knocking against the table and grabbed the edge of it tightly with his hand. "Come on, Cate," he said to himself quietly so only he could hear. "Don't leave me hanging."

As if in response to his plea, a sharp squeal rang out, like metal scraping against metal. The screeching came not just from the living room, but from all around the house, blasting from all directions. Heely covered his ears, but the sound was too loud to keep out.

"Cate!" yelled Heely, worried something terrible was happening. He sprang to his feet and ran into the living room where he found a creature made of crystals, holding a naked baby. A beam of light shone from the center of the creature's forehead, and it pointed directly at the newborn's face.

"Is that you, Cate?" Heely asked, even though he knew his words couldn't be heard over the terrible screeching.

He looked around the living room in an attempt to figure out the strange scene. The blankets that had been wrapped tightly around Serena were now strewn across the floor, and the creature, who resembled a sparkling, crystalized giant, was kneeling on a wool rug in front of the chair where Serena Cate had been sitting only moments before. The giant was half again as big as Serena and made of tiny, multifaceted crystals which covered every part of its form. And though it was somewhat hard to discern, the creature appeared to be in the shape of a woman.

Heely watched, suddenly drawn in by the brilliant ray of white light that ran from the creature to the small baby. The ray twisted and turned in sync to the continuous shrieking, and it occurred to Heely that the beam might be the source of the sound. The baby squirmed and stiffened as if in distress, but Heely couldn't see the child's face from his position in the doorway or hear its angry cries.

After another minute passed with Heely transfixed by the strange scene, the light moving from the creature to the baby stopped twisting, detached from the crystalized woman's forehead, and gently floated into the baby's eyes where it was absorbed. The horrible sounds ceased, and Heely removed his hands from his ears as he shook away the spell he'd fallen under.

Almost instantly, he regretted this decision when a second later, an otherworldly voice bellowed at him from the creature's mouth. "This is your daughter. I chose you to be her father because I knew I could trust you to watch over her all of your days. You will not disobey me!"

Heely knew for certain now that this creature was his precious Cate, and he nodded. "I will look after our daughter until my very last breath, but not because you've ordered me to. I will do it because I love her, and because she deserves all the happiness that I can give to her and more."

Serena Cate nodded too. "What will you name our daughter then?"

Heely thought for a moment and said, "How do you feel about the name Mene?"

"Mene?" Serena asked. "Yes, that is a strong name, but not

quite the one I was expecting you to pick. How about we call her Mina? It's a more pleasing name and one she's likely to feel comfortable with"

Heely took a step towards them. "May I hold her?"

Serena looked at Mina. The little baby had fallen asleep, but Serena was still holding her out in front of her like she was a squirming dog instead of a baby. She lowered Mina into Heely's arms, and Heely gazed down at the dark-haired, rosy-cheeked, slumbering babe.

"Yes, Cate," he said smiling. "I think Mina is the perfect name for our beautiful girl."

Again, the scene began to pull apart into an array of colors as it jumped forward once more.

Serena was holding Mina who was now a young girl. She sang a sweet song to her while rocking her back and forth and caressing her hair. Heely watched his family from the doorway of Mina's room, smiling wistfully at the scene, wishing that the days they spent together could last longer.

As the young Mina learned to walk, she began to play outside in the grass near the cottage with her new puppy, Bonkers. However, it was soon after Mina became mobile that Serena became more and more absent from Mina's life. During the long periods while her mother was away, Heely took Mina on walks along the shore or through the forest by their home. He taught her about their world and told her stories of the years he'd spent all alone, and of the different places he'd seen while traveling across the entire planet.

He also took her around town to see the new people and places that had appeared right after Mina was born—just as Serena Cate had promised they would. But Heely never mentioned to his daughter that these people and places were just as new to their world as she was because he knew the truth was forbidden. Plus, he wasn't sure how Serena Cate's magic worked, and he worried that if the people found out they didn't really belong to their world, the spell might be broken.

Mina loved spending time with her father and listening to his stories, but around the time she turned four, she began asking a lot of questions about why her mother was always gone. Of course, no answer ever satisfied her. And soon enough, whenever Serena went missing for a day or more, Mina would go into hysterics, sometimes becoming despondent after she finally settled down. It was a difficult decision for Heely to make, but he knew that the time had come for Serena to either choose to stay with them or leave for good.

One night, when Heely and Serena Cate were getting ready for bed after she'd returned from an exceptionally long absence, he confronted her.

"You've been clear from the start what this relationship is, and you owe me no explanation. But still, I feel the need to ask. Where is it you go that is more important than being right here with your daughter?"

Serena Cate sat down on the end of their bed and sighed. "As you know, Heely, you live inside of a crystal world—a relic left over from when the Earth was still alive. When your parents betrayed me, I did my best to preserve all the life I could, along with the best parts of my creations. The result of this was that hundreds of lesser worlds came into existence. They are beautiful and full of life, but they operate on a much lower level of energy than the original world I created, Ortus.

"Ortus has been stripped down to a barren land because when I created Earth I did so by transferring most of Ortus' energy into the mighty universe where Earth existed. However, when the Earth died, the energy it had taken from Ortus didn't return back to Ortus in the same way—the way your parents had hoped it would when they defied me. Instead, it broke up, fragmenting into hundreds of tiny worlds like yours.

"One day, these crystal worlds will disappear altogether,

and the only pieces of my creations that will be left will live in the original but desolate world of Ortus. When your parents turned on me, they did so in hopes of recreating the paradise that Ortus had once been, but that was never possible."

Serena Cate stood up and took Heely's hand.

"So then, you go to Ortus whenever you leave us?"

She nodded and led him to the bedroom window.

"Look up there. The moon that you see isn't' really a moon at all. It's another dimension. All the crystal worlds have the same moon in their sky, but none of these moons are actually a giant rock circling a planet. They are inter-dimensional portals that lead straight to Ortus. Hidden inside the fabric of each crystal world is a one-way ticket to travel to the one, all-encompassing dimension. This was true of Earth too, but I was the only one who ever knew the secret. Not even the time gods were allowed to know."

Heely looked away from the silvery moon and focused on Serena again. "So why did we bring a life into this world if one day this world will cease to exist?"

"Because, Heely. I have a plan to fix all the wrongs. And Mina is a part of that plan. One day, she will join me on Ortus to help fight those who would try to stop me."

"I don't like the sound of that, Cate. Mina is a sweet child. She shouldn't have to fight anyone."

Serena frowned. "I'm sorry, but you don't get a say in this, Heely. Mina will live a good life with you and remain a child for longer than any other child. Time moves slower here than on Ortus, and although you have nothing to compare it to, you and Mina will get to spend a very long time together.

"Also, you may have already noticed, but our daughter ages much slower than you. For that reason, and for several others, I am stationing two guards here to act as her parents. But please don't worry. They'll never love her the way you do. They will believe that she's their own child, but they won't feel true parental love for her."

Heely protested. "That's awful, Cate! You and I should be the ones to take care of her, not some guards who don't even care about her! And what are you planning to do with me, anyway? There's no way I could ever forget that Mina's my daughter. She's more important to me than anything else in any dimension in the universe!"

Serena shrugged. "This is why I didn't tell you until now. I knew it would be upsetting, which wasn't my intention. I do love you and Mina, but I have elves and a shifter being to take care of back on Ortus."

"You mean you have pets? These other creatures are more important to you than us?"

"No, darling. But they are important. They, too, will play a role in my plan. Especially my shifter, although the life I'm setting him up for will lack any true meaning to him. I have set him and his loved one up to live worthless lives in order to get what I want in the long run. However, there will be good moments for my sweet Ragher too. He and the wolves he'll eventually join will just have to learn how to make the best out of some truly terrible situations. But alas, I digress."

Serena Cate took a step towards Heely, but he turned his face away in anger. She sighed. "You are right, my darling. It is time. Maybe I have already stayed in your lives too long. I'd hoped we could be together one more year, but I see now that the longer I am present, the harder this will all be."

Backing away from Heely, Serena raised both her hands above her head, readying herself to cast her spell. Heely looked back at her, realizing what was about to happen. He flew at her, and they toppled to the floor, but Serena had already begun to speak the primeval words, words that no one else had ever known except for her and the time gods.

The spell sounded like a beautiful, ancient melody and as

Serena continued, the lights all over the planet dimmed, and a powerful wind rushed towards them from each corner of the world. Then everything went dark except for Serena Cate, whose skin began to glow in a pale blue light.

Heely could feel his thoughts beginning to jumble and twist in his brain, like the beam of light that had shone from Serena's forehead the day Mina was born.

"Please, Cate," he pleaded, but she didn't stop.

Heely leaned over her as she lay on the ground and touched her lips with his fingertips as they spoke the final words that would steal his memories of her away forever. Tears filled their eyes as they stared at one another for the last time, and Heely kissed Serena Cate's face like it was the final thing he would ever do.

And in a way, it was.

CHAPTER 21

RAGHER'S DILEMMA

Ragher had been pacing back and forth for nearly twelve hours. Never in his long life had he been in such turmoil over what to do next. For hundreds of years, he'd done whatever the oracle had told him to do, though he knew very well that the woman in the ice labyrinth wasn't an oracle at all—or even a woman for that matter. And while it would have been appropriate to call her a goddess, she wasn't exactly that either.

During his era of captivity, Ragher had known her as Serena Hecate, but mostly he just referred to her as Serena. This name was the one she had told him to use in his earliest memory of their time together. But he wondered now if this had really been their first encounter, or if it was just the first encounter Serena had allowed him to remember.

Ragher was well aware of how Serena manipulated the memories of mortals and gods alike. He knew what she had done to Theia and Theo. She'd shown Ragher visions of the ways in which she'd altered their realities, just like she'd done to Ragher and the ones he loved. And while Ragher was back in the confines of Serena's ice fortress, wandering the labyrinth with Axel and Fred for nine years, Serena had shown him the truth about Fred too. It turned out that Fred was the reincarnation of one of the most ancient creatures on the Moon, although Ragher doubted whether Serena had shared this truth with Fred.

Serena had forced Ragher to keep many of her secrets for hundreds of years, but she also kept plenty of secrets from him, too. He had been her loyal subject. He'd wanted to please her and had even worshipped her like she was his god, but all she'd ever done for him was bring him heartache. When she sent him out to protect Neriti, Ragher thought Serena was finally allowing him to live freely. He hadn't realized what Serena actually had in store for him—a relationship between Neriti and him that would bring them both years of suffering and unimaginable grief.

Serena hadn't warned Ragher that Theo might suspect he was a Moon Walker, and therefore, it was an awful surprise when he realized that Theo's minion was constantly stalking him. Serena had shown Ragher many visions of Theo killing the Moon Walkers by sucking out their energy, yet she had never bothered to inform Ragher that she'd put a spell on the remaining Moon Walkers—before they were transformed into wolves and bryobane—that prevented Theo from stealing their energy anymore.

That bit of information alone would have prevented so many of the mistakes that Ragher and Neriti made over the years when trying to protect their family. But Ragher knew that it was no accident Serena had withheld this important information. He had seen the depths Serena was willing to go to at times to change the course of the Moon creatures' lives. He had seen alternate timelines while in the ice tunnels and knew that Serena had a way to analyze and weigh the outcomes of events. He had seen her do it when deciding whether to exterminate the bryobane. And later he realized that Serena had shown him a projection of what Neriti's life would look like before she was even born.

This meant that Serena had known Neriti was destined to bring great healing to the wolves, but instead of allowing it to happen, Serena had sent Ragher to unwittingly destroy this timeline. And while Ragher hadn't known it then, he now understood that the ripples he created in Neriti's life had transformed it into a much different version of the one he'd seen in the tunnels. Instead of a life full of purpose, Neriti's life had often been full of tragedy. And the knowledge that he'd played a part in ruining her life was devastating to Ragher, causing him to wonder if Serena might actually be pure evil.

At the very least, it was evident that she was playing games with everyone's existence, like a devious chess master carelessly allowing most of her pieces to be taken before pulling off a grand maneuver during the endgame.

And once again, Serena had set him free to do her bidding. She had sent Ragher to find Axel so he could trick his son into fighting Theo. Serena's plan was for Ragher to volunteer to go tell Theo that the wolves wouldn't fight him—that they wanted to stay neutral going forward.

But in reality, Serena had ordered Ragher to sacrifice himself to the dark god in order to draw the wolves into the fight. Serena had told Ragher that this was the only way to prevent the wolves from being annihilated, and she promised him that if he did as she commanded, she would allow Axel to inherit the Moon realm along with Serena's own child.

The problem was that Ragher didn't know if he believed any of this. Serena had lied to him many times as a way to get him to do what she wanted, and it had cost him everything. Plus, he'd never known Serena had a child, and knowing what he did about her, Ragher found it hard to believe.

So now Ragher was stuck worrying about what to do next, and after a full day of contemplating whether to follow Serena's commands, he'd worn himself ragged from all the pacing and stress. Without even thinking about what he was doing, he soon succumbed to his exhaustion and lay down to sleep.

It was impossible to know how much time had passed while he was sleeping, but when he awoke there was a beautiful, white wolf standing over him, nudging Ragher's foot with her nose. "Wake up, Ragher. You can't sleep. We need to move on from here quickly."

Ragher was confused about what was happening, and assuming it was just a dream, he began to fall back asleep.

"No," snapped the female wolf. "I told you we need to get going. We have a mission to complete."

Ragher raised his head a little and opened his eyes again, trying to sort out whether this pushy voice really did belong to a dream or not. But this time when he laid eyes on the wolf, he knew he wasn't dreaming. Instead, he thought he was staring at a ghost.

"Imgu?" he asked in a frightened tone.

"No, Ragher. Imgu is dead, remember? I'm Imgu's daughter, Elu, the leader of the underground wolf pack. Now get up. We have to move."

Ragher finally understood he wasn't dreaming, and he stood up to face Elu. "But why are you here? What mission are you talking about?"

Elu looked around. "We have to go to Theo right away. Neriti has been sending me messages for several weeks, and she says this is what we must do. But we have to hurry. Otherwise, your friend who lives in the ice tunnels will find out and try to stop us."

"She's not my friend," Ragher replied, and as he said it something inside of him snapped, as though hearing himself say these words out loud suddenly broke a spell he'd been under for centuries. He realized that of course he wasn't going to obey Serena's orders. He had no idea if he could trust Elu or believe that Neriti was somehow sending her messages, but he didn't care because any path forward that didn't involve Serena was the path he knew he should take.

"Okay, I'm with you. Let's go," said Ragher, and the two wolves took off down the hilltop towards the Darkside, racing in the direction of Black Ice Glacier.

Once they reached the bottom and were headed into the darkness, Ragher asked, "How did you know where to find me?"

Elu answered, "Neriti. The messages she's been sending have been through dreams and visions. She showed me where you would be."

"Alright. But then how did she know? I only just left the ice tunnels and was trying to decide what to do next. A day ago, I didn't even know I would be there."

Elu waited a second and then said, "Look, I know this is going to be hard to hear, but I think the dark spirit is the one who told her. Some of the messages I received seemed to be coming not just from Neriti, but from Theo, too."

Elu was right. Ragher didn't like the sound of this. "How can you be sure that it wasn't Theo alone sending you these messages? He could be trying to lure me back in. I assume Axel told you stories of Theo when he tried to get your pack to unite with the others. But I promise you, those stories pale in comparison to what Theo is truly capable of."

"It wasn't just Theo. The first vision was definitely from Neriti. She appeared to me and the other healers in our pack during one of our healing circles and recited ancient chants that only she would know. It is true that she was using Theo's powers to communicate with us, but she assured us that the dark god is weak. After this manifestation, she continued to come to me privately to tell me some of the things she's learned during these years that her energy has been bound to Theo's. And I believe Theo shared some of this, too, because

I was able to see into his past, to a time when he lived on Earth.

"Neriti wants you to hear all of this for yourself, however. She said it's important you no longer follow Serena's orders."

Ragher felt a little more confident that Elu's story was real, but he wanted to be careful. "I believe you, but I think we should transform ourselves before we face Theo. Axel taught you how to shift when he visited your pack, right?"

"Yes, he gave us back our voices and taught us how to embrace our Moon Walker powers."

"Good. Have you practiced enough to hold your shape at will?"

"Yes," confirmed Elu.

"Okay, then I think we should shift into humans before we get to Theo. He hates wolves, and the last time I saw him was right before I made my escape from Black Ice Fort, which means he might not be thrilled to see me. And if it turns out this is all a trick, a disguise could buy us some time to leave the glacier before Theo can catch us."

Elu let out a sigh. "Humans, though? Do you really think that's necessary?"

"Yes, I do. And I think it would be best if I took on the shape of Betsy and you of Dale. I happen to know that Betsy is able to see Theo, unlike the other humans, which means it won't seem strange for me to address him as her. You may be able to see him, too, now that you've discovered your Moon Walker powers, but we don't want to take any chances, just in case you can't."

Elu didn't like this idea. "Couldn't we shift into something less offensive? A couple of talking slugs, perhaps?"

Ragher laughed. "I don't think Theo would believe that a couple of talking slugs had arrived at Black Ice Glacier randomly, seeing as how there are no talking slugs on the Moon."

"That we know of, anyway," argued Elu. "Until a few weeks ago, I was under the impression that the Moon only has one god and that the Moon Walkers had disappeared ages ago. But now I know that none of that is true. We were the Moon Walkers. And the Moon has three gods, who seem to be at odds with each other, which feels like it might not bode well for the rest of us."

Ragher agreed. "Yes, that may be an accurate assessment of our situation, which is why I think we should take precautions when we go see Theo. Because who knows? Maybe it isn't even Theo luring us to the glacier. It could be some other force entirely, and we don't want to show up in wolf form to meet Theo if we're unwelcome."

Elu thought about this for a moment and said, "Okay. But this feels strange. What if Betsy and Dale aren't welcome either?"

"They may not be, but I doubt Theo will harm them because Betsy is Theo's daughter."

"Ah. That explains a lot about her character. But Dale? You don't think Theo would harm him either?"

Ragher responded, "No, I saw visions of Dale before I left the tunnels. He works for Betsy now. The worst-case scenario is that Theo might take Dale hostage as leverage against Theia, but I doubt it very much."

Elu asked, "Why would that give him leverage?"

"Because Maude was Theia, although she didn't realize it for most of her life. All of this was Serena's doing, the god who lives inside the underground ice fortress."

"Well, that certainly aligns with the messages Neriti has been sending me. Look, Ragher. Let's meet Theo face-to-face as ourselves. I know you've been through a lot. Neriti's messages showed me how much control the gods have had over your life. I understand that you feel the need to protect yourself by hiding. This is what my pack and I have done, too, for many years. We have hidden underground to avoid being targeted like before. Axel tried to get us to join the other wolves on the surface again, but we refused.

"When he left, I felt conflicted about the decision my pack made. At first, I thought it was right because we had agreed that it was our best chance to survive the evil that has plagucd the Moon since the Moon Travelers arrived. But now that I know the truth about what you and Neriti were put through by the gods, I can see that there is no use in trying to hide.

"The evil is much bigger than what we imagined, and it will find us no matter where we choose to hide. The only choice we have now is to face it together, but we cannot do that until we truly know what we're up against. That is why we are going to see Theo and Neriti. It is a dangerous risk, but I am tired of being overly cautious and hiding. Aren't you?"

Elu's words moved Ragher, and he smiled bravely, even though Elu couldn't see him in the pitch black.

"Yes. I am tired too. It's time to be brave. That is how I'd hoped to live my life all along, but so many times I was forbidden from doing so. You're right, Elu. The wolves need to face this evil together, and not the evil that Serena would have us believe in, but the true evil in this world. No more hiding. For better or worse."

CHAPTER 22

THE AFTERMATH

Two days had passed since Betsy's army had attacked Rebelton in the middle of the night. Nearly half the homes had sustained some kind of damage, from burned roofs to blown apart walls. Luckily, there had been no casualties or serious injuries, except for the ones Mina sustained.

Fred hated himself for not having done a better job of protecting her. He'd watched in horror as she'd shoved a man with a primed grenade. Like a fool, he'd started to run towards her to pull her back, but there wasn't enough time.

When Mina had shoved the man to the ground, she had prevented the grenade from completing its intended trajectory, which meant that it had landed close. When the grenade exploded, Mina was thrown through the air by the blast, and the man, who by all accounts should've been dead, survived without so much as a scratch. In fact, all the witnesses who watched the scene unfold swore that before the grenade even went off, the man was picked up by an invisible force and thrown down the street where he promptly stood up and took off running.

Mina, on the other hand didn't fare so well. Some of the shrapnel from the grenade lodged itself in her back before she hit the ground and was knocked out cold. Miraculously, once Evelyn removed the shrapnel, Mina's skin healed incredibly fast, and less than thirty-six hours after the ordeal was over, there weren't even any battle scars left to mark what had happened. However, after forty-eight hours, Mina was still in a coma, which meant that not every part of her had healed so well.

Fred worried that Evelyn might be suspicious of Mina's amazing healing power. But if she was, she didn't show it. At the end of the first two days, Evelyn said to him, "Don't get down. Mina has been through worse than this these last couple of months and dealt with it very well. I am sure she'll be healthy again soon. She's young and has quite the talent for healing. Plus, the coma she's experiencing is most likely the kind of coma associated with the brain needing time to heal from a bad concussion.

"In the meantime, Bob and I will be back tomorrow to go through the motions of fitting Mina with the new arm. We might as well get some practice in now so that when she wakes up, we'll be ready to go." Then she patted Fred on the shoulder reassuringly and left.

Fred lay next to Mina now on top of Evelyn's bed, speaking to her whenever he thought of things to say. "If you were ever trying to stay incognito, you sort of blew your chance, so to speak. Half the town thinks you had something to do with the attack because they saw you for the first time at the meeting that night. And also, they're idiots.

"The other half of the town suspects you might really be an angel and that the wings you wore when you first came to the Moon were real. Of course, none of them have any explanation for why you no longer have wings or seem to remember that I once had wings also. But you know, it's something for them to talk about."

Fred stared at Mina's silky, dark hair spread out across her chest and thought of the scenes he'd watched of her while he was in the ice tunnels. He could remember how much his heart ached for her then. She was beautiful and kind and smart, and he wanted more than anything to hold her.

He wrapped his arm around her waist gently and spoke again. "Evelyn and Bob got the votes to build the robot. There was a lot more debate after what happened, but they were able to make their case. I think what it came down to is that nobody wants what happened the other night to happen again. And the mega-robot is the only way to prevent Betsy's goons from having another crack at the city.

"Oh, and I almost forgot. Some of the people who wanted to stop construction to build weapons are telling everyone that Bob and Evelyn are responsible for the attack. They say they hired the New Waldoff thugs to come here and shake things up so that everyone would vote for the robot. Obviously, they're just sore losers."

Fred felt emotionally exhausted. He hadn't slept since the night Mina got hurt; he wanted to be there waiting for her when she awoke. Yet as he held her, he began thinking about where in space and time Mina might be, and soon he drifted off to sleep.

When Fred came to again, he was walking through a white haze. He couldn't see more than a few inches in front of his face, but he continued to push through the fog, hoping if he walked far enough, the world around him would become discernable again. There were no sounds to guide him, and he wasn't able to see his feet, so he moved carefully.

A second later, he heard voices and the haze evaporated. He was standing next to John and Maude in the valley while they discussed how to start construction of the new city. Fred looked around and noticed the man he and Mina had seen on horseback with Dale the day Fred brought Mina to Rebelton. He was hurrying towards John and Maude with dark storm clouds in his eyes.

"I need to talk to you right now!" Max demanded as he came within earshot of the couple. Then looking at John, he added, "Privately!"

John didn't like his tone. He put a hand on Max's chest as if to create a barrier between him and Maude. "You need to take a step back, lad. That's no way to be speaking to a lady."

Max snapped at John. "This doesn't concern you. You've already played your part in all this, helping everyone keep the big secret all these years. You can go now. I only want to speak to Maude."

John looked over his shoulder at Maude. "Do you believe this joker? What's he going on about keeping big secrets? I certainly must have done a mighty good job of it since I can't even remember what it was!"

Maude smiled. "You can go, John."

John frowned. "Not a chance, Maude. Not until this clown calms down by will or by force."

Maude shook her head. "That won't be necessary. I can handle Max, even in the state he's in."

John lowered his hand from Max's chest. "Well, I have no doubt about that, but I still say this fool shouldn't be speaking to you in such a manner. As far as I can tell, you've done nothing wrong to fill him with such piss and vinegar."

Then to Max, he said, "You better be respectful to Maude, young man. Or I'll come right back over here and teach you some proper manners."

Max stared at John but said nothing, waiting to have his turn to speak with Maude alone. John walked away, and Maude said, "Alright, Max. Let's have it out."

Max sighed, feeling a little less worked up than before. "I

remember everything, Maude. Ever since we left New Waldoff, I've been having trouble sleeping. But last night when the sun went down behind the mountain, I fell into a deep sleep, and everything came back to me. Only, it doesn't feel like it happened decades ago. It feels fresh, like it was yesterday. How could you keep it from me all this time? I loved her, Maude! I love Helen, and now she's dead!"

Maude's eyes filled with tears, thinking about her lost child. "I know she is Max. But it doesn't feel fresh to me. I loved Helen too, and it has been far too long since I've seen my darling girl. You need to understand something, though. Nobody here tricked you into forgetting Helen, because nobody who knew about you two remembers you were ever in love. Only you and me.

"But I didn't remember either until recently. I got my memories back before we left New Waldoff. I know who I am now; I'm Theia. But I'm not the only god on the Moon. Serena and Theo, my siblings, are also gods. Serena is more powerful than Theo and me. She's the one who cursed you so that you and everyone else on the Moon would forget about the relationship between you and Helen."

Max shot back. "I didn't just forget! Those memories were stolen from me. But now it all makes sense! You got your sister to do your dirty work in the greenhouse that day—to keep Helen and me apart!"

"No, Max. What Serena did to you—to all of us—was wrong. She's the reason I spent decades with no memories of who I was or where I came from. I've been waiting for you to remember. I thought once I got my memories back that you might start to, also. Clearly, Serena wants us to remember everything, but I haven't figured out why. Can you think of what she said before she took your memories? Anything that might explain why?"

Max shook his head. "No, Maude. Stop trying to confuse

me. You kept Helen from me. If you and Bob hadn't tried to tear us apart, none of this would have ever happened! And now she's dead, and I'll never get to see her again! Never get to even say goodbye!"

"Stop, Max! You can't let yourself go down that hole. We need to work out Serena's plan and figure out why she did this to you and Helen. What was her motive?"

Max's face grew tense. "I'm not staying here to work anything out with you. I'm leaving tonight. By hell or highwater, I'm going to find Serena. That woman's deranged, and someone needs to stop her. The fact that you're a god, yet you're just hiding away up here in the mountains instead of going after your sister to avenge Helen's death speaks volumes. You might not be deranged, but you're certainly not much of a god!"

Maude looked stunned, but before she could react, Max turned around and stormed off.

Suddenly, Fred became very aware of himself again, standing next to Maude watching Max walk away in a hurry. Then something profound happened. Maude looked right at him and said, "If you're here, then you must be a time god. Is that right, Fred?"

Fred looked down at himself, surprised to find that he was fully visible and not a ghost. He nodded at Maude. "Yes. Serena never told me I was a god, though. You did a few weeks from now when we meet again. We're going to break Bob out of prison and build a machine to bring Mina back after Serena releases me from the ice tunnels. That's where I am right now, or at least the version of me that exists in this time."

"I see," said Maude. "Okay, I think I have this figured out. Thank you for your help."

Maude started to walk away, but Fred thought for a second and then called after her. "There's something else, Maude."

Maude turned around and looked at Fred questioningly. He said, "Serena is planning to turn you back…"

But all of a sudden, Fred felt himself suffocating as he was jerked forcefully out of his dream state. He sat up in bed, gasping for air.

"It's okay, Fred" he heard Mina whisper to him sweetly.

Startled, he looked to his left and saw Mina sitting next to him propped up against the wall. "How long have you been awake?" he asked breathing hard.

Mina smiled and brushed his dark hair across his strong brow. Then she kissed him on the lips. "A while," she said. "I had a vision while I was out. I saw my parents on the day I was born. It was pretty incredible, to be honest. What my mother is capable of is horrifying. I wish I could've seen more, but I'm glad I got to witness that one day, at least. It's good to finally know the truth about where I come from. Why I'm here."

Fred looked stunned. "So you know, then? Why your mother brought you here?"

Mina shook her head. "Not exactly. I know how I got here, though. My mother made it clear on the day I was born that I'm an old soul. She also mentioned to my father that his parents had something to do with ruining her creation. I'm not sure what she meant, though. Do you know anything about that, Fred?"

Fred's heart skipped a beat. For a second, he'd hoped that the biggest secret he'd been keeping was finally out. But unfortunately, Mina still had no clue why Serena had summoned her. He shook his head and prayed that Mina didn't question him any further as the knots in his stomach grew. Being torn between two loyalties was breaking him.

Mina sighed. "How's that man? The one I tackled?"

"He's fine," said Fred, "although it's hard to say for sure since he ran off after the explosion. I think you saved his life. He flew out of the way before the grenade went off, like he was being thrown by an invisible hand. I think you have a lot of the rebels worried that you're some sort of witch now, but I'm sure Bob and Evelyn will help us sort it out."

Mina bit her lip. "Maybe they won't have to. I think it might be time for us to leave. You said you were going to visit the wolves, so let's go. I'm starting to feel restless like we're not supposed to be here anymore. Sitting around waiting for the rebels to work out their politics can't be the reason Serena wanted me back on the Moon. And I want to find out what my purpose is for being here. Unless maybe you already know."

Fred shook his head. "I'm not taking you away from here until Bob and Evelyn have attached the prosthetic, and you've given yourself a few weeks to learn how to use it. Surely, you see now how dangerous it can be after what happened the other night."

Mina frowned. "I'm a demi-god, Fred. I would think that having two good arms is overkill when you're a demi-god. I mean, you saw me throw that man without even using one arm."

Fred laughed. "Okay, well when you can replicate that on command, I'll concede. But until then, I'm not going anywhere with you 'til you know how to use your new arm. I don't want to risk putting you in danger."

"Fine," Mina gave in. "I'll let Bob and Evelyn attach that metal monstrosity to me as soon as it's ready to go."

"It's ready now. Evelyn and Bob were planning to come over tomorrow to practice fitting you with it, but now that you're awake, I bet they can go ahead and attach it."

Mina sighed. "They should've just attached it while I was sleeping. At least it probably wouldn't have hurt that way."

Fred lay down and pulled Mina next to him, and they stared into each other's eyes for a moment.

"You know I was really scared while you were in that coma,

Mina. I wish I'd protected you better. I shouldn't have let you go after that man."

Mina rested her hand on the side of Fred's face. "You don't have to protect me, Fred. I should've been more careful. But I was scared that people were going to get hurt if I didn't do something fast."

Fred inched his face closer to hers, and Mina smiled.

"When I fell asleep earlier, I went back in time and saw a conversation between Max and Maude. It must have taken place right after the rebels fled New Waldoff. They were talking about how Serena stole the memories of Max and Helen's relationship—from *everyone*. But Max and Maude got their memories back a few weeks before Serena let me out of the ice tunnels. And I get the feeling that Max might not actually be on Betsy's side despite the fact that we saw him with Dale on our way here. I think you were right that there's something we don't know about him."

Fred wasn't finished telling Mina everything that had happened, but out of nowhere she started kissing him with more passion than either of them had ever shown each other before. Max ran his fingers up and down Mina's back underneath her shirt.

A second later Mina pulled her head away, and Fred stopped. "Sorry. Was I getting too carried away again?" he asked. But Mina shook her head. "No, Fred. It's okay. I want you to get carried away this time."

Then Mina pulled Fred on top of her and slowly, tenderly, they began to kiss again as though for the very first time.

CHAPTER 23

THE OPERATION

"Ow!" Mina winced.

"Sorry," Evelyn apologized, looking over the top of Mina's head and locking eyes with Bob. She tilted her chin towards a bottle of pain relief ointment while using her piercing-blue eyes to point Bob in the bottle's direction. Bob was holding Mina's arm in place, but he let go and reached for the jar, then handed it to Evelyn, who smiled at him appreciatively.

"Here, Mina. I'm going to rub some more numbing cream on your arm, now that I have the metal rings secured in the right spots."

Mina nodded but didn't say anything. Beads of sweat were collecting along her hairline. She looked down at the dark, metal forearm Bob had built to replace her own. It had thick metal coils that wrapped around the upper part of her arm—the part that hadn't vanished—all the way to her shoulder. Mina thought the metal appendage looked like it belonged to a primitive robot, like the ones she'd seen in films.

Fred hovered in the corner of Bob's small living room, which had been transformed into a workshop after Fred and

Mina began sleeping at Evelyn's. Fred hadn't wanted to get in the way of Evelyn as she carefully measured and adjusted the metal arm, positioning the coils so she could affix them to the correct muscles with the little wire screws that Bob had invented. But now that all the fitting work was finished, Fred moved across the room to be by Mina's side.

Mina smiled at him, but she was clearly nervous. "Remind me again what the screws do," she said to Bob.

"Of course, Mina," Bob replied. "In theory, once the tiny screws are inserted through the coils in your arm, you'll be able to move the metal limb by moving the muscles in your upper arm. The screws will then sense the muscles' vibrations and send this signal through the special silver headband that I made for you to wear. The signal will be interpreted and sent back into the screws, causing more vibrations deep inside your upper arm muscles. These vibrations are meant to simulate the feeling of movement so that your brain can interpret sensations from your bionic arm."

Mina already knew all of this, but she was having trouble wrapping her head around what it all meant. Her stomach felt sick. She thought about asking Bob and Evelyn to stop, but she knew it would be better to get it over with. So she kept her thoughts to herself.

"Are you ready?" asked Evelyn as she picked up the small drill that Bob had built for her to insert the twenty plus screws deep into Mina's arm. Mina looked at Fred nervously, and he crouched down next to where she sat so that his head was close to hers. He pulled her hand to his lips and kissed it.

"Let your mind wander. You can squeeze my hand as tight as you want to," Fred said soothingly.

Mina nodded and looked at the space between Evelyn and Fred, towards the wall. She took a deep breath and held it, trying to force her consciousness to abandon her body for the time being. Evelyn readied the drill.

Mina moved the air in and out of her chest, concentrating on the high-pitched drilling sound. She felt Bob's hands pushing firmly against the top of her shoulders, ready to hold her in place if she tried to pull away. The first thin piece of wire penetrated her skin. It felt like a tiny, hot insect burrowing into her muscles. Mina felt like she might throw up. She heard Fred begin to hum, and she knew what he was doing. He wanted her to hum back, to harmonize just like they had done together in the narrow tunnel years earlier, and in the ocean before Mina left her home again.

But the pain was too intense. Mina couldn't take her mind off the searing, electrical heat that was causing her muscles to twitch and jerk on their own. She wanted to be able to hum the right notes, but all she could manage was to hum a low, guttural tune that was more in harmony with the drill than with Fred.

Evelyn paused for a moment and looked at Mina's face. She said, "That's half the screws, Bob, but Mina looks like she's going to faint. Let's take a break."

Mina shook her head and ordered, "No! Keep going! I can take it!"

Evelyn looked at Bob questioningly, but Bob only gave a slight nod, keeping his hands positioned on Mina's back. Evelyn looked again at Mina's pale, sweaty face and then at Fred, as though wanting a second opinion. Fred nodded too, although his expression indicated that he wasn't so sure. Evelyn hung her head in defeat and started the drill again.

Before she could insert the next screw, though, the ground began to shake back and forth, lurching them from side to side. For a few seconds, the movement was intense, but then it quickly stopped. Evelyn released the drill's trigger and grabbed ahold of the table just as everything around them went still again.

"What was that?" she gasped.

Fred, who'd remained focused on Mina, responded, "It felt like an earthquake—" His voice trailed off as a memory came rushing back to him.

"What is it, Fred?" asked Bob.

Fred looked up at Bob from where he was kneeling at Mina's side. "In the labyrinth, right before the oracle set me free, the ground shook. I'd almost forgotten. It happened when Serena finally revealed the exit out of the tunnels."

"Are you saying you think the oracle had something to do with the tremor?" Evelyn asked.

But before Fred had the chance to respond, Mina's entire body stiffened, and her arms and legs began thrashing wildly. Her eyes rolled to the back of her head, and Bob quickly grabbed underneath her arms as Evelyn took hold of Mina's legs. Fred leapt out of their way, and they moved Mina off the chair and onto the floor.

"What's going on? What's happening to her?" Fred asked in a frightened voice.

"She's going into shock," Evelyn answered loudly, even though they were right next to each other. "I was worried this might happen if we kept going. Fred, run to Bob's bedroom and grab the red blanket folded on his bed. We need to warm her up fast."

Fred did as he was told, although part of him made a mental note of the fact that Evelyn knew there was a folded, red blanket on Bob's bed.

"What do we do?" asked Bob. "Do you think the metal screws are doing this?"

Evelyn shook her head. "No. She was in bad shape before we even started the procedure. I should've postponed it."

"Don't blame yourself for this, Evie. Mina wanted us to go ahead with the procedure."

Fred was back with the red blanket. He laid it down on top of Mina. She had stopped shaking and seemed somewhat conscious, although she looked delirious. Fred walked to the table and grabbed a pair of gloves and the bottle of numbing cream. Then he knelt down next to the metal appendage that was halfway attached to Mina's arm. He pulled the gloves on, and slowly, he began to rub the deadening lotion onto all the bright red spots where Evelyn had drilled the wires into Mina's skin. When he was finished, he moved on to the rest of Mina's arm until it was completely coated in the lotion. He looked at Mina's face again and saw that her eyes were at half-mast.

"How did you know to do that?" Evelyn asked. "It seemed like the numbing cream was barely working before."

Fred shrugged. "Just a hunch. I thought if the lotion soaked into the spots where you drilled, it might do a better job of providing some relief."

Bob placed a finger over his lips and pointed at Mina. Her eyes were shut, and she'd begun taking deep, rhythmic breaths. Bob stood up and walked to the front door, motioning for Evelyn and Fred to follow.

Once the three were outside, Bob asked, "What do you two think we should do? She's resting now, but I'm worried she might get worse if we leave her arm the way it is now. I think we need to consider removing the prosthetic and coming up with a new idea to help Mina."

Evelyn looked at Fred. "I agree with Bob. I know we'd all hoped that this bionic arm would solve her mobility issues, but it's clearly causing a major shock to her system. I think we need to get it off of her while she's relaxed so we don't do any further damage."

Fred looked at the ground. He knew that it was on him to make the final decision, and he understood his friends' point of view, but his gut told him they should wait. "I know that this isn't how any of us hoped this would go, but unless things start to get worse, I think we need to let Mina decide how she wants to proceed."

Evelyn and Bob looked at each other to see how the other would react to Fred's decision. Bob spoke first, "I know you want to give Mina the choice, Fred, but I don't think it would be safe to continue attaching the arm, even if that's what she decided she wanted."

Evelyn chimed in, "We gave it our best shot. Bob's design was ingenious, but we need to tweak a few parts, including how we secure the arm to Mina's body. We always knew this might not be the final solution, and we were straightforward with Mina about that. Everyone here knew there was a chance we were going to have to abort the procedure and return to the drawing board."

Fred glanced over his shoulder at the front of Bob's house. Everything that Bob and Evelyn were saying made sense, but he still had a feeling they should wait.

"Look, I have to make the journey to see Axel soon, but I'll wait until Mina's doing better. Let's at least give her some time to recover from what she's just been through. You can remove the arm when she's in better shape. I told her I wouldn't leave here with her until she'd learned to use the prosthetic, but I've changed my mind. I'll take her with me to see Axel while the two of you figure out what to do next. That way she can put some space between this whole ordeal and whatever you two come up with next. Alright?"

But before Bob or Evelyn had time to respond, a deafening shriek erupted from Bob's house. The three friends turned in the direction of the screeching sound.

"Mina!" Fred yelled as he ran to the front of the house. Flinging the door open, he darted into the living room, but he couldn't see Mina. An array of colorful lights bounced playfully around the darkened room, making it nearly impossible to see anything at all.

"Mina!" Fred shouted again over the loud metal screeching as he carefully made his way to the spot in the living room where they'd left her on the floor. He heard Bob calling to him from the front door. "You have to get out of there! Whatever sound that is, it's picking up steam! It sounds like something's about to explode!"

Fred ignored Bob. There was no way he was going to leave without Mina. He yelled her name over and over again while moving farther into the room, through the blinding lights. Once he felt certain he'd reached the area where Mina should be, he knelt down and began running his hands over the floor, hoping he could feel his way back to her. He closed his eyes to block out the strobing lights that were making him ill.

Fred's heart pounded as he moved his arms back and forth along the floor, panicked that he wouldn't be able to find her before something terrible happened. The shrill, metal noise had reached the same pitch as a ripe kettle of tea, and Fred froze in terror waiting for the explosion that he sensed was imminent.

"That's enough," a soft voice commanded, permeating the lights and sound.

Fred knew the voice belonged to Mina, and his heart leapt, knowing she was awake and alive. The shrill sound began to relent, and Fred could tell through his closed eyes that the lights were beginning to fade too. He moved in the direction he'd heard Mina and reached out his arms, but his fingers quickly jammed against a piece of curved metal.

Just then, the lights and sound vanished, and Fred was faced with a shocking sight.

"My god, Mina! What happened?"

Mina knelt before him. Her right arm was made entirely of metal from her shoulder to her fingertips. And around the crown of her head sat the halo-shaped headband Bob had built for her to control her arm.

The sight was unexpected, but it wasn't the reason Fred was stunned. He shook his head and rubbed his eyes to make sure he was really seeing what was right in front of him, wondering if the flashing lights had caused his vision to falter. He stared hard into Mina's face, trying to focus on her beautiful features, but there was nothing to focus on.

Just like the colorful, strobing lights, Mina's face refused to hold shape or any permanent features at all. It quickly morphed, spun, and flashed through hundreds of different lips, noses, eyes, cheekbones, and hairlines. Fred was in awe of the strange occurrence. He reached out to touch the area where Mina's face should be, but before he could, he heard Evelyn scream.

He turned around and saw her and Bob staring at Mina in horror.

"What the hell is going on here?" Bob asked in a tone that sounded angry, though Fred recognized it as fear. Fred looked back at Mina. Her features had returned to normal, and he could see that she looked dazed, as if awaking in the middle of sleepwalking.

Fred took Mina's new metal hand and held it tight. Then he looked at Bob and Evelyn. It was happening. Everything that Serena had told him would happen had come true, and now more than ever, Fred knew he had to protect the mission she'd given him. This meant diverting attention away from what had just happened—taking Mina out of the city, away from all the suspicion and conspiracy theories that were already swirling around her. They would go to the wolves, he thought.

"Bob. Evelyn. Thank you for all your help, but it's not safe here for Mina anymore. I'm taking her away. We'll leave tonight."

CHAPTER 24

THEO'S MEMORIES

When Elu and Ragher arrived at the glacier, Ragher noticed it seemed different. The crystals at the foot of the enormous ice mountain normally glowed in bright red tones that grew darker along the path to the top of the glacier. But now the crystals' shine was dimmer and not just red, but different shades of amber, blues, and greens. Ragher wasn't sure what this meant, but he was certain there was a reason the glacier wasn't lit in the same ominous way as before.

When the wolves reached the long, flat stretch at the top of the glacier, Ragher saw the ruins of Dan's fort off in the distance at the lower end of the glacier's icy top. He shuddered as he remembered some of the despicable acts he'd carried out there, inside the now crumbling walls. There had been so much torture and so many wicked deeds, and Ragher wondered if the dark energy that had collected within the fort had been exorcised once the cannonballs ripped it apart.

"This place is creepy," Elu whispered.

Ragher looked down at where they were walking. He'd forgotten how the light from the crystals made the dark ice look like it was moving. He saw Elu pulling her legs up higher than necessary as she walked, and he knew she must be feeling disoriented from the slow-moving lights spread across the ice beneath their paws.

They continued down the trail along the top of the glacier until Ragher saw the familiar red glow of stacked crystals. The piles formed a circle that opened up towards the path Ragher and Elu were on.

"That's where he lives," said Ragher. "It doesn't look like he's there right now."

"What should we do?" asked Elu.

Out of nowhere, two giant hands grabbed Ragher and Elu around their necks and lifted them, six feet off the ground. Elu squealed, but Ragher didn't make a sound.

"What are you doing here?" asked a deep, sinister voice.

Ragher gasped for air, trying to respond, but he couldn't. Then suddenly, the hands let go, and Ragher and Elu landed hard on their sides. Ragher stood up quickly to get his bearings again. But as he did, he heard Neriti's voice.

"You knew they were coming, Theo. If you want to be taken seriously, then you need to play fair."

Elu and Ragher turned to face the dark god. Elu gasped, and Ragher knew this meant that she could see Theo too. However, Ragher was almost as surprised by the sight of him as Elu. Theo was different now. The malevolent spirit stood before them not in the form of a strong, smoky god, but as a fleshy, slender creature with yellowed skin that looked old and diseased.

He wore a long, white robe, which seemed odd since he looked neither like a human nor any of the other mortals Ragher had ever seen. It was obvious he'd been transformed into a weakened state, although he was still over ten feet tall. Yet even so, his narrow stature, combined with his elongated height, only added to the impression that he was now feeble.

Ragher looked Theo's pitiful body up and down, clearly searching for Neriti. The last time he'd seen her, she'd emerged from the smoke that formed the dark god's body. But Theo no longer possessed this sort of body. And Ragher feared he might find his beloved's head plastered to the side of Theo's weirdly shaped torso like a grotesque, animated tumor.

He was relieved when Neriti walked around from behind Theo's back to greet the wolves. Neriti's beautiful, transparent body was lit up in a white glow, though her light was dim. Ragher noticed that the light surrounding Neriti's body seemed to move from Theo's body towards her. The light flickered at times, and Ragher sensed this was because Theo's weakened energy was tied to Neriti's somehow.

Ragher was overcome with emotion. He moved towards his wife, the mother of his two pups, to nuzzle her. But Theo stopped him.

"You can't touch her. We might as well clear this up from the start so that it doesn't become awkward later. Neriti is dead. The only reason she isn't *dead* dead is because she played a dirty trick when she sacrificed herself, which made her a part of me. She's like a leech I can't get rid of. She keeps her own energy from vanishing by continually feasting on low doses of mine."

Ragher snickered. "Well, that serves you right considering how many Moon Walker souls you feasted on over the years."

Theo hissed, "Delighting in irony is just an excuse for enjoying someone else's misery. I suppose that makes you no better than me, wolf."

Ragher fired back, "Except for all the killings and tortures and attempted mass extinctions."

Theo glared at Ragher with his dark, beady eyes. "Oh really? You think you're so innocent in all of that? Aren't you the wolf who betrayed your own kind? If I recall, you played a prominent role in all those things too."

Ragher growled. "I did it to protect my kind! I gave up years to keep you and your deplorable minion and doltish thug in check, and if—"

Neriti interrupted Ragher before he could finish. "That's enough! Bickering will get us nowhere, and despite the fact that Theo is quite clearly an imperfect, warped god, he isn't our biggest threat. Nor are we his."

Elu, who'd remained calm through all the back-and-forth exchanges asked, "Then what's our biggest threat, Neriti?"

"The biggest threat to all of us is Serena, the goddess who lives in the ice. She's extremely powerful. She has the ability to control memories, which makes her a master at manipulating the creatures of this realm, as well as all the creatures in the crystal realms."

"Crystal realms?" asked Elu.

"Yes, there are many tiny worlds that are contained inside the Moon's crystals," answered Neriti. "They were formed from the leftover atoms of Earth. Ages ago, Earth existed on a different plane that was connected to the original realm—our realm on the Moon, or Ortus as it was once known."

"But how do you know all of this Neriti?" Ragher asked.

Theo interjected, "It's like I was saying earlier. When Neriti killed Gryobe, she undid the spell I cast to create him. And by breaking the spell, she was able to dismantle his parts. Then, once Neriti and the other murderous wolves freed the bryobane and wolf spirits that I'd trapped inside each of Gryobe's antennas, a piece of my own flesh appeared to Neriti. I'd implanted this piece of me inside Gryobe as a way to guide his actions."

"I want to be the one to tell this part," Neriti said to Theo. Then to Ragher, she said, "First, you should know that when you revealed what Serena had told you—that Theia was gone —I realized the visions I'd been receiving couldn't be from Theia.

"For a long time after that, I believed the visions were coming from Theo instead. I thought he was pretending to be Theia in order to manipulate me and the other wolves. But I went along with the charade to find out what he wanted. I thought that knowing this would help me plan my revenge against him for the terror he'd put us through all those years, and for what he'd done to Tahissi's pups, our grand pups.

"One day, you, Axel, Ruth, and I went to visit Maude. You escorted me there so I could tell Maude about the crystal that had appeared during a vision quest the healers performed inside Crystal Crater. But when Maude touched the crystal that day, it transformed her into a ball of light. She was possessed by a spirit, who not only foretold of the birth of the human children born to the first Moon Travelers, but also of the eventual arrival of the girl and boy angel. Then the spirit sent a silent message straight into Ruth and me. It was this message that showed me what I had to do to kill Gryobe and go after the dark spirit."

"But if Maude was Theia, then who was the spirit that spoke to you?" asked Elu.

Neriti answered, "I believe it was Serena. At the time, I thought she was trying to help me on my quest for vengeance against the dark spirit, but I no longer believe that to be true. By exploring Theo's memories, I've witnessed the long history of Ortus and the Earth realm, and this has led me to the conclusion that Serena means to do us all harm."

Theo, who didn't like to wait idly by while someone else did all the talking, took over again. "I never planned to create Gryobe. It wasn't until my sisters united against me and killed all the bryobane that I decided to create a minion. It was their betrayal that inspired me to bring Gryobe to life. The bryobane were supposed to be off limits. Years earlier, I was forced to give up the hold I had over the Moon Walkers who'd joined my side. Serena said I was abusing my position as a god by seeking ultimate power.

"She objected to the fact that I'd found a way to steal their energy. Of course, I only stole the energy of the walkers who didn't obey me. But Serena insisted there had to be balance on the Moon, and she said I'd upset this balance by murdering Theia's followers.

"It was complete bollocks, of course. Serena just didn't like that I was becoming more powerful. Unfortunately, I didn't have access to my earliest memories at that time to know this. So, I went along with the compromise.

"I was given the bryobane, who were recreated from the Moon Walkers to my liking, though they were less intelligent than I'd hoped for. And in turn, Theia got the wolves, who were made to her liking—loyal pets, essentially.

"Naturally, Theia got huffy when some of her pets were enslaved by my subjects. But there wasn't anything unfair about it. It was merely a matter of 'finders keepers.' The bryobane found the wolves in their poorly constructed, collapsed tunnel, and therefore they got to keep them.

"I thought it was understood that I hadn't broken any of the rules of the compromise, since I didn't hear a peep out of Serena or Theia about what had occurred. In fact, they didn't even have the courtesy to tell me they wanted me to give the wolves back before plotting their scheme to punish me!"

Ragher scoffed. "Has it even occurred to you that you're presently in the company of the kind you kept enslaved? Or are you so ignorant of your own bias that you'd believe us wolves to take your side on this?"

Neriti responded, "Don't let pride get in the way of seeing the big picture, Ragher. It's true Theo is blinded to his own prejudices, but that's partly because he's a god. He sees things on a larger scale and therefore believes his own divinity is more important than that of mortals' concerns.

"But as I've stated, he's not our biggest threat. Serena is also biased towards her divinity, but unlike Theo, she's able to use her powers to deceive and manipulate with such prowess that her victims are clueless to who is torturing them and why. So, for now, just listen to Theo's explanation without anger. Otherwise, you won't gain the insights that you'll need to know what we're up against."

Neriti looked back to Theo, encouraging him to go on. Theo shrugged indifferently but spoke again, "I communicated with the bryobane the same way I later communicated with Dan—through thought osmosis. I planted ideas in their tiny, atrophied brains. First, I ordered the bryobane to have the wolves mine for crystals. Then I had the bryobane melt the crystals inside a giant crater on the Darkside so that when they cooled, they would form together and make an even bigger crystal.

"Once the crystal was as big as a lake, I was able to escape the confines of my glacier without forfeiting my powers. I apparated back and forth between the crystal and the glacier, which made it much easier to rule over the bryobane.

"When I realized that my herd of beasts had taken it upon themselves to have their slaves build an underground tunnel that led to the Dayside, I was delighted. Finally, I thought, everything was coming together. I had a more strategic position to work from, and I could order the bryobane to attack the wolves on the Dayside after the tunnel was complete. But Serena must have known what I was planning to do. I'm certain she was the one who convinced Theia to sacrifice the enslaved wolves in order to kill my subjects.

"I guess you take the wolves side in the matter, but I had every right to be furious. Serena stacked the deck against me when she put a spell on the Moon Walkers so that I couldn't steal their energy anymore. Then she changed my clever Moon Walkers into brainless monsters. The entire herd contained the collective intelligence of a jellyfish! They were all predator but with zero cunning.

"So in my rage over what Serena and Theia had done, I decided to take matters into my own hands by making the best of a horrid situation with the creation of my very own hench-man. Unfortunately, I had to use up all the power from the giant crystal to bring him to life, but I knew it would be worth it if I made him the right way. And Gryobe was truly a master-piece if I do say so. He had the cleverness and stoicism of the wolves, the brute force of the bryobane, and the ability to make devious and sinister decisions like me."

Neriti stopped Theo again. "Right, and now that you two know all of this, let's go back to how I became attached to Theo."

Theo grimaced. "I want to tell them more about Gryobe first!"

Neriti shook her head. "How would that help? Most of Gryobe's life was devoted to making the wolves' lives worse."

"Fine!" Theo shouted in a tone of childish frustration.

Neriti ignored him and continued. "After Serena showed me how to destroy Gryobe, I tried to kill the thing once when Ragher and I found it spying on us outside of our den. Ragher held me back, but I threatened to rip Gryobe's antennas off, which I think alerted Gryobe to the fact that I knew how to kill it. I wanted the thing to fear me, but my plan worked too well. After that day, I hunted for Gryobe many times but could never find it.

"Years later, once I knew Dan and his followers were coming for me, I used the relationship Ragher had been fostering with Dan to finally end Gryobe. The vision Serena sent to me in Maude's living room showed me mutilating Gryobe by slicing each of its antennas off and cutting open its throat as the healers recited a counter spell to free the spirits of the wolf and bryobane that were trapped inside of Gryobe.

Then once the two energies were freed, a slimy, pus-filled ball emerged from Gryobe's throat. Serena's vision showed me eating this disgusting morsel and killing Gryobe for good."

Theo interrupted, "What my sister *didn't* show this wolf was that the ball contained the piece of me that was implanted in Gryobe to guide him. It's what had tethered us to each other. So, when Neriti ate it, it was now her energy that was tethered to my own. And if that idiot, Dan, hadn't killed her, I would've fixed our little problem by ripping out Neriti's throat and taking back that piece of me. But once she was dead, her physical form ceased to exist, and the spell became mostly permanent."

"Mostly permanent?" asked Elu.

"Yes, well if I had my full range of powers back and were able to find a way to create another massive crystal, I could undo the spell. But alas, I continue getting to get kicked in the crotch over and over again by the women in my life—figuratively speaking, anyway. As you can see, I've essentially become a sterile version of my former self with barely enough power to scare away a small pack of rats like you all."

Elu spoke again, "But why would Serena want your energy tied to Neriti's?"

Theo groaned. "This is going to take forever if we have to explain everything. I guess I might as well sit down. I hate freezing my ass on the ice, but I'm tired of standing. Why don't you explain this one, wolf?"

So, Theo sat down and crossed his spindly, jaundiced-looking legs in front of him. It wasn't a pretty sight, but it made him a more manageable height for the rest of them to look at. Neriti sat beside Theo, and Ragher thought this made her look like Theo's faithful companion. It made him cringe inside.

Neriti replied to Elu, "I don't have an answer for why Serena would want me tied to Theo. Possessing him has enabled me to see his memories. All of them, in fact. Even the ones he'd long forgotten, which I've since helped him remember. It's like the part of Theo I'm attached to is the same part that rules his memories. If Serena knew this would be the outcome, then I'm clueless as to why she wanted it to happen. Having access to Theo's memories has made it painfully obvious the lengths that Serena is willing to go to make us all suffer."

"Like what?" Ragher asked. "What memories of Theo's could possibly paint anyone else in a worse light?"

Neriti began to reply, but Theo stopped her. "No, wolf. They're my memories, so I will be the one to share them."

Neriti nodded, and Theo responded, "In the beginning, there were five gods. There was Serena, who's a creation god and the only one of her kind. And then there were four gods of time: me and Theia and two others who Serena eventually murdered. The five of us lived here on Ortus, or the Moon realm as you know it. The time gods loved each other and Serena, and she loved us. It wasn't a romantic love per say, at least not in the beginning, but more of a carefree, blissful love that revolved around the utopian existence we all shared."

Ragher interrupted. "Neriti, are you sure this is right? I'm having a hard time picturing Theo living a happy, "kumbaya" existence, even if it was the beginning of time."

Neriti scolded him. "You need to listen to Theo, Ragh. You're already being skeptical when you haven't even heard the beginning of his story yet."

Theo leaned back, shifting his weight to his large fists. "That's right," he said in his deep voice. "And my patience is wearing thin, so keep your comments to yourself until I'm done."

Ragher looked peeved, but he didn't say anything back.

Theo went on, "The time gods were content to live eternally in the paradise Serena created for us, but she didn't feel the same way. With each century that passed, her mood grew darker. It seemed she'd become bored with having everything, and we did have everything because Serena created whatever we asked for.

"We thought up all kinds of paradises and scenarios, hoping one of them might make her happy. We lived inside of cloud worlds with rainbow roads, palaces made from pure light, and we had griffin servants that fetched anything we pleased. We lived in tropical water worlds with the bluest seas you've ever seen, and extravagant mansions filled to the brim with riches, and we had food so decadent it was like nothing your mortal brain could comprehend. Serena created hundreds of worlds inside of Ortus, all at our request. We hoped that one of them would cheer her up, but none of them were ever good enough.

"Eventually, Serena pulled away from me and the other gods and began to spend all her time by herself. There was a little cottage that she liked to stay at when she wanted to be alone. It was located in a forest clearing next to a body of water. She asked us to give her space, and we did as she asked since we were perfectly capable of entertaining ourselves in one of the hundreds of paradises she'd created. However, after enough time passed, I suggested to the other gods that we check on her. And when we did, we found that Serena wasn't alone at all.

"While we were away enjoying our time together across various utopian landscapes, Serena had been busy creating actual sentient beings. Not just a few insignificant animals to enhance the sea and forest that she liked to frequent most, but willful, complex beings, similar to us. Make no mistake, however. These beings were no gods; they were elves.

"The other gods and I were horrified when we realized what she'd been up to. Serena had manufactured these hideous, little creatures in all shapes and sizes. They were jubilant and silly, if not downright mischievous at times, and they seemed to have the same passion for life the five gods had once shared. But they were also crude natured and too eager to please, and very few of them wore any clothes at all.

"The time gods were furious over this betrayal. We told Serena she would have to destroy the elves. It was only fair since she should've consulted with us before making new creatures that we would have to share Ortus with. But Serena was outraged by our demands, and instead of banishing or killing the elves, she made more.

"I was so mad I could've killed her. I traveled back through time to stop Serena from making the new elves, but I couldn't go back far enough. Serena wasn't able to travel through time, but somehow, she'd found a way to zap the elves into existence even further back than when time began. I didn't realize it until much later, but what Serena had actually done was erase our memories from before the elves existed so that we couldn't travel back to the time before they lived.

"I went into a mad rage once I realized Serena had beaten us, that there was no way to get rid of the pests. I began tearing apart every elf I could get my hands on. The other three gods joined me in killing the elves, although they didn't seem to have the same passion for the job as me. If they'd worked a little harder or shown more flare for the work, it might have proven to Serena that we were a force to be reckoned with. Especially if we'd been able to exterminate all of her creatures. But when Serena found out that we'd begun slaughtering her elves, she quickly put an end to it by stealing our memories. Before then, none of us had known she was capable of memory theft."

Elu questioned, "But if she stole your memories, how do you remember any of this now?"

"The wench didn't erase our minds," Theo explained. "She merely denied us access to whatever sets of memories she wanted to keep from us, like a spell she put us under for however long it benefited her. It gave her total power over us. We were the gods of time, and yet she was the one who could control our past, present, and future by determining what we could and couldn't remember.

"The first time she used her memory spell, she made us forget we'd ever lived on Ortus without the elves. Then, she separated the four of us and gave each of us our own elf kingdom to rule over. For a time, this kept us occupied, but eventually we each became depressed. The elves were worthless little wretches, always coming to us with ridiculous problems and demanding that we solve them.

"I'm sure it will come as no surprise to any of you that I was the first god to break. I couldn't take the elves' snively, little faces anymore, so I decided to scare the hell out of them by eating a few. It worked, but Serena didn't like my heavy-handed approach to ruling, so she stole my memories again and banished me to one of the tropical paradise realms she'd created within Ortus. The other three gods realized what she'd done to me and told her to undo her spell, but instead, she stole their memories, too, and banished them to their own separate paradise realms.

"I'm not sure how long this lasted. During my exile, I believed myself to be the only being that had ever existed, which I mostly enjoyed, although it was a lonely business sometimes."

Neriti added, "This was one of Theo's most interesting memories to watch. With his own two hands, he created an entire army out of palm fronds and coconuts that he pretended to lead into battle on a daily basis. He was quite skilled at making these plant soldiers, and it felt revealing to watch him deal with his loneliness by building an army instead of friends."

Theo scoffed at the idea. "Friends? How would friends have been useful? Building an army is like building another set of arms. There's unlimited potential to what an army can achieve. Indulging in friends is like mortals' indulgence in fatty foods. The fleeting experience is mildly pleasurable, but it comes with awkward, long-term consequences."

Ragher asked, "Wait, I'm confused. Were you eating your make-believe, army friends?"

Theo glared at the wolf. "Stop distracting me, wolves! Back to business!"

Ragher grumbled, "I'm just saying that for an immortal being, who has an infinite amount of time to think of ways to solve problems, you're pretty clueless. I mean, you rely on eating mortals as a way to solve most of your problems."

Theo snapped, "For a supposedly clever wolf, *you're* pretty clueless. Like you said, I'm an immortal being. I don't need to win over mortals, and if eating a few from time to time helps me deal with my stress, then so be it! Now, shut up and let me finish!"

Theo glared at **Ragher** and then continued. "At some point, Serena restored all our memories and reunited us. Then she announced she'd come up with an idea to build a mega world for the gods that was neither paradise nor hellscape. But to pull it off, she had to reclaim the energy she'd used to create the different paradise realms on Ortus. That meant destroying them and leaving Ortus in a total state of ruin.

"The other gods and I were extremely skeptical of Serena's plan, but we were also careful how we approached her this time, knowing she could zap away our memories if she felt so inclined. We asked her why we'd want to live anywhere besides a paradise, hoping we could reason with her by making her see how absurd her idea was. But she wouldn't budge. She said that this was the compromise she'd come up with to keep everyone happy. We knew that wasn't true, though. Serena was only interested in keeping herself happy. The rest of us wanted to live in paradise, but Serena said she could never be satisfied in a utopian world. She needed to live in a world with complexity. So, that's what she made."

"What happened to the elves?" Elu asked.

Theo sat up and began to rub his large knuckles that he'd been pressing into the ground. He smiled coyly. "Oh, they're still around. Serena recycled some of them into the early humans; the rest stayed behind. While the gods were away on Earth, they lived alone on Ortus in the hellish conditions that Serena had left for them. When she diverted all her energy into creating Earth, it wiped away Ortus' lush sceneries and left the barren world that you know today."

"But then how did you end up back here? Did Serena change her mind again?" asked Ragher.

"No," replied Theo. "The five gods lived together on Earth for thousands of years. In the beginning, we traveled everywhere together, but eventually that cold-hearted shrew abandoned us again. She told us she still wasn't happy despite all the suffering she'd put us through on Earth. I mean, sure it was nice at first, exploring Earth and being worshipped like the powerful gods we were. But the humans quickly became as intolerable as the elves, which I suppose makes sense considering the first humans had once been elves.

"So then, shortly after Serena declared her newfound displeasure for the Earthly life she'd forced on all of us, she came to the conclusion that to truly be happy, she needed to *become* a human. The other gods and I thought she'd gone completely insane. Here she was, this extremely powerful god of creation, but instead of finding satisfaction in her ability to create anything she desired, she chose to go play dress up. And in a human suit no less!

"I told the other gods to ignore her. By this time, I'd decided that Serena was unstable. I figured she would go a few centuries, maybe a millennium tops, playing "human." Then she'd grow bored of it just like she had everything else.

"However, Serena did the unthinkable. She blocked her own memories so that she was able to incarnate into a real, honest-to-goodness person with no memory of ever having existed before, and definitely no memory of being a powerful goddess. And as if that weren't enough, she put a spell on herself so that she would continue to reincarnate as a human over and over again.

"She was born to human parents, lived, died, and then started the absurd process over again. It was grotesque, and worst of all, we had no idea how long she had cast her spell for. As far as we knew, it could have been a permanent spell that lasted forever.

"The gods and I had been betrayed before, but this felt far worse than the other betrayals. Serena had forced us out of our home to live among dumb mortals, and then she'd abandoned us to fend for ourselves, stranded in her godforsaken universe with no way home to Ortus.

"After waiting around a hundred years, hoping Serena would remember who she was and return to her senses, we decided to do something. The gods of time formulated a plan. We would use our powers to track Serena down and then force her to remember who she was as many times as it took until she let us go back to Ortus.

"Unfortunately, all we managed to do was anger Serena each time we forced her to remember who she was. She got better and better at hiding from us each new incarnation, which meant we had to become more skillful at finding her each time, traversing all of time until we did. The last time we found her, we spent years planning a way to get her to give up on Earth and return to Ortus with us."

"And your plan worked?" asked Elu.

Theo looked angry. "Not in the way we had hoped. In the end, we did succeed at getting Serena to give up on Earth. But she didn't just give up and go home. For a while she fought us.

She tried to hide again, but it wasn't easy for her anymore. We had figured out a way to keep her alive so she couldn't reincarnate, although I'm not sure she wanted to by this point.

"After years of massive bloodshed and fighting, Serena finally made the decision to sacrifice everything she had created in order to get her way. The other time gods and I wouldn't let her live how she wanted to, so she decided to destroy us. But the only way to destroy us was to extinguish the Earth and its entire universe.

"I didn't see it coming. I didn't think she had it in her to destroy something she loved so deeply. I guess it was her hatred for us that fueled her. She hated us more than she loved the world she'd created, and in the end, that's what drove her to burn it all down."

Ragher asked, "But if Serena destroyed the Earth in order to destroy the time gods, how are you and Theia still alive?"

"We're not alive in the same way we were before. When Serena destroyed everything, the energy from the Earth and its universe didn't just vanish. Energy can't be destroyed; it can only change form. In this case, the energy that Serena used to create the Earth embedded itself back into the origin world, Ortus. The crystals that are scattered across the Moon's Darkside are fragments of the Earth's energy. They contain remnants of all the life Serena brought about when she created the Earth.

"I assume this was an unintended consequence of Serena's hasty decision. She must have known that even if she demolished everything, it wouldn't just go away. But I don't think she knew just how that would play out. When she realized that the Earth's remains and inhabitants were scattered across the darkest parts of the Moon, trapped within the crystals, Serena began to search every crystal world, looking for any sign of our continued existence. Probably hoping to confirm that she'd turned us into dust.

"Eventually, she found Theia and me. We had each been reborn into a separate crystal world, and we were just beginning to rediscover our divine powers. That's how Serena found us. She went to each world and asked the elves, or humans, or humanoids if there was anyone among them who had great powers. Serena found Theia when she was told of the invisible woman who lived in the mountains.

"When Serena approached Theia, she quickly realized that my sister's memories of her former self were gone. Just like Serena had chosen to incarnate as a human on Earth, Theia, too, had become human, except that she was aware of her powers. She realized that she could move through time by focusing her mind. But whenever she did so, her body disappeared, which is why the other humans had dubbed her 'the invisible woman.'

"I imagine when Serena found me, it was much easier for her to confirm my identity. I had already conquered all the creatures in my world by using my rediscovered powers to subdue and torture all those who challenged me. Half the crystal world was on fire when Serena arrived."

"So when Serena realized you were the time gods, she brought you back to the main surface, to Ortus, or the Moon realm, or whatever it's called. To what? Keep tabs on you?" Ragher asked impatiently.

Neriti replied, "No Ragher. She didn't bring them back here right after she found them. First, she tortured them for hundreds of years, moving them in and out of different crystal worlds, testing them, observing their reactions to various scenarios, and manipulating their memories over and over again. It wasn't until a couple of millennia ago that she brought them back to Ortus—again, with no memories. She made Theo and Theia believe that they and Serena were new gods, that they'd manifested on the Moon together from out of the ether. It was like she'd hit the reset button on their first existence on the Moon, except now there were only three gods."

"If that even was our first existence all those eons ago," said Theo.

Elu asked, "You mean there may be memories you still don't have access to?"

"Of course!" Theo yelled. "Haven't you been listening to the story? Serena isn't a goddess of creation; she's a goddess of deception. Yes, she can bring worlds and creatures into existence, but that's not what she chooses to focus on. Our entire existence, she has been toying with Theia and me. She knew she could have whatever she wanted, that she'd always have the upper hand. But instead of ruling over us outwardly, she chose to pretend she was our equal, all the while studying us and controlling us."

"Why would she do that?" asked Ragher skeptically.

"Who knows, wolf! It's probably all a game to her. Why did she keep you locked up all those years in the ice tunnels? And before that, why did she go around attempting to fool herself into believing she was human? None of it makes any sense! I'm telling you, Serena is mad! Cunning, yes. Calculating, absolutely. But stark raving mad!"

Ragher shook his head and looked at Neriti. "Is this what you believe too?"

"I don't know exactly what to believe, Ragh," Neriti replied. "It's been hard to draw any conclusions based on Theo's memories, but judging by the lengths Serena has gone to, I think it's fair to say she has it out for the two surviving time gods. In Theo's memories, I watched Serena put Theia and Theo together multiple times so that they would become lovers. Then once they were bonded, she would introduce some sort of conflict that would tear them apart. They even produced a child together, which in the end, Serena stole from them. I can't think of any reason she would do this unless it was to punish them endlessly. And we both know how miserable she made our lives. I don't know if Serena is crazy, but she's certainly cruel."

Ragher thought about it for a moment and then said, "Yes, she is cruel, but I think there might be more to all of this. Why would Serena spend thousands of years punishing Theia and Theo for some perceived wrong that happened a bajillion years ago?"

Theo laughed in a mocking tone, "She blew up the entire universe she created to get rid of us. I think she's capable of holding a grudge for a few millennia, even if it's just so she can finish the job she started."

Elu piped up. "I agree with Ragher, Neriti. You and Theo are biased towards Theo's perspective because it's the only way in which either of you have witnessed the conflict between the gods. But as each of you has confirmed, Serena is quite calculating. If she were only interested in seeking revenge, she could have continued to torture the other two gods within the crystal realms for eternity. Yet she brought them back to the Moon's surface and gave them a chance to be gods again. Why?"

"It's just another way for her to abuse us," said Theo

However, Ragher picked up Elu's train of thought. "That's right, Elu. Plus, there's something else that the rest of you don't know. Serena sent me away from the tunnels to find Axel. She wanted me to tell him that I was going to go to Theo and convince him to let the wolves remain peaceful in whatever war the humans are about to start. But what she really wanted was for me to convince Axel of my good intentions before I went off and did whatever I had to do to get Theo to kill me. She said this would draw Axel and the wolves into the fight that's coming."

Neriti scolded, "Ragher, how could you?"

"I didn't, Riti. I'm here, aren't I? When Elu found me, I was trying to decide what to do next, but I already knew I couldn't go through with Serena's plan. Not this time. There's one more part you should know, though. Serena also told me that the only way to save the wolves was to follow her plan. She promised that if I sacrificed myself to Theo, she would make sure that Axel and her own child ruled the Moon realm together.

"Her own child?" asked Theo. "That's nonsense! She doesn't have a child. Unless…"

"Unless what?" asked Ragher.

"Unless she's talking about my son. The one she stole from me!" shouted Theo angrily.

Elu asked, "Would he even be alive still after all this time?"

"Yes, it's possible," Ragher replied. "Serena seems to have some ability to control aging. For instance, Fred aged while we were down in the ice tunnels. And the Moon Travelers never seem to grow a day older."

"Moon Travelers? Ha! Such a stupid term. Those recycled elves didn't travel here anymore than I did. They were summoned by my sister, the siren. Pulled from their comfy, cozy crystal worlds into this freakshow of a reality," grumbled Theo.

Ragher and Neriti weren't listening to Theo, though. They were watching Elu who suddenly seemed disturbed by something.

"What is it, Elu?" asked Neriti.

Elu looked at the other two wolves nervously. "I think I may have figured out what Serena is really after."

Ragher was stunned. "What she's after?"

"It's like I said before," Elu went on. "If Serena wanted to continue seeking revenge, she could have tortured the other gods inside the crystal worlds forever. But she brought them here. What if the reason Serena is trying to draw the wolves and humans and gods into a fight is so they destroy each other? Theo said Serena already tried to kill the other gods once, and she had no problem destroying an entire world filled with creatures while she made the attempt on her siblings' lives. What if she's trying to achieve the same result again, but this time she's manipulating all of us into destroying each other?"

Ragher and Neriti looked at each other, waiting to see how the other would respond, but it was Theo who broke the silence, with loud, maniacal laughter. "I always knew you wolves were clever, but this one takes the cake. I should have made *her* my minion."

Ragher rolled his eyes. "This isn't funny, Theo. If Elu's right, then we're all going to die, and possibly very soon."

"What should we do, Ragh?" asked Neriti

Ragher looked at Theo and said, "You need to call off whatever you and Betsy are planning. Serena is counting on us all to go to war with each other, but that can't happen if Betsy doesn't initiate the fight."

"You're beginning to sound a lot like my sisters—trying to stop me in my pursuit of domination. Why should I care if we go to war with each other? As far as I'm concerned, it would finally settle things and maybe get rid of all these lesser creatures running around all over the place. It's a damn infestation of sub intelligence is what it is!"

Neriti moved around to face Theo. The light radiating from her ghostly body twinkled brightly.

"You should care because you're in no condition to go to war. Look at yourself, Theo. You look like a piece of rotting celery. Call off the fight for now, at least. Give us some time to learn what Serena is up to so we can formulate a plan that doesn't involve total annihilation."

Theo looked down at himself as if to confirm whether he did in fact look like an expired piece of celery. "Fine. I'll have Betsy postpone the fight. But only temporarily. The second I have my powers back, all bets are off!"

Neriti, Ragher, and Elu took a collective sigh of relief.

Unfortunately, what they didn't realize was that Theo had already made his own plan, which didn't involve aligning himself with the wolves, or any other mortal. When Theo had regained access to his memories and become familiar again with how duplicitous Serena could be, he decided it would be best to set his sights on an alliance with his deceptive sister. As far as he could tell, it was the only way he could keep from being outmaneuvered by her. This time instead of trying to beat Serena, he would do his best to join her and gain her trust. Then he would beat her. It was the best way, he decided, to finally fulfill his innate desire for total power. And this time, no do-gooder group of mortals was going to stand in his way.

CHAPTER 25

METALLICIZING MEMORIES

Hours before the procedure began, Mina thought about how it might go and worried some over how painful it would be. Yet her concern about the pain and the odd procedure—or even the excitement she felt about regaining an arm—weren't at the forefront of her mind the day of the operation. Instead, Mina was preoccupied with the sense that she was being watched. The feeling was familiar. It was the same one she'd had in Waldoff Market years earlier after she'd found the strange note pinned to her wings. And it was the same feeling she'd had many times on Earth after her grandfather died and her parents abandoned her—including the stormy day in the forest when she'd run home to find Bonkers gone for good.

It wasn't that she felt like she was being spied on. It was more of a feeling that something or someone was calling to her from just beyond her realm of existence, as though there was a big, invisible sign flashing neon letters above her head, but she had no way of seeing it. She only sensed it was there. It was a feeling that there was something more she was supposed to know, but she was too blinded by her own senses to figure out what was being whispered to her from this place beyond her understanding.

And though the feeling had been festering for years, it had only recently grown into more than just an inkling that something was askew. No longer was it a ghostly tapping on her shoulder or a glimpse of an apparition. On the day of the operation, this feeling had become much bigger. An impending doom hung over Mina as she began to realize that the giant she'd long suspected was lurking in the shadows had suddenly shown up on her doorstep and was ready to be let in.

So though it was true that Mina was worried about the operation and her own well-being, what she really feared was the metamorphosis she was about to undergo from her comfortable state of mind, that was rooted in ignorance, into this mysterious new place of understanding. She didn't yet know what this would mean, but she worried that once she crossed the threshold everything would change for the worse.

"Ow!" Mina winced as Evelyn prepped her upper arm before she began to attach the prosthetic.

She heard Evelyn and Bob talking to one another and she sensed Fred's presence nearby. But Mina wasn't focused on them. She was caught up in her own anxieties. The beast was pounding to be let in, but she had no idea how to open the door or what that might entail.

With no other choice, Mina forced herself to live in the moment, even though that meant facing the physical pain head on.

"Are you ready?" asked Evelyn, picking up the drill to begin.

Mina looked at Fred, unsure of what Evelyn was really asking. Her vision had started to blur, and even though she could hear Evelyn's voice, she was certain she was looking at Dan. His blistering, red skin and dark black eyes came into focus, and she saw him holding up a vile of bubbling liquid in front of her face.

Mina felt a wave of panic. She looked at Fred, who looked back at her reassuringly. "Let your mind wander, and if you'd like, you can squeeze my hand as tight as you want to," he said soothingly.

Upon hearing Fred's words, Mina knew that the vision couldn't be real. After all, Fred was even more terrified of Dan than she was. No, this was all part of the strange state of mind she had been caught up in. She knew she could trust Fred as well as Bob and Evelyn. So, she nodded and allowed her mind to wander, hoping she could shake the vision of Dan while escaping some of the pain she knew was coming.

The sound of the drill pierced every pore of her consciousness, but Mina didn't recognize the high-pitched hissing as the sounds of the machine her friend was using to attach her new bionic arm. She interpreted it as the fizzling dark purple serum that Dan was inching towards her face. "This isn't real," she told herself over and over, but the sound of the hissing liquid made her doubt whether that were true.

The tiny, metal screws boring into her skin were excruciating, but Mina's brain interpreted the feeling as Dan grabbing ahold of her arm with his hand which looked like a giant raven's claw. He dug his talons deep into her flesh, and with his other claw, he raised the poison filled vile over her head. Mina knew what was coming next. He pulled her head back and poured the liquid into her mouth. She tried not to swallow, but some of the cold liquid slid down the back of her throat.

Mina felt sick. She knew this couldn't be real. It had to be a weird hallucination, possibly brought on by the pain relief ointment and the stress of the operation. She heard the sound of Fred humming to her from somewhere outside herself. She latched on to the sound and tried to create an answer to it by harmonizing with him, but the only noise she could make sounded like the terrible hissing sound of the bitter tasting poison in her mouth.

Then, simultaneously, the humming and hissing stopped. Mina spit out the poison and the vision of Dan faded. She heard Evelyn suggest that they take a break, but Mina didn't want to. She wanted to get through the rest of the operation as quickly as possible.

Through clenched teeth, she ordered, "No! Keep going! I can take it!"

Evelyn started the drill again, and suddenly Dan was standing right in front of Mina once more. The dark, black pools in his eyes swirled menacingly, and he smiled an evil grin. "Back for more, princess? I thought I turned your insides into goo years ago. Or was it the other way around? No matter! You won't survive this time!"

Mina yelled back at the red-faced demon she knew was Dan, "I already have! Remember? You're dead! Helen killed you, and your poison is all gone!"

Dan laughed maniacally and lunged closer to Mina's face so that their noses were practically touching. The black whirlpools in his eyes were spinning faster and faster, and Mina felt like they were pulling her in. "Are you sure about that?" Dan asked.

From out of nowhere, Mina could feel the poison filling her mouth again. She tried to spit it out like before, but she couldn't open her mouth. Panicked, she looked around the room, searching for signs of Fred or her friends who she knew *should* be there. But everything beyond Dan's oozing, scabbed face and freakish eyes began to slowly melt away.

Mina tried to open her mouth—to scream for help and expel the poison that was threatening to choke her. But her jaw was paralyzed. She watched the dark green walls of Bob's living room break apart into beads of liquid and eventually evaporate into the dark abyss that lay beyond. As the last droplets vanished, Mina felt herself begin to choke on the poison. She gasped for air through her nose, but it didn't do any good since she was unable to cough the liquid out of her throat and lungs.

Soon, her body began to convulse, and as it did, she found herself descending from the sky above the Darkside of the Moon. She fell quickly, and the air pushed up around her, reminding her of the many times she had fallen before. She continued to breathe through her nose as she looked down. It was dark below, but she could see a large stone structure that was aglow in dim, red light. And well beyond the structure's borders, she saw flashing lights and knew these were the same flashing artillery lights she'd seen years earlier from the top of Dan's fortress.

As she hurtled towards the stone tower she'd nearly died on nine years ago, she instinctively closed her eyes and stiffened her body, bracing for impact. But as soon as her eyes were closed, the sensation of falling stopped. She opened her eyes again and found herself back in her thirteen-year-old body, kneeling atop the tower, still holding the poison in her mouth. Only this time, Mina knew that it really was the lethal concoction. Dan was standing above her holding the ladle he'd used to pour the poison into her mouth, looking giddy.

Mina bent over. She knew she should be fine. The lunar dirt would work its magic and absorb the poison, just like it had the first time. Dan walked to the side of the tower while Mina waited to feel the poison dissipating. But it didn't. Again, Mina panicked. She spit out the cold liquid, but she couldn't get every drop. Within seconds, her heart began to beat sporadically, and her stomach and intestines started to burn like they were on fire. Mina coughed and gasped for air. The pain was so intense she didn't feel like she could breathe anymore. Dan didn't look back at her, but he laughed.

She didn't understand how, but she knew this was the end

of her life. Somehow Dan had dragged her back in time to replay these events so that this time *he* would be the one to survive. The last thought she had as the darkness closed in was that all this pain and defeat she felt seemed awfully familiar, like it was a memory she was reliving. She lay down on the cold stones and closed her eyes, ready to let death wash over her.

But nothing happened. The burning intensified for a few more seconds, and then suddenly, it stopped. Mina opened her eyes and realized she was kneeling on top of the roof. And again, Dan was standing above her, holding the poison-filled ladle. He grabbed her hair and pulled her head back and poured the concoction into her mouth. She coughed and spat and waited to see what would happen, but when the excruciating pain started to creep into her stomach this time, Mina snapped.

"No!" she screamed defiantly.

Dan, who was walking towards the tower wall, turned around and caught her eye. "There's nothing you can do about it, little girl. That loser sister of mine never stood a chance, not against my brainpower. You picked the wrong side, but it doesn't matter. Pretty soon, there'll be nothing left of your insides except for an acidic goo, and all the Moon's creatures will be dead."

Mina took deep breaths through the pain. Her long hair hung in front of her thirteen-year-old face, and she stared at Dan, seething with anger. She'd heard every word he'd said and was well aware of how confident he seemed, but she also noticed that his face told a different story. His deranged, black eyes didn't look quite as menacing as they had before, and Mina thought that he almost looked scared.

Mina closed her eyes. She suspected she was in some sort of lucid dream, and that the only way to avoid the pain of her melting insides was to wake up. She concentrated on turning her waking mind on, but to her surprise she was only able to succeed at resetting the scene. This time, though, she was watching Dan as he stood atop a stool, lowering his ladle into the vat.

This was good. It meant she'd have time to dig the dirt out of her pocket and shove it into her mouth. She reached for the dirt, but her pocket was empty. She searched her other one, but there was nothing there either. "You forgot to grab the dirt, Mina! You idiot! You have to go back and get it!"

But Dan was already walking across the roof now, carrying the full ladle and sprinkling the purple beads into it from the vial he'd pulled from his pocket. She stood up to try and run down the staircase that led to Dan's bedchamber, but he leapt at her and grabbed her around the waist.

"Stop!" Mina shouted, and to her surprise, he did. In fact, everything did. The loud sounds of cannons firing at the fort and the fizzing sound of the potion too.

Mina's heart was pounding. She pulled herself away from Dan and stared at him. He was completely frozen mid-assault. Angry and confused, she grabbed the ladle out of his hand and flung it over the side of the tower.

"What the hell?" she asked as she looked out over the horizon. There were bright white lights dotting the darkness beyond the fortress, and it quickly dawned on Mina that these were the flashes from the firing cannons, only they were frozen in time too.

Mina didn't know what to make of all of it, but she knew she needed to put an end to this hellish nightmare-memory she was caught up in. "I've got to get the dirt," she told herself. But then, suddenly, her heart sank as she remembered that the dirt wasn't all she would need. She reached her hand around to the back of her wings, to the spot where she knew the tantrum needle should be hidden. Yet, just as she'd feared, it wasn't there.

She looked at Dan again as though she half expected to see

him coming out of his deep freeze. He didn't move. Mina felt like she was reverting to her thirteen-year-old self again at the thought of having to go all the way back to the Sheep Spa to fetch a tantrum needle. "There's no way I can make it all the way there and back without him waking up and killing everyone! I give up!" she yelled and threw herself on the ground.

Angry and frustrated, Mina pounded her hands on the stones in front of her. Her hands throbbed, which was strange, she thought, since she hadn't felt any sensation in her missing hand since it disappeared. "I have to find a way out of here," she said.

She closed her eyes again and concentrated on waking, and before she knew it, she realized she was floating. She opened her eyes and saw herself hovering right above a different version of her thirteen-year-old self. This Mina was walking down the path between the tantrum cactuses, with their long, sharp needles, heading towards the Sheep Spa while hunched over the map in front of her.

Mina remembered this time well and knew what was about to happen. Then low and behold, ten seconds later, this other Mina had her wings caught in the cactuses. Except she didn't know that's what had happened. She'd been so nervous approaching the spooky, metal building that she'd just assumed she was being grabbed.

Mina lowered her body so she was standing in front of this other version of herself, curious to see the situation up close.

From right behind the spot where she was standing, watching herself pull away from the cactuses, she heard a familiar voice in her ear. "She's not paying attention!"

"Holy crap!" Mina shouted, startled by the voice.

She turned around and saw a beautiful woman with dark tan skin and dark eyes.

"You're Helen!" Mina gasped, surprised to see her in her physical form.

Helen nodded. "That's right, and you're Mina, only you're not the Mina that I know. You're much older now, aren't you?"

Mina nodded, stunned by how real everything suddenly felt. It was one thing to watch a memory play out from different angles, but talking to Helen didn't feel like it was part of a memory. It felt like something new.

"I don't know what to do with her…well, *you*," said Helen. "You need to get down to the bottom of the hill before the guards see you, but you've stopped looking at the map."

"Why don't you just jump inside my head and tell me what to do?" asked Mina.

Helen shook her head and looked past Mina at the thirteen-year-old struggling with the cactus. "We're not there yet, remember?"

Mina looked over her shoulder, then back at Helen. "Maybe I can help? I mean, I am her after all."

Helen nodded. "It's worth a try."

Mina walked up to her younger self and put her hands on her shoulders as though to push them back. Her hands, however, went right through her like a ghost's.

She tried a different tactic. "Come on, Mina. You need to push backwards to get free."

And just as Mina spoke these words, her younger self seemed to have an epiphany. She shot up straight and lunged two steps backwards, freeing herself from the lethal cactuses.

"Wow! I didn't think that would work," said Helen. "I'm impressed. I guess it's a good thing Serena brought you here."

"Serena?"

"Yes, your mother, Serena,'" replied Helen

Mina frowned. "This isn't real, is it? If you were real, how would you know that?"

The other version of Mina was starting to walk down the path again. She walked right through Mina and Helen, who in turn began to follow her as they talked.

Helen explained, "Serena told me a long time ago who you are. She's who had me set the plan in motion to bring you and Fred here originally. And she's been giving me all the instructions to guide this other version of you towards facing Dan. She also told me she suspected you would arrive along our journey in an older form. And she said to let you know that it's time you realize you can do whatever you put your mind to."

"Whatever I put my mind to? What is that supposed to mean?"

Helen shook her head. "It's not for me to say."

Mina asked, "How do you know Serena?"

"She's who I spoke of as Theia. Before you learned who Theia really is. She's spoken to me my entire life, like an imaginary friend whispering in my ear. But you're the first person she's ever given me permission to tell this to."

Mina replied, "I see. But why didn't you tell me before?"

"Those are her rules. She said this other version of you isn't ready yet."

Mina looked at the other version of herself. She had stopped to stare at the creepy-looking factory.

Helen said with frustration, "This younger version of you gets distracted a lot. And look at that! You have tantrum needles sticking out of your wings! It's sort of amazing that you managed to grow up at all."

Helen's comments suddenly reminded Mina of why she was there. "No wait, that's important! You have to tell me to keep one of them hidden—for later."

Helen was surprised. "Why? You know, they're incredibly dangerous. If it pokes her, it will paralyze her, and it seems like she's already good at paralyzing herself." Helen looked at Mina, who was still frozen, staring at the Sheep Spa.

"No, you have to make sure she has it on her when she faces Dan. It's extremely important. Also, tell her to keep some dirt in her pocket. Promise me!"

Helen nodded. "Okay. I promise. This is why Serena brought you here, you know? It was always part of how she planned to fight Dan and Theo."

"But I don't really understand. If all of this has happened already, then how am I able to have an impact on the past?" asked Mina

"The gods of time don't just control time, Mina. They are time. Time only exists because they exist. This means that they can shape time any way they want; it doesn't have to be linear the way the rest of us experience it."

Mina looked shocked. "You know, whenever I think I'm getting the hang of this place, a giant truth bomb explodes in my lap."

Helen laughed. "That's how this place works. Anyway, I have to get back to your other journey before you get yourself into trouble. I think you can handle things from here. Don't you?"

But before Mina could answer, she was back on top of the tower, facing Dan again. He pulled her head back with the ladle positioned above her lips, but this time she was relieved to find that the back of her mouth was filled with lunar dirt. The poison flooded her mouth but was quickly absorbed by the powdery, dry dust. Dan backed away as Mina spat and gagged, doing her best to rid herself of the poisonous mud, but also trying to make it seem like she was really suffering.

Suddenly, the outer wall of the fort was blasted apart by back-to-back cannonballs, and Dan snickered. "Well look at that! Maybe you'll get to see the main event after all! Probably not, though. That poison only takes a minute to do its magic. You should feel your major organs melting into a fiery puddle of goo right about now. Do you feel it? Just give me a thumbs up if you do."

But before Dan could get an answer, everything fell silent. He looked over the tower wall to see what was going on, and

Mina used the opportunity to stand up and arm herself with the cactus needle which, this time, was right where she expected it to be. Stumbling at first, she took several steps towards Dan, positioning herself next to him.

Dan spun around, baffled over why the cannons had stopped firing. He stared at Mina in horror. "How did you do that?" he asked.

Mina raised the hand that was holding the tantrum needle and thrust it into Dan's neck.

He screamed. "Nooo! I'm invisible! That's not possible! How did—" but before he hit the ground, a dark, smoky presence manifested in front of her like a black tornado with two red beams peering out from its center.

"What are you?" Mina screamed as the smoky presence began to take shape in the form of Dan, but with glowing red eyes. The dark spirit reached out and clutched Mina around the throat, lifting her off the roof. Mina grabbed Theo's hands in an attempt to pry them off of her, but she realized that she only had one hand again. She looked at where Dan lay atop the roof and saw that she was no longer playing the part of her thirteen-year-old self. That version of her was standing over a paralyzed Dan, just like she'd done years earlier.

Back in her present body, there was nothing Mina could do to fight off the dark spirit, and he laughed at Mina's pathetic attempt to release herself from his grip. Mina asked again, though the words came out hoarse, "What are you?"

Using one hand now, Theo continued to hold Mina by the neck, hanging her out over the side of the tower so that she was hovering above the spiky crystals at the bottom of Black Ice Fort.

"What a risky game my sister is playing, sending you to me like this," Theo said in his deep, crisp voice. "Tell me, how did you move through time? Are you Theia or just some lowly half-breed god?"

Mina could barely breathe and realized she might soon pass out. Theo loosened his hold a little, and Mina gulped for air. In a strained voice, she replied, "I'm not Theia. I'm Mina from Earth."

Theo growled, "You're lying! Earth hasn't existed for thousands of years."

He tightened his grip again, but Mina pleaded, "It does exist! I traveled here from Earth twice through different dimensions! And all those people Dan was trying to kill, the Moon Travelers, they're from Earth, too."

"They're not from Earth, Mina the half-breed. They're from the different crystal worlds my sister created after Earth was destroyed. She's been toying with you—making you all believe that you made some big journey to get here. When the fact of the matter is you were always here."

"That's not true!" Mina yelled at the smoky giant who'd finished taking on Dan's appearance and now looked like a demon-possessed version of her original adversary. "I flew here from Earth!"

"Oh, you did?" asked Theo. "And the other Moon Travelers, they believe they walked across a bridge tethered to another planet? But you see, that's her way. The portal to and from the crystal worlds is up there," he said smiling Dan's smug grin as he pointed towards space.

"When you leave your tiny worlds, the only place you can end up is here, and so here is where you are. She made the transition easy on your lot. After all, no one wants to believe they're a tiny piece of space dust, even though that's exactly what you all are—the tiniest particle of dirt, from worlds so small and insignificant that it's hard to believe they actually exist.

"It was a simple trick for Serena to pull off. In fact, not much of a trick at all, really. You're either locked in a crystal world, or you're here. It was the way that she brought you here that was duplicitous. My sister is a master at deception. She's deceived us all at one time or another. Even now, I suspect you might be one of her deceptions."

Mina continued to struggle while holding tight to Theo's hand, trying not to fall or be choked.

"And you're scared of her?" Mina asked, although she wasn't intending to taunt Theo. "Is that why you're worried she brought me here?"

Theo didn't like what Mina was insinuating, and he loosened his grip around her neck. Mina shrieked, believing she was about to fall to her death.

"You either know more than you're saying or you're a fool! And I intend to find out which it is!" Theo shouted.

The dark god wrapped his hand tightly around her neck like a boa constrictor strangling its prey. Mina struggled with her one good hand, but it was no use. Theo was much too strong, and she began to suffocate.

Her eyes rolled back as everything went dark, but before she lost consciousness, a thought flashed across her mind. "You're not really here. Go back to Bob's tiny home in the valley! Find Fred!"

Mina hummed, concentrating on the arm that was half gone. She pictured the metal prosthetic that Evelyn had been trying to attach and reached her hand over to see if she could feel it. But there was nothing there.

Theo brought his other hand to her neck and squeezed even tighter than before. But Mina continued to feel around for her metal arm. "I know it's there!" she thought. "If I just connect to it, I can bring myself back to the present."

Using every bit of energy she had left, she focused her mind until the bionic arm appeared out of thin air.

"Damn it!" she thought. Pulling the prosthetic arm back into the past wasn't what she'd intended to do. Mina didn't have a second to waste thinking about the implications of what she'd done, though, since Theo was close to forcing the life out of her. Quickly, she attempted to raise both hands to Theo's arms to fight. Only, it didn't work; Mina had no way to control the bionic arm. It just hung to her side like a useless appendage anchor.

"Holy hell! I don't have the controller!" she thought.

Again, Mina focused her dwindling energy on what she needed, willing herself to connect with the metal headband that Bob had made to control the arm. She reached her arm out in the direction of where the table would be if she were still in Bob's living room, and even quicker than before, the ring appeared in her hand. She shoved the halo down over the crown of her head and raised both arms to grab Theo's wrists.

Theo laughed. "It would seem there's more to your story than you were letting on. But I have a secret too. I was going easy on you."

With his hands still wrapped around Mina's throat, Theo began to transform into an even larger form—a muscular, horned man with a narrow, pointed face and devilish eyes. As Theo grew, so did his strength, and Mina felt her chance to save herself slipping away.

She continued to hold his wrists, wishing she had a way to match his superhuman strength. Her neck ached horribly under the crushing weight of Theo's enormous hands, and she was no longer able to breathe.

But before Mina's life faded away, she heard Theo shout, "What's happening?!"

She opened her eyes to find a beam of light shining from her forehead. She gasped for breath and realized she was able to breathe again. Theo stared at her with a look of dismay, and Mina soon understood why. Her hands were still squeezing his, but her metal arm had become much more solid. It covered her entire arm, all the way up to her shoulder, in a series of metal plates that fit perfectly together.

Theo screamed in pain, and his arms began to sizzle and smoke like they were on fire. Mina knew the dark spirit was being burned, but she had no idea what was causing it. He pulled away from her in fear, but Mina didn't fall. Instead, she hovered effortlessly in front of Theo. Without thinking, Mina punched her metal arm into his smoky stomach. Theo roared and grabbed at Mina's arm, but he couldn't pull it out of his body.

Multi-colored lights began to radiate inside Theo's smoky form. At first, they were faint, but as Mina continued to shove her arm deeper into his stomach, they grew brighter. Theo begged of her, "Stop! I understand! I know who you are now! Don't kill me, most powerful demi-god!"

Mina nodded, and said, "That's enough!"

Then without warning, the scene changed. She was back in Bob's living room, kneeling on the floor in front of a visibly distraught Fred. Bob and Evelyn were there too, and they looked terrified.

Mina ignored her friends' expressions. Fred was holding her metal hand and saying something to Bob and Evelyn, but Mina wasn't listening to him. She already knew what came next. "I have to go see my mother now. It's time to learn the truth."

CHAPTER 26

MISTER AL & GENERAL MAX

Mina raced out of Bob's house with Fred on her heels.

"Stop, Mina!" he begged as she began walking down the valley's sloped street that led out of town. "Please, wait! You can't go to Serena!"

Mina kept walking fast. "Why not?" she asked.

"Because she doesn't want to see you!" Fred blurted out, desperate for Mina to stop.

Mina spun around to face Fred. He looked worn out and upset.

Evelyn and Bob caught up to them a second later, and before Mina or Fred spoke again, Evelyn asked, "Mina, what was all of that back there? And why do you have to go see your mother so fast? I didn't even realize your mother lived on the Moon."

"That's because I've never met her," said Mina angrily. "Or at least not that I remember. Why don't you ask Fred your questions. He knows a lot more than I do. More than all of us, actually. But he's chosen to keep us in the dark."

Fred spoke calmly, "That's not fair, Mina. I'm trying to do the right thing here. For all of us."

"Or you've chosen to align yourself with the most powerful god on the Moon because you're afraid of what she'd do to you if you defied her."

Fred shook his head. "That's not it. I swear."

Mina paused and stared at Fred as if trying to decide whether she believed him.

Bob said, "I think we need to have this conversation somewhere more private, Mina. We're beginning to attract unwanted attention."

Mina looked around and saw several groups of people standing outside their homes, staring at her. "What is it!?" she yelled at them. "You've never seen a girl with a giant metal arm lose her mind before?"

Evelyn laughed, but Bob glanced at Evelyn with a stern expression.

"Oh, relax," Evelyn told him. "Mina is still recovering from being in shock. And honestly, I don't love how much this town reminds me of the last two Moon cities. We may have left the autocrats behind, but our citizens seem to have just as hard a time keeping out of other people's business as the citizens in New Waldoff.

Evelyn moved closer to Mina. "Look, I've seen some strange things in my day, Mina, but what happened back there is beyond comparison. I think it's clear you're not entirely tethered to our reality. I'm a woman of science, so I hesitate to believe that you're a part of something divine without absolute proof, but at the moment, I have no other explanation for how this could all happen."

Evelyn glanced at Mina's metal arm. "I'm glad the prosthetic is attached, although it appears not to have many of the original components from Bob's design. May I?" she asked.

Mina shrugged but nodded. "Sure, go ahead."

Evelyn ran her hands over the sectional plates that made up the arm. "Can you feel when I touch the arm?" Evelyn asked.

"Yes." Mina replied. "But it doesn't feel like it did before. I can feel tiny vibrations wherever you move your hand along the metal and that's about it."

Evelyn looked at Bob and shook her head. "How is this possible? Do you think the prosthetic is actually synched with the halo she's wearing? I mean, they don't really look that similar to the ones you made."

Bob seemed nervous. He looked at Fred, who hung his head and said to Evelyn, "Mina's a demi-god, Evelyn. I know it's hard to believe, which is why we didn't tell you before. Her mother is a powerful goddess who controls the Moon realm. Her name is Serena. What happened back there in Bob's living room happened because Serena wanted it to."

Evelyn looked shocked but excited too. "This is real? You're not pulling my leg?" she asked.

Fred shook his head, and Bob replied, "No, Fred's telling the truth. Maude was a goddess, also. She was Theia, the goddess that the wolves worship. We didn't know it until right before she died. Serena put her in human form and erased her memories. Then when it suited her, she killed Maude—turned her into dust as far as I can tell." Bob didn't try to hide his bitterness.

Evelyn looked at Mina's arm again. "Mina, I can see you have questions that you want answered immediately, but in light of everything that's just occurred, I have to ask. Do you think you could afford to stay with us a little while longer? Help us work on the mega-robot? I have a feeling that with your assistance, we might be able to significantly cut the work time down."

Mina looked frustrated. "How so?" she asked.

"Well, I'm not sure yet, actually," Evelyn confessed. "But

would you at least be willing to see if you're able to help us save time? Maybe we could spend a couple of days testing your abilities and see if this new arm or…" Evelyn looked around to see if anyone was close enough to hear her, then continued, "Or possibly some newfound powers might help us create the robot quickly. After all, we know Betsy will eventually send more people to attack us. What happened the other night was just a test run to discover our vulnerabilities."

Mina sighed. "Okay, I'll stay a couple of days just to see, but I can't promise that I'll stay until the end."

Mina saw Fred's face relax, and she said to him, "As soon as I want to, I'm going to see Serena, Fred. I don't care that she told you to keep me away. She brought me here for some purpose, and I'm tired of sitting around waiting to find out what that is. This is my life, and if you won't tell me what her intentions are, then I'll have to find out for myself."

The next few days, Evelyn and Bob spent hours running tests to find out what Mina could do with her new, powerful prosthetic. Fred wanted to help too, but Mina insisted that he give her some space for the time being. The truth was that she had realized she had avoided pushing him for information too much because she didn't want to push him away. But she knew that she deserved answers. And even though they loved each other, she also knew this might not be enough to keep their relationship going. Especially if Fred continued to hide the truth from her.

Fred was devastated to be shut out like this. His heart ached with the knowledge that he had hurt Mina, and it didn't help any that he'd also let Serena down by losing Mina's trust. So, on the third night that Mina didn't show up at Evelyn's to sleep, he decided it was time to leave. Serena had told him he needed to go to the wolves eventually, a task he'd been avoiding because he was going to have to deliver bad news. Without saying goodbye to anyone, Fred set off on foot in the early morning hours, headed towards the wolf pack that lived on the wolves' ancestral land.

In the meantime, Mina spent every moment of the day pushing herself to new limits, spurred on by what Helen had said to her outside the Sheep Spa. "You can do whatever you put your mind to." Mina was a little skeptical of these words because she knew they were a message from Serena. However, after her encounter with Theo on top of the tower, she suspected that there must be something to her powers.

The tests that Bob and Evelyn designed were mostly meant to test Mina's strength, speed, and coordination to find out whether she had any superhuman qualities that involved these traits. What the two scientists were stunned to learn was that not only did Mina have the ability to move at lightning speed and lift objects ten times her weight, but she could also heat anything she touched to extreme temperatures.

The day after Fred left, Mina felt ill at ease. She knew she'd hurt him by giving him the cold shoulder for a few days, but she still thought it was spiteful for him not to leave a note. Bob asked Mina if she wanted to go after him, but she declined. She was pretty certain Fred had gone to the wolves like he'd been planning to do the last two months, and she had no interest in following him now. Not while she had more important things to accomplish, like helping Bob and Evelyn build their robot, and confronting her mother.

So, for several weeks, Mina kept her focus on doing everything she was asked to do in order to bring Bob and Evelyn's mega-robot to fruition. They brought several others in to help with the more menial tasks, but Mina was in charge of all the heavy lifting, bending, and welding. John and his sons were the only other people allowed to be around when Mina used her powers, since Bob trusted them to keep Mina's secret safe.

One afternoon while the group was busy working, John's

son, Samuel, asked, "What's this then? The robot has a name?"

Evelyn and Bob stopped what they were doing and looked over at Samuel, who was staring at a set of plans for the mega-robots left foot.

Evelyn asked, "A name? What do you mean, Samuel?"

The young man replied, "It shows here that his name is Mr. Al. Is that short for Albert?" He pointed to the top of the plans.

Bob burst out laughing, and Samuel's face flushed with embarrassment, realizing he'd made some kind of error.

Evelyn moved to where Samuel was standing and looked down at the plans. "I see what you did there," she said. "It actually says M.R.A.I., which stands for Moon Realm Artificial Intelligence. The writing is a bit smudged, though. It was an easy mistake." She glared at Bob, who was still laughing.

But the name stuck. From then on, the group referred to the mega-robot as "Mr. Al." And once all of Mr. Al's larger parts were assembled, Mina moved them down the mountain in the middle of the night, hauling a large wagon that Bob had built for the occasion.

Over the next few days, Mina wasn't needed as much. Most of the remaining work involved sensors, circuitry, Mr. Al's control system, and so on. Every once in a while, Mina was asked to move a few giant parts or weld a couple together. But soon, it became obvious that the work was almost done, and she approached Evelyn and Bob to say goodbye.

Evelyn gave her a hug and said, "Thank you, Mina. Your selflessness saved us so much time. Because of you, the whole city will be able to rest easy starting tonight."

Mina nodded. "I was happy to help. But I need to tell you something before I go. I have a feeling that the power on the Moon is shifting. I'm nervous this means that Betsy is gaining an edge over Serena somehow. I waited until now to tell you because I didn't want to worry you or make you think I was trying to discourage you from finishing the project. Just be careful. And maybe don't rely solely on Mr. Al, okay?"

Bob nodded and wrapped his arm around Mina's shoulder. "Of course, Mina. You know me. I'm never happy unless there's more to solve. We'll get Al up and running and then put together a committee to discuss contingency plans in case Mr. Al fails us."

Mina sighed. "I'm going to miss you guys. Take care of yourselves. If anyone asks, I guess just tell them I went to find Fred."

Evelyn asked, "And if Fred shows up again? What should we tell him?"

Mina looked deflated, but Bob stepped in and said, "I don't think we need to worry about that. He knows what Mina's plan is; he can figure it out for himself."

Bob pulled his arm from Mina's shoulder and turned to give her a big hug. "I want you to take Grimbolt, Mina. I know he's a bit tired looking, but I think having a horse will come in handy."

"No, Bob!" Evelyn said a bit scoldingly. "Not that old thing! Give her one of the others."

But Mina replied, "It's okay. I wasn't planning to take any of the horses, and Bob's right to want to hang onto the fast ones. You might need them. Besides, Grimbolt helped Maude escape from New Waldoff, right? If he was good enough for Maude, then he's good enough for me."

Mina began to turn to walk back up the mountain where the horses were, but as she went Bob called after her, "Oh, and Mina! Don't forget to say goodbye to Jacques before you go. We'll never hear the end of it, otherwise!"

MAX STEPPED off the elevator onto Betsy's floor and noticed two things—the air was overwhelmingly humid, and there was a lingering stench that smelled like plant innards. Being back in City Hall brought back bad memories. Even returning as one of Betsy's trusted servants, Max felt nervous about being there after spending months locked away in the building's bowels.

He walked down the hallway alone towards Betsy's office. She had sent her guards to his home the day before to request that he meet with her the following day. Max was surprised at the timing of the guards' visit considering they arrived shortly after Betsy's incredible—and very public—transformation.

Max heard all about it at his local corner shop. People were huddled inside, discussing the implications of what Betsy's newly discovered powers would mean for the citizens of New Waldoff. Unlike the rest of the shoppers, Max wasn't surprised by what he overheard. Ever since regaining his memories, he'd known what might happen—that Betsy would one day receive a crystal that would make her all-powerful.

He had already spent months worrying about what might happen if Serena followed through with the promise she'd made to Betsy in the greenhouse decades earlier. He'd thought about trying to stop Betsy before the crystal ever arrived, but he knew that wasn't the right way to handle the situation. He'd already formulated a plan; he just needed to stick to it. No matter what.

When Max entered Betsy's office, he was surprised to find her in her usual form—lumpy, warty, and oddly dressed. She sat behind her desk, talking to a couple of guards who were speaking to her in hushed tones. He thought he heard one of the guards mention Mina's name as he walked in, but he couldn't be sure.

No one seemed to notice his presence, so Max hung back and looked around the room. The vines that normally covered the place had been rearranged to form large, spiral pillars that reached from ceiling to floor. Max wondered if Betsy had organized the vines in Romanesque columns because she wanted her office to have a stately jungle vibe, or if they were like this so she could force the pillars to close in around her visitors and imprison them.

"Probably both," he thought.

A few seconds later, Betsy dismissed her guards and turned her attention to Max.

"Come here," she said waving him towards her desk.

Max walked to Betsy, steeling himself for whatever she was about to say or do to him.

"Geez, Max. You look like you're about to shit your pants. I was going to ask if you'd lead my army, but maybe I should find someone with a sturdier spine."

Max was shocked. Now that Betsy was all-powerful, he thought she might try to finish the job she started all those years earlier in the greenhouse. As far as he knew, she didn't really need him around. Of course he'd been helpful when he'd revealed Theia's identity and the rebels' location, but he didn't think Betsy was the type to get overly sentimental about a couple of good deeds. She seemed more like the type to keep you alive only as long as the good deeds kept coming.

"Me?" Max asked finding it difficult to hide his surprise. "What about Dale or one of your guards?"

Betsy scowled. "You saying you don't want the job?"

"No," Max responded. "I'm just not sure I'm qualified for the job."

Betsy shook her head. "You were a soldier before you came here, right?"

"Well, I was a seaman, actually. But I never saw any fighting. Wouldn't you prefer one of the men or women who actually served on the Moon to do it?"

"No," Betsy stated bluntly. "All the highest-ranking soldiers were on the council, so we know they can't do it. And I don't trust any of the others. I'm certain that some of them still feel more loyal to those dead losers than they do to me, and I don't have time to weed out the traitors."

"And Dale?" Max asked a bit tentatively. Dale had been missing for a couple of months, but Betsy had told anyone who'd asked that he'd been given a secret assignment she couldn't discuss. Max had initially suspected that there might be something more sinister behind Dale's disappearance, however.

Betsy smiled. "I thought I told you. He went to the other side of the Moon."

"Right. I just figured you might want to give him the honor, since he's one of your most trusted allies."

"Nope," said Betsy. "He's all tied up at the moment. Maybe permanently. Who knows?"

"Okay. Then what would you like me to do?" asked Max.

"I want you to be my general. Organize an army and get them into shape. Get them ready. And I mean ready for anything. What I have planned won't be easy," she explained.

She unhooked one of the buttons at the top of her dress and pulled out the crystal that Serena had given her. Max looked at it with great interest. It looked just like Ruth's crystal, the one Ruth used to trick him into taking her to see Maude on the day Mina departed the Moon.

"So you're wearing it as a necklace?" Max asked.

"That's right. You remember what this is? You remember that day in the greenhouse all those years ago when I used you to get to Helen?"

Max felt a pain in his heart, hearing Betsy say Helen's name.

"I remember," he said.

Betsy went on, "Serena told me you'd help me in my quest to seize power. I didn't believe most of what she said that day, but her promises came true. So, will you lead my army?"

"Against whom?" asked Max.

Betsy tapped her chubby fingers on the desk. "Whom do you think?" she asked coyly.

"Serena?"

Betsy nodded, obviously uncomfortable over the thought of confirming Max's guess out loud.

"Okay, I'll lead your army," he said.

Betsy asked, "And there are no hard feelings about me trying to eat you?"

Max shook his head. "No. The only hard feelings I have are for Serena. She stole Helen from me when she erased our memories. She let her die without giving me a chance to say goodbye, and then restored my memories so that all I can do now is grieve. If I can help you kill her, I'll do it."

Betsy smiled devilishly and patted the crystal dangling from her neck.

"That's what I wanted to hear," she said. "But first, I should warn you that Serena has made this far too easy up until now. For instance, giving me this crystal; I don't trust it completely. We'll have to find a way to outmaneuver and out strategize her if we're going to overthrow her. If she figures out we're coming for her, she'll erase our minds, or worse. Lucky for us, I think I know her weakness."

"Oh really?" Max asked. "What's that?"

"Mina."

Max was startled. "Mina? Why would Serena care about her?"

"Are you sure you want to know? It's a pretty big secret. One I'd be willing to kill you over if you ever let it slip to anyone."

Max thought this sounded more like what he'd come to expect from Betsy. "Who would I let it slip to? I have no friends."

"Good! Friends are a useless waste of time. I have reason to believe that Mina's a time god like Theia and my father—and a powerful one at that. Even more powerful than Theia and Theo. Serena brought Mina here with Helen's assistance. It's why she didn't want you and Helen involved anymore. She used Helen to push Mina into a fight against Dan. It's how Serena got Dan out of the picture.

"But there's something else that happened the day Mina and Helen faced Dan at Black Ice Fort. A future Mina traveled through time from somewhere in our current timeline, sometime that's close to now. And when she did, she nearly killed my father. I think it's all part of some big plan Serena has for the Moon realm."

"What kind of plan?" asked Max.

"I don't know," Betsy replied angrily. "To be honest, I sent Dale to Serena a while back to find out what her plan is, but he hasn't returned. He's probably dead. But I don't want to worry about Serena's plan anymore. My father has become obsessed with forming an alliance with his sister because he thinks it's the best way to usurp her power in the long run. However, I've given up on all that. I want to seize power *now*, and I'm willing to bet that killing Mina is a good way to start."

Max nodded. "Of course. That's clever. So, we'll begin by attacking the rebels' city then?"

"Yes, I sent a group of guards there last night on a secret mission," said Betsy. "They attacked the entire town, threw grenades at homes and flushed people out. One of my men got eyes on Mina. Or to be more accurate, she tackled him to the ground before he got away. But we know for sure she's there now, and a couple of the guards have stayed behind, hidden, in case she leaves.

Max asked, "When do I need to have the troops ready by?"

"A month, tops!"

"A month?!" asked Max bewildered. "How am I supposed to train an entire army in a month?"

Betsy laughed. "I don't care how you train them. Just make sure they know how to fire their weapons in the right direction and not at each other. I'm sure some of those no-brains out there probably don't know one end of a cannon from the other. In the meantime, you and I will spend our nights strategizing on how to squash the rebels while making sure that Mina doesn't escape."

"And once Mina's dead?"

A glimmer of evil flashed across Betsy's cold eyes. "And then the party begins."

CHAPTER 27

A DISTRACTION

While Fred was in the ice tunnels, he spent most of his time learning things he didn't want to know. He learned secrets about Serena's purpose for Mina. He learned first-hand what happened to the wolves at the hands of Dan's followers. He learned that when Serena created the Moon Walkers, and subsequently the bryobane and wolves, that her intention hadn't been for them to have purposeful lives or freewill. Her intention was to hand them over to the time gods as a means of distraction. These creatures were merely toys to occupy Theo and Theia's minds, since for a while both gods believed that having ultimate power over their subjects meant having ultimate power over the Moon.

Fred also learned that Serena had tasked him with one day divulging this information to the very creatures it affected the most—the wolves. He'd asked Serena why it was important to reveal such a horrible truth after all this time, but she told Fred not to question her motives. Serena said he should be proud to play the part of liberator, for he was giving the wolves freedom by offering them the truth. Fred asked how he was giving them freedom, and Serena answered that the wolves could finally live their lives without being beholden to any god. After some thought, Fred decided that what this really meant was Serena no longer wanted the wolves to worship Theia.

On the journey to see the wolves, Fred thought a lot about whether he'd made the right choice leaving Mina behind. He loved her so much that his heart ached for her, but he also knew that things were changing. Serena had explained that Mina would gain all the memories of the Moon realm and become powerful. And she also told Fred that if he gave Mina space to grow into who she was meant to be, then their relationship would persevere any troubles it faced. Fred held onto those words like a security blanket, reminding himself of them whenever he realized he was becoming too protective.

Still, he worried that leaving Mina in Rebelton wasn't what Serena had intended when she'd told him this. After all, he knew he was supposed to offer Mina some amount of protection as well as guard her against confronting Serena. Then again, part of him wanted Mina to confront Serena, sensing it was the only way for Mina to finally learn who she was supposed to become.

When Fred reached the wolves' ancient lands, he was stunned by what he discovered. Thousands of elves of various shapes and sizes were scurrying around all over the place, mostly playing games or dancing.

"What the heck?" Fred asked himself as he waded into the sea of elves. Loud, squeaky laughter and high-pitched elf languages assaulted his ears everywhere he went, and with no wolves in sight, Fred began to wonder if the elves had invaded the wolves' territory and booted the wolves out. Eventually, Fred came across an elf who was removed from the rest. He was leaning against a cliff, looking irritable and pouty.

Fred nodded at him in greeting and asked, "Do you speak my language?"

The squatty elf who was half Fred's size rolled his eyes and said in a mocking, shrill tone, "Do you speak my language?"

"Okay," said Fred, not exactly sure what to make of this grouchy elf. "Do you know if the wolves still live here?"

"Zimzor doesn't know or care. All Zimzor want to do is play babbauley ball with friends. But they say no! Zimzor can't hold onto ball good."

A few seconds later, another elf approached Fred from the side and introduced himself. "Hello, hello, hello, human man. I am Exigor, the designated elf speaker. Can I help you with something?"

Fred nodded. "I'm looking for the wolves. I've come to deliver a message to them."

"Oh wonderful!" squealed Exigor. "Is it from the empress? Is she going to let us return to our homes now? Is the fighting over?"

"No," said Fred. "It is from the empress, but I think she told me the message before you left your homes. What fighting are you referring to, though?"

Exigor looked sad. "Oh, I hoped this was it. The empress told us to leave our homes and move in with the wolves for a while. We had to lie to the wolves and say we were kicked out so that they would feel bad for us and take us in. It was fun at first like a big moon doggy sleepover. But the wolves are grumpy and don't like to dance. Some of the pups play games but only when they're allowed to. So now we're bored."

"And the fighting?" Fred asked again.

Exigor replied, "Yes, when the fighting is over, we can go home. Do you know if it has started yet?"

"To be honest, Exigor, I don't know about any fighting. I'm just here to give my message to the wolves."

Sighing, Exigor said, "Okay, okay, human man. I understand. But will you let me know when the fighting is over?"

"Sure," said Fred. "If I find out about the fighting, I'll let you know when it's over. By the way, this child here, Zimzor, says his friends won't play babbauley ball with him. He said it's because he has trouble holding onto the ball."

Zimzor looked angry and stomped his foot. "I no ask you for help! Zimzor being alone fine!"

Exigor laughed. "Well, that is true, I guess. Zimzor does have trouble holding onto the ball, but that's only because he keeps eating it. Also, Zimzor is an adult elf and the leader of his elf tribe."

Fred looked back at Zimzor. "Oh, I apologize, sir. I didn't realize. But maybe you should consider not eating the babbauley ball if you want the others to play with you."

Zimzor shouted, "You don't realize because you stupid man! I leader. I eat all babbauley balls I want to!"

Fred nodded at the elf and said, "Alright, Zimzor. Good luck with being alone then."

He continued to press on through the gatherings of elves until finally the elves thinned out. He entered a valley with steep canyon walls on both side that stretched on as far as the eye could see. Here the wolves roamed about in small groups, in and out of dens that were carved into the canyon walls. Compared to the elves, the scene seemed tranquil—quiet and without chaos.

This changed rather quickly, however, when the first wolf spotted him.

"Intruder!" cried a large, white wolf with gray paws.

Suddenly, all eyes were on Fred. Every wolf in the valley stopped what they were doing and stared at him. And the wolves who'd been in their dens came out to see what was going on. Fred put his hands out in front of him to show the wolves he was unarmed. "I've come to deliver a message from one of the gods. I'm not here to hurt you. I don't even have any weapons!"

"Ha!" said the wolf who'd first spotted him. "You're a man.

Where one of you goes, others follow. Maybe the others have weapons."

"No," said Fred protesting. "Nobody is following me. My name is Fred. I was trapped in the ice tunnels with Axel and Ragher."

Just then, Axel appeared from one of the dens in the middle of the valley.

He spoke to the rest of the wolves, "It's okay. He's telling the truth. Fred was the boy child who was brought here years ago—the one with wings. Dan tortured him, and then after Dan was killed, Fred spent nine years trapped in the ice tunnels with Ragher and me. He's my friend."

"The only human that was ever a true friend to wolves was Helen, but she's dead," said the wolf with gray paws.

Fred answered, "But Helen brought me to the Moon and guided me. Do you think she would've done that if she thought I would hurt you. Look, I'll admit I didn't treat the wolves right when I first arrived. I was scared of you. But being down in those tunnels for nine years changed me. I would never do anything to hurt anyone now—wolf or human or even those annoying elves back there."

Fred saw several of the wolves nod their heads and heard a few confirm that the elves were indeed annoying. Axel asked, "Why are you here, Fred?"

"I have a message for you, Axel," replied Fred. Even though the message was intended for all the wolves, Fred was too nervous now to deliver it to the whole pack. They were obviously deeply suspicious of him, and he didn't think it would go over well if he told them he'd been sent there to announce that their entire existence had been meaningless.

Axel nodded and looked around at the others. "Go back to your business! He's not staying. He's only here to speak to me. I'll walk him out the way he came in."

One of the wolves near Axel said, "You can leave with him

if you'd like, and take all those annoying pests with you while you're at it."

A few of the wolves snickered at the comment, but Axel ignored them. When he reached Fred, the two friends walked side by side out of the canyon and back towards the elves' new territory. Axel spoke first, "It's good to see you on the outside. I worried what had become of you after you left the tunnels."

"Yeah, it's good to see you too. I heard you were supposed to be uniting the remaining packs against Theo. How's that going?" Fred asked earnestly.

Axel laughed. "Not so well, considering I gave up. The wolves are tired of all the fighting. We've spent decades getting tangled up in human affairs. And even though Theo is a god, we feel like this isn't a fight to involve ourselves in. Let the humans battle him and each other if they'd like. We've decided we will sit this one out."

"I see," said Fred with a concerned expression. "Did the oracle ever tell you she's a god too?"

Axel looked at Fred, and they stopped to face each other. "No, but I've since learned. The elves have a high opinion of the mad goddess, or 'empress' as they like to refer to her. Despite the fact that she kicked them out of their homes!"

Fred shook his head. "She didn't kick them out. She told them to tell you that so you'd let them stay. The one named Exigor spoke to me on the way in. He said that Serena wanted them to come here until the fighting stops."

Axel looked confused. "Why? Is there already fighting going on?"

"Not that I'm aware of," said Fred. "But there's something else—a message she sent me to give to the wolves. I think I better tell the whole pack, though. Will you go talk to them? Ask them if I can relay the message? And maybe remind them I'm just the messenger?"

"What's it about?" asked Axel.

But Fred frowned and said, "I'm sorry, but I think it's better if I tell you all at once. It's not going to be pleasant, and I'd prefer not to have to say it twice."

Axel looked suspicious but gave in. "Fine. But this better not be about trying to unite the packs against Theo, Fred. We aren't doing it. You understand?"

Fred nodded. "I promise, Ax. It's not about that."

"Okay, come on then. You might as well go with me. They're not going to tear your throat out. At least not yet."

So, Fred followed Axel back to the canyon. The wolves who were still outside barely noticed him this time. One of the largest they passed snickered and asked, "Back so soon, Axel?"

Axel didn't look at the wolf, but replied, "We need to see the council. The message is for everyone."

Fred moved around Axel so he could walk next to him. "I thought I was going to tell the wolves all at once," he said.

"This is how we do this, Fred. You tell the council what the crazy goddess who kept us captive for nine years wants us wolves to know. Then if they decide it's worth it, they'll tell the rest of the pack."

"And the other wolves?" Fred asked. "I mean, the other two packs?"

Axel shrugged. "Word travels."

They had reached a secluded den at the farthest back section of the canyon. Axel stopped in front of it. There were two wolves sitting on each side of the entrance, but the opening was wide enough for Fred to see inside. Ten wolves sat in the shadows at the back of the chamber. Fred could see their heads which were bathed in a blue light that was cast by the fire they were huddled around.

"Is Chaxtan here?" Axel asked one of the wolves at the entrance.

The guard nodded. "Yes. Most of the council is here today, but they're busy. Come back another time."

Axel spoke again. "Can't. This human is here to see them. He says he has a message for all the wolves."

The other guard scoffed, but the first guard kept his cool and said, "I don't care if Theia is here to see the council. The human will have to come back another day."

Axel looked at the guard like he was being dumb. "So you're saying you want to turn this human away so that he can come back next week and bring all of his human friends with him?" Axel asked loudly.

"That's not what I said, old wolf!" shouted the guard as he moved towards Axel and got in his face.

By this point, however, Chaxtan had moved to the front of the den. Fred saw the silvery wolf eyeing him as he moved out of the darkness and into the light. "What's the meaning of all this?" he asked turning his attention to Axel.

Axel motioned his head towards Fred. "This is Fred. He's the human I was trapped inside the tunnels with for years. He brings news from the oracle. It's a message for all the wolves. I thought you'd rather hear it now than make Fred return another time," he said glaring at the guard who hadn't moved out of Axel's space.

Chaxtan sighed. "Of course. Come in both of you. I imagine this won't take long. The council has been working around the clock to figure out what to do about our elf problem. But we could probably use a quick distraction."

Fred leaned down a little as they entered the den so that he could fit inside.

"What do you mean?" asked Axel. "I thought you granted the elves temporary asylum on our land."

"Yes, well true. But it's temporary, right? The elves mouthpiece, that Exigor elf, he seems determined that none of them can go home until there is some sort of battle. Yet he doesn't seem to know when this fight will take place or what it will be about. And we're worried that these creatures are trying to trick us so that they can set up permanent colonies in our ancestral land."

Fred interjected, "I don't think that's what they're doing, sir. I think that they're just as confused about these fights as you are. Exigor asked me on my way here if I knew whether the fighting was over. He seems as eager for them to return home as you are to see them go."

The three had reached the back of the den where the other wolves had stopped talking and were waiting on their arrival. Chaxtan spoke to them, "Axel has brought us the human, Fred. And you'll all be happy to know that Fred has solved our problem. He says the elves are honest creatures that can be trusted. They will all leave whenever this mysterious fight is done."

The other wolves laughed, but Fred defended himself. "That's not exactly what I said."

Chaxtan ignored him, though. "Axel says this man has a message for the wolves that comes from the oracle who they say kept them imprisoned."

Fred spoke again, "Just to be clear, she's not an oracle; she's a goddess. The dark god, Theo, and your goddess, Theia, are her siblings."

Several of the wolves on the far end of the council's circle started to speak quietly to each other.

Chaxtan stared at Fred for a second, but then said, "Sit down, Fred."

Fred did as he was told and took a seat a foot back from the opening in the circle, right next to Axel. Chaxtan stayed standing, pacing back and forth now. "For ages, the wolves have surmised that there were two gods on the Moon. Of course we knew of Theia since she was our own god, but we suspected there was an evil presence here too. And yet now you say there are actually three gods? Or are there even more we should know of?"

Fred shook his head. Even though he knew there were

more than the three, he didn't think it a wise idea to complicate matters further. "Not on the Moon," he replied.

"Well, where else are these other gods hiding then? On the Earth?"

"No," replied Fred. "This is part of the message I was sent here to tell you. There hasn't been an Earth for thousands of years, and when it existed, this wasn't its Moon. We live on Ortus. In the beginning, it was the only world that existed. The Earth you're accustomed to seeing is a mirage, or I should say a portal to other dimensions—dimensions that exist here on Ortus inside of crystals.

"These crystals contain thousands of miniscule worlds and millions of creatures, but none of them live in the true world. Ortus is the only true world. At one time it was ruled by five gods, but two of them are thought to be dead, leaving only Theia, Theo, and Serena."

"This feels like blasphemy," protested one of the female wolves in the circle.

Axel quipped, "How can it be blasphemous if it's true? Theia is aware of the other gods. She just didn't tell us about them."

Another of the wolves replied, "But maybe there was a reason for that. I mean, you claim to have been imprisoned by this third god, Axel. Maybe Theia has been protecting us from these other gods."

Fred shook his head. "This is the second part of what I've come to tell you. Serena hid Theia inside of Maude. Serena can erase memories. She's done it to the creatures and gods many, many times. She erased Theia's memories when she trapped her in human form. After this, whenever you spoke to Theia through the crystals or during ceremonies, it was really Serena you were speaking to, pretending to be Theia."

The wolf named Dalia exclaimed, "It's a miracle! Serena sent us our goddess in the flesh during the ceremony to bring back Neriti's grandchildren! We were just too foolish to see that she was an answer to our prayers."

Axel who looked just as confounded by this news as the rest of the wolves said, "So, that's what Serena meant when she told Ragher Theia was gone. What a dirty trick to play on her own sister. But Maude knows who she is now? You've told her?"

Fred hung his head. "No, Axel. She already knew. When I found her after I left the tunnels, she already had her memories back. Serena gave them back to her a few weeks before she killed her."

All the wolves except for Axel gasped. "What do you mean? Theia is dead?!" asked Dalia. "Impossible! She's a goddess!"

Fred replied, "I'm sure that Theia still exists somewhere, but Maude is no longer here with us."

The wolves looked around at each other like they'd been completely deflated. Eventually, Chaxtan spoke for the entire group. "Thank you, Fred. But we will need some privacy to reflect on your message."

"I'm sorry," said Fred, "but I'm not quite finished. There is one last message from Serena."

None of the council looked like they wanted Fred to speak again, but he continued anyway. "The last message is the hardest to tell you, and please understand that it's not one that I take any pleasure in passing along."

"What is it?" asked Axel nudging him to get on with it.

"Serena wants me to tell you that she is the creator of all. From elves, she created Moon Walkers, and from Moon Walkers, she created the bryobane and you. However, she says that the only reason she chose to do this was to give Theo and Theia a distraction so they would never figure out her plan to destroy the whole world. Your lives have no other meaning except to keep the other gods from discovering her secrets."

"My god! We were elves?" cried Chaxtan in a horrified voice.

"Wait! Serena is going to destroy the whole world?" asked another council member. "What does that mean, Fred? How do we stop this?"

Fred nodded. "I have been asking myself that very same question for several months, and I don't have a good answer still. But I do think that this fight the elves are referring to has something to do with Serena's plan. Most likely she assumed that once I gave you her message, you would choose to confront her."

Axel said with a hint of panic in his voice, "Then clearly, we shouldn't confront her. It's probably a trap. She sent you here to tell us all of this to lure us to her. Maybe she's planning to imprison all of us because we didn't follow her orders to fight Theo."

"I see," said Chaxtan sounding concerned. He looked at Fred. "Thank you for telling us all of this, Fred. But like I said before, we will need some time to reflect on our own. Axel will show you out."

Fred and Axel left without saying another word. But once they were well beyond the council's den, Axel said, "I hope you know what you've done. If the council confronts Serena over this, she will have won."

Fred shrugged, though. "Axel, Serena is a force much bigger than you can imagine. I greatly disliked her after everything she told me, but I also knew it was the truth. So with time, I've come to accept that there's no use in fighting her or disobeying her. She isn't going to win if you decide one option or the other. She'll win because she has already. Everything has already been planned out. All we can do now is see where we land when the dust settles."

Axel stopped. "You're saying this is all fate then?"

"No, Axel. I'm saying that Serena is larger than life and has already mapped out every move. She's not able to see the future, but she's come pretty damn close. Whatever the council decides to do, she's already expected it for decades, maybe centuries."

Axel asked, "And you're sure about this, Fred? You don't think she just tricked you into believing this so you'd do what she told you to?"

Fred threw his hands up. "Who can say for sure? But if everything she showed me is true, then no. I don't think it was a trick."

"So what's the end result? What does Serena want?"

Fred stopped and turned to look at Axel. Then he looked around to make sure nobody could hear him. "She wants to rip this world apart, Ax. She wants to end everything we know, and she's planning on getting Mina to help her do it."

Axel grumbled, "I see. We have no choice then. Damned if we do and damned if we don't. But we'd be cowards to go down without a fight. I'll go talk to the council again and try to persuade them. You go tell the elves that they'll get their homes back soon, but only if they're ready and willing to fight."

THROUGH THE MELTING ICE

Mina's heart was beating fast as she sped across the Darkside atop Grimbolt, the old gelding who had come to life again under Mina's command. As he galloped through pitch black, Grimbolt seemed determined and happy to be serving an important master, trusting her to guide him, even though he didn't know of her newly discovered power to see in the dark.

A fire had been growing inside of Mina since she left Rebelton. She was angry with Fred for having kept so much from her. She understood that he thought he was doing it to protect her, but she still felt betrayed. Worse, she felt angry over all the heartache and suffering she'd been forced to endure since being swept away to the Moon nearly a decade earlier. However, she knew this wasn't Fred's doing. It was her mother's.

Hearing the truth from Theo about where she and the Moon Travelers really came from was upsetting. She knew it didn't exactly change anything about her past, but it made her feel like her whole life had been lived inside a fishbowl—a fishbowl controlled by Serena. She wanted answers about why she'd been lied to her entire life and what Serena's big plan was.

Mina found the entrance to the ice labyrinth without any trouble. Along with all the memories that her mother had forced on her, Mina had gained a large bank of knowledge which included the layout of the Moon. Mina suspected that this was a "gift" from Serena just like the memories, but just like the memories, Mina didn't understand why she possessed it.

After dismounting Grimbolt inside the large dome of light that surrounded the entrance, Mina got down to business. She spent a second peering into the dark sloped, tunnel. Then without giving it any thought, she hopped in and rode the slippery ice to the bottom.

Once inside, she found herself in a dimly lit room. She looked over her shoulder, expecting to see a large sheet of ice sliding into place to block her exit, but nothing happened.

"Baaaaaa! Baaaaaa! Black sheep!" She heard a spooky tune being sung from somewhere off to her left. A shadowy piece of the tunnel broke apart next to her, and the dance of the ice walls began. Mina moved into the space where the gap behind the wall had appeared; however, the tunnel that was forming around her wasn't brightly lit either, not like it had been in her dream or in the memories she'd been given. As in the first room she'd entered, there was a low light that made the ice look like it was cloaked in shadows.

The tunnel walls snapped into place, and Mina felt her stomach drop. Her nightmare had come to life. The floor of the tunnel sloped down into a big, dark hole below. She thought about turning around, but she knew there was no escaping. She looked down at her body to make sure it hadn't disappeared. It was still there.

Then out of the darkness, Mina heard the song being sung

again. *"One for the master. And one for the dame. One for the little boy who lives down the lane."*

This time though, three different voices took turns singing the song, and Mina recognized who the voices belonged to. "Okay, guys. You got me. Come out now."

Nothing happened for a few seconds, but then Mina saw movement inside the darkness. The three sheep became clearer as they approached, although at first it was hard to see them because they were fully black from head to toe.

"Did you like our song?" the first one asked Mina.

"We used to sing it to you when you were still inside the tree. Do you remember that?" asked the second. "We sang it to your father too when he was a little lad."

The third bleated loudly in the second sheep's face and said, "Of course she doesn't remember that! She wasn't even born yet!"

Mina shook her head. "I'm sorry, but I don't remember. Look, I need to speak to my mother. Can you take me to her?"

"Well, that's just dandy! We spent the best hundred years of our lives looking after this twerp, and she doesn't even remember us!" the first exclaimed.

"Seriously!" said the second. "And she didn't even have the courtesy to mention our new coats! Your mother gave them to us as a reward. We thought you'd like them."

The third sheep looked even more annoyed now. "Serena didn't give them to us as a reward, you nitwit. She scorched our wool as punishment for taking so long to get the crystal to Betsy, and for bringing her that dead girl's scalp! I told Wensley to get rid of that foul-smelling thing before we left the city!"

Mina sighed. "I'd really like to talk to my mother now. You know, I've never actually laid eyes on her before. Could you guide me in the right direction? Is she down there?" Mina pointed at the dark hole.

"Never seen your mother? Of course you have, child! You

spent hundreds of years with your mother before she abandoned you and your father down there!" The first sheep motioned his head towards the ground.

The second said, "That's right. She made us guard you for several hundred years. You treated us like your pets, even after Serena tried to draw your attention away to that mangy mutt. I still say it was bonkers she attempted to replace us in your heart with that long-eared monstrosity!"

"We've been over this, Balwynn," said the third. "Serena gave her that dog because we were getting too attached. Anyway, she erased Mina and Heely's memories before she abandoned them. That's why Mina doesn't remember. It's not actually her fault."

Mina frowned. "If all that's true, then how come you three didn't remember me either the last time we saw each other? When we were at the Sheep Spa together?"

"What Sheep Spa?" asked the first sheep.

"Oh, that sounds luxurious! I could use a day of relaxation and a good hoof scrub!" exclaimed the second.

"And they wonder why I always have to talk so much," said the third. "These two knuckleheads don't remember much of anything most of the time. Serena has erased their minds to the point of senility. They have moments of clarity, but the moments are always fleeting. That day we saw you at the Sheep Spa, I remembered what I was told to remember. Serena had a plan, and she made sure we followed it by putting us under a spell."

"But surely, it wasn't hundreds of years at least?" Mina said questioningly. "I mean, nobody lives that long. Right?"

"Wrong!" shouted a voice that sounded like it was coming from inside the ice wall next to them.

Suddenly the tunnel floor began to shake violently, and the three sheep were tossed end over end back down into the dark hole. Mina was able to hold her ground, but the jerky movements were taking their toll. She began to feel sick.

"Stop it!" she demanded of the ice wall. "This isn't how you greet your long-lost daughter! Don't you think I've undergone enough by your hand?"

Vapor poured over the ice wall nearest Mina, and soon water began to drip down the ice. The wall thinned out and became translucent like a wavy pane of glass. At first it seemed as though there was only darkness behind the ice wall, but then a giant head made of glowing violet crystals appeared on the other side of the melting sheet. Its eyes were black and shiny, and reminded Mina of Dan's.

Serena's giant head spoke to Mina through the layer of ice, and as her face moved, the crystals rubbed against each other, which created the sound of tapping.

"Why are you here?" she asked.

Mina felt anger rising in her chest. Her mother's words were the same as they'd been in her nightmare—the one she'd had before all the memories began pouring into her.

She replied heatedly, "I'm here because you brought me here! It would seem based on the information I've gathered from the sheep and Fred and Helen and Theo and all the memories you've thrust into my brain that you have been very busy conspiring to bring me here. So tell me! Why am I here?"

"No. I mean, why are you here?" asked Serena. "I told Fred not to let you come here. You should go."

Mina's anger quickly turned to pain. "My whole life has been plagued by lies and hurt because of you! Father and I were doing fine on our own. You should've left our memories intact and left us alone after you abandoned us. But you're cruel! You let my father die, you moved my pretend parents far away, and then, when I only had one companion in the whole world, you stole Bonkers away too! You're a monster!"

Calmly, Serena said, "It would seem we need to have a

reckoning. I thought that the memories I sent you might help you understand your own role in all of this, but maybe I was mistaken because *I* didn't do any of those things that you accuse me of. That was all you, my dear."

"What is that supposed to mean? I didn't kill my father or kidnap my dog!"

Serena replied, "Well, yes and no. But let me explain something first. Your role here is not of my long-lost daughter, although I understand why it might appear that way to you. However, I am in the midst of settling an ancient score and reconciling a mistake I made ages ago. That is why you are here on the Moon—to help me do so."

Mina began to yell, "I would never—"

But Serena stopped her. "With regard to who's to blame for the loneliness you endured after you left the Moon, that truly was you. When you first set foot onto Ortus, your energy began to align with my own. It was like a great yet undetected awakening inside of you, freeing you from the constraints I'd placed on you in that crystal world with your father. I wanted you to have a happy childhood, which is why I set everything into motion the way I did. To fulfill your responsibilities here, it was important for you not to know who you really were or where you actually came from.

"You spent millennia in that happy clearing by the sea with your pretend parents, and father, and Bonkers. Of course it didn't feel like that long because that was part of the magic of the particular crystal world you were in. It was also well hidden in case either of the time gods ever detected you or your father's existence. I transformed two of the most ruthless type of elves into your parents and put a memory spell on them so that they believed they were your parents. They were only meant to guard you; I made it so they would never love you deeply as parents often do love their children. That way their guardianship didn't interfere with your father's immense love for you.

"As a gift, I allowed you to retain some of the memories of Heely and I taking care of you when you were very young. To keep these memories from being confusing, I transposed your other set of parents into the memories. But, Mina, when you left the crystal world to come to Ortus the first time, your home world and everything in it was closed off to you forever. There's no way back through the portal into the crystal worlds, except through me.

"However, something unusual began to happen when you arrived on Ortus. You picked up some of my powers almost right away without realizing it. You vanished into thin air when you were trying to make your way into the market and two other times when Dale's men were chasing you. None of this should've been possible so soon. I hadn't done anything to transfer my powers to you. I decided to test it by giving you the chore of finding your way through the market to meet your secret contact, Theia—or Maude as she was known to you then.

"I told Helen to suggest the plan to Maude after I watched you become invisible the first time. It took quick maneuvering, but Maude was able to get a silver bird over to your welcoming committee. Originally, they were meant to take you straight to Maude, like they did with Fred. But as I said, I wanted to see what else you were capable of.

"Using our intertwined energy, I manifested that message that was attached to your wings. But you were the one who brought that vine to life and made it drop you right where you needed to be. It was delightful to watch.

"All of this to say, it was you who created the world you went back to, Mina. I needed to know how powerful you were, and you certainly showed me. When you flew away, I was worried you might parish. But you soared, and it was magnificent. Without even realizing you'd done it, you brought an entire world into existence inside of an empty crystal. You created your own dreams, your own reality, and your own nightmares too. You made the world you were comfortable with, but then you tested yourself when you sensed it wasn't real by drawing on the energy we share—including my own memories of my time spent with you and your father—to push yourself out of your comfort zone."

Mina shook, listening to her mother's words. She felt them inside of her, saw the memories of what had happened, and knew it was all true. There was a sense of relief that she'd finally heard the truth, but hurt and rage that she had been unwittingly allowed to create so much trauma for herself.

"And Father?" she asked in a strained whisper. "He and Bonkers, are they still alive?"

"You cannot go back, Mina. Not now. Not ever. Therefore, there's no way I can answer that question to your liking. So I won't."

Mina lashed out. "You are a cold, heartless goddess, and I will never do what you ask of me! Never!"

Suddenly, the ice began to crack, and Mina took a step back, worried what might happen next. Her mother's giant crystalized head hadn't really frightened her at first, but she knew she'd feel differently if the ice that separated them broke apart.

"There is nothing left for us to say to each other then. You can fight me if you so desire, just like the others have chosen to do, but I suggest you go out and discover more answers on your own since you clearly don't like the ones I've given you.

"There's a trove of ancient papers, the ones that the Moon Walkers gave to the wolves and the wolves gave to the humans. You can recall memories of them if you wish to verify what I'm telling you. Many of them were destroyed in the New Waldoff explosions. But Dale secretly kept a large supply of the papers, ones he stole from his parents when he was still a boy, believing they might be worth something one day.

"Before he was hauled away to prison, he paid one of his guards to stash the papers into a military supply crate. The papers are still in this crate inside of City Hall in New Waldoff. Go read them if you wish. They will fill in the memories you know are missing, the ones I have not given you access to. The choice is yours, however."

Mina was skeptical that the answers she wanted could be found so easily in some old papers, but she had no time to voice her skepticism. A second later, her mother's giant head disappeared, and the ice thickened so that it was opaque again.

"Great," said Mina sarcastically, although she was experiencing a mixture of feelings because of what had just happened. A tiny spark of hope had ignited inside of her that her father and best friend, Bonkers, were still alive, even if she couldn't get to them. She also felt a little relieved that her mother hadn't demanded anything of her since she was certain that it was Serena's intention to control her.

The tunnel walls broke apart, opening up a pathway that led to the room Mina had first entered. "Okay," she thought. "I have free will to do what I want." But Mina thought it in such a way that it was more like she was trying to convince herself of the idea than she actually believed it.

She climbed back out of the sloped tunnel, deciding what to do next. Absentmindedly, she hoisted herself onto Grimbolt and began to ride. But for the first time in a long while, she had no idea where she was headed.

CHAPTER 29

A REUNION

The sky lit up in pink and violet flashes of electricity as Theia descended from space, riding a blue beam of light as she entered the atmosphere of the teeny tiny world below her. The world wasn't the Moon realm or the Earth realm either. It was somewhere else. Somewhere Theia recognized. Somewhere she'd been stranded before.

When she reached the surface, she looked around. Golden-green fields stretched out for miles in every direction, reflecting the rays of the late afternoon sun. Yet along the horizon, the fields seemed to taper off, curving downward—an indication that Theia had been dropped onto a planet with a pathetically small circumference.

The air was different than the Moon's, thicker as though the sunlight and the planet's dust had intermingled in a way that didn't quite make sense. The world didn't seem real, Theia thought. But then again, it never had. Theia understood why the world looked surreal. It was merely a crystal world, meaning a world within one of the many crystals on Ortus, or the Moon Realm as the mortals now called it.

Theia looked up at the sky. Deep blues bled into the black

of space as the day melted away with the fading, red sun. It was all beautiful, but it was all essentially pretend.

"She's banished me again. But this time she's left my memories intact. Why?" Theia asked herself.

The tall goddess knelt in the grass. She was youthful looking with milky white skin and long, red hair that sparkled magically in the light of the setting sun. Helplessness crept through her body, invading her thoughts while anger and darkness sank their claws deep into her heart.

"How dare you!" she screamed at the sky above. "How dare you take me away from what's left of my family! How dare you trap me in one of your hell forsaken crystals again! You cowardly wench! When I find my way out of here, I'm going to make you pay for everything you've done! Do you hear me, Serena? Do you HEAR ME?!"

Theia's chest heaved under the weight of her anger and sorrow, and the sobs she'd been holding back finally broke free.

All of a sudden, she felt a hand gently touch her shoulder from behind. Theia sprang forward as she leapt to her feet and spun around. There, standing before her, was a tall woman with tan skin and dark, flowing hair. The woman wore a silky, white sundress that Theia thought made her look like an angel. But she knew better. This beautiful woman was no angel; it was her daughter, Helen, in the flesh.

Helen's eyes and lips smiled lovingly at her mother, but she didn't speak.

Theia whispered in shock, "Helen? Is that you?"

Helen nodded. Her long, dark hair bounced playfully across her shoulders. Theia couldn't stop smiling. It had been years since she'd seen Helen's face, and she couldn't believe how beautiful this older version of her daughter was. She had her father's dark complexion and calm eyes, but her stature and her smooth, flawless skin looked just like Theia's.

"Yes, Mother," she replied. "It is me. But look at you! You're young again!"

Theia's anger towards her sister vanished as her heart swelled with love for her darling, lost child. She threw her arms around Helen and asked, "But how? How is it possible? I thought you were dead. I thought Serena had murdered you and absorbed all your energy after the battle against Dan and Theo."

Helen pulled away from her mother's embrace. "So, you know then? Your memories have returned?"

Theia nodded. "Yes. Nine years have passed since the fight against your brothers. In fact, I think a new war is about to begin. Before I got my memories back, I spent all my time obsessed with finding out what happened to you and how I arrived on the Moon all those years ago with no memory.

"When Ruth gave me your letter, I was furious. I tried to cut her out of my life for betraying me. But then the day we sent Mina home, Ruth confronted me again. Theia stepped forward and took hold of her daughter's hands. "Here, hold on tight, and I'll show you."

The two women were pulled away from the tiny planet and thrown through time and space. Seconds later, they stopped abruptly. They were standing next to Ruth and also Theia, who was in the form of Maude. The two were facing each other, and thirty feet away stood Bob, Max, and Jacques, talking to each other out of earshot.

Helen asked, "This is the conversation you had with Ruth after Mina left?"

Theia nodded. "Yes, I didn't believe anything she said at first."

Maude was staring at Ruth with a sour expression. "So you want me to believe I was possessed by a spirit that told you whatever *truth* this is that you keep going on about? That makes no sense, Ruth! If that were true, why wouldn't I remember it? Or why wouldn't Neriti have ever told me this story?"

Ruth shook her head. "Sugar, you have no idea how frightening it was to be visited by that thing. It felt like we were being seen by our very maker, and that message it zapped into my brain! Well, lordy, Maude! It was terrifying! And I've been living in fear of what this spirit could do to me ever since. It can erase minds! Heck! The only reason I'm even telling you all of this now is because it told me to.

"After it revealed the truth about our world, it showed me that if Mina tried to leave, I should stop her by any means necessary. Even if that meant telling you the truth about that day. Heck, Maude! I know I sound like a blithering, old fool, but the spirit even showed me that we'd be having this very conversation right now! I mean, this all here is a real freaky little case of déjà vu!"

"Calm down, Ruth!" Maude barked. "You're right. You do sound like a blithering fool. But honestly, even if every word you're saying was the truth, I don't see the point of you telling me now. You said we weren't supposed to let Mina go, but she's out there!" Maude pointed over her head towards outer space. "And right now, all you're doing is keeping us from rescuing her!"

Ruth looked up at the sky. "No, honey. She's already gone. Can't you tell? I didn't make it here in time, and maybe I wasn't supposed to. I don't know. This spirit is tricky. I'd say that I reckon she's a dozen steps ahead of us in this game she's playing, only I think she might be playing a million different games at once with all sorts of different folks involved. And probably it'd be more accurate to say that she's a thousand steps ahead of all of us in each of them games."

Maude sighed. "What games, Ruth? Seriously, I don't have time for this nonsense! Bob! I'm done with her!" she yelled towards the men.

But Ruth looked at Bob and shook her head. Then she said to Maude, "Not yet, you ain't. Look here, Maude. I guess I'll just have to be frank about it. Helen weren't acting alone when she did what she did. Your little girl had been in cahoots with that spirit for a long time. It's how she learned to use my crystal to control me. But I'm pretty sure that this spirit had even more control over your baby than the control Helen had over me. When it showed me how this world works, it also showed me glimpses of Helen's life before she was ever born. It showed me how Helen would be controlled by something bigger than herself, something beyond her own will—like an invisible giant tugging at her strings."

Maude raised her eyebrows. "I see. Well, you're too late to break the news, Ruth. Helen told Bob that it was Theia who helped her carry out her plan. It was all done as part of a warning to let the humans know that they needed to honor the Moon's energy, like the wolves do. Otherwise—"

Ruth interrupted angrily, "This spirit ain't Theia, Maude! And I know that for a fact! This crystal has been giving me visions for years now." Ruth held up the crystal so it was dangling between them.

"And gosh darn it if I don't know more than I ever wanted to. And one of those things I know is that the spirit was tricking Helen if she told her she was Theia! She was telling your girl fairytales! Why? I don't know. But probably so she could get Helen to do what she wanted her to! Or maybe she wasn't lying at all, and it was your girl who was lying to keep us all safe!

"Listen to me, Maude." Ruth took a step towards her friend, lowering the crystal. "That day that Neriti and I showed up to talk to you about the problem you was having not being able to get with child, Neriti told you that the wolf elders were going to hand all those ancient papers over to the humans. You remember?"

"Yes, why?" Maude asked curtly.

"Because one of the things that spirit told me—that she whispered in my ear many times through this dang crystal—is that you will finally know who you are once you learn how to read those papers. Those papers hold secrets about this realm that nobody else knows. Maybe them Moon Walkers knew the secrets once upon a time too, but they ain't here to tell us whether they did or didn't. So what I suggest, if you still want to know why you're here, why any of us is here, is that you get to work on figuring out them papers. Or what's left of them, anyway."

Maude looked down at the crystal that hung by Ruth's side. Both Helen and Theia followed her gaze, catching a slight glimmer that shone from the crystal for a fraction of a second. It could've simply been the crystal reflecting a beam of light, but when Maude looked back at her old friend, her countenance had changed. She seemed relaxed.

"That's right," she said dreamily. "I remember now. Neriti said that the papers were part of the vision that she and the other healers saw during their circle. Maybe there actually is some truth to what you're saying, Ruth."

Then suddenly she became cross again, but this time not with Ruth. "Blast it! What have I done? I erased so many of them! What if there's not enough markings left to figure out the language?"

Ruth shook her head and reached her hand out to hold Maude's. "Nah, sugar. It's gonna be okay. You've been through enough mourning already. Don't focus your mind on what you can't undo; focus it on what you can do going forward."

Maude nodded at Ruth, and Theia and Helen saw tears filling Maude's eyes. Ruth spoke comforting words to her friend and moved forward for a hug, but before Theia and Helen could see the reconciliation, they were jerked back to the tiny crystal world filled with grassy landscapes.

"Do you think Ruth hypnotized you with her crystal on purpose, Mother? I never would've thought my sweet, purple-haired godmother capable of such trickery." Helen laughed.

Theia shook her head. "No, I don't think Ruth was the one using the crystal to make me change my mind. Most likely it was my sister, Serena, considering how devious she is. Wouldn't you say?"

Theia stared at her daughter expectantly, waiting for her to confirm what she'd suspected ever since her memories had returned. Waiting for Helen to tell her the secret she felt sure her daughter had clung to her entire life. A secret that made Theia wonder if her darling daughter had ever even had the chance to be herself—the chance to explore her own identity outside of the role that had been thrust upon her.

Helen hesitated. Theia's eyes were staring at her knowingly. as though they were trying to pry into her very thoughts. Theia prompted, "My sister, Serena…"

Helen took a deep breath, as if nervous about what her mother might say next.

"She was the spirit Ruth spoke of, wasn't she? She was the one whispering in your ear, telling you to fight your brothers? Telling you how to orchestrate a way to lure Fred and Mina from the crystal worlds to the origin world—to Ortus?"

Helen nodded, letting out a deep sigh. "Yes, Mother. It's true."

"I'm so sorry, Helen!" Theia embraced her daughter again. "If I knew how to get out of here, I'd go after Serena and end her. She's destroyed everything good in all of our lives, erased memories, tortured the gods and mortals for eons. Her evilness knows no bounds!

"Tell me, what did she threaten to do to you? And why didn't you come to me in secret and tell me what she was putting you through?"

Helen hung her head. "She was part of me, Mother. She

was the voice inside of me before I even knew how to speak, the biggest influence in my life. And yet my biggest secret too. I tried to push her out of my head several times, but she wouldn't allow it. She had big plans for me from the beginning."

"Like what?"

"Oh, I can't tell you everything. But she used me to carry out important parts of her plan, like guiding Fred and Mina and taking on Dan, even though she already knew how it would all turn out. On the other hand, she said that if I didn't do everything perfectly, then her plan would be ruined. So, I had to sacrifice. Do what she wanted even if it wasn't what I wanted."

"And Max? Was he part of the sacrifice she wanted you to make? Or do you even remember how you used to feel about him?"

"Yes, Mother. I suppose he was one of the sacrifices I was forced to make."

Theia looked at Helen oddly, as though something suddenly seemed off about her. Helen looked up and met her mother's eyes, but as Theia continued to gaze at Helen, a look of suspicion crept across her face.

"What's with all this 'Mother' nonsense? Call me what you've always called me."

Helen shrugged. "Haven't I always called you 'Mother?'" she asked a bit coyly.

Theia's eyes narrowed. Then a second later she gasped. "Oh my god! You're not Helen!"

She took a few steps back, distancing herself from the woman who looked just like her daughter. "It's *you!* Isn't it?"

Theia seethed with anger as the tall, tan-skinned woman who looked like Helen laughed a sinister laugh.

"It is, yes. If you only knew how many times we've lived through some version of this scenario, my precious Theia.

You've always been so clever. Even when you didn't remember who I was, you still detected when you were being deceived. Truly, I've never grown tired of watching that expression on your face, the one you get whenever you realize you're being duped."

"You're an awful creature, Serena! The way you casually flaunt your power over everyone else, it's disgraceful. Why couldn't you have been a goddess of mercy and love? Fate was brutal when it assigned you the role of creator in our realm."

Serena scoffed. "Ha! You don't even know of what you speak. I was loving and merciful, but you and the other gods forced me to become this way! I never sought to punish you for what you did, however. My only goal has been to make things right again."

"You haven't sought to punish us? Really? Then why when I came to you and asked you to stop Theo's deranged pet from killing those pups that horrible day on the Darkside, why did you erase my memory and turn me into Maude?"

"Who says I was punishing you?" Serena smiled darkly.

"If you don't think that having your very essence stolen away from you over and over throughout eternity isn't punishment, then maybe you should try it sometime. It's a living hell!"

Serena looked serious. "I did try it. Don't you remember? I created the Earth for us to escape the boring, the mundane, the infinite paradise I'd created for us on Ortus. We needed more than paradise to truly thrive. We, the five original gods, we weren't happy here despite the narrative that you and Theo have tried to convince yourselves of again and again. We warred with each other because we had nothing better to do. We needed distractions, complications, good, bad, beautiful, ugly, pleasure, torture. We needed all of it to truly exist. But you two couldn't stand it, so you made me burn it to the ground by forcing my hand. It took you ages, but you finally found a way to back me into a corner I couldn't escape from.

"Before that, I spent millennia running away from my divinity, because the only way I could be happy was to forget who I was and what I was capable of. I found my happiness amongst the ordinary mortals, but you and Theo couldn't let me be. You were willing to do whatever it took to get back to Ortus, no matter how many times I warned you that it would never be the same. In the end, you forced me to destroy the Earth, even though the paradise you once knew on Ortus was forever gone.

"So, yes. I stripped away your memories many times over, but I've done so only as a way to right the wrongs you caused. And the day you came to me demanding that I protect the wolf pups, I wasn't punishing you. I was giving you a chance at redemption—something you denied me again and again when you kept me from living blissfully unaware as a mortal."

"All of that is crap, Serena! Spare me your righteous indignation! You didn't only strip away our memories for thousands of years, you stole Theo's and my child. Then later, you allowed Theo to manipulate my son, Dan, while you controlled Helen to the point of preventing her from living a normal life. A life which you eventually stole from her, no less!"

"Actually, that's just the half of it, dear Theia—it's only what you remember, anyway."

Theia's hatred for her sister was intense. She felt herself about to go into a rage, but she forced herself to keep her cool. She realized now what she needed to do. And the only way she could accomplish her plan was if she still had all of her memories intact.

Serena mocked Theia, "Are you scared? Is that why you stand there silently like an angry scarecrow? Because you know you can never beat me? I've always been and will always be the most powerful god in this universe. As long as I exist, you will always lose!"

Serena seemed to be waiting for a response, but Theia dug her heels in, unwilling to make any sudden moves and risk having her mind erased.

"Fine, I will go then," said Serena. "But you know where to find me if you decide you want to face me in the real world." Serena looked over her shoulder at the full moon that hung in the sky.

"Just make sure you're ready to handle what's up there. Time moves slower here, which means it's been a few months since you've left Ortus. Not so long, you might think. Yet long enough for your man to move on with another woman. Tata, Theia!"

Serena smiled wickedly and snapped her fingers, vanishing into thin air.

Theia screamed at the space where her sister had stood and stared up at the Moon with fury. She was done living this absurd way. Serena had left her no room for contentment in life, as she continued to interfere with everything that Theia cherished about her own existence.

She knew it was time to break free of Serena once and for all, even if that meant the end of her very long life. She could no longer shy away from her fear of death when practically everyone she'd ever cared for was already lost to the eternal void. It was time to embrace her fear and follow her loving daughter into the darkest shadows. But she wouldn't sacrifice her life in vain like her dear, sweet Helen. Because Theia had decided that when she died, she was going to make damned-well sure to take Serena with her.

CHAPTER 30

CHASING MEMORIES

As Mina and Grimbolt crossed the border between day and night, Mina was shocked when she looked out on the horizon and spotted thousands of elves migrating in her direction. She saw quite a few wolves mixed in with the herd as well, but their numbers paled in comparison to the amount of little gray creatures hopping along towards her. When she got closer, she realized she'd overlooked Fred, who was towering above the others.

Mina climbed down from Grimbolt and waited for the giant group to catch up to her. Fred ran to reach her before the others, and when he got to her, he threw his arms around her tight. "I'm so sorry, Mina. I shouldn't have left you the way I did," he said looking back over his shoulder at the army approaching them.

Mina bit her lip as he pulled away. "I'm sorry too, Fred, although I'm still upset about how much you kept from me. I've just ridden back from the ice tunnels."

Fred nodded. "Did Serena tell you everything?"

Mina snickered. "No. She sent me away to find out about

the memories she's still withholding. She's not exactly warm and fuzzy, is she?"

"No, not really." Fred laughed. "So, what are you going to do?"

Just then, a taller elf walked up to them and introduced himself. "Hello, hello! I am Exigor, mouthpiece for all elves! And you are her! I am so honored to meet her! Serena told us about you. You have come to save us!"

Mina looked at Fred questioningly. To Exigor she said, "I'm not sure what you mean, Exigor. Why do you think I'm here to save you?"

Exigor giggled. "You are Mina! Serena told the elves about you before you were born. We used to ask her night and night and day and day for a thousand years when she would fix our home, the moooney Moon. She said she had a plan, and you were her plan! And now you are here! Hooray!"

The elves who were close enough to hear Exigor shouted, "Hip hip hooray!"

Then soon, all the elves were shouting, "Hip hip hooray!"

Mina was surprised by Exigor's declaration; however, she didn't want to confirm or deny it since she didn't know anything about it.

Changing the subject, she asked, "Where are you all going?"

Fred started to explain as Exigor rejoined the group of elves that were walking past them. "I visited the wolves and gave them Serena's message. They didn't take it well."

"And the message was?"

Fred sighed. "That Serena created the wolves to be a distraction for Theia and Theo. Their only purpose was to keep the gods from interfering in Serena's big plan."

"Yikes, Fred. That's extremely harsh. What are the elves and wolves planning to do now?"

But before Fred could answer, she heard a deep voice from behind her. "We're planning to unite against Serena in a last-ditch effort to prevent your mother from using you to end the world."

Mina turned around. "Axel!" she shouted before bowing her head deeply.

Axel bowed his head at Mina in return. "It's good to see you, kid, although you're not exactly a kid anymore, are you? Fred told me about the arm, but you look better than ever."

Mina shrugged, "Thanks, Axel. I'm still getting used to the arm and this band around my head," she pointed at the metal ring. "I feel like a cyborg, honestly."

"A cyborg?" Axel asked.

Mina smiled. "Yes, like a human who's also part robot."

"I see," said Axel. "So you're part goddess, part robot, and part human. You've become quite the overachiever."

Mina said, "When I was just in the ice tunnels, Serena told me she was planning to use me. Why do you think it's to end the world? That elf, Exigor, just told me the elves think I'm going to save the Moon. So, which is it?"

Fred spoke, "It's the first one, Mina. I wasn't able to tell you until I told the wolves. Again, I'm sorry. I should've gone to them sooner, I guess, but I didn't want to leave you after you came back.

"Serena told me she brought you to life so you could help her end the world. I guess she didn't want to scare the elves by telling them the truth. I can only imagine how annoying it would be to have a bunch of freaked out elves running around for a few millennia like the sky is falling."

Axel snickered. "Do you really think it would be any worse than it is now?"

"Okay," said Mina. "But if the elves think that Serena is going to save them still, then why have they united with the lunar wolves against her?"

Axel replied, "Because they want their homes back. Serena

kicked them out and told them to live with the wolves until the fighting stops. So, basically, they've decided to fight so that they can then stop fighting and go home."

"Right," said Mina. "And you're sure this is the best plan? The elves don't look like they'd make very good soldiers. Plus, it doesn't really sound like they know what they're getting themselves into."

Axel agreed, "No, they don't, and they won't be, but the wolf council decided to take a stand anyway. Serena's message resonated with them. The wolves were never important to her. She abused us by allowing the time gods to toy with our lives and even slaughter us—or have their minions do so. She also meddled in our affairs when she pretended to be Theia for decades.

"My father, Ragher, is a perfect example of the mistreatment she's shown us. He served her for centuries, yet she never gave him any respect. She could have at least allowed him to live one full lifetime with his family, free of her harassment and control, but instead she put our entire family through hell.

"My parents lived in fear because of the orders Serena gave my father not to confront Theo. If Serena had allowed Ragher to turn himself over to Theo, Ragher would have found out years earlier that Theo wasn't going to kill him. Tahissi's life and my life were greatly impacted by the lies our parents felt they had to tell to keep us safe. And if that wasn't enough, Tahissi's partner and pups paid the ultimate price. Because our father loyally obeyed Serena like a good servant, my niece, my nephews, Tahissi, and Tegelro are all dead now.

"The wolf council was persuaded to fight because they see that it is wrong to sit idly by, knowing we are not the masters of our own fate. Like our ancestors who stood up to the bryobane many years ago, it is time to say, "enough." It is time to demand our freedom so that we may live our lives in peace without interference from the gods!"

"Wow, Axel," said Mina. "I didn't know all of that. But I can certainly see why you feel like it's time to confront my mother. I only worry that you're greatly outmatched. Do you think it would be wise for me to come with you?"

"No!" said Axel and Fred in unison.

Fred explained, "I think it would be better if you search for the memories Serena told you to find. Let the elves and wolves fight her first. Who knows? Maybe they'll weaken her enough so that she'll no longer have the power to put an end to our universe. How are your powers, Mina? Did you figure out if you're able to do anything exceptional with your new arm?"

"Yes, but not just with my arm. I seem to have taken on some of Serena's energy too. I'm able to do lots of things I couldn't do before, although maybe I could but didn't realize it. I'm not exactly sure. Serena said that her energy began to blend with mine the moment I arrived on the Moon the first time."

Fred nodded. "That's good. I think. Hopefully, your powers are catching up to Serena's. If we let the army attack first, then maybe we can catch her off guard with a sneak attack once she's committed herself to the fight."

Mina bit her lip. "I don't know, Fred. I get the impression that she doesn't care what I do. I suspect that means she's ready for anything. What if it doesn't even matter how we play this? What if Serena is so powerful that she already knows she can beat us no matter what?"

"Then heaven help us all," said Axel. "Anyway, you two be careful doing whatever you decide. I have to go now. I'm off to try and recruit the underground wolves to our cause before the army reaches the ice tunnels. I'll have to hurry, though."

Mina bowed at Axel again. "You be careful too, friend. And don't worry. Fred and I will come up with some way to help."

Axel took off, and Fred spoke again, "I know how easy it is

to feel like we're already beat because of how powerful Serena is. But one good thing I know is that she needs *you* to complete her plan. That means we still have some leverage over her. Did she tell you where to go to find the answers you're looking for?"

Mina nodded. "Yes. She said Dale had one of his guards stash some papers in an army crate. I know where it is. I've seen it in some of the memories Serena gave me. I would have to go all the way to New Waldoff to find it, though."

"Okay," said Fred. "Then let's go to New Waldoff. I've made it in and out of there before without being detected. I'm sure we can find a way to do it again."

Mina looked worried. "I don't know, Fred. I feel anxious leaving the wolves and elves alone to fight her."

Fred replied, "I know. I'm scared too, but I think we have to exhaust all our options. We didn't give up when we were trapped together in the well years ago; we worked together to call for Axel and the wolves to help us escape. If we go to Serena now, we're toast. But maybe there's something in those papers that can help us. If there's even a slight chance that's true, then we need to find out."

Mina sighed. "Okay, Fred. We'll go to New Waldoff. But I think we better hurry. I can already feel that we're teetering on the precipice of something big, and I want to be able to help if our friends are in trouble."

Fred nodded. "Agreed. Let's go!"

Mina and Fred rode off together to New Waldoff, which was a long journey, even with Grimbolt going full speed most of the time. Mina rode in front of Fred, just like she had on their way to Rebelton, and it made her think back to the conversation they'd had then.

"You know, Fred. I've thought of Mattie every day since I met her. I know I said I'd put her out of my mind, but I can't. Serena told me that when I left here before, I didn't go back to the crystal world I was born in. She said I created my own world inside of an empty crystal and brought to life everything that I knew from my childhood. I suppose if that's true, then it could also be true that nothing was actually real after I left Earth, just like you said. I guess that means that Mattie might not have been real either."

Mina started to tear up. "I suppose I should be happy that Mattie isn't out there somewhere missing her parents and hoping I'll return someday, but honestly, I'm heartbroken. I wanted her to be real because there was something about her that felt special. It's hard to explain, but there was part of me that really felt like she was my own daughter."

Fred wrapped his arms tighter around Mina and kissed the back of her head. "I love you, Mina. I'm sorry for what you've had to go through. Maybe someday, if we're able to make it through the next few hours and days, we can start a family of our own."

Mina squeezed Fred's arm with her hand and whispered, "Maybe."

When they arrived at the sloping stone entrance that led through New Waldoff's outer wall, Fred asked, "Okay, are you sure you can stay invisible the entire time we're walking in?"

"Pretty sure," said Mina, vanishing and then reappearing to test her power out again.

"Good. The guards are probably going to want to ask me some questions, but I think I can convince them that I'm one of Dale's men. If it comes to it, I'll tell them I'm Max and hope that works. Remember, you go on without me when we get up there. If I don't catch up to you, it means I've been arrested. Just break me out later after you find what you're looking for. Okay?"

Mina nodded, and they walked up the path to the large entrance. Halfway up, Mina hung back for a second, and when Fred looked back, she was gone. He kept walking. Fred noticed a second later that the large gate to the city was open, which meant he could walk right in. When he passed through the wall, however, he was surprised to find that no one was on the other side. The city streets were empty.

"Who goes there?!" shouted a voice off to Fred's left. Fred turned and saw a single guard perched on a stool, leaning against the large stone wall behind him.

Fred answered, "I'm one of Dale's men. I was part of the team who went to check on the rebel city a few months ago. Dale told me to stay there and keep watch over the rebels from a safe distance. I've returned to report back. Where is everybody?"

The guard laughed. "You're a day too late, son. The others have gone off to fight the rebels."

"The whole city?" Fred asked in disbelief.

"Damn near all of it," said the guard. "The general drafted every able-bodied person to fight. Betsy ordered him to. Said it was the only way to ensure the safety and freedom of the Moon realm."

The guard eyed Fred suspiciously. "Funny you didn't cross paths with them on your way here. What did you say your name was?"

Fred stalled by asking, "How come if every able-bodied person was drafted, then you're still here?"

The guard sat up straight and puffed out his chest. "I have an important job here. Betsy brought me into her office and personally asked me to stay here and keep a look out."

"A look out for what?" asked Fred.

The guard looked all around like he was making sure no one was listening, which Fred thought was strange since there didn't seem to be anyone else for miles.

"Well, just between you and me, there's a wanted fugitive on the loose. Three days before everyone left, some men showed up who'd been keeping an eye on the trail that leads up to that dang city of fools in the mountains. Kind of like you were doing, I guess.

"Anyway, that angel Mina, who was here a long time ago, well, she's back now. She was living with all those dimwits up there in the mountains. But then those two men who were spying for Betsy, they ran back here and said that Mina left for the Darkside a few days ago.

"So, Betsy asked me if I thought I could recognize Mina on account of the fact that I was the one who let her into Waldoff Market years ago. And I said, 'sure I could recognize either of those angels from before!' I mean, who wouldn't be able to recognize them? They have wings, you know? But I guess she wanted a competent guard like good old, Neil, to be in charge. Did you hear that I was the one who arrested that fugitive, Bob?"

Fred shook his head and said seriously, "I've heard she and the boy don't have wings anymore."

Neil frowned. "Is that right?"

"Well, that's what I hear, anyway. So what are you supposed to do if you find Mina? You think you could take her into custody all by yourself?"

Neil shrugged. "Yeah, I'm sure I could take her. She's just a woman, after all. If she does come around here, I'll knock her out so I don't have to deal with some sort of hysterical woman fight. Then I'll throw her in prison and wait for Betsy to return so she can admire my catch."

Fred laughed. "Well, it seems like you've got it all figured out then. I guess I'll just be on my way."

Fred turned, but before he could walk away, Neil stood up from his stool and said, "Wait just a second. You still haven't told me who you are."

"The names Fred," said Fred with a roguish smile. "And that woman standing behind you is Mina."

Neil spun around in shock and came face-to-face with

Mina, who lifted her metal arm above her head and brought it down hard against Neil's temple. He fell to the ground with a thud.

Mina stared down at Neil. He was knocked out cold. She snickered. "How's that for a hysterical woman fight?" Then to Fred, she said, "I never did like this guy. He wouldn't even let me borrow a pen the first time we met. Yeesh!"

Fred nodded. "Thanks for sticking around to help me out."

Mina replied, "Of course, but how did you know I was standing behind him? I hadn't appeared again yet."

"I just had a feeling," said Fred, shrugging it off. "Mina, I think I better warn the others about Betsy's army. If I go fast, I might be able to get around the army and sneak up the trail before they reach the base of the mountains. An army that size can't be moving at a very quick speed. I think I still have a shot."

Mina bit her lip. "Okay, Fred. But what should I do after I find the papers?"

"Leave the city and head back to the Darkside, towards the tunnel with the bryobane remains. I'll find you along that path somewhere."

Mina walked to Fred and kissed him on the lips. "You're a very brave man with a good heart, Fredrick."

"Fredrick?" Fred asked as he pulled away from Mina.

Mina smiled. "Just trying out new pet names. I mean, what better time to try something new than when the whole world's in jeopardy, right? But seriously, I love you. Promise me you won't do anything stupid."

Fred leaned into Mina and kissed her gently. "I promise. I love you, too, Minuet."

"Minuet?" she asked cheekily.

"Yes, I think it goes rather nicely with Fredrick."

Fred squeezed Mina's hand and then turned and took off through the city wall. He looked over his shoulder one last time before he disappeared down the stone path towards Grimbolt, and Mina waved.

"Okay," she thought. "Let's find these papers and get out of here."

Mina worried that she might have a long walk ahead of her back to the Darkside if she couldn't find a horse. Wandering her way up and down the winding streets of New Waldoff, she learned which way to go by studying the memories in her head. Sometimes it was hard to identify buildings and streets from the memories because there were entire blocks that had been blown apart and huge vines that covered nearly every square foot of the cityscape now. Mina took a few wrong turns, but she was able to correct herself before getting too far from the right path.

Eventually, she wandered into an area of town where the narrow streets gave way to an open space. Mina realized from what she saw that she had found the city's courthouse. During her walk, there had been a few shadows lurking in windows, reminding her that she wasn't totally alone in the old-timey town. Yet when she reached the front of the courthouse, she was surprised to find a large man sitting on the steps, staring sadly off into space. From her memories, she recognized the man. His name was Cary.

Cary looked at Mina as she stopped in front of him. "Is it over yet?" he asked her.

Mina was confused. It seemed like Cary was familiar with her as well, which was a bit startling since she was sure they'd never met before. "Is what over?" she asked.

Cary sighed and hung his head. "Everything. The annihilation of our very souls."

Mina looked at Cary with an even more puzzled expression.

"I couldn't go with them, you know? Not this time," he said. "It went too far. She changed the children into elderly folks. Did you hear that some of them are even senile now? These people went from spending decades as children to becoming senior citizens in the snap of a finger. With no in-between! And they're being forced to fight along with everyone else!

"My family and friends don't even understand why they're fighting. They think it's to retain their freedom, but hell! How can you retain something you don't even have? Bob's friends didn't hurt anybody, but Betsy and her guards say they did. So they're going to go slaughter a bunch of innocents! Just like we slaughtered the wolves. It's just plain wrong!"

Mina sat down next to Cary for a minute and put her hand on his shoulder. "You're right. It is wrong. But if it makes you feel better, one of my dear friends is on his way to try and warn Bob and the others."

Cary raised his head and looked at Mina. "You mean, Bob's alive? I heard Betsy killed him after she tortured him."

"No, he got away," Mina explained. "Maude helped break him out. I guess Betsy didn't want anyone to know."

Cary smiled. "That's a pretty big secret. Are you one of the rebels?" he asked looking at her arm and halo.

"Not exactly. I guess I'm not really aligned with any of the groups on the Moon, to be honest. But I'm definitely more of a rebel than anything else," Mina said with a smile.

"Yeah, I guess I'm not aligned with any group either, now that everyone's abandoned me to go fight the others."

Mina nodded. "I have to get going, Cary. I just wanted to make sure you were okay. You looked so sad sitting here all by yourself in this empty town."

"I'll be okay," said Cary. "I'm sure my people will find me again. Even if I have to sit here and wait on them for a few hundred years." He laughed.

Mina laughed too. "Okay then. Good luck. I hope you don't have to wait for too long!"

She left the courthouse behind and walked a little further until she found City Hall. With everyone gone, Mina wondered if it might be locked, but she pushed the door open and walked right in. She looked around the lobby and found a stairwell which she took to the basement. Once she left the stairwell, she entered a long corridor. All the way down the hall, there were dozens of barred doors on each side. But unlike the prison above, these doors led into multi-sized storage units.

Mina's shoes scuffed along the cement floor as she raced down the hall, looking at the numbers on the doors as she passed. When she reached the door marked '814,' she stopped and put her hand on the doorknob. It began to glow bright red, and a few seconds later, the knob fell right off. She pulled the door open, then squeezed herself between two large wooden crates.

At first, she tried to lift the top with her hands, but she couldn't get her metal fingers under the rim. So she smashed her metal fist through the top of the crate and made a giant hole. She repeated the motion again and again until she had full access to the contents inside the large box.

There were several layers of black army uniforms folded and stacked at the top. Mina pulled all the clothes out and tossed them behind her, digging down towards the bottom. Soon, her metal arm knocked against something hard. She grabbed ahold of the solid item and pulled it out too. It was a box. Mina opened the box and found a dozen silver birds. She grabbed a couple and put them aside to take with her later. She kept digging through the contents of the crate, past a bunch of metal gadgets that Mina thought were probably taser guns.

At the very bottom of the crate, she noticed a large leather satchel. She brought it out of the wooden box and tugged on the leather flap that lay across the front. Then she reached into the bag and pulled out a ream of old papers. She smiled as she began to look over the strange symbols. It surprised her at how easily she could read the made-up language. It came so naturally that it was almost like she was channeling the Moon Walkers who'd created the odd script.

Mina stood for a while, flipping through the sheets and stuffing them back into the satchel when she was through with each one. Very quickly, it became apparent that she was reading a history of creation from Theia's perspective. There were tens, if not hundreds, of summarized reports relating to how Serena had stolen the time gods' memories over thousands of years. Before and after they lived on Earth, but not during.

Mina was fascinated by the accounts, but soon something struck her as odd. It began to dawn on her that Serena's so-called 'punishments,' as Theia continually referred to them, were more methodical, more calculated than simple, run-of-the-mill punishments. Mina didn't know exactly how she understood it, but the more she read, the more certain she became that these punishments weren't actually punishments at all. They were tests.

Suddenly, Mina had a vision of the giant gear wheel she'd seen in the crater while leaving the Moon years prior. She'd assumed it was part of the mechanics that kept the Darkside and Dayside running, but what if…

Like a bolt of lightning, Mina's thoughts led her to an answer that she knew was right. "Serena can't control time. So she built a giant computer on Ortus to help her predict the future. That's what all the wheels and underground conveyor belts are really for. Serena has been using her power to erase minds in order to test and retest how the gods and mortals will react in a million different scenarios, running the situations over and over with different variables. Then she captures the memories from her tests inside her computer and analyzes the data until she knows with absolute certainty what every outcome of every situation will be."

A wave of fear suddenly pummeled her. "That means she

already knew I would choose to come here and that Fred would leave me stranded. Oh my god! I have to get out of here before it's too late!"

Mina grabbed a couple of silver birds and stormed out of the storage unit. She knew she was panicking, but she didn't have time to calm down. Even if there was nothing she could do that Serena wouldn't already know about ahead of time, Mina needed to get to the wolves and elves to let them know they were walking into a trap. She needed to tell them that the best thing they could do was the most unexpected thing of all —nothing.

Mina practically jumped up the entire staircase and ran back to the lobby on the first floor. She left the building and ran down the street, passing Cary who was still seated on the steps outside the court building. She stopped for just a second and yelled, "Cary! Do you know if Betsy's army took all the horses?"

Cary shrugged. "I imagine so. You could look around, though. There might be one or two left."

Mina thanked Cary and then sped off again. She told herself she didn't have time to locate and search every stable. But just as this thought left her mind, Mina had a strange feeling come over her. She felt light and airy and tapped into the energy around her. Then right as the most tranquil wave of electricity flowed over her, Mina's mind focused in on a series of images, showing her where to find a horse nearby.

Mina ran in the direction of the building she'd seen, and sure enough, in less than three blocks, she found a white mare alone inside a one stall stable. A few minutes later, Mina had saddled the mare up and was riding out of town. She passed by Neil, who was still flat on the ground.

"Lucky jerk," she said as she directed the mare down the long slope and out onto the Moon's surface. "We should all be so fortunate to get to sleep through the apocalypse."

Once Mina was back on firm ground, she kicked the mare forward, and they took off across the dusty, gray terrain. "I hope it's not too late to warn the army," Mina thought. But just then, a thunderous explosion erupted from the direction of Rebelton—the direction that Fred had gone just an hour earlier.

Mina looked towards the mountains, but she couldn't see anything from so far away. "He's okay, Mina," she told herself. "They're all okay, probably. Think about the wolves and the elves. You still have a chance to save them."

Mina tried for a few more seconds to turn her attention from the frightening explosion, but it was no use. Without warning, she pulled the horse's reigns and turned the mare towards the mountains. She'd done her best to fight it, but in the end, she couldn't resist following her heart.

CHAPTER 31

A HARD STONE

The day the army left New Waldoff to fight, Max witnessed something unexpected. Betsy showed up to lead the charge wearing a dark red, velvet suit instead of her permanent long black dress with the high collar. In addition to the change in wardrobe, Betsy had accessorized her ensemble with a large green vine that was wrapped around her neck like a well-fed python.

Max had spent the entire month following the six thousand orders Betsy had given him on how to recruit and train the new army. To say he was the most micromanaged general in the history of armies would've been an understatement. But luckily for him, Betsy only bossed Max around during their evening strategy sessions when they planned out tactics for taking the rebel valley by surprise. Or at least that's what they did whenever Betsy wasn't telling Max how to run the next day's training exercises.

He knew he should have been relieved that the month was over and that it was time to leave New Waldoff, but instead, Max felt like a raw bundle of nerves. He had been thinking of Helen nonstop the last few weeks, and whenever he had the chance to sleep, he willed himself to dream of her.

Betsy rode up on a large black stallion, donning her new outfit and pushing her way through the soldiers. Until then, the soldiers had been lined up in columns of three, ready to exit the city in an orderly fashion. Max sighed as he watched Betsy undo his morning's work in a matter of minutes.

Betsy asked, "These soldiers ready to march?"

Max shrugged. "Well, they were, but I guess we won't worry about an orderly exit now."

"Fine. Fine," Betsy said loudly as she surveyed the troops. There hadn't been enough time to make uniforms for the thousands of people they'd drafted, so Max had told everyone to wear gray clothing in order to blend in with the lunar landscape.

After Betsy completed a full circle on her horse, she asked, "Why are some of these soldiers wearing burlap sacks with holes cut out of the sides and bottom?"

Max answered, "I told them to wear gray. I guess that was the only gray cloth some of them had access to. Supplies have been tight since we transitioned everyone into all day training."

Betsy looked stern. "Don't lecture me on supplies! It doesn't matter what they wear! What do I care if they're pleased to die in a potato sack?"

The troops looked at Max and each other nervously, but Max reassured them, "She doesn't actually mean that! You're all going to be fine! The rebels will never know what hit them! Am I right?!"

The crowd cheered with mild enthusiasm, which annoyed Betsy. She added, "We're going to blast those bastards' city apart just like they blasted ours! Are you ready for revenge?!"

This time the soldiers cheered much louder, and Betsy nodded at Max as if to say, "And that's how it's done."

Soon, the army was on the move. Neil stood at the gate and

saluted the newly anointed soldiers as they exited through the city walls. Betsy and Max rode together at the front of the militia which spread out and formed units after they were free of the city's narrow streets.

Max reflected on how this was a much different trip than he'd taken with Dale just a few months earlier. Unlike Dale, Betsy wasn't interested in talking to Max, which suited him fine, except that he needed something to distract him from his nerves.

"So, we've really settled on splitting the army up once we set the mountain town on fire, then? I know you want to move on to Mina quickly, but I'm worried that without knowing where she is, we'd be cutting our strength in half with no gain to show for it."

Betsy waited a beat and then asked, "Do you know why I decided to get dressed up today?"

Max shook his head.

"It's because today is the day I crown myself ruler of the Moon. Ruler of my father, ruler of my aunts, and ruler over all you puny, self-absorbed lifeforms. We don't need an entire army, Max. The only reason I've had you training these bozos is because I need it to seem like we need an army to get the job done."

Betsy pulled her crystal out from under the velvety, buttoned top she was wearing. "This right here is all I really need. But I don't want Theo to know just how powerful I am yet. Serena knowing is fine because I have her weakness figured out. When we get to the valley, I will go in first and neutralize the rebels with my powers before setting the town ablaze. That's when we'll send the fastest of the soldiers towards Serena. She'll think they're planning to fight her, but really, they'll be distracting her while we go after Mina to kill her."

Max asked, "So why didn't you tell me you were planning

to use your powers on the rebels? Like maybe during one of those endless strategy sessions you made me sit through?"

Betsy scoffed. "I didn't tell you because I didn't want you to know. It seems like it should've been fairly obvious, though. Did you really think I would trust you to build a competent army in just a month? Or *ever*, for that matter?"

Max didn't respond. However, he did change his mind about how this trip compared to the last one. Heavy doses of egotism and last-minute changes to strategy made this trip exactly like the one he'd taken with Dale.

After traveling for an entire day, the army got to within a half mile of the trail leading to the rebels' valley. At this point, Betsy stopped the march and said to Max, "The spies who told me Mina was gone also informed me that the rebels have been working on some large weapon at the base of the mountain. I'm going to send my friend along ahead of us to see what they've set up."

Betsy pulled the thick, green vine from around her neck and tossed it to the ground. Then to Max's horror, once the vine hit the dirt, it grew a large eyeball out of one end and began to expand in length. It wriggled back and forth as it moved, like some grotesque earthworm. Max looked at Betsy. She was holding the crystal in one hand and smiling wickedly.

Max asked, "How did you know how to use the crystal?"

Betsy rolled her eyes. "Please, Max. I'm a demi-god; it's easy for me. All I have to do is hold it in my hand and let it sense what I want from it." She looked at him suspiciously. "Why? Are you thinking about stealing it?"

"No, of course not," he replied. "I just never believed in magic. It's hard to wrap my head around."

Snickering, Betsy said, "Well, you wouldn't be able to control it anyway. You're just a regular mortal. You'd probably blow yourself up if you tried to harness its powers."

Max shrugged and slipped into a memory of Helen. A few

minutes later, Betsy broke him from his daydream by clapping giddily. "You won't believe it, Max!"

Max was startled but asked, "Won't believe what?"

"The vine told me there's a giant robot walking around the base of the mountain. I guess those dopes up there aren't so dopey after all. But I wonder what they'll think when I turn their machine against them." She laughed maniacally.

"Come on. We'll need some front row seats for this."

Max felt his heart begin to pound. He knew Betsy was planning to kill the rebels, but knowing it wasn't the hard part. Now that they were close to enacting Betsy's evil plan, Max felt queasy.

The army began to march again, and Max ushered his horse forward. Ten minutes later, he laid eyes on the robot. It was massive—much bigger than Max expected—and for a moment, he worried it might wipe out their front line if given the chance.

He whispered to Betsy, "You do have a plan, don't you?"

Betsy nodded. "Of course I do. Now shut up!"

They neared the robot as it paced along the bottom of the mountain, perpendicular to them. When they got to within striking distance, the giant humanoid spotted them and began to charge. It raised its left arm, and Max realized that it was pointing a weapon at them. The hole inside the robot's arm started to glow, and instinctively, Max raised his arms to shield himself. But before the robot could fire, Betsy held her crystal above her head, stopping Mr. Al in his tracks.

A young woman and man suddenly appeared from behind a large boulder thirty feet away, sprinting as fast as they could towards the trail up the mountain. Max guessed they were the rebels who'd been in control of the robot seconds earlier.

"Watch this, everyone!" Betsy shouted to the soldiers nearby.

The giant machine stood still another few seconds, but then

it came to life again, turning in the direction of the trail. The fleeing couple was almost around to the other side of the mountain when the robot began blasting lasers in their direction.

The army hollered and whooped in delight, egging the robot on. But then for no apparent reason, the lasers stopped, and the robot began to shake. Bolts of electricity shot out of the robot's joints, creating an electrical field that engulfed its entire body. Soon, black smoke was pouring from out of its neck, and Mr. Al wavered back and forth until finally it fell to the ground with a loud *boom*.

Betsy grunted. "Stupid rebels!" she shouted as she rode up to the side of the robot to examine its remains. "They've gone and fried their only line of defense! Well, no matter, I suppose. It would've been fun to watch those losers die at the hand of their own creation, but then again, I've always enjoyed knocking skulls together and grinding up bones.

"Come on, Max! Let's lead this slapdash dumpster army of yours up the mountain. The sooner we sauté the rebels and find out where Mina is, the sooner we can go after her."

Max didn't respond, though. Betsy looked around and saw that he was clutching his heart. "What's going on with you? You having a heart attack or something?"

Max spoke the words, "No longer will these feelings hang over my heart like a hard stone. I love you, Helen."

Betsy's eyes suddenly widened. She lifted her crystal towards him, but before she could fully react, a fireball exploded around them like an atomic bomb going off. It was so large that it engulfed the army in a millisecond. The sound of the blast traveled for miles, even farther than the sound from *The Day Theia Shook*. The flames were so intense that they incinerated every living thing they touched. And when the smoke cleared much later, all that was left were the melted remains of the fallen robot and two sparkling crystals lying on the ground.

TEARS BLURRED Mina's eyes as she flew across the Moon on the back of the white mare. After she made the decision to go after Fred, the missing memories of Max magically appeared in her mind. The first memory was of Max decades earlier at the greenhouse with Betsy, Helen, and Serena. When Betsy had lured the lovers into her trap, only to be thwarted by Serena. But there was another memory that came after, which explained Max's role the last several months. And this one, Mina played over and over.

"Wait, Max! Stop!" yelled Maude.

She ran down the center of the mountainous valley, chasing after Max and passing several worried looking groups of people as she went. It had taken her a minute to piece together what Max had meant when he told her he didn't understand why she wasn't going after Serena to avenge Helen's death.

"Stop, Max!" she yelled again, speeding up as much as her old legs would allow. But Max kept walking, faster than before, unwilling to wait for Maude to catch up.

Maude stopped and looked around the undeveloped city where all the refugees from New Waldoff had settled. Maude saw only clusters of empty tents. Everyone was farther up the valley, just finishing their work for the day. Sensing no one was near, she transitioned into her youthful form and took off after Max again—faster than any human could have run. When she reached him, she threw herself in front of him and slapped her hands against his chest to stop him.

"Wait, Max!" she said. Her light red hair flew wildly in every direction as she came to a stop.

Max looked frightened. "Maude? Is that you?" he asked.

"Yes. It's me, just like you knew me before I drank the

poison Dan sent me. Or had you forgotten that this is how I once looked? And that I drank Dan's poison to find out what happened to Helen so I could save her? You aren't the only one who loved her, Max! And I had nothing to do with the memories my sister erased.

"But I want to know what you meant back there. What do you mean you're going after Serena to avenge Helen's death? You think Serena killed her?"

Max frowned angrily. "Of course I do! The only reason Betsy didn't eat me alive that day in the greenhouse was because Serena popped out of Helen's head and stopped her. Serena wasn't trying to protect me, though. She was protecting Helen because she needed Helen to do her bidding!

"If Serena could protect Helen from Betsy, then why didn't she protect Helen from Dan when Dan made Helen disappear? Or keep Helen from dying in the end? It's because that's what Serena wanted to happen! She used Helen and then discarded her so that Helen could never reveal all the secrets she knew!"

Maude looked shocked. "My god, Max! You're right. I didn't want to see it before, but you're right. Ruth told me after Helen died that a spirit had been controlling Helen, but I only figured out that this 'spirit' was Serena after I got my memories back. And then I was so focused on what Serena had done to *me* that I never thought about what she'd put Helen through."

"So, you're telling me you really didn't know that Serena was responsible for Helen's death?"

"No. Do you think I would've been okay with Serena killing my only daughter?"

Max sighed. "No, I guess not."

"What I don't understand," Maude began, "is why Helen wouldn't have told me what was happening to her before it was too late. Why did she let Serena use her and then throw her away?"

Max shrugged. "She didn't tell me either. But she had to have a reason to keep such a big secret. Serena must have convinced her it was a secret worth keeping."

"Or she was manipulating her," said Maude coldly. "Serena has manipulated the gods and humans and Moon Walkers and wolves for as far back as time goes. She erases memories on a whim just to watch what will happen. She's nasty and cruel. She once stole a child from Theo and me, our precious baby, Heely. And I'll probably never know what became of him."

Maude suddenly realized how much she'd revealed to Max, and she looked around to make sure they were still alone. Then, changing back to her older appearance, she took Max's arm and began to pull him farther away from where the rest of the rebels had made camp.

"I'm sorry, Max. I shouldn't have told you all of that. But I think I know now why Serena was using Helen. Serena has spent millennia punishing Theo and me for a wrong she thinks we committed long ago. I think manipulating Helen was one more way she found to torture me."

Max shook his head. "I'm sorry for what you've been through, Maude. But I'm not sure that's it. I remember now what Serena said in the greenhouse before she took my memories. She talked about a time calculator that hadn't predicted Betsy's existence. She said that Betsy had always been a thorn in her side and that instead of killing her she was going to make her a deal."

Maude looked at Max puzzled, "A time calculator? I don't know what that is. Did you hear what Serena offered Betsy?"

Max nodded. "She said if Betsy protected the winged children from Dan and Theo, then she'd give Betsy a crystal that would make her extremely powerful. She also said that one day Mina would become Betsy's enemy and that I'd help Betsy with her plans to rule over the Moon. But that's ludicrous!"

Maude nodded, "Yes, of course it is. What else?"

Max continued, "Well, then Serena used some insane idea to justify why she was stealing my memories! She said, 'it's important that these feelings you have no longer hang over your heart like a hard stone.' Whatever the hell that's supposed to mean!"

Max felt angry reliving these moments from his past, but as he did, Maude's eyes grew big. "Max! You're right. There was more to it! Serena was sending you a message!"

Maude tugged at the neckline of her dress and then pulled out a leather necklace with a crystal dangling from the end of it.

"This is Ruth's necklace. A hard stone hanging over your heart. Ruth gave it to me before she died. I told her I couldn't take her necklace, but she insisted. She said she'd always known that the crystal was meant for me one day, and she told me to take it and go after the truth. But I think you're the one who's supposed to have it now."

Maude pulled it up over her head and placed it in Max's palm.

"I don't know what the hell Serena's playing at, but I'm sure we can both agree that it would be catastrophic for Betsy to have the kind of power Serena is planning to give her. I doubt Serena wants Betsy to have that kind of power either, to be honest. It's why she let you know that day in the greenhouse about the deal she was making with Betsy. It sounds like she wants someone to stop her. That's why you've got to take this crystal and go after her. Hide it however you can. Betsy can't know you have it, or she'll try to steal it from you.

"This crystal has a great deal of power. I imagine it's even more powerful than the one Serena plans to give Betsy. I don't know what a time calculator is, but it sounds like it's part of some bigger plan Serena has. And now *you're* part of that plan too. It's probably why Serena told you that you'd help Betsy one day. Maybe her time calculator showed her that you would figure out her message and go after Betsy."

"So then what do I do?" asked Max.

"Hmm," Maude thought out loud. "Betsy is still serving Theo, but I've traveled through time and watched Betsy closely. If you're willing, I think I know a way you can ingratiate yourself with her."

Max nodded for Maude to continue.

"Go to New Waldoff and let the guards arrest you. You'll have to keep the crystal hidden somewhere they can't find it. I've recently been told that Serena is planning to release me from my human form soon, and when she does, I'll find a way to send you a message. That's when you tell the guards you want to speak to Betsy. Then tell Betsy you know who Theia is and where the rebels are hiding. She shouldn't be surprised you're helping her because Serena already told her you would one day."

"But what about Serena? How do we stop her? She can't just get away with all the horrible things she's done!"

Maude nodded. "I know. That's why I want you to wait before you do anything drastic. See if there's a way you might be able to go after both Serena and Betsy—kill two birds with one stone, so to speak."

Max said, "Fine, but what if Betsy starts to suspect that I'm up to something?"

"She might," replied Maude. "You'll have to stay on your toes. Remember that all of New Waldoff is set up to spy on its citizens. Live everyday as if all you care about is pleasing Betsy. Do what you have to do and say what you have to say to keep her happy. But then, when it's not possible anymore, and you know it's time, you have the key to your exit right here." Maude patted Max's hand where he was holding the crystal.

Max looked at Maude seriously. "And we're doing this for Helen?" he asked.

Maude nodded. "For Helen."

Mina screamed into the wind. Each time she replayed the memory she asked herself why Max had been used as a pawn by her mother. Then, finally, she allowed herself to watch the newest memory of Max. The one from just moments before when he'd killed Betsy and the soldiers and himself.

After it was over, the answer to Mina's question became clear. Serena had used her powers not to *see* the future, but to carefully plan the future through trial and error. Max's role hadn't been that of a sacrificial pawn exactly. He'd been more like a knight sent to take down Betsy—"the thorn" in Serena's side, as she'd once put it. Betsy was the demi-god, whose existence Serena hadn't foreseen. And therefore, Serena was forced to find a way to outmaneuver Betsy in order to protect her big plan.

After several hours of riding, Mina caught up to Fred. They slowed their pace and exchanged sad glances. "Did you hear—"

Mina nodded. "Yes, I heard it. I had just left New Waldoff. It was Max. He blew up Betsy's army and himself too. He did it for Helen because he thought it's what she would've wanted —to protect everyone."

"The missing memories showed up then?" he asked.

"Yeah, but not until after it was all over. I found the hidden papers also. They're a recounting of Theia's memories. She had the Moon Walkers create them for her in a secret language so that whenever Serena erased her memories, she could find them again. At some point, Serena found out about them, but for whatever reason, she hasn't destroyed them—or at least not all of them."

"What did they say?" asked Fred.

"Theia believes that Serena has spent the last few thousand years punishing her and Theo because they did something long ago that caused Serena to destroy the Earth. I think this means that besides being my aunt and uncle, Theo and Theia are my grandparents too. It's all so messed up, Fred, but I think I'm more than a demi-god. In fact, I know I am. Helen basically said as much during the vision I had after Evelyn drilled the screws into my arm. I was just too afraid to admit it to myself. I'm one of the time gods that Serena brought back to life."

Fred nodded his head. "Yes, you are, Mina. I couldn't tell you before. Serena said you had to figure it out for yourself. But I wouldn't worry too much about the incest factor. I'm not sure it works the same way with gods as it does with mortals. And just so you know, I imagine that Bob and Evelyn have it figured out that you're a god too. After you woke up from your vision, your face was completely gone. Or rather, there were a bunch of different faces morphing together where your face should've been. It was eerie looking and not something that would likely happen to a mere mortal, or even a demi-god."

Mina frowned. "That must've really scared them. I'm surprised they didn't say anything about it."

Fred laughed. "They probably didn't know what to say. 'Pardon me, Mina, but your face seems to be possessed by a bunch of other faces. Could you make it stop please?'"

"Okay, I see your point. So, if I'm a time god, then does that mean that you're…" Mina paused and waited for Fred's response.

"I think so," said Fred. "But it's strange. Maude asked me if I was a time god in the vision that I had of her and Max talking. I guess I'd gone back in time somehow while I was asleep. The weird thing, though, is that Maude was the one who told me I was a time god when I first arrived in the valley. I guess I'd already told her somehow, even though that dream hadn't happened yet."

Mina said, "I went back in time too during that vision I had of Helen after the operation. I was at Black Ice Fort facing Dan, but I wasn't prepared to beat him. So I went even further back to when Helen was guiding me at the Sheep Spa using the map. I saw my old self and told Helen what I would need to beat Dan. She explained to me then that the gods of time *are* time."

"But what does that mean?" asked Fred.

"I don't know exactly, but I think it's why we're able to traverse time so easily without even intending to. If it's that easy for us, then maybe that's why Serena put such strict rules on Theia and Theo when she finally brought them to the Moon. And why she keeps having to steal their memories. If she'd allowed them to have too much power *and* their memories, then they could have gone back in time to try to prevent her from controlling them altogether."

"I bet you're right," said Fred. "So what do we do now? Go help the elves and wolves or go warn the rebels that the end of the world is nigh?"

Mina looked in the direction of the mountains. "I already sent a silver bird to Bob and Evelyn, telling them we would head to Serena's after I found you. I think we have to help the wolves and elves. Serena clearly knows what choice we're going to make, so it doesn't really matter what we do. But I hate to drag the rebels into this if we don't have to. There isn't an army of mortals big enough in this universe to take down Serena. In the message I sent, I basically told them goodbye. The only chance we have to beat Serena is if we find a way to alter the timeline somehow."

"Do you really think Serena would have given you all the memories you need to unravel her plan?"

Mina shook her head. "No. But I hate to think we're already beat before we even try."

"Agreed, so let's go try something."

And with that, the two gods went galloping across the Moon to face a destiny that had been waiting on them for several thousand years.

CHAPTER 32
NEGOTIATIONS

At Neriti's request, Ragher and Elu spent several weeks at Black Ice Glacier brainstorming ways to find out what Serena's plan was. Early on, they hit a dead end with their strategy to prevent Betsy from starting a Moon war when Theo revealed that he'd tried contacting his daughter to no avail.

He told them, "I've sent that little mutant a thousand calling crystals, but she hasn't touched even one! I filled her whole, damn office with the things, but she refuses to talk!"

Elu and Ragher seemed skeptical at first, but Neriti confirmed that Theo was telling the truth and suggested they move on. So, the three wolves discussed ad nauseam how to trick Serena into revealing her secrets. First, they came up with an idea for Elu and Ragher to disguise themselves as different creatures, but they decided that there probably weren't any creatures that Serena trusted enough to spill her entire plan to.

Another strategy they thought of was to go to the remaining wolf healers and have them contact Theia in hopes that Serena would impersonate her sister again. The idea was that they might be able to guilt Serena into telling them the truth when they caught her in the act of lying to them. But no matter how many different ways they spun this idea, they all agreed it was implausible that Serena would allow herself to be guilted into revealing her secrets.

Another thought they had was to recruit all the Moon creatures to help them destroy the crystals in hopes that this would get Serena's attention. Then they'd force Serena into telling them the truth by warning her that they would destroy every single crystal on the entire Moon if she didn't disclose her plan.

Theo reminded them at this juncture that it hadn't bothered Serena when he melted the crystals down to make a giant crystal. Ragher pointed out that it might've been because he hadn't used the crystals in Crystal Crater, but Theo scoffed at this.

"Spoken like a true wolf. The crystals in Crystal Crater aren't more special than the crystals anywhere else. That was a stupid assumption the wolves came up with because of their relationship to my sister, Theia. Such snobbery your kind embraces over a completely fabricated notion! Anyway, I'm tired of listening to you all think of a million ways to trick Serena. Why don't the two of you who aren't currently feasting off my energy go to the ice tunnels and ask Serena to tell you what she's planning?"

Ragher pushed back, "We can't just go there and ask! If she never told me in all the years I lived with her, then why would she divulge her plan now?"

"Did you ever actually ask her to tell you her plan?" asked Theo condescendingly.

Ragher stopped to think about this, but then he said, "Well, no. But she's lied or withheld the truth so many times, there's no reason to think that she'd be honest now."

But Elu spoke up in favor of Theo's idea. "You know, Ragher, there might be something to what Theo is suggesting. There's not much likelihood that we're going to be able to trick

Serena, considering how powerful she is in this realm, but maybe we can appeal to her sense of decency by being direct about what we want."

Theo rolled his eyes. "That's the stupidest thing I've ever heard. My sister doesn't have any sense of decency. Go to her and ask her what her plan is but do it under the guise that I want to form an alliance with her. Tell her I'll give up my hold over Black Ice Glacier if she's willing to fold us into her hair-brained scheme. But leave out the hairbrained part."

Neriti looked at Ragher and Elu and said, "I hate to admit it, but I think Theo has just come up with the best idea so far. If you approach Serena as though you've come to negotiate on Theo's behalf, she might be willing to tell you what her endgame is. Or at least some of it."

"What do you think, Ragher?" asked Elu.

Ragher sighed. "I think it's a suicide mission. For me at least. I betrayed Serena, which means if I set foot in those tunnels, she's more likely to kill me than let me leave again."

Neriti said, "Maybe not, Ragh. Tell her you didn't think her plan to draw the wolves into the fight would work because you doubt that Axel actually cares much for you after you lied to him his whole life. Tell her you're offering Theo's obedience instead and that if she agrees to align with him, then the two of them can create whatever war they want. Hopefully, she'll think you're trying to help her, and if she agrees to the offer then maybe she'll reveal her plan at that time."

"That's a big assumption, Neriti," said Ragher. "She could just as easily see through our charade and strike Elu and me down on the spot."

Neriti's light began to glow a little brighter. "Do you know what I thought about the most when I lived with Theo for nine years inside the crystal he was using to control Goodman?"

Ragher shook his head.

"I thought about us and our family and how different

things could've been if Serena had stayed out of our lives. It was during that time that I began to explore Theo's memories in depth, and I watched people on Earth through his eyes. Theo is a grizzly, old god, but even he has a soft spot for families. Maybe it's why he's so angry—because he never felt like that was part of his existence."

Theo grew angry. "That's horse crap! I did have a family! My siblings were my family! They were just bad at being my family."

"Right," continued Neriti. "Anyway, I thought about how Serena tormented Theia and Theo by taking their child away, and how she basically put us through the same situation when she made us think we had to give up Axel and turn you into a pup to hide you from Theo. If we had just ignored her, then maybe—"

Ragher interrupted, "But Neriti, you were the one who came up with that plan. Remember? I tried to fight you, but then Serena told me to go along with it."

"That's what I'm trying to tell you, Ragh. Serena controlled you for hundreds of years. She was the other female in our relationship from the beginning. I came up with the idea to hide our family because I was always terrified of losing you to Serena or Theo. It was gut wrenching giving up Axel and hiding ourselves the way we did, but it was the only way I thought I could keep you from Serena. She was like a drug you couldn't stay away from. And you proved that by going to her and telling her my plan when you disagreed with it. Instead of staying and talking to me about our options, you ran off to *her*.

"In my heart, I wanted us to be brave and stand up to the gods—not to sacrifice ourselves or hide. It took me a long time to realize how hurt I was by the way you treated me when we were together. You put her first in our lives and took it for granted that I would always be there, even though you never considered what was really good for us as a couple or as a family."

Ragher pushed back, "Riti, I tried to do what was right for our family. I was prepared to give myself over to Theo before you came up with that plan."

Neriti shook her head, though. "But Ragher, leaving me with pups to raise by myself wasn't right for our family either. If anything, that was a coward's way out. I wanted you to fight for us."

"Well, you never told me that," said Ragher.

"I know, Ragh. I was young and in love, and I didn't want to do anything that would push you away. I worried you would leave me if I told you to betray Serena. But I wish now that I had said those words I was so afraid to say. Maybe everything would've been different."

Neriti smiled sweetly at Ragher. "The reason I'm telling you this now is because you need to stop worrying about how Serena will react. You continue to give her power over you by constantly considering what her thoughts and actions will be whenever you do anything. For once in your long life, you need to care only about how you feel and what you want and not care about how any of that relates to Serena."

Ragher looked sad. "You're right. It has been a hard habit to break, Riti. Serena has set me up to fail and be miserable many times over and yet I continue to hang on to this relationship despite how toxic it's become. It's hard for me to change. Serena trained me to care for her and obey her during all those years in the tunnels. I don't really know how to be anything else but her servant—even if I'm a resentful one."

"I know," said Neriti, "And that's why facing Serena will be a good test for you. You have lived to do her bidding for ages. It's time to turn the tables. Go to her and convince her that you are still acting in good faith. Then find out whatever you can to help us stop her."

Theo grumbled, "Maybe the female wolf should go alone. I don't think this pansy wolf is going to pull it off. He'll do something stupid or probably say too much. Clearly, he has the hots for Serena."

Ragher snapped, "That's disgusting, Theo! I have never had romantic feelings for Serena. If anything, she was like a mother to me all those centuries she was holding me captive."

Theo laughed. "Sounds like a classic mommy fantasy to me."

Ragher looked like he wanted to pounce on Theo's long, yellowish torso and rip him apart. But Neriti intervened by saying, "Just let it go, Ragher. Theo doesn't like not being the center of attention. It's why he's acting out."

"That's not true!" growled Theo. "And why would I care about getting attention from you furry mongrels, anyway?"

Neriti looked at Theo. "Because despite what you think about yourself, the reason you are this way is because of how desperate you are for any type of love or attention. You just prefer to have the attention directed at you like a spotlight instead of sharing it with others. The hole inside of you is so deep that you feel you have to beat people into loving you so that they'll help you fill the bottomless pit where your heart should be."

Theo hissed, "Watch it wolf, or I'll—"

"You'll what?" asked Neriti. "Force me to rewatch all the horrific things you've done to others? Been there and seen it already, Theo. And while it's all quite disturbing, the effect has worn off over time."

Theo mumbled some words under his breath that the others couldn't hear.

Elu asked, "Are you ready to try this, Ragher? If we succeed, we might be able to stop Serena from destroying the whole world."

"Of course," he said to Elu. "I'll do my best."

Then he looked at Neriti and said, "I'll stand up to her, Riti, and I won't let her control me this time. I should've done it for our family decades ago, but I'll do it now for you and Axel and myself. I love you. I hope you know that. I've loved you for hundreds of years. And I'll do right by you, even if it's too late for us now."

Neriti's light dimmed a little, and she said, "I know you will Ragher. And who knows? Maybe there's another life waiting for us beyond this one. Maybe one day, we really will have a second shot at all of this."

Theo groaned disgustedly. "You two are so pathetic and simple. There's no other life waiting for you beyond this one. You're either here, or the crystal worlds, or your nothing and nowhere. So can we speed this up? You may think I'm an attention whore of a bottomless pit, Neriti, but I'd rather sit here alone with my thumb up my butt for all of eternity than have to be a part of your emotional garbage-athon."

Ragher said to Neriti, "I'm so sorry you can't come with us. I'll try to make a deal with Serena to set you free from Theo if it's possible."

Neriti shook her head. "Don't worry about me, Ragh. I'll be fine. Just keep your focus on finding out what Serena wants. It's our only chance to save everyone."

Ragher nodded, and although it was hard for him to leave Neriti, he and Elu began their journey through the dark towards Serena's underground ice labyrinth.

When they arrived, they were dumbfounded by the massive army of elves and wolves camped out inside the light that surrounded the entrance to Serena's lair.

"What's all this?" Elu asked.

Ragher shook his head. "I have no clue, but it looks like we may be just in time."

They neared the white domed entryway that stuck out of the ground, and Ragher spotted Axel sitting close to the dark doorway next to another wolf, who Ragher recognized as Chaxtan.

"Axel!" Ragher called to him, unable to hide the exhilaration he felt upon seeing his son.

Axel turned his head towards his father, then quickly walked to him and bowed. "Ragher, how did you get here?" he asked excitedly.

"Serena let me out of the tunnels several weeks ago," explained Ragher. "I've been with your mother and Elu at Black Ice Glacier. Elu and I have come to speak to Serena."

Chaxtan joined them at Axel's side. "How can that be, Axel? You claimed your mother is Neriti, but Neriti has been dead for many years."

Ragher answered, "Neriti isn't actually deceased, Chaxtan. Her energy is attached to the dark god, Theo. Elu and I were with both of them up on the glacier."

"I see," said Chaxtan skeptically, but the other wolves ignored him.

Axel spoke to Elu, "I went to recruit your pack to join the fight, and they told me you were gone. I was surprised because I thought you were determined to stay below ground. How did you end up at the glacier?"

Elu responded, "After you departed, Axel, I began receiving messages from your mother. She told me to go to Ragher and take him to the glacier. She wanted us to know the history of the world we live in. She's been able to access Theo's memories and see what has happened over a great span of time—not just here on the Moon, but thousands of years ago on Earth too."

Chaxtan asked, "So why have you two come to see Serena, then?"

Ragher looked at Elu, not certain how much he should say, but Elu spoke for them. "We are here to try and prevent Serena from destroying the world."

Axel looked surprised. "You just spent the last several weeks with Theo, and he let you leave to come here to *stop* the world from being destroyed?"

Ragher laughed. "I agree that it does seem ironic, but yes."

Chaxtan spoke a bit haughtily. "I hate to say it, but you're too late. The wolves and elves have decided to join together to fight Serena. She's been planning this whole event from the beginning, you know. She's aware that we're all here, and she's already planned on how to deal with us."

Elu asked, "If that's true, then why did you bother to come here? Why not stay on your land and continue to live your lives instead of facing Serena?"

Axel answered Elu. "Most of us have come here because we still have hope."

Elu smiled at Axel. "Well, if you are planning to fight her, then what are you doing standing around?"

Chaxtan shook his head. "No one can get in. Hundreds of us have tried. We've taken turns walking down the tunnel into the dark cave below, but there's nowhere to go from there. It's a dead end."

Ragher furrowed his brow. "The tunnels are gone, Ax?"

"Yeah, I've been down there the most times. I keep thinking maybe something will be different, but Chaxtan is right. There's nobody down there and no light either. It's just a small dark room. But it's not like the void because you can feel the walls."

Ragher looked at Elu. "Think we should try?" he asked.

Elu nodded. "Sure. Otherwise, we came all this way for nothing."

Axel and Chaxtan walked Ragher and Elu towards the entrance to the ice labyrinth. Elu looked down into the darkness and shivered.

"Funny," she said. "I've never been afraid of the dark

before, but this feels different. It's like something's calling to me from inside the tunnel."

Axel and Ragher exchanged glances, knowing full well what that might portend.

"I'll go first," said Ragher before jumping into the sloped tunnel.

"Here goes nothing," said Elu following Ragher down.

When they reached the bottom of the slope, Ragher said, "I think this is different than what Chaxtan and Axel were talking about, Elu. I can't find a wall anywhere. Follow my voice. I'm going to keep walking."

Elu followed Ragher in the direction he was speaking. A second later she said, "Ragher, I see a light up ahead. Do you see that? It's beautiful!"

Ragher felt the hair on the back of his neck stand up straight. "Look away, Elu!" he ordered. "It's a trick. She's trying to hypnotize you, just like Theo's monster hypnotized my grandpups!"

But Elu was already mesmerized. She couldn't take her eyes off of it. The colorful light was bouncing playfully towards her, and Elu sat and stared at it."

Ragher closed his eyes, and called out, "Knock it off, Serena! We've come here to talk to you, which clearly you want, or you wouldn't have let us into your void!"

Childish laughter erupted from every direction as the ball spun over Elu's head. Elu began to laugh too, but then the multicolored light disappeared, and Elu sighed with disappointment. Seconds later, a voice startled her from behind.

"Oh, Ragher. You've come to talk, have you? And here I was under the impression that you'd come to play games."

Elu turned around, and Ragher opened his eyes. A tall woman made of pure white light stood before them, hovering in the air. Her hair and clothes looked as if they were submersed under water because of the way they flowed around her.

Ragher said to Serena, "We're not here for games. We've come on behalf of Theo to negotiate a deal. He wants to align himself with you. He's willing to give up his hold on Black Ice Glacier and become your subordinate if you'll let us help you."

Serena laughed boisterously. "What hold does he mean? Is he really so naïve that he thinks he owns some part of this realm? At best, he's been leasing that frigid glacier he calls home. And from *me*, no less! Tell him, 'No deal!' And just to put a finer point on it, tell him this ludicrous negotiation is the reason he just lost his memory charm."

Serena snapped her fingers, and Elu stared at Ragher in disbelief.

"Neriti!" Ragher screamed. "Noooo! What have you done? You promised—"

Serena interrupted, "NO! *You* promised me you would sacrifice yourself to Theo to draw Axel and the wolves into a fight against him. But you haven't delivered your end of the bargain, so now that offer has expired!"

"No! *NOOO!*" Ragher yelled. "You can't do that! You never said you would kill Neriti if I didn't do what you asked! You never said—"

Serena interrupted him again. "Don't play dumb, Ragher. You know who I am. You know what I'm capable of. I tortured you for years. Just because you enjoyed it doesn't mean I'm not a monster."

Ragher leapt at Serena, but he passed right through her and fell hard on the ground behind her.

Elu tried talking sensibly to Serena. "Axel and the elves and wolves are out there right now ready to come after you. Ragher and I can stall them for a while, though. If you align yourself with Theo, then you'll get what you want. When they find out you're on the same side, they'll come after you both."

Serena replied, "I didn't say that I wanted them to come after me, though, did I? I can see that you're a clever wolf, however. So what's in this for you? It's hard to imagine why *any* wolf would choose to help Theo."

Ragher stood up and ran back through Serena. He yelled at Elu. "Stop it! She killed Neriti! We aren't doing this anymore!"

Elu ignored Ragher and answered Serena, "We want to know what you're after. And we want you to bring Neriti back. Not as part of Theo, but in her own body."

Serena replied, "You seem to have me confused with a former version of myself. Thanks to Theia and Theo, I'm no longer able to create new life, not even in the crystal worlds where I'm most powerful. The best I can do is reincarnate Neriti into a new life, although once you hear my plan, I think you'll understand how that isn't exactly advantageous to you."

Ragher yelled hysterically, "Let's go, Elu! We'll tell the wolves and elves to do their worst! Hopefully, they'll tear this place apart! It's probably what she wants anyway!"

"No, Ragher," Elu snapped. "She'll kill them if we let that happen."

Serena smiled. "She's not wrong, Ragher. My plan is and always has been to dismantle this world. It was never meant to exist after I destroyed the Earth. Not like this."

Ragher shouted, "Lies! If that were true, you would've done it already!"

Serena threw her arms in front of her towards Ragher, and he flew out of the way—a hundred feet into the void where they couldn't see him anymore.

"Get your friend under control when he returns!" Serena ordered Elu. "I have no interest in talking to him any longer, and the next time I have to discipline him, it will be much worse."

A few seconds later, Ragher leapt in front of Serena. Barring his teeth.

Elu yelled, "Stop it, Ragher! She's doing exactly what we asked her to do. She's telling us her plan."

"No, she's not! She's full of lies! Even now with an army out there knocking at her door, she can't bring herself to tell the truth. Despite the fact that doing so would save lives. She has no use for us mortals, so she tosses us around and treats us like scum!"

"Why would I lie?" asked Serena. "The reason I haven't dismantled this world yet is because I need help. That's where Theo will come in handy. He and the other gods are going to surrender their energy to me. That's how I'm going to finish the job I started. With help from them."

"They would never do that!" yelled Ragher.

"They would if they thought I was going to take something precious from them. They can either give me their energy willingly and keep their memories, or I'll just go ahead and take their memories and convince them to give me their energy when they no longer know up from down anymore."

Elu looked horrified by this. "You're right, Ragher. We should go."

"So soon, Elu?" Serena asked mockingly. "I know you were trying to trick me into giving you information you could use to save the world. Did you not like what you heard?"

Elu looked at Ragher pleadingly, but Ragher shook his head. "We can't leave. I forgot. There's no way out until she lets us out. We're trapped in here."

Suddenly, the ground rumbled, and a beam of light entered the void from a few feet away, leading up a short path.

"You were the ones who wanted to see me. I have no interest in holding you here. But you might as well know, if we're being honest, that Theo was only tricking you into doing his bidding. He has been planning to form an alliance with me ever since Neriti helped him get his memories back. He thought he could beat me by gaining my trust. Theo was using you as his unwitting minions to secure the alliance with me in hopes that I would set him free from Black Ice Glacier."

Elu and Ragher were halfway through the exit, but before he left, Ragher looked back at Serena and said, "I never mattered to you, did I Serena? I did everything you ever asked of me except for one thing, and now you've taken everything in my life that was good except one thing. If you have any compassion at all, you'll leave me and my son alone. Forever."

A second later Elu and Ragher found themselves back outside in the open, surrounded by elves. "Oooohh! Spooky Moon Doggies playing whacky game of hide-and-go-seek! How you play peekaboo like that Moon Doggies? I can't even see where you was hiding!" exclaimed an impish-looking elf, who was standing in front of Elu and Ragher.

Ragher ignored the elf and stormed off in the direction of the entrance to Serena's fortress with Elu following behind him.

"Ragher, we need to be on the same page about what happened down there. Now that we know her plan is to steal the other gods' energy, we have to get the elves and wolves to help us stop it!"

But Ragher stayed focused on finding Axel and Chaxtan. When he reached the white dome, Chaxtan seemed surprised to see him. He looked towards the entrance that led into the dome. "Well, I'll be," he said. "You two must have gotten a lot farther than we did if you found another way out of there."

Ragher didn't react to Chaxtan's amazement, though. Instead, he asked, "Does anyone here have a way to create fire?"

One of the elves who was nearby squeaked, "Brexley does! He can start fires with his dry, ugly feet. All he got to do is rubs them together real fast!"

Elu spoke, "Ragher, we can't fight her! We need to make a plan to keep the other gods away from here! It's the only way to keep Serena from stealing their energy! She really is going to destroy us all if we don't figure this out! Don't let your anger over Neriti cloud your judgement!"

Axel asked, "Why is Ragher angry about my mom?"

Ragher looked at Axel sadly. "Because Serena killed your mom, Axel! While we were in there, she killed Neriti for good!"

Axel recoiled as though the news had hit him in the head. Even though Neriti's energy had been attached to Theo, Axel had believed he would get to see her again one day. But now he was losing her all over again, and he hadn't even had the chance to come face-to-face with her since finding out that she was his mother.

Axel yelled at the elves around him, "It's time to fight! Your empress has fired the first shot. It's time to go to war! Go out beyond the light and grab as many twigs as you can! We're going to firebomb the tunnel and smoke her out of there!"

Elu turned her attention to Chaxtan. "Chax, I'm a pack leader, just like you. We can't let these two speak for everyone. From what I learned down there, I can say for certain that we are all doomed if we don't do something to prevent the other gods from coming here. Serena is going to steal the other gods' energy in order to end the world. There's still a way to stop this! Please help me!"

But Chaxtan only shrugged and hung his head. "Leader Elu, I understand your concerns. But my council and I have already determined that the only way for us to move forward is to fight this god."

The little elf called Brexley sat in front of Ragher and Axel rubbing his feet together as a few little sparks jumped out from between his limp, curved toes. And the wave of elves who'd heard Axel's orders were off searching for kindling to set a fire in Serena's home.

"This is outrageous!" Elu screamed in frustration. "You are doing exactly what Serena wants you to do! She may be a master manipulator, but you are all fools!"

Just then, several of the elves who were further back behind them began shouting feverishly and pointing at the sky.

"A space witch is coming!" one of them shrieked.

Elu looked to where they were staring and saw that way off in the distance, against the dark backdrop of space, a woman made of turquoise-colored crystals was walking across the sky. It appeared she was headed in their direction, like a female-shaped comet.

Elu squinted as she looked closer. The woman was walking on top of a shiny blue surface that was expanding out in front of her as she stepped. Chaxtan looked in the woman's direction now too and said, "Oh my goodness! Is that the neon bridge?"

Suddenly, the ground beneath them began to shake uncontrollably, and the entrance to the underground void collapsed into the ground. A giant hole opened up where the white dome had been, and even more of the ground broke apart and fell into the sinkhole.

"Run elves! Run Moon Doggies!" cried Brexley as he blew out his feet. Thousands of elves were running in every direction, away from the land that was being swallowed into the growing pit beneath the Moon's surface.

Elu, Chaxtan, Ragher, and Axel took off running too. For a split second, Elu looked back over her shoulder and saw the top of a dark-violet head rising up from the space beneath the Moon where the hole had appeared.

She looked back and Chaxtan yelled, "That's Theia! Theia's in the sky. Our ancestors said she can appear in crystal form. Maybe she's coming to save us!"

Elu looked up and saw the blue crystal woman walking across the neon bridge as it appeared in front of her. Then she heard a deep laugh off in the distance away from all the action. Her stomach sank. She recognized the laugh because she'd heard it many times over the last few weeks. It was Theo.

"Oh my god! It's too late!" she yelled to the other wolves as they hurried away from the apocalyptic scene. "The gods are headed right for each other! No one can save us now!"

CHAPTER 33

THE CONVERGENCE OF GODS

Mina and Fred were halfway across the Darkside to the ice tunnels when they unexpectedly ran into a group on horseback. It was Bob, Evelyn, Jacques, John, and John's two sons, Samuel and Egan, all of whom wore a headlamp.

Mina, who could see in the dark, called out to them to get their attention after realizing who they were. "Bob! Evelyn!" she yelled.

The eight friends greeted each other as they rode towards one another.

Fred asked, "How did you know where to find us?"

Bob replied, "We got Mina's silver bird shortly after the explosion. She told us she was planning to ride back to the ice tunnels once she found you, so I pulled out one of my old maps and estimated the path you would take, then triangulated our own path with yours so that we would eventually cross paths at some point."

Evelyn laughed. "He's pulling your leg. This was just luck. We wanted to help out when we heard that the elves and wolves were going to battle Serena. Judging by what we saw when we rode down the mountain, we just narrowly escaped fighting our own battle. There's a charred crater at least half a mile wide at the base now. And I'm sorry to say that Mr. Al is a smoking pile of melted metal. All of that work for nothing."

Samuel said sadly, "Rest in peace, sweet robot."

Mina nodded. "I had a vision of what happened. Max sacrificed himself for you guys once he realized there was nothing he could do to prevent Betsy from attacking Rebelton."

She looked towards Bob, "He did it to honor Helen, Bob. He clearly loved her very much. The reason that no one remembered it was because Serena erased everyone's memories of their relationship until a few months ago."

The little chef gasped, "A tricky devil woman?! Who is this Serena you speak of?"

Fred explained, "There are five gods on the Moon. Well, really four now because one of them was banished. But there were five—Serena, Theia, Theo, Mina, and me. Mina and I didn't know that we were gods, though, until very recently."

"Mon dieu!" exclaimed Jacques. "This is fantastic! You ate my cheese, Mina! That means my cheese is good enough for a god!"

"I'm pleased you're taking the news so well, Jacques," said Mina.

"Well, that explains your incredible talent for lifting and welding," commented Egan.

Samuel added, "It surely does. My bet was that you were some kind of dragon fairy on account of the wings you used to have."

John chimed in, "Wait, so if you two are gods, and there's a god missing, does that mean what I think it does? Was that fiery, red-haired wife of yours a god, too, Bob?" John pointed his head so that Bob was directly in John's spotlight.

Bob shielded his eyes. "Yes, Maude was a god. She was

Theia. Or is Theia, somewhere out there, I guess. I didn't know it until just before she died, though."

Fred asked, "Did Bob and Evelyn tell you all where you wcre going?"

Jacques shrugged his shoulders. "No, they said we were going to help Mina. That was good enough for me."

Mina smiled at the chef. "Thank you, chef. Thanks to all of you, in fact. However, you should know that what you're about to face will be the biggest challenge you've ever experienced. Serena is the most powerful god that has ever existed as far as I know, and she already has all of our moves figured out. Whatever we do, she knows we're going to do it already. The fight may already be over, but I still plan to confront her, just in case there's anything I can do to change her mind."

Egan asked, "Change her mind about what?"

Mina bit her lip. "Serena is planning to destroy the world, and she thinks I'm going to help her do it. That's what her plan has been for several thousand years. But I promise you that I won't help her willingly."

Evelyn sighed. "Well, even though this has been about the weirdest existence I would've ever expected to have, I feel like I've lived a good life. If the choices are either to go and fight the god who's trying to kill everyone versus going home to take one last nap, then I choose to fight."

"Me too," agreed Bob, John, Egan, and Samuel.

"How about you, Jacques?" asked Mina.

The little chef blew a raspberry in the air as he thought about it for a second. Then he said, "Well, I'd always planned to die while cooking one last glorious meal, but what the heck? I guess that roasting up a goddess will have to suffice."

The group looked at each other for one last moment. Then they pointed themselves in the direction of the ice tunnels and took off together.

Back in Serena's domain, the ground above the ice labyrinth continued to collapse into a pit that grew wider by the second. The elves and wolves were still running for their lives. And out of the pit, Serena emerged in the form of a dark-violet, crystal giant, towering hundreds of feet above the chaos. Her dark crystals glowed just enough to cast a dull aura over the Moon's surface.

In the sky across from Serena, Theia descended down a rapidly appearing bridge sparkling in neon blue. She, too, was in the form of a crystal giant, but the light that shone from her multifaceted crystals was a bright blue.

From the east, a steady pounding of footsteps foretold of Theo's ensuing arrival from his glacier home, although it was unclear as of yet what form he had taken.

Serena's deep voice boomed across the land for all of the Moon creatures to hear, "I understand that the mortals have joined forces against me, although the mass hysteria I see below indicates that they've had a sudden change of heart."

She waved her long arm out in front of her, and suddenly the wolves, who were fleeing the scene, became indistinguishable from the elves that they were running alongside. She looked off in the distance and saw Mina and Fred riding with the others on horseback towards the bedlam. They were still a few miles away, however, so Serena commanded, "Be here now!"

A second later, Mina and Fred and their friends, who had also turned into elves, appeared before Serena, inches from the massive pit where she stood.

"One more tweak before the other two gods arrive," she spoke loudly to the whole world. Then she reached both shiny crystal arms in front of her and strained briefly as though lifting something heavy.

"There," she said pleased. "I have opened up the portals to all the crystal worlds. We will soon be joined by quite a few more of my creations."

A second later, Theia reached the end of the bridge as it connected to the Moon's surface several miles back. However, Theia was as large as Serena, so it took her only a few moments to cross the space between them.

Fred asked Mina, "Do you think Theia will be upset about Bob and Evelyn?"

But Mina looked at Fred as if he were insane. "That's what you're worried about right now? How would Theia even know that's Bob and Evelyn?" she asked pointing at the two elves sitting on horseback next to them.

"I'm Jacques!" squeaked the elf next to her. "And I'm John!" squeaked the other, both sounding quite offended by Mina's misunderstanding.

Mina dropped her head all the way back to stare up at Serena's face. "What are you doing?" Mina yelled at her mother. "Why have you changed all the mortal creatures into elves?"

Serena's crystal body creaked a little as she gazed down upon her daughter. "Haven't you guessed, dear? I'm taking us back to the beginning, just like Theia and Theo always wanted me to do. Isn't that right, Theia?" She asked looking across at Theia, who was standing much closer now.

Theia shouted at Serena in her own loud voice, "For thousands of years you have punished me and my brother for wanting to go back to the beginning, yet that has been your plan all along?! You truly are a dark soul, Serena!"

Serena laughed. "You have no idea. But as I told you in the crystal world I sent you to, I was never punishing you for your crimes. There has never been a way to take us back to the beginning until now."

From the darkness off to the east, Theo appeared as a hundred-foot tall, sickly yellow creature, just like the way he'd looked before, only much larger. Yet even with his grandiose stature, Theo still stood much shorter than Serena and Theia.

"The group is all here now, then," said Serena to the other gods. "I'd have thought that more of you would've arrived on horses in honor of the apocalypse. But no matter."

Theo looked down at the group sitting on horseback in front of the pit. "I always did have a taste for horse," he said to himself as he reached down to grab Mina and her horse.

But Serena shot a bolt of electricity at Theo's arm from her outstretched hand, and he backed away. "No, Theo! Behave!" she ordered him like a dog.

Theo nursed his smoking arm for a second and then glared up at Serena's dark face. "Always a pleasure to see you, sister," he said through clenched teeth. "Did those wolves tell you of the deal I was willing to make with you? My domain for information? Well, you can forget that now! Theia is back and no longer tied to Crystal Crater, so I suppose that means each god for themself. May the best one win!"

Serena looked down at Theo's large, shriveled body. "And you think that means you?" she asked him tauntingly. "Look at yourself, Theo! My daughter, Mina, drained you of your power years ago, and you can never recover from that! She stole your energy because, unlike the mortals, you don't have to give your permission to have your energy taken away by a time god! How about that!? Oh, and also, your daughter Betsy is dead, so you have no more minions to do your bidding!" Serena laughed at Theo like he was nothing.

Theo screamed at Serena, "You horrible bitch! I'll make you pay for everything you've ever done!"

"Stop Theo!" yelled Theia and Mina at the same time, but

it was too late. Theo dove towards Mina again and tried to grab her, but Fred was ready for this second attack, knocking Mina out of the way and positioning himself under Theo's outstretched hand instead. "I'm a time god like you, Theo! Do your worst!" he yelled.

"No!" shouted Mina. She ran at Theo's large hand as it wrapped around Fred.

"Don't mind if I do," said Theo, and he tossed Fred into his mouth, consuming him whole.

Mina lay on the ground where she'd jumped at Theo's hand but missed. She stood up shaking with rage, ready to do whatever it took to punish him for what he'd done. She yelled at her friends, "Run, everyone! Give me room!"

Bob, Evelyn and the other humans-turned-elves rode away from the large pit to a safe distance before turning back again. Mina looked towards space, then harnessing all of her energy, she grew into a dark-violet crystal giant just like Serena.

Theo reacted by immediately using the energy he'd gleaned from Fred, turning himself into a black crystal monster with large horns and red eyes. He raised his hands out to his sides, and the Moon's surface began to shake as Theo's loud voice shouted, "Look upon me all you sniveling peasants! I am your dark lord! Your one and only god!"

Mina wasn't sure what Theo was doing until she looked off in the distance. Gigantic waves of dirt lifted high over the Moon's surface in all directions. The entire terrain rose and fell as though rolling over mountains. Hundred-foot tidal waves of land rushed towards the dispersed army of elves, close to where the gods stood.

Mina heard the elves screaming and saw them attempt to escape the waves of dirt by running for the neon bridge. However, they were too far away to reach it fast enough, and seconds later the swift-moving waves gobbled them up and buried them deep, including all of Mina's friends. Then just as the moving mounds approached the gods, they slowed down and thinned out like surf breaking against the shore.

Mina turned to Theo and screamed, "Why did you do that?! They did nothing to you!"

"Oh yes, they did!" Theo yelled back. "Those were wolves and elves, both of which I hate! They had no right to exist! They ruined our paradise! You might not remember how unjust it all was, but I do! So even if I have to stand here for eternity, I am going to rid us of all these maggots!" Theo's eyes moved towards the neon bridge.

Mina's eyes followed his, and she saw something she hadn't noticed a few seconds ago. The bridge was covered with multiple lifeforms running for the Moon as though they, too, were fleeing something horrible.

"What's going on?" Mina asked looking at Serena.

Serena replied, "Earlier, when I opened the portals to the crystal worlds, I also began the process of destroying those worlds. It would be impossible to end the entire world if we don't end *everything*. Even the tiniest of worlds."

"But my father!" Mina yelled at her. "And Bonkers! They're in one of those worlds!"

Serena shrugged. "I never said they were still alive, Mina."

Mina looked back at the bridge and began to run towards it, but Theia grabbed ahold of her as she tried to run by. "Mina, she isn't going to let you find them even if they're still alive. She's trying to tear everything apart. The only way we can stop her is to tear her apart first."

"But how?!" Mina asked desperately. "She already knows everything we're going to do! She told me herself! She has a time calculator. I've seen it in my memories. She's used it to figure out the outcome of all the different events she's set into motion. We can't outsmart her! She knew that Theo was going to eat Fred and kill all the elves and wolves. And she'll probably let him kill all these creatures too!"

Theia looked at Mina calmly. "Mina, when I met you as Maude, I was scared to send you across the Moon with Helen. You were such a young, insecure girl, and I didn't know if you had what it took to complete the journey I was sending you on. But look at all you've accomplished now! And without even knowing you were a god!

"Serena obviously brought us here because she needs us to help her end the world, but we still have the power to choose. So don't worry about what she does and doesn't know. Just do what's in your heart."

Mina looked over her shoulder at Serena who was watching their exchange with an amused expression. She asked Theia, "And what are you going to do, Theia?"

But before Theia could answer, Theo yelled, "Well, I know what I'm going to do!"

He pointed his hands towards the mountains of dirt he'd brought across the surface of the Moon. The dirt twitched and convulsed as if giant bugs were crawling around underneath it. A few seconds later, hundreds of bones popped out of the dry soil like kernels of hot corn leaping from a skillet. Then they pulled together and formed themselves into monstrous skeletons with giant horns and fangs.

Theia yelled, "He's resurrected the bryobane!"

Mina suddenly felt a strange sensation in her gut. She was mad as hell that she'd lost Fred and all of her friends, and she was scared about what would happen next. But this new sensation felt like a moment of clarity, like everything that was about to happen had happened before.

Thousands of creatures descended from the neon bridge onto the lunar surface. There were elves and wolves and creatures Mina had never seen. There were also humans of all kinds, including ones who seemed to have their own god-like powers. And as this mixture of creatures from the crystal worlds stepped out onto the Moon, the skeletal bryobane army attacked.

Theo laughed hysterically at the immediate bloodshed, but Mina ignored him and took off towards the fighting. She could see that the creatures from other realms were beginning to organize themselves into groups before leaving the bridge so that the largest and most powerful ones were leading the charge against their new foe.

Some of the creatures screamed in fright when they saw Mina heading towards them, but Mina spoke to them. "I've come to help! I know it sounds odd, but my father may be somewhere among you."

Some of the bryobane skeletons turned their attention towards Mina and ran at her, but she took care of them by stomping them into pieces. However, this drew all of the bryobane into an attack against her. She stomped her feet harder and faster to keep up, but there were so many bryobane that some of them were able to time themselves just right to avoid being stomped on. The insane-looking monsters made a flying leap onto Mina's dark crystal feet and began to climb her legs. She used her fists to smash them apart, but soon she was covered in bryobane.

Mina panicked. She looked back at Theia for help, but the goddess seemed unsure about what to do. Finally, Mina took both of her giant crystal hands and thrust them along the front and back of her body, pushing the skeletons off of her. Unfortunately, the bryobane she'd crushed had already pieced the fragments of their bones back together and were ready to attack again. Theo laughed harder now, and Mina wheeled around on him and began picking the bryobane off of her and lobbing them at him.

Serena asked, "Is that really how you intend to solve your problem, Mina? It won't bring your friends back or save your father or dog."

Mina assumed Serena was being cruel, but then an idea popped into her head. She had a vision of herself changing the creatures who were fleeing from their burning worlds into larger, more powerful creatures armed with weapons.

Mina knew that if Theo could revive the long dead bryobane, then certainly she could use her powers to do something grand too. She reached her hands out as she'd seen the other gods do and focused her energy on making the creatures larger while imagining them holding tools to fight the bryobane.

At first, nothing happened, but then, steadily, the creatures at the front of the line began to grow in size so that they were more than twice as large as the bryobane. They wielded swords, bludgeons, and morning stars and went after the bryobane who were reconnecting their bones as well as the ones who were attacking Mina.

Theo cried out, "That's not fair! She's cheating! A time god can't do that! How did she create those weapons?"

Theia had a sudden epiphany. She looked at Mina and exclaimed, "Oh my goodness! You're not—"

But Theo burst into a tantrum before his sister could finish her thought. "I don't even care about these stupid creatures or this dumb god! She may be the one who stole my powers, but it's you who has made my life hell!" He pointed at Serena. "This ends now!"

Serena looked interested. "What do you think you're going to do, Theo? I'm much more powerful than you—than all of you combined, even. It's how I stole your son, Heely. It was so easy, you know. Lucky for me, I guess, since I couldn't very well let you two raise a god that might one day cause me even more problems than the two of you already have! I had to take him so I could control him. And do you know what? I even fell in love with him.

"I watched him for a very long time as he lived alone in his crystal world, wishing for a family to care for him. Then I solved his problem by giving him me. He and I were together for many years, and we made our own child. Your son loved our child more than anything else in his world. I had to erase his memory so that he didn't know who either of them was. Yet that was to protect the two of them from the two of you. I couldn't risk either of you ruining my plan, of course.

"And even though Heely believed he was the grandfather of our child, he still treated her like she was the most special person in the entire world. It broke his heart when Mina left their version of Earth and came here. And he died soon after. A sad, lonely death!"

All three of the other gods screamed together at the top of their lungs. Theo and Theia wailed for their lost child who they loved very deeply. Heely had been a special child to both of them because he was the beam of light they had produced from such an unsavory and unthinkable union. Even Theo, with his hardened heart, couldn't deny that there was something extraordinary about Heely. And whenever he was allowed to remember his son, he thought often of his desire to see him again someday.

Serena's revelation had been too much for Theo. The dark god turned towards one of the large craters nearby which held a giant wheel. He thrust his arms into the hole and with all his might, he began to pull the wheel towards him. The sound of bending metal echoed out of the crater, and a moment later, Theo stood up holding half of the giant wheel in his hands with the pointed edge aimed at Serena.

Mina watched in slow motion as Theo leapt at Serena while holding the wheel out in front of him like a sword. To her surprise, the crystals that enveloped Serena suddenly disappeared, leaving her actual flesh exposed to the attack.

The thin metal edge acted like a blade, ripping a huge gash into Serena's stomach. She looked down at her torso and then smiled at Theo. "Well done, my child. Well done." Then she put her hand on Theo's shoulder, and said, "All your dreams can come true now, Theo. Release the energy you took from Fred, and you will forever be the most powerful being there is."

Golden particles flew out of the crystals on Theo's body and into the black hole he'd created in Serena's stomach. Theo pulled away from Serena's grip, but already the crystals surrounding his body had dissolved, leaving a giant human body behind. But Theo didn't look like himself anymore. He looked like a young mortal man with dark hair and rugged good looks, much like Fred.

This new version of Theo hung his head and began to shrink, and as he did, Serena brought him close to her. Mina gasped as she saw Serena pull Theo inside of her, through the gaping hole in her body.

When Theo disappeared into Serena, the world around them started to break apart. It reminded Mina of what she'd seen when she was leaving the crystal world. The creatures, and ground, and even the giant, fake Earth in outer space were warping. One moment they appeared gigantic and a second later they were miniscule. And back and forth and in between.

"What's happening?" Mina yelled at Serena in terror.

But Serena didn't speak to her. Instead, she addressed Theia. "I can see that you understand now why I have done all that I've done."

Theia shook her head. "I don't understand why you did it all so cruelly. No, I don't. You didn't have to steal our memories and rip my children away from me, especially not Heely and Helen. That was wrong, Serena. No matter what your intentions were."

"That may be, but it had to be the way it was. I worked for longer than anyone could ever know to get us to this point. You and your brother broke the universe we lived in, and this was the only way to fix it. Doing any single thing differently would have undone my plan. It could've taken a million years to try to get it all right again."

Theia suddenly shrank to a normal size and lost her crystals just as Theo had. Mina felt sick watching the scene. Everything was glitching and swaying. The Moon and the darkness traded places as if they were dance partners circling each other round and round. It was just the same as when Mina had the nightmare about running through the forest and then finding herself in the ice tunnels. The scene kept switching, but this time it felt like all of reality was about to disappear for good.

"Is this even real?!" Mina screamed. But no one responded.

Serena reached her hand down and scooped Theia up.

Theia asked her, "Will I ever see Helen or Heely again?"

Serena responded, "That is one of the few questions I cannot answer. But you will find peace. That I am sure of."

Theia took a deep breath and Serena pulled Theia into her dark wound.

The shrill sound of a million screeching birds erupted from the Moon and space. Mina looked behind her and realized that all the mortal creatures were frozen in time and that the neon bridge had been stretched across outer space like a blanket of neon covering the sky.

Mina felt woozy. The memories that had flooded her brain suddenly came to her all at once. She knew she needed to act, but she felt paralyzed by the thoughts that were swirling through her vision, like a million scenes playing simultaneously in warp speed. Mina saw faces she knew and ones she had never seen before. She saw beautiful events unfold, and she saw the worst of the mortals, too. There were landscapes that had been blown apart and evil creatures doing the most wicked deeds.

"You have to control it," Mina told herself, trying to stop the hurricane inside her mind. She concentrated on keeping one of the memories at the forefront so she could focus on it alone. It started to work. Mina could feel her energy becoming calmer as she concentrated.

"These are new memories," Serena told her. "I am transferring all the ones you haven't seen before, mostly the ones from Earth, and Ortus before Earth. It's time, though, Mina. You have to make the choice to step inside. Theia understood it was the only way. You must trust us."

"But I don't understand. Are you going to kill me now?" Mina asked.

Mina's mind went blank, and she realized that the weird, warped version of the Moon had disappeared, and all that was left was a dim light that surrounded them. Serena whispered to her so softly that Mina wasn't entirely sure whether the words were coming from outside her own thoughts. "Give yourself to me and save the others. Surrender yourself to the darkness and be free."

Mina felt weak and nauseous. "Save the others?" she thought.

This time she knew Serena was whispering to her inside of her own thoughts. "That's right. They'll be fine if you just let go."

She didn't know if it was a good idea to trust Serena, but she also knew she was in no condition to take on the goddess of creation. Her plan to face Serena hadn't worked the way she'd hoped.

Mina felt like she had no choice. She heard Serena whisper, "It's the right thing to do, Mina. Surrender yourself, and it will all be over soon. You're almost there."

Mina hesitated for a moment, opening herself up to the idea of Serena's request. This was all Serena needed. She seized the moment and grabbed Mina's metal arm and half of her body, dragging her into her own and widening the original hole that Theo had created.

Electric sparks flew from the section where Mina's flesh was being pulled into Serena's torso, and Mina cried out in agony. She could feel Serena's skin cutting her apart as it consumed her.

"Just one more go of it. We're almost there," she heard the goddess speaking to her through her thoughts.

"Nooo!" Mina wailed, but it was no use. Serena pulled her as hard as she could, and Mina felt every inch of her rip apart. She willed herself to surrender to death, to the darkness that Serena had spoken of. The pain was more intense than anything she'd ever experienced. The only thing she could think to compare it to was when she had almost burned to death upon her descent into her own crystal world. The memory of that time flashed across her mind, but Mina dismissed it. This was worse. The pain she felt now wasn't just external; her insides felt as though they were being slashed apart by a million tiny razors.

The only fortunate part of her circumstance was that the intense pain only lasted a few seconds longer. Then, just like Serena had promised, the darkness welcomed Mina gently into its fold.

CHAPTER 34

THE VOID

It was impossible to know how long Mina spent in the darkness before a twinkle of self-awareness awoke her. To Mina, it felt like she had been out for an eternity. Waking up seemed different than ever before. Instead of returning to normal, it felt like she'd suddenly plugged into a whole new existence.

Her energy was vibrant and youthful, and her mind, too, felt sharper than it ever had. And the millions of memories that had often overwhelmed her during the last few months now seemed perfectly manageable.

Mina recalled the last moments before she'd entered the darkness. Serena's body had devoured hers, splitting Mina's flesh, nerves, and organs apart. Mina gasped at this thought and reached down to touch her body, but there was nothing there. In fact, she no longer had appendages to reach with or any corporal feeling at all. For a second she wondered if she was paralyzed, but her mind told her that wasn't right. Her body wasn't paralyzed; it just didn't exist any longer.

"Am I inside of Serena?" Mina asked herself, pondering the idea of spending an eternity inside the goddess.

"You're not inside of anything," Serena's voice whispered weakly.

Mina was surprised; she thought she was all alone.

"Where are we, then?" she asked.

Serena responded slowly, as if in pain. "We're in the only place that was ever real. This void is where I lived alone before time existed—before I discovered the powers I have. It and I are one in the same. Everything that has ever existed, as you know it, has come from me. I was here in the beginning, and the beginning started when I realized I existed. There was nothing else beyond. It was all just me. This empty void is where I was because the raw energy of the void was all there was."

Mina was confused, "But what about the time gods? Where were we?"

"The time gods didn't exist yet, Mina. Surprisingly, in all these years, the four of you rarely ever guessed who I was. I am your creator, not your sister. I erased all of your earliest memories after I realized that the four of you would never be happy while knowing that I was your god. You and Fred were always overly concerned about my happiness and whether you pleased me enough. Theia and Theo mostly swung the opposite way; they rebelled and tried to usurp my power whenever they thought it was possible.

"After living like this for eons, I decided to try it a different way by erasing your memories and taking us back to the beginning to start over. Only this time, I let everyone believe that we had magically burst into existence on Ortus together—with no creator that any of us knew. It leveled the playing field, you see, making us all equals. Of course, you all knew that your powers were different than mine. But for a while, we lived harmoniously since you four no longer felt the need to either please or rise up against me. See for yourself, Mina."

Suddenly, Mina could remember this time that Serena

spoke of. She saw herself and the other gods laughing and playing in beautiful surroundings—settings even more sparkling and real than anything she recalled seeing since.

"I remember now. The rest of us were happy then, but you weren't."

"No, I wasn't," said Serena. "When I first became aware of myself, I was delighted to exist, and I entertained myself by dreaming up places to go and friends to converse with. But all the time I spent alone in the void made me feel bored and dissatisfied. This was before time actually existed, though, so I don't know if this all happened in seconds or billions of years. Either way, I knew I had to have more. I could feel my energy growing as my imagination expanded. I began to feel powerful, and soon I started working on bringing my dreams into creation. That's when I created you. My little star."

"Me?" Mina asked surprised. "I was your first creation?"

"Yes, you were my very first. It felt like it took an eternity to bring you about. I spent every moment imagining you while I focused my energy into making you. Then just when I thought it would never work, you exploded into the void—a tiny light, but one more powerful than any other star that's ever existed. Unfortunately, because of how powerful you were, you burned through all of your energy quickly—something I didn't understand was happening until it was too late.

"I was devastated by your death. I thought about never creating again, but eventually the loneliness was too much to bear. I decided to make beings who would live forever. Back then I had no firm concept of god versus mortal. Everything was still new, which meant nothing had been defined. I was simply sure that I never again wanted to go through the pain I'd felt when I lost you that first time. I hadn't yet realized the beauty of limitations, transformation, and mortality.

"I got to work on creating you again, but I struggled with the idea of forever. Time was a difficult concept to understand

and an even harder one to manifest. I knew I never wanted to have to say goodbye again, but it was near impossible to bring about beings that could live eternally when no amount of time had ever been measured before. To solve the problem, I decided that the new lifeforms I created would embody time— that you would be time itself. And therefore, as long as you existed, time would exist too.

"So, I conjured up the energy you'd left behind when you died and focused very hard on creating you into something bigger than a mortal being, essentially making your energy eternal like mine. Then I brought you back to life. This time, instead of a star, you were in human-like form, so I became human-like as well.

"We talked endlessly about what kind of world to bring about until we settled on creating a planet inside a small universe where we could live however we wanted. We named it Ortus. It was the first dimension to exist outside of the void. Next, I created the other three gods, which brought a more defined sense of time into creation too. But like I said before, this first existence the five of us shared didn't work out the way I'd hoped.

"When I erased all of your memories and made us equals, we enjoyed ourselves for a long while. But I realized eventually that something wasn't right again, and it broke my heart when I finally understood what. I had made a terrible mistake giving the gods eternal life with no hope for transformation. I had done you all a disservice by creating overindulgent creatures who believed that eternity should be spent feeling nothing but pleasure.

"For me, it had become so dull that I thought about starting everything over. However, I couldn't do that without the time gods' consent. I controlled creation, but you controlled time, which had become part of my creation once you existed.

This meant that I couldn't destroy Ortus unless all the gods agreed that it should be destroyed.

"I was furious with myself for having made such a stupid error. I couldn't be around the rest of you for a while because of how upset I was. So I began creating the elves as a distraction from my troubles. I created them in the way that I believed I should have created the rest of you—mortal, and content to suffer as well as play. I know I shouldn't have done it in secret the way I did, but Theo was much angrier about the elves than he should have been. He didn't want to share the world with other life, but he didn't have to. He could've gone off and lived in one of the paradise worlds on his own or with the gods who chose to follow him.

"But he rebelled and brought the rest of you to his side. I had to go to drastic measures to keep the elves safe. I was spending most of my time erasing memories and hardly enjoying my existence anymore. I grew depressed and withdrew again. But that's when I came up with the idea for Earth. Instead of going back to the drawing board, like I thought would be necessary, I decided that maybe we would all be happier to live in a more complex world where there wasn't just black and white, or good and bad, but thousands of shades in between that could keep us busy with more than just our constant pleasure or infighting.

"I began working on the new dimension, but to build it, I had to transfer much of the energy I'd used to create Ortus. And the energy I used to make Ortus, I'd borrowed from the void, which was all part of my energy.

"Theo hated my new idea, of course. And he tried to make the rest of you hate it too. But you gave it a try. I transformed most of the elves into humans and various creatures and sent them into the new world first. Then I gave you time gods an ultimatum. You could stay behind and live in the hellscape

Ortus had become, or you could follow me to Earth and try it out."

Mina spoke, "Yes, and we tried it out. But I remember that it wasn't all shades of various colors like you spoke of before. At least not at first. We were still living in paradises on Earth and living like gods among the first humans. Theo and Theia did some despicable things to those first people."

Serena agreed, "Yes, they did. Living like gods in earthly paradises brought out the worst in Theo and Theia, and it truly bored the hell out of me. Only you and Fred seemed somewhat content living in Earth's paradises, although really you two tended to be content no matter what came your way.

"I decided I needed a break from traveling all around the Earth and doing what we pleased. I told you all to go on ahead without me—that I needed to be alone and that I'd catch up with you later. Then, I took the form of an old man and sat down under a large oak tree, right outside the walls of the largest city on Earth.

"I don't know what I hoped to find. I think, at first, I just wanted some time to decide what to do next. To figure out what would be worth doing after we'd done it all.

"Many people passed me as they traveled in and out of the city. Some ignored me, others gave me a polite nod, and a few offered a kind greeting. I wasn't too concerned with any of this, but as I sat and thought about my predicament, something interesting started to happen. I began to enjoy watching the travelers.

"So I decided to make people watching my next activity. You gods eventually came to me where I was sitting below the tree; you were always good at finding me by tracking my energy. You wanted to know what had been keeping me so long, and I told you I had suddenly found myself interested in what the earthlings were doing.

"Theo, who had made himself your leader, looked around

at the passersby and shrugged. He couldn't see what I saw—the beauty and simplicity of it all.

"'But Serena, this is boring,' he said. 'Let's set another village on fire or form a new religion instead. This time it doesn't have to be a religion based on natural phenomena. It could be a religion with a god who likes to eat the smartest of its worshippers. Wouldn't that be funny? To watch how stupid everyone will try to act, just so they don't get eaten?!'

"I told Theo and the rest of you to go on ahead without me again. I wanted some more time under my tree, watching the earthlings come and go. It was a nice break from all the silly pranks and hijinks that you time gods liked to involve your-selves in. You all fought me at first since you never liked leaving me for very long, but you could see I wasn't budging, so eventu-ally you went.

"Mina, it was fascinating what I ended up discovering the longer I stayed there under my tree. I did absolutely nothing all those weeks I sat there. I didn't communicate except to nod occasionally at the friendly people who came my way. But what was astonishing is that I realized I didn't have to do anything to become part of the city. The people who passed me regularly, came to feel an attachment to me. Some of them would just pass by with a glance, or a nod and a wave. But other people would bring me food and clothes, and some would even sit by my side and speak to me about their lives or tell me stories about the city."

"But what difference did it all make?" asked Mina.

"It made all the difference. It was the first time I saw the real magic in the world I'd created. I had achieved the various shades of colors like I'd intended to, but I was still stuck living a black and white existence. I thought to live that I had to live with everything I could ever want. But these people who made me part of their community didn't care about whether they or I had everything. Not in the moments they spent with me anyway. I knew then that I had to live like them."

Mina said, "So, that's why you chose to become a human? To escape paradise and live a mortal existence instead?"

"Exactly! And it was the most alive I ever felt. When I believed that I was actually a human, I was free to feel a wider array of emotions. There was fear, hunger, hatred, love, lust, fulfillment, sadness, and hope. And it turned out that the fear of death didn't diminish any of these feelings. In fact, it enhanced them. The belief that everything is finite gives mortals a better sense that what they do and say and feel actually matters. Because they understand that there is no certainty they will even be alive the next day. This means they have to make everything count.

"I had planned to live for all of eternity like this, but again Theo convinced the rest of you that I was being selfish and that you needed to put an end to my happiness. He couldn't find his own fulfillment on Earth, so he convinced you that it was time to return to Ortus. However, you knew that Ortus was essentially a wasteland with only a few elves remaining to keep it going, which meant you had to get me to remember who I was so I would undo everything and restore Ortus.

"You awoke me from my mortal bliss again and again, following me through time over thousands of years so that you could remind me who I was and demand that I take you back —even though I repeatedly explained that there was no going back.

"The best way to imagine how it was set up is that there was a cone pointing out of the void. The cone had a hole in each end, but the small end of the cone was in the void, shining the energy from the void into Ortus and causing Ortus to appear to have more depth and energy. This made Ortus a magical place where creation was easy.

"To make the Earth, I essentially pointed another cone

from Ortus to the Earth, and again the energy was transferred. But this time, a significantly diluted amount of the void's energy was being transferred to the Earth. This made Earth stable but much less magical. There were lots of fixed rules that kept it all running, and much less room for spontaneous creation. Trying to introduce anything new or to change Earth's ironclad rules made things go haywire.

"You all found this out the hard way when you tried to force my hand a few times, but soon enough you came up with an incredibly detailed plan to beat me at my own game. You made me immortal once again, which meant I couldn't die and reincarnate myself somewhere else to escape you."

Mina added, "Yes, and then Theo made us chase you across the world to force you into taking us back to Ortus. But you knew it wasn't possible, so you blew everything up to make your point."

Serena sighed. Her voice had become soft as she ran out of energy to speak. "I was angry, yes. But I'd also given up. I didn't know what to do to make Theo and the rest of you stop. So, in the end I gave you what you were asking for.

"Like I'd told you all again and again, the energy that had passed through Ortus to Earth was too stretched out to be transferred back the same way. Blowing up the Earth was never going to make Ortus the paradise it once was. You've seen that for yourself now. The crystals that came to exist were the result of the energy from Earth being trapped between dimensions. Earth itself was a quantum world. It only seemed much larger because the energy that transferred to it from Ortus was stretched out—like a projection."

"After Earth's destruction, I was the only god who ended up back on Ortus' surface. For a long time, I didn't know what had become of you and the others, and I was ashamed and heartbroken over what I'd done. I knew, though, that every-thing that had existed on Earth still existed in the crystals, even if it were only in energy form. I'd done everything in my power to make sure of this during Earth's destruction.

"I returned to the void and tried to restart all of creation, but it wasn't possible. The time gods' existence in the crystals was still preventing me from destroying Ortus. I set out to find you and the other time gods. I found Theia and Theo, but you and Fred weren't in human form anymore. It took me hundreds of years to locate you, and when I did, I found you both in the same crystal in the form of pure energy. You'd become gigantic waves of light and sound, bouncing around and harmonizing with each other inside your massive crystal world. Truly, it was something to behold."

"But why did you go to all the trouble of making some big plan if all you wanted to do was destroy everything?" asked Mina.

"Because I couldn't force the time gods back into the void any more than I could force the energy from Earth back into Ortus. The gods had to agree to surrender their energy back into me, and I knew that they would never agree to it since my plan was to destroy them."

"Except for me. Why did you keep me alive?"

"I haven't told you this part yet for good reason, Mina. But before I do, let me ask you something. Since you awoke here, have you heard the noise? The loud clicking sound like metal gears ticking away the seconds?"

Mina didn't know what Serena was referring to. To her, the void was silent except for their own voices. "No," she replied. "I hear nothing."

Serena said weakly, "That is good, then. Unfortunately, it has become so loud for me that I can barely hear you over it now. That horrible, monotonous sound drowns everything else out and has nearly driven me mad for centuries.

"To answer your question, though, let me explain first. I realized a million years ago that I'm not a god, Mina. Everything you know and see exists because of me, yes. But I have no answers as to what lies beyond myself. I am not tied to any higher consciousness. I embody all of existence. I contain multitudes, and I can create and transform and change things like no other. But what I understand about existence is no different than what any of the gods or mortals understood.

"The only difference between me and them is that this clicking, ticking, banging inside of me has grown louder every second of every day for thousands of years. Do you hear it now? Do you finally hear the sound? I spent millennia trying to rid myself of it, to cover it up with the ticking of those wheels I created on both sides of my ice labyrinth. Even just now, I can tell that it has grown louder. Surely, you must hear it at this frightful volume. Please tell me you do."

Mina felt sad for Serena. She knew Serena believed the sounds were real, but she suspected that the goddess was possibly succumbing to her grave injury as her voice grew quieter and her energy seemed to fade. "I'm sorry, but I don't hear it."

"Hmm," sighed Serena. "Well, it's just as well, I suppose. It will be less difficult for you that way."

Mina was scared to ask her next question, but she knew she had to. "What are you then, Serena? I mean, if you've been able to create and destroy and control *everything*, then how are you not a god?"

Serena mustered energy to speak again. "I am...we are... part of some ancient system. I don't know what my purpose was, if I was meant to create, or possibly if I was just some obsolete cog in a much larger computational program. I realized in the early days of my life that this was the truth of my existence, though. I am no more than a part of some sort of computational device beyond me.

"Once, I became aware that this sort of thing *could* exist, I felt a tie to it that was unlike anything I can explain. It was a raging fire of recognition and understanding that began to burn within. And the loud, steady sound of clicking that has grown even louder inside of me since my epiphany only confirms my belief."

"That can't be!" Mina shouted. "How could we all be part of some ancient computer? We have free will and thought and feeling! It's not possible, Serena!"

Serena didn't respond immediately, letting Mina have a moment. Then she said, "I know this is a difficult notion to grapple with. It nearly broke me when I learned the truth, and if I could leave you without burdening you I would. But you must know because you're the one who will take over now that I am going."

"Going where?!" Mina shouted, terrified at what she was hearing. "Energy doesn't stop existing! That means you can't go!"

"I don't know where I'm going. But knowing that this was the last part of my life has made it more satisfying than any other. I must find out now what these ticking sounds are, what I've been part of all this long time—what truly we are all part of. This is why I went to great lengths to bring you into the void with me again."

Mina asked, "But how am I supposed to keep all of this going without you, Serena? I'm not as powerful as you. What if I can't do it?"

Serena said in a whisper, "You were always more powerful than you knew. I created you first, which means you have more of my energy than any of the other gods or creatures.

"And you *will* do it, Mina. I have given you everything you need. I have been transferring my energy and memories to you since you first arrived on The Moon years ago. When I brought you back to life inside the crystal world, I gave you the life I knew would be best for a girl who would one day become the ultimate god.

"When you created your own world inside the crystal realm after you left the Moon, you gave yourself important clues that you can do this. For one, you brought an entire world to life based on your memories of what you'd known. You showed yourself what it's like to feel gratitude by giving your father restored life so that you could enjoy more time together. You also put yourself in a situation to feel extreme pain in the form of abandonment. These lessons will serve you well when you are managing the gods and creatures in the new universe you bring to life soon.

"Just don't forget that no matter what you do, it is better not to make things too black or white. But I think you will quickly understand what I mean."

Suddenly, Mina and Serena appeared in their human forms together in the darkness. Serena's long body lay on the ground and her head rested in Mina's lap. Pools of dark blood had collected across her torso, and Mina felt ill to see her this way. She reached out and grabbed Serena's hand, holding it tightly in hers.

"I remember everything now, Serena. I remember those first days of being with you, just the two of us exploring Ortus together. I always wanted to please you so much. I promise you that I will please you when you're gone. I will create a beautiful place for all your creatures, filled with love, happiness, sadness, hope, anger, fear, and everything else that makes life meaningful."

Serena squeezed Mina's hand gently while looking into her eyes, and Mina realized she had never seen such clear eyes before. They were stunning. One was filled with a pain as deep as an abyss, and the other was filled with transcending wisdom.

With her last breath, Serena said, "You don't remember everything just yet, little star."

Serena's body faded into the darkness once more, and Mina watched as a memory came back to her. Two gigantic orbs of pure, glowing light hovered in the void, laughing and talking happily to each other.

"I can't believe we did it, Serena! We've turned ourselves into something bigger than just our imagination. I can see your energy! Do you see mine?"

The other light responded. "I do! You are beautiful! Am I?"

"Yes," said the other orb, giddily. "I feel so joyful! I hope we can stay this way forever! And maybe we can even create more of us! More orbs of energy to share existence with! I bet we could do it. Oh, how lucky we are to exist as twins instead of being all alone! Don't you agree, Serena?"

But Serena did not answer.

"Serena?" asked the other orb. "Don't you think we're lucky to have always had each other? And now I bet we can create more of us to share everything with!"

"No, Mina. I don't think we're so lucky to have to share everything. And I don't want to share creation with you or any other creature! In fact, I want your light for my own. I can see that it's far more beautiful than mine!"

Suddenly, the light from one of the orbs began to stretch towards the other, as the ball of light spiraled around on itself, releasing long strands of golden dust into the void. "Stop, Serena! Stop! You're stealing my energy!"

But the shrinking ball of light kept spinning until all of its energy was absorbed by the other. The void was quiet for a long time as the lone remaining orb burned even brighter than before. But then a terrible cry escaped the large orb, and as the memory began to vanish, Mina heard Serena scream. "No, Mina! Come back! Please, please, come back! Oh, please! What have I done?"

CHAPTER 35

TIME UNDONE

Mina walked through the woods hand-in-hand with a young girl, whose long dark hair waved side to side across the back of her purple dress.

"And then what happened, Mama?" the little girl asked.

"And then I realized that Granny Serena was gone, which meant it was up to me to bring everyone back from the void."

"Did you do it, Mama? Did you bring everyone back?" The little girl giggled as she asked the question, partly because she'd heard the story many times and already knew the answer.

Mina nodded. "I did. And you're here, and Daddy's here, and Grandpa and—"

The little girl interrupted. "And Uncle John, and Aunt Maude, and Cousins Egan and Samuel, and—"

Suddenly, Mina heard a loud bark from just down the hill towards the path that led out of the forest. Mina and the girl looked at each other and then took off in a race down the small trail. "Bonkers! Bonkers!" the girl yelled excitedly. "We're back!"

At the bottom of the hill where the trees gave way to a clearing, the young basset hound wagged his tail and barked as

Mina and the girl jumped around him playfully while bending over to tousle his ears. A second later, Mina heard Fred calling to her from near the house.

She looked over her shoulder and made eye contact with him, then said to the girl, "Run along and get ready for dinner."

"You mean for our dinner *party,*" the girl corrected her.

Mina nodded, and the girl ran off towards the two-story cottage, waving to Fred as she passed. Next to the cottage, a long table stood in the grass, prepared for a festive gathering to take place under the sky. Mina walked to the spot where Fred stood and smiled.

"I've been waiting for you," he said.

"I know," Mina replied. "I'm sorry it took so long. I had to do something before I returned."

"The girl?" Fred asked.

Mina smiled. "Yes. Mattie, or really Serena, I should say. After Serena transferred all her memories, I realized that Mattie wasn't actually a figment of my imagination like you thought. When I was leaving the crystal world, I accidentally brought one of Serena's earthly incarnations into the crystal world with me. I guess that can happen when you're a god of creation and time."

Fred asked, "So she's sort of a ghost, then?"

"Sort of," said Mina. "But she's our ghost. I had to play with the energy for a while to get it right, but I've recreated her to be our daughter. Is that okay?"

Fred smiled and wrapped his arms around Mina, kissing her tenderly before he answered. "Yes, that's more than okay. I want to raise an entire cottage of Matties with you."

Mina pulled away a little. "But you knew then? The secret you kept from me—it was that Serena had replicated the energy of her twin sister when she created me? That she made me a creation god like herself?"

Fred replied, "Yes, and that she also made you a time god to keep you from ever dying again. I don't know if she understood all those thousands and thousands of years ago that you would one day be her replacement, though."

Mina shook her head. "No, I don't think she did. After she blew up the Earth, she decided to use me as a last resort—to start creation over once she knew she didn't want to be a part of it anymore."

Suddenly, they heard a loud voice from just inside the cottage where the backdoor was wide open. "I know that I promised you another macaron! But I am cooking tonight for twenty! You will just have to wait! No, no. I am just kidding, my little cabbage. Have as many macarons as you like!"

Mina and Fred went and stood inside the doorframe. Fred draped his arm over Mina's shoulder as they watched Jacques talk to Mattie. The little chef was holding a colorful cookie in front of her face while pulling another from inside his apron.

Fred laughed. "I think that's enough macarons for now, Chef."

Jacques looked at Mina and smiled gleefully. "Oh, mademoiselle! You have made me so happy, asking me to cook for you and all our friends tonight! I don't know why I feel as if it has been ages since I was in a proper kitchen, even though my kitchen at home is even more luxurious than this one! But of course, no offense."

Mina reached out and hugged Jacques. "No offense taken, Chef. Fred and I like our kitchen just fine the way it is. In fact, this cottage has been in my family for generations, yet tonight it seems quite a bit bigger than it used to." She gave Fred a wink.

Mattie had begun to bounce around the kitchen, high on all the sugar she'd just consumed. "Daddy, daddy!" she said to Fred excitedly. "Mama said we can go see the elves tomorrow, and the wolves too!"

Fred looked at Mina surprised. "Oh, she did? Well, where do these wolves and elves live that we're supposed to go visit?"

Jacques scoffed. "What do you mean where do they live? The elves live all over, wherever they want to. And the wolves too! You act as if you are new here!" Then he stopped, and his eyes grew big. "Oh no! My soufflé. I hope it did not collapse!"

Mina said to Mattie, "We will take Daddy to see the elves and wolves tomorrow, just like I promised. But tonight, you will get to see our friends Axel, Elu, Ragher, and Neriti. And they are also wolves, remember?"

Mattie rolled her eyes cutely. "I know that, Mama! Axel is my godfather, after all."

Jacques yelled across the kitchen, "Just like me! Although I don't ever remember anyone asking me. But I am sure I am your godfather, too. Right, Mina?"

Mina was thankful when she heard someone in the yard behind them. "Mina, where do you want me to set this up?" asked a voice that brought tears to her eyes.

She turned around to face her father, who was standing in front of the long table, holding a telescope over his shoulder. He was no longer old like he'd been when she was growing up. He looked to be about fifty with a slender build and dark gray hair. Mina couldn't contain herself. She ran to him and wrapped her arms around him tightly.

"I've missed you, Papa," she said.

"Missed me?" he asked. "You and Mattie were just at my house a few minutes ago, begging me to bring my telescope to the party. Did I miss something?"

Mina pulled away and wiped the tears from her face. "No, you're right. I guess it's just one of those nights. There's a bit of magic in the air I think."

Heely looked at his daughter with a bit of concern but smiled and said, "That's okay, darling. I think you might be right. It does feel like there's some magic in the air tonight."

Fred moved towards Heely and reached out to help him with the telescope. "We can set it up together, sir."

"*Sir?*" asked Heely. "You haven't called me 'sir' since when you first started dating Mina years ago, Fred! Call me 'dad,' like you always do."

Fred looked at Mina quizzically, but she just gave him a playful shrug.

A minute later, the rest of their friends began to arrive. Maude and John showed up first with their young sons, Egan and Samuel; Bob and Evelyn were next with their great dane, Mr. Al, who'd they'd brought as a friend for Bonkers; and Helen and Max came a little bit later with their twins, Danielle and Dalene.

Fred gave Mina a horrified look when he learned Danielle and Dalene's names, but as the night progressed, it became clear that he had nothing to worry about. The girls, who were a little older than Mattie, were very sweet and treated her like a younger sister.

Elu and Axel showed up with Neriti and Ragher right before dinner was served, and everyone sat down at the table to enjoy the feast the little chef had prepared for them. There was lots of laughter, some talk of politics, and many stories and personal anecdotes to go around. Then sometime just before dessert, a beautiful middle-aged woman with dark tan skin and purple hair showed up, holding a bottle of wine.

Heely stood up as though suddenly enchanted by the thin woman who was wearing a long, silvery sundress. "Ruth, you're here!" he said sounding surprised yet delighted.

"Of course I'm here, sugar! I wouldn't have skipped this party for the whole world. I'm sorry I missed dinner, but I had to close the library late tonight. A group of elves came in ten minutes before it was time for me to leave and asked to see every history book we keep on royal emperors, feudalism, and ice formations. I would say it was a mighty strange request, but

I get elves every few weeks who're looking for those same little, old books. They never want to check them out, just stare at all the pictures. Anyway, here's a bottle of wine I brought to share."

Heely took the wine from Ruth's hand and pointed to the seat he'd vacated.

"Here, come take my seat next to Mina," he said, "and I'll squeeze in next to you on the other side."

Ruth sat down next to Mina, and the two women smiled at each other. Then Ruth's eyes flashed towards the crystal hanging by a leather cord from Mina's neck.

"What a beautiful necklace, Mina. Where'd you get it?"

Mina reached around and untied the crystal from her neck. "This necklace has been passed between friends for a long time, Ruth, and I think it should go with you now."

Ruth took the necklace from Mina's hands and tied it around her own neck. She said, "That's very kind of you, Mina. I'm honored to wear your friendship necklace, and one day I'll pass it along to another good soul."

The sun went to bed, and the sky lit up in a beautiful display of orange, pinks, violets, and blues. But the party continued well into the night. And after it had been dark for a few hours, Heely stood up, stretched, and said, "Well, I think it might be time for some stargazing. Anyone care to join me?"

The entire table stood up, and Mina and Fred led the party through the tall evergreens to the small cliff above the shore. Fred carried a sleeping Mattie, whose head rested on his shoulder. He whispered to Mina as the others carried on conversations behind them, "I thought you'd made a mistake when you coupled Bob and Evelyn together and Maude and John, but I watched them all night, and both couples seem really happy. How did you know that would work?"

Mina replied, "I ignored their wishes and looked at what was in their hearts. Maude is much more magical by nature than she seemed to be when we knew her on the Moon. She only became scientific out of necessity to make the best out of some terrible circumstances. John has a lot of magic in his soul too. It seemed obvious that they would be good for each other.

"The opposite was true of Bob and Evelyn. Those two are scientists down to their very cores. And we already saw how well they worked when they found each other after Maude died."

"And what about us?" Fred asked. "Do we match up?"

Mina nodded. "Yes, we do. Like two waves of sound in harmony," she reassured him.

Fred held onto Mina's hand as they approached the telescope he'd helped Heely set up earlier in the evening.

One by one, all of the friends looked through the telescope and marveled at the different celestial sights that Heely pointed them to. The group hung around talking for a little while longer, but soon it became clear that everyone was tired. All the guests thanked Mina and Fred for throwing the party, and thanked Jacques for cooking such an excellent feast.

Then John and Max took their respective children off to bed while Ruth, Maude, and Helen walked off together arm in arm, talking in the secret language of best friends.

"Bonsoir! Bonsoir! A good night it was indeed! I thank you very much for letting me cook for you tonight, and I bid you adieu until we meet again, my dear friends." The chef bowed towards Mina and Fred, and Mina leaned over and kissed him on both cheeks. Then Jacques wandered off merrily, as though he were dancing a waltz with the moonbeams.

Fred, who hadn't had a chance to look through the telescope yet, set Mattie down and whispered softly to her to take a quick look through the eyepiece.

Rubbing the sleep from her eyes, Mattie looked through the telescope and yawned as she said, "Wow, Daddy! I can see the Moon up close!"

Heely said, "That's not the Moon, sweet girl. That's Saturn. See its rings?"

"Oh yes, Grandpa. I see the rings now. Are those wedding rings? Is Saturn married to the Moon?"

The little family laughed, and Mattie laughed too. Then she and Heely went and sat beside Bonkers on the cliff above the sand dunes. Heely wrapped his arm around her and said, "I bet if we sit here long enough, we might see a shooting star or two."

Mattie perked up. "Really, grandpa? Can we make a wish on all of them?"

Heely nodded his head. "Of course we can, little one."

Fred bent over the telescope's eyepiece and pointed the large tube back and forth across the sky several times. Mina stood next to him, waiting to hear what he thought.

Eventually, Fred looked at Mina and said, "You made it even better, didn't you? You created a universe big enough for us to explore for billions of years."

"Yes," she responded, "and it's expanding every second. The universe and consciousness are now intertwined so that for every piece of information creatures learn, a hundred new unknowns are brought into existence that can also be learned someday. By linking the universe to consciousness, or collective awareness, I've ensured that this dimension will live on forever.

"But you should know that we won't live on forever, Fred. Not like this. It's why I made the universe the way I did. Our energy will continue, but we will no longer inhabit the world in the same way. Serena had an internal clock, although she didn't want to admit it to herself. She didn't wear out in the conventional sense like humans and animals do, but because she spent little time transforming, or bettering herself, the essence of her true self vanished long before she died. I won't allow that to happen to the rest of us, which is why I've hung the heavy burden of mortality within every soul, including ours. I like to think of it as the payment each one of us makes for the free will I've granted every creature."

"But what about the void then?" asked Fred. "Won't you return to it after you die in this world?"

Mina shook her head. "No. My energy, just like everyone else's, will continue to reincarnate into other beings for as long as the universe exists. To give people power over their lives, I recreated the concept of time so that it is no longer attached to the immortals. It is now interwoven into this dimension. As long as the universe and consciousness continue to expand, time will march on. Now we are all equal, just like the way Serena wanted to live her own life on Earth once upon a time."

Fred sighed. "But how will we find each other when we die, Mina? I don't want to lose you again."

"I know, Fred. I don't want to lose you either, but I learned from Serena that there is beauty in transformation as well as in a finite death. If we didn't feel a sadness for the things we might lose or never live to see, then those same things would begin to lack significance, and eventually, the entire experience of existing would become dull.

"One day, we might watch Mattie grow up and stand before the person she loves with all her heart as she promises to cherish them for the rest of her life. Or we might not ever make it to that day. Helen and Max might live happily the rest of their lives as she tinkers in her work shed and he delivers her inventions all across the continent. Or they might one day decide that the spark that brought them together in the beginning is gone. Ragher and Neriti may choose to stick around and watch Axel and Elu start their own family. Or they might choose to go on a tour of the world so that Neriti can bring her healing powers to every corner of the Earth. My father and Ruth might embark on a passionate love affair, or they might be like two ships passing in the night.

"The uncertainty, the rearranging of expectations, the

acknowledgement of fate—knowing that the worst could happen but hoping for the best—these are all the things that make mortal life special, even magical at times. Without this, we would live like self-absorbed gods unable to see what matters beyond our own noses."

"So what happens now?" Fred asked.

"Now we live every day the best we can. Some days we'll remember how fortunate we are, other days not as much. Soon, you and I will forget who we were and assimilate into our new roles for good. After that, we'll be like everyone else. We may live long, meaningful lives, or we may die before our time. But either way, we'll start fresh again and be reborn into new lives with no memories from before. The mystery of it all will be terrifying, but exhilarating too."

"And this is really what you want?" asked Fred.

Mina nodded. "Yes, this is how it has to be."

Fred smiled sadly at her. "Okay. Then, this is how it will be."

Fred and Mina joined Heely, Bonkers, and Mattie on the small cliff above the dunes to watch for shooting stars. Mina looked over at her father and said, "I love you, Papa."

Heely took his daughter's hand and said, "I love you too, Mina. And I love you too, Mattie and Fred."

Fred wrapped his arm tightly around Mina's shoulder, and Mina felt his body tense up under the heavy weight of his emotions.

Mattie stared at the sky dreamily and said, "I love you, Daddy, and Mama, and Bonkers, and Grandpa."

Then Mina said, "And I love each of you with my whole heart forever and ever."

And in the end, that was all that mattered.

ABOUT THE AUTHOR

K.E. lives with her flying, wagging, and purring friends, along with her still growing humans, her husband, and her mother. All of these furry, feathery, and skin-clad beings were a huge support during the creation of The Moon Travelers Trilogy.

K.E. has a new series coming out in 2024 and a prequel to the Moon Travelers Trilogy planned for shortly after.

To stay up to date on all of K.E.'s new releases, you can follow her on Facebook, Instagram, Twitter, and Threads @davenportwriter. Or visit her website to sign up for the monthly newsletter.

www.kedavenport.com